THE BOOK OF THE DEAD

ALSO EDITED BY JONATHAN STRAHAN

Best Short Novels (2004 through 2007)
Drowned Worlds
Eclipse: New Science Fiction and Fantasy Vols 1–4
Fantasy: The Very Best of 2005
Fearsome Journeys
Fearsome Magics
Godlike Machines
Life on Mars: Tales of New Frontiers
Made to Order: Robots and Revolution
New Adventures in Space Opera: From The New Space Opera to Here
Revolutions in the Heart: Stories in Honor of Ursula K. Le Guin
Science Fiction: The Very Best of 2005
Someone in Time: Tales of Time-Crossed Romance
The Best Science Fiction and Fantasy of the Year: Volumes 1–13
The Book of Dragons
The Book of Witches
The Infinity Project 1: Engineering Infinity
The Infinity Project 2: Edge of Infinity
The Infinity Project 3: Reach for Infinity
The Infinity Project 4: Meeting Infinity
The Infinity Project 5: Bridging Infinity
The Infinity Project 6: Infinity Wars
The Infinity Project 7: Infinity's End
The Starry Rift: Tales of New Tomorrows
The Year's Best Science Fiction Vols 1–2
Twelve Tomorrows: Communications Breakdown
Twelve Tomorrows: Life in the Anthropocene
Under My Hat: Tales from the Cauldron
Revolution in the Heart: Stories Inspired by Ursula K. Le Guin
Vaster than Empires

With Lou Anders

Swords and Dark Magic: The New Sword and Sorcery

With Charles N. Brown

The Locus Awards: Thirty Years of the Best in Fantasy and Science Fiction

With Jeremy G. Byrne

The Year's Best Australian Science Fiction and Fantasy: Volume 1

The Year's Best Australian Science Fiction and Fantasy: Volume 2

Eidolon 1

With Jack Dann

Legends of Australian Fantasy

With Gardner Dozois

The New Space Opera / The New Space Opera 2

With Karen Haber

Science Fiction: Best of 2003

Science Fiction: Best of 2004

Fantasy: Best of 2004

With Marianne S. Jablon

Wings of Fire

THE BOOK OF THE DEAD

AN ANTHOLOGY

EDITED BY
JONATHAN STRAHAN

ILLUSTRATED BY
GALEN DARA

HARPER
Voyager

Harper*Voyager*
An imprint of
HarperCollins*Publishers* Ltd
1 London Bridge Street
London SE1 9GF

www.harpercollins.co.uk

HarperCollins*Publishers*
Macken House,
39/40 Mayor Street Upper,
Dublin 1, D01 C9W8
Ireland

First published by HarperCollins*Publishers* Ltd 2026
1

Designed by Natalie Nguyen
Illustrations © Galen Dara

A catalogue record for this book is available from the British Library.

ISBN: 978-0-00-880956-0 (HB)
ISBN: 978-0-00-880957-7 (TPB)

Printed and bound in the UK using 100% renewable electricity by CPI Group (UK) Ltd

MIX
Paper | Supporting responsible forestry
FSC® C013604

CREDITS

For Marianne, with love and thanks

CONTENTS

ACKNOWLEDGMENTS

Any project like *The Book of the Dead* is the product of many hardworking, talented people doing their best to create something special. I'm indebted to David Pomerico, my editor, the fabulous Isabella Ogbolumani, who was essential helping to bring this one home, and to everyone at Harper Voyager. Thanks also to Galen Dara for the incredible cover and artwork. A special thanks to Garth Nix, who was instrumental in coming up with the idea for this book early in the winter of 2023. Assembling anthologies is a strange and awkward business with many, many factors affecting whether writers are able to deliver stories on time or at all, so I'd also like to thank all of the writers who took part in this project for their generosity and kindness.

INTRODUCTION

Jonathan Strahan

In early 2023 I had just completed *The Book of Witches*, which would go on to win the World Fantasy Award the following year, and was thinking about what I could possibly follow it with. There were several strong candidates but an idea emerged during a trip to Hobart, Tasmania, that autumn that I could not let go. On a rainy evening some friends and I met in a Mexican restaurant to discuss books and other things, but throughout the evening my eye was repeatedly drawn to a display of calaveras—Day of the Dead skulls. It showed sixteen highly decorated skulls, each of which seemed to me to imply a world of stories about what had happened to the owners of those disparate heads, how they'd happened to come to be there, and why some of them seemed quite so happy about it.

Those ideas began to coalesce during that trip and I started work on assembling the book you now hold. *The Book of the Dead* itself belongs to another culture, as does the Day of the Dead, so I knew that, despite taking inspiration from those things, any book I assembled would have to draw on different sources, so I began to think about representations of death, dying, and the dead in science fiction, fantasy, and horror. There are countless lands of the dead and a range of personifications of death as a character. My favorite, and possibly the most famous, of these is Terry Pratchett's Bill Door, talking in ALL CAPS and sharing kindness and wisdom as he moves through what is a difficult job, though there are others. In Garth Nix's *Sabriel*, necromancers descend through nine perilous precincts of death, each one a darker and more dangerous stage of the journey and are guarded from its perils by magic. In Ursula K. Le Guin's *Earthsea* cycle, the land of the dead is a place of silence and shadow, a bleak mirror to the living world where the price of power is paid in mortality. Tolkien, too, placed mortality at the heart of Middle-earth, from the gift and doom of Men to the Undying Lands beyond the reach of Elves.

Science fiction, on the other hand, rarely treats Death as an end in itself. Instead, it focuses on how death might be deferred, cheated, or technologically transformed. In Mary Shelley's *Frankenstein*, death is challenged through reanimation—an early, gothic vision of scientific hubris later revisited by authors from Poe to Lovecraft. Later, writers like James Blish in *A Case of Conscience* or Philip K. Dick in *Ubik* pushed the idea of suspended lives and half-lives, where technology blurs the line between living and dead. In *To Your Scattered Bodies Go*, Philip José Farmer famously and colorfully imagined Riverworld, where every person who had ever lived is resurrected and lives again. Lededje Y'breq escapes death in Iain M. Banks's *Surface Detail* when her mind is transferred into a new body so she can investigate her own murder, something echoed in more recent works like Richard K. Morgan's *Altered Carbon* and the short fiction of Greg Egan. And the notion of escaping death by uploading into a virtual world or a matrix has been virtually a convention of cyberpunk or post-cyberpunk fiction since the 1980s.

Horror keeps death close at hand. Sometimes it is the quiet inevitability that waits just beyond the frame, and sometimes it bursts forth in blood and terror. Vampires offer the fantasy (and curse) of life beyond death. Zombies, once a symbol of slavery or mind control, now embody our fear of meaningless survival, bodies without selves but with insatiable appetites. Ghost stories linger in the space between memory and loss, between terror and romance, sometimes conquered by love and sometimes simply refusing to stay politely buried, as in W. W. Jacobs's classic "The Monkey's Paw" and its modern variants like Stephen King's *Pet Sematary*. And then there are the countless tales of serial killers, revenants, haunted houses, and other cursed places where death is both the threat and the consequence. In horror, death is never abstract—it is the very thing you can't look away from.

So what of *this* book of the dead? As you might expect, the stories draw on all these genres, and sometimes challenge their boundaries. This started for me with the arrival of Stephen Graham Jones's tale of two construction workers on a late shift when something very strange happens, and finally came together with Tamsyn Muir's very different, and appropriately

Egyptian-inspired, account of funerary practices on Mars. If you choose to read the stories in order (not everyone does), the journey begins with Indrapramit Das's tale of a young woman on a train faced with terrible choices and ends with Kaaron Warren's depiction of a family deeply familiar with death, but who occasionally need to escape it. In between you'll find Daryl Gregory's stark horror tale of animal experimentation, Jeffrey Ford's gentle posthumous fantasy about a chance to visit a lost love, Paolo Bacigalupi's violent assassin tale, Garth Nix's powerfully moving return to his Old Kingdom, and many more. What each of these writers, along with the other two dozen brilliantly talented contributors have done, is to offer a kind of vast mural of death in many incarnations—sometimes loving and ruminative, sometimes unsettling and horrifying, but always deeply human. Here are our greatest strengths and most terrible weaknesses all laid out in one of the oldest, most persistent, and most universal themes of story.

Jonathan Strahan
Perth, August 2025

THE BOOK OF THE DEAD

PASSENGERS

Indrapramit Das

We sat in the close quarters of a winter-cooled train compartment, huddled together for warmth. Boys and girls, closer to each other's bodies than we'd ever been. Our feet nestled next to each other, thighs and hips brushing. It was the first time most of us—class nine students all—were traveling without parents, the first time I would travel beyond Calcutta with friends. Beyond the windows was blackness, the scratched glass shutters engraved with our reflections, distant villages in invisible countryside flying past like fireflies. Cold air rushing from the gaps under the shutters with the dewy smell of earth. Eight teenagers in a compartment with six berths. Too many—the illicit thrill of breaking rules. But we wanted, needed, to be close. Puberty had changed everything, much to the anxiety of teachers chaperoning for the trip. Blankets covered a multitude of legs as warm, damp paper boxes of Indian Railways food were passed around and earphones shared from a circulating Discman, music and conversation overlaying the rhythm of the train's clattering beat and motion. We played bluff with cards on the sagging valley created by a blanket stretched over two rows of seats.

Watching Yamini shiver in the chilly air from the windows, I wanted to be the one to give her an extra jacket. But Abhishek, the boy she had *her* eye on, beat me to it. Such a romantic gesture. Everyone smiling, charmed. Yamini's best friend Reya, sitting opposite her, gave her a knowing glance of approval. It felt like everyone in the compartment was coddling Yamini, because of her misfortune—as we were all boarding at Howrah Station, the seat number called for her ended up being in a compartment with no other kids from our school. She'd gotten stuck alone. The teachers said it was a mistake, but there was nothing to be done. I'd seen her face amid the chaos of the announcements on the platform, pale with disappointment, since everyone else got to sit with their friends. I was disappointed too, because I'd wanted her to sit with us. But once the train started moving, she'd quickly found Reya, and the two of them joined us boys in our compartment.

Yamini wrapped Abhi's puffy blue-and-green windcheater around herself. It was too big. Mine would have fit better. I wondered at the cruelty of genetic fate, that would have Abhi be tall and athletic and blessed with body hair, and me be small and frail, a poor excuse for a man to be, sitting with the girls and watching the other boys play football and cricket on our school field, secretly relieved to be among them but still uncomfortable.

So, unrequited love it was. The celebratory rush of any sign of affection, potentially misconstrued. An unusually warm smile. The brush of a hand against my leg. Yamini sitting next to me, her thigh against mine. Was it luck, or was it waiting, timing things just right to slip into the right spot next to her on that blue bunk. It was enough for now. Abhi on one side of her, me on the other. For the journey from Kolkata to Siliguri, and then by bus to our hotel in the Himalayan foothills, I wanted to be close to her. To see Darjeeling and stand on Tiger Hill to witness the sun rise and illuminate the snowy peak of Kangchenjunga for the first time by Yamini's side. It was enough.

Throughout the coach, tentative young heads were laid on shoulders as evening turned to night across the hinterlands of Bengal. The lights went out, darkening the compartments and leaving only the soft glimmer of aisle lights, the murmur of students too intoxicated by one another's presence to fall asleep. The comfortable gloom, interspersed by the flashing orange glow of rural stations, eased our intimacy. Girls and boys cuddling were prodded silently by friends in warning, and sprang into sitting position as patrolling teachers passed us by like jailers. Reya, the other girl in our compartment, went back to her berth. We were still seven in our compartment, and Yamini was the odd one out. Mrs. Bose, our math teacher, one of our chaperones, came up to us, wrapped in her shawl. Everyone sat up, backs straight, Yamini's head leaving Abhi's shoulder.

"Yamini, bedtime. Enough chatting. You have to go to your own bunk now," she said. I felt Yamini squirm next to me, shrinking into Abhi's jacket like a turtle. "But, ma'am, can't I just stay here?"

"With the boys? Absolutely not."

"But it's not fair I'm all alone at the end of the coach," said Yamini.

"I know, dear. It's terrible your seat got mixed up. But it's not so far from everyone else."

Yamini paused, hesitating. "The uncle on the opposite bunk keeps looking at me. It feels creepy." She had already told us about the man leering opposite her berth, with the bloodshot red eyes. All us boys had promised to defend her, to kick his ass if he tried anything. She had laughed, blushing, secure in the attention of her friends, of boys growing into men. Now, we sat meek and silent, just boys again.

Mrs. Bose's expression softened. "Yamini, dear, there's people all around, nothing will happen. This is India, everyone stares. You're a big girl now. You have to get used to these kinds of things. Your friends are nearby, we are nearby. Are you still scared?"

Yamini's eyes darted to all of us, embarrassed. "No, Mrs. Bose," she said.

"That's right. Just come wake me or one of the other teachers if you need anything or get frightened."

There was a titter from Dhruv, sitting by a window. Yamini stuck her tongue out at him. "You wanna change places with me?" she taunted.

"No switching," said Mrs. Bose. "I'll have half the students on the train asking to change seats to sit with this friend or that friend. Come, Yamini, enough fooling around. Be a good girl and go to sleep, in the morning you can join your friends again."

Abhi's hand on Yamini's arm, brief, so Mrs. Bose's gaze wouldn't melt it away. "Keep the jacket," he said softly. That would have gotten an *oooh* from the boys if Mrs. Bose wasn't standing there. "Thanks," Yamini whispered back. Like a warrior departing for battle she tied her long black hair into a high ponytail, gathered her Jansport from under our legs, and left the warm knot of our bodies to follow Mrs. Bose.

"Mrs. Bose, I can take Yamini's bunk," I said before I could change my mind. "She can take mine and sleep here."

"Soumik," said Mrs. Bose in stern exasperation. "I already said no. Now go to sleep, all of you. Come, Yamini."

Yamini solemnly waved goodbye to all of us as if we'd never see her again. But her eyes caught mine—gratitude, like when Abhi offered her his jacket. A thrill like a knife, straight through me. But I knew I'd dared to ask because Mrs. Bose had already said no. I didn't want Yamini to sleep alone among strangers, but *I* didn't want to either, thinking of her sleeping near Abhi, maybe even crawling into his bunk in the dead of night. My courage was only half real. But not in Yamini's eyes, I told myself, a bittersweetness simmering in me.

I couldn't sleep, thinking of Yamini lying alone in her berth, being watched by the man with red eyes. I was in my own middle berth, surrounded by people I knew above, below, across the canyon of floor littered with our sneakers. My backpack was a hard pillow, the restless motion of the clattering train keeping me from relaxing between the chlorine-scented sheets and blanket given out by the Indian Railways; the lit aisle a dim twilight in that shaking chasm of bodies upon bodies, stacked and vulnerable in uneasy sleep. I kept thinking of Yamini, what it would have been like to sleep next to her, a body supine next to mine for the first time. There was a man with red eyes opposite her, thinking. What was he thinking? What was she thinking? Was she awake too, wondering what thoughts were running behind those red eyes? Was she thinking of when I, reedy Soumik, the shortest boy in class, her casual friend, no tall and dashing Abhi, offered to take her place in that lonely berth opposite the malevolent leer of the man with red eyes? Was she thinking that maybe Soumik was the one she ought to depend on, to have a crush on, not Abhi who didn't offer to go alone among these strangers in the dark instead of her? Was she lying awake right at that moment, waiting for me to make my way down the coach with its snoring passengers, its haze of dreams, to find her, to check that she was safe? The idle erection against the uncomfortably tight crotch of my jeans felt dirty in such a public space, among friends. But I couldn't stop thinking about Yamini's glance of gratitude, of how much more grateful she might be if I slid up to her bunk, blocking that man's view of her. In her relief, she might let me sit in her bunk to keep her company.

I poked my head into the corridor, peering at the narrow, jittering line of night-lights, the rows of berths. There was no one walking in the aisle. I slipped off my bunk stealthily, placing my sock-clad feet on the handlebars by the aisle and using them as a ladder down. I looked at the blanketed cocoons of my friends in the compartment. No one said anything. If any of them was awake, they weren't showing it. I looked for my sneakers among the litter of shoes between the berths. Never mind. The linoleum floors were cold through my socks, and probably disgustingly dirty. But I could be quieter this way.

I had a rough idea of where Yamini's berth was—somewhere near the end of the coach, three or four compartments down. I had seen her sit down when we were all boarding the train. Like a thief I crept down the aisle, compelled to dance by the train's sway, passing each compartment as if it were a darkened exhibit in a long museum, human life packed into this metal tube, a showcase of its hive-like proliferation, limbs and torsos and breath of dozens and hundreds from coach to coach fogging the glass panes of the shutters. I the only visitor to this museum, alongside the darkness outside peering in through the windows. Or perhaps alongside the many, many eyes on this train, wet spheres sliding in their sockets, hidden by lids or watching each other, watching their fellow exhibits on the shelves opposite, examining those bodies under blankets. Yamini the prize exhibit.

I was nervous as I made my way down that narrow corridor, and I didn't quite know why. I told myself it was because of the chaperones. But I knew they were at the other end of the coach. And I could just say I was going to the toilet. No, there was something else to this uncertainty. My mouth tasted of dozing half awake, remnants of the greasy puris and aloo dum in those Indian Railways boxes sour between my teeth. I hadn't brushed. It felt wrong, being awake and creeping down this coach. But I kept going. Then, abruptly, I recognized Abhi's blue-and-green windcheater, lying crumpled like a pillow in a dark lower bunk of the compartment next to me.

Yamini's berth. I leaned down toward the shelf of the bunk, the lowest in the bay of three on the left side of the compartment. It was empty, the bright windcheater in a pile with Yamini's felt jacket. The bunk was bare—the sheets were still folded at the foot of it, under the window. Her blanket was piled at the end of the bunk. I looked at the lowest berth opposite, at the dark shape of, I assumed, the man with the red eyes. He was sprawled in his bunk, one leg falling off the side, another on the bunk. Khaki trousers, bare feet sticking out toward the aisle, soles dark with dirt. In the shadows, I could make out that his blanket covered his upper body. A fly was crawling over his toes. Multiple snores competed from the other berths.

The man was here. Yamini wasn't. My heart was racing like the tracks under us, invisible behind barriers too. The toilet. She had to be there. I made my way down the coach, my socks damp. There were muddy marks all over the aisle, water tracked from the toilets probably. The dirt mingled with what looked like paan spit under the dim lights, rusty red. I grimaced, trying to stay on tiptoes.

The thundering machinery of the train was louder at the end. I could see nothing but blackness beyond the entry door, which was propped open to the night air like in many non-AC sleeper cars. The slipstream billowed through it, ruffling my clothes, carrying the bark of the train echoing back from the empty landscape. I stayed away, not wanting to tumble out. The toilet door beyond the entryway was shut. Light underneath it. My terrible mouth dry, I knocked on the door. No response. Afraid to wake people up, I knocked harder, relieved at the roar of the train, which was going fast, jerking me back and forth. "Yamini?"

Nothing from behind the door.

"Yamini, it's me. Soumik. Are you in there? Are you okay?" I asked, in a half whisper through my cupped hands, face against the cold door despite the stench hovering around it. A sharp click made me snap back. The door opened a crack, revealing a thin slice of Yamini's face, her wide eye.

"Soumik?" she whispered, as if she couldn't trust herself.

"Yamini, are you okay?"

She whispered something I couldn't hear.

I bent closer to the crack.

"What?"

"Are you alone?"

I nodded. Her eye was darting. Cheek wet. Washing her face? Tears. She opened the door and grabbed me by the chest, hand clutching the front of my T-shirt. A shock, the rough physicality waking every nerve in my body. I was pulled into the toilet. We were together, a tangle, her arms around me, and I wondered if she was embracing me but no she was shutting the door behind me, and then we were two of us staring at each other in that cubicle, our doppelgängers in the flecked mirror, the harsh blue light shining on Yamini's wet face and wide eyes, the roar of the train incredibly loud in the closed space. The smell was hideous. Yamini wasn't wearing her T-shirt. She was in her bra, peach but grayed with sweat or water. My jaw opened and closed. I didn't know what to say, details flicking against my brain like thrown pebbles. There was no space, so she was very close, wedged against the metal sink in her jeans. My socks were soaking through in the muddy mix of urine and water on the floor. I felt like throwing up. She already had—I could smell vomit, see the wetness around her mouth. And there was blood, diluted red water among the slick of the floor around the raised bumps where you place your feet and piss or shit into the Indian-style steel toilet in the floor. Or it could just be—the walls were covered in old rust-red streaks of paan spit.

"Soumik," she said, syllables cut by her teeth, clashing like mine now. Her freezing wet hands grabbed my T-shirt. I could see the T-shirt crumpled in the sink. Her T-shirt. It had been white, and was now darkened with red. My first thought was that Yamini was having her period. I didn't think why the blood would be on her T-shirt instead of her jeans. Her minty breath was on me, and we were so close. She had brushed. It was impossible. This was fantasy, decaying second to second. The rotten smell howling up from the black hole right beside our legs, the funnel into open darkness, to angry night. She leaned close to me, like she was moving in for a kiss. So I could hear her over the noise.

"I kih," she spat out.

"What's wrong—"

"I killed I think I killed him."

I stared at her. I wanted to ask, what do you mean? But I knew. The man with the red eyes. Sprawled on his bunk. It wasn't period blood on her T-shirt. It was a stranger's blood, a man's blood, a man whose leg was dangling off his berth and on the ground just some dozen feet away from the toilet. I gulped back nausea as the train swayed us. I was dancing again. We were dancing. Trying to avoid the gaping steel mouth of the toilet in the floor, Yamini had given up and was holding me, for strength, for balance, who knew. Her arms around my narrow torso, those freezing fingers interlocked behind my back, against my spine. I was frozen too. "I'm here. I'm here," I said, like heroes in movies who find someone bloody and afraid. I felt as bloodied. I held her at the hips, her jeans against my fingers, like we were at a party. We danced. The train made us. "Help," she said. "What do I do," she said, her words dissolving in the clashing of mysterious levers and gears and wheels below us.

I swallowed. "Okay. It's okay. I'm here," I said again, because I couldn't find other words. She shuddered. "He kept looking. Wouldn't stop. I knew something would happen. I had the knife, kept it beside me. I . . . think. I f . . . fucking knew something would happen. No one believed me."

"How . . . He's dead?"

She shuddered again, as if in waves, her fingers clenching against my back. "Don't know. I think so. Hit him with the knife. In the neck. I think. What do I do? Help. Help."

"I need to . . ." I said, and clenched my jaw tight. "Are you okay?" I asked, swallowing spit and bile.

Her head twitched, but she said nothing, her eyes glazed and directed downward, at my chest, through me, looking out into the darkness beyond me, the door, the walls of the train. Stupid question.

"I'm here, Yamini," I said, a parrot parroting, a record skipping. "Look at me," she said. And I did, shocked, her bare skin strange and unnatural to my eyes. I had never seen a real girl up close without her shirt on. In her hunched posture, her seizing, caved stomach, there was nothing of the women I'd seen in magazines and movies wearing lingerie or bikinis or nothing, their chests held out and backs arched. But my thoughts raced to those images nonetheless, to the fact that I was holding a partially undressed girl, the way her skin shone with damp, her lips quivering with what could just as easily have been desire. "Is there blood?" she stammered, leaning toward me every time she spoke. I saw the gooseflesh all across her arms and shoulders, reminding me uncomfortably of plucked chicken skin. I couldn't find any blood on her. It was all on the T-shirt. I shook my head. She'd acted quickly.

She took the T-shirt, leaving the knife in the sink, and began wiping the diluted pink and red on the floor and the sink, the stains recalling wet stone floors in fish markets after scaly bodies were de-gilled and chopped.

"Let me," I said. She stared for a few seconds, crouching by me, and held out the now vile rag of the shirt. "Thanks," she said, and crouched over her Jansport, tucked under the sink. She took out a fresh green T-shirt and put it on. I wiped down the sink and watched as fabric covered her skin, her torso, again, a pang of disappointment vanishing under the wheels of my hurtling thoughts. The bottoms of my socks were drenched. For once, gratitude for the dirtiness of train toilets, which had mingled with what blood Yamini had dripped while washing her hands and torso so it mostly looked like mud, or the paan spit that painted the cubicle like a Pollock. I filled the plastic mug on the sink with water and washed the floor until there was no red. There was still the shirt. I looked at the single window, which had an opaque white pane that couldn't be opened. The entry door outside was open—but there was the risk of being seen.

The stench shifted something in my head.

"The toilet. Yamini. Throw the knife down there. And the T-shirt," I said. "Quick."

Her eyes widened with a flash of hope. She turned on the tap again, holding the Swiss Army knife under the water and soaking the shirt. The knife seemed clean, like she'd been washing it earlier. She unfolded it very carefully, her hand movements compromised by adrenaline, like my own. It was anointed, after all, with death. Clenching the shirt in her other hand, she began to tear the blade through the scarlet-dyed cloth. I imagined the small blade doing the same to human skin, slicing through flesh and cartilage. How had she killed him? Stabbed his neck in frantic terror as he loomed over her, like I had done over her empty berth. Blade snagging on his vocal cords. Is that why he hadn't screamed, drunk and dizzy and shocked that there was a blade in his throat instead of a pliant teen girl under his hands? Is that why he had staggered back to his bunk to bleed out? Was his blood pooling down under the berth as we spoke, drowning cockroaches?

I watched Yamini rip her shirt. Clever. So it would fit down the hole and not get stuck. "Here," I placed my hand on her fist, which held the tool of death, and moved it away. Picking up the tattered shirt, I gritted my teeth and tore it into strips with the help of the weaknesses she'd slashed in the fabric. She took the pieces of cloth and fed them to the stinking maw at our feet. Once the last strip vanished down the shit-stained hole, I noticed tears crawling down her cheeks, catching the harsh blue fluorescent light. She nodded, and looked me in the eyes. I nodded back. She took the knife and turned toward the mouth of the toilet, jaw clenching visibly against its hellish breath of excrement. She crouched down and held her arm over it, hand over the hole. Its black throat seemed to swell with eagerness for the residue of blood now in the crannies of the folded blade, the roar of the train monstrous in that metallic cubicle. She opened her hand. There was a startling bang that made us both gasp, muscles tightening. She startled upright, grabbing my arm. And then, nothing. It was gone, the little Swiss Army knife ricocheting down a lonesome stretch of train tracks in the middle of Bengal. Together we washed our hands in the sink, pumping on the chemical soap dispenser until it was near empty, our four hands becoming one tangle under the pink slime, slippery with foam. We held hands, letting each other wash the filth from our fingers, knuckles, palms. Hers seemed so soft, so small, so incapable of what she had done. But there were bones underneath, and we could all be so reduced by each other. When we were done, we hesitated, our hands dripping, and wiped our hands on our jeans because there was no towel.

"I have to go back," Yamini said. "I have to sleep in that bunk." She was holding my arm tight. I hesitantly moved closer, and she acquiesced. She was against me, in a tight hug. We absorbed each other's shivering, as the vibrations of the train passed through our bones. I couldn't tell if she was sobbing, because of the noise and fury, the constant dance. She might have been. I held her tight, disbelieving. "Thank you," she said, her face inches away from my own. Her words electric through my body. As we began to separate, I touched her lips with mine, pushed gently. Her mouth was warm and soft, unlike her cold hands. She jerked back and pulled out of my arms, thumping against the sink. One second. My first kiss. Maybe hers. Her eyes and face—I recoiled at the horror there. She was terrified, not meeting my eyes. Behind her, in the mirror, my own face loomed, clammy and dazed. What had he done, that man with the red eyes? What had she done to him? What had I done? In that moment. "Sorry. I thought, sorry," I said. She was shaking her head. "It's fine. We have to get out of here, someone will notice." Her arms were folded against her torso, hugging herself, her eyes darting to avoid mine. "I have to go back."

"I'll sit with you. Until morning. I can go back to my bunk before people start waking up."

I saw the hesitation, the dread in her face. The lifeless man in the opposite bunk, going cold in the winter air. Her alone in hers with me, her classmate, who had helped her cover up a killing, and then kissed her as if it were a first date.

*Carefully we crept out, welcoming the bracing, icy wind from the open coach door*way, letting it gush into our mouths and nostrils to wash out the smell of the toilet we'd shared for, what? Ten minutes? It had felt like an hour. I peeled off my disgusting socks and hurled them out of the open door, out into the black. I followed Yamini already down the aisle, both of us soft on our feet, her wearing her Jansport, hair untied and messy over her shoulders, in her fresh green T-shirt, as if nothing at all had happened, as if we'd just snuck away to kiss in the toilet. And we had, I thought, feeling sick again. I had. For that one irrational second when I touched her mouth with my own, all that had happened that night seemed worth it. Now, a man lay dead, and I was an accomplice. A hot panic engulfed me. I could go to jail. She could. Not together, nothing romantic—each of us in a separate prison, in shared cells as big as a train compartment, with a toilet as dirty, unable to see our devastated parents, our families. I thought of the dead man's parents, staring at us in a courtroom, faces twisted in grief, hatred, fear. We were children. How did we end up here? I couldn't fathom how Yamini had mustered the strength to keep going after what had happened.

I nearly walked into Yamini as she halted by her berth. The floor was still muddy around it. Paan spit and mud—or not. The man opposite—his feet still facing the aisle, one still on the ground. I couldn't tell if the smell of the toilet had followed me, or whether it was radiating from him. There was a dark wet patch between his legs that I hadn't noticed earlier. I looked away instinctively from this indignity.

Amid the snores of our co-passengers, Yamini and I crawled into her bunk. Because the middle bunk was down and occupied, there was no space to sit. We lay down together, awkwardly, her backpack a shared pillow, our sides touching. I was on the open-facing side. She didn't tell me to leave.

Despite my kissing her, she didn't want to be alone. She wore Abhi's colorful jacket and zipped it up, its puffiness hiding her new shirt. The chemical-scented railway issue blanket pulled over us. We were stiff as corpses, muscles aching. One body, male and female, united by violence, by the blood in the great forests of veins that enmeshed the world. I dared not turn to face her, nor she to face me. I could scarcely breathe. I wanted to disappear, and I wanted to stay there forever in my rotten love. "Can you hold me," whispered Yamini, words broken by a trembling that I could only share. So I did. She had crossed her arms across her chest. I crossed my own arm across her limbs. She didn't turn to face me. I felt a terrible yearning.

I crept out of Yamini's bunk at the edge of dawn, when blue light began to lighten the windows, dividing the night of the passing earth with the approaching day of sky. I woke in a panic that I'd be discovered with her, from a sleep that probably lasted a few minutes but felt like eternity.

In that sleep I traveled in the train for years, forever, with Yamini my co-passenger.

All the other passengers were dead in their bunks, each coach a catacomb, including the man with the red eyes opposite us. Amid their hosts of flies and cockroaches, they lay silent, sometimes moaning, tossing and turning their rotting bodies. They resented Yamini and I for our life. The train traveled across a shadowed land, never ending, a blackness beyond the windows howling with spectral winds, dotted with distant lights. We knew our fellow passengers would tear our warm bodies to shreds if we left our bunk, so there we lay in each other's arms, our clothes rotting to dust as time passed. Yamini looked older as time passed, a grown woman instead of a teenager—I was as well, my muscles grown into my skin to shape my limbs out of the stick-like frailness of the body I'd left in the waking world. Naked, we tasted the lifespring in our mouths, and we fucked, desperately, like we'd never done in our distant, forgotten waking lives. Sometimes I was Yamini, and she was me, and in my hands her, my cock was a stone. We came, over and over. We fucked to hold on to life, as the man with the red eyes watched, the wound in his throat gasping in the shadows of his tomb opposite. He masturbated, coughing with mocking laughter as our clumsy motions became practiced, in time, as the landscape passed by the window a black tapestry embroidered only with those distant lights of cremation fires, or stars. When I was Yamini and she me, or both of us indistinguishable, I felt inside myself for a child, for anything created in this place, but there was only the stickiness of my own cum limning the mouth to a void inside me, holy and lightless, a gemstone of nothing inside our flesh. Our two bodies one, Yamini and me and me and Yamini. Sometimes Yamini and I would shout at the man opposite in his bed of decay seething with cockroaches and centipedes. "You deserved it, you fuck," we'd cry, and spit our life at him, the waters of ourselves, his own befouled waters seeping out of him in rivers to trickle down the aisle of the coach. He would be pleased, and chuckle with his wound. One day he said, gurgling breath through his throat, "Look, the train is turning. You are no different than me. We are passengers. Look upon our rider."

We looked out the window next to our bunk, through the grill. The train was turning, shaking, the parabola of its body curving and visible now, dotted with the lights of its windows. It was as long as a thread, looping in that empty desert of dark matter. At the head of the train, we could finally see what pulled us forward through space-time, the engine of its eternal motion. The coaches were harnessed with chains to a titanic buffalo that galloped through this desert, head down and horns sparking. Under its hooves was thunder and lightning, the track upon which it galloped a bridge of light waves through the dark, extending forward, or up, or down forever. Upon the hillock of the buffalo's back was a rider. The rider's flesh was void as the eternity behind them, visible because their skin rippled with the warp of gravity, their body a singularity, their shape humanoid, genderless. Two arms held the reins to their beast, two raised up totems—a rod and a flaming noose that lashed through the un-night a permanently looping solar flare. On the rider's head was a crown gemmed with blazing supernovae too far away to blind our mortal eyes. The rider turned to look at us, and we could see their eyes clearly even across the distance from our window to the front of the train, which was infinite. The rider's eyes shone with the unlight of failed stars, their smile jagged with curving tusks that were the sharp crescents of arid lifeless worlds in the irrational constellation of their bounded form. "Yes," the man with the red eyes hissed in his bunk. "Look!"

"Look away," I told Yamini, and she told me, and we wrested our gaze from the rider, who was too far away for us to ever see, yet close as the sky to earth, pulling our train on that track of light through the desert and its dunes of dark matter and its cremation fires that crept into the sky so above and below became one, toward a city on the invisible horizon that had no proportion, its immense arched gate rippling with swallowed light, its geometries unseen but teeming with immense gravity, a land of no return in which shadows were so deep even light could not escape.

"We have to get off," Yamini said to me. "Now." We agreed. We weren't meant to be passengers here. This was the wrong train. It had to be.

We had sex one last time, two made one again, that black space in our womb flaming with invisible light. And we finally sprang from our bunk, after untold years. The man with the red eyes lurched out of his to chase us eagerly, slavering blood with his smiling wound, followed by other passengers. We ran, the man swift on our heels, his long nails gouging flesh from our back. We ran, as the rider's buffalo sounded through the desert, a mournful vibration that would shatter our waking eardrums. We ran, and leaped out of the open door at the end of the coach, out into the hurtling winds of time.

When I woke, Yamini was awake on her side. She was staring at me. I was sweating despite the cold, and so was she. "You should go," she said. The toilet stench in the compartment was stronger. The gray shape of the man opposite us resolving as the shadows lightened. I didn't look too closely. I started to get off the bunk, hoping the shocking stickiness in the crotch of my jeans wasn't visible. "You were dreaming," Yamini whispered, hand on my arm. I turned. Her eyes were glittering in the gloaming. "I was too," she said. "We were still in the train, going forever. He was there. He chased us out." Her face suddenly childlike again, cheeks still rounded with what adults called baby fat and shining with the waters of our mysterious bodies, a ghostly loveliness in the birthing dawn. "I think I dreamed the same thing," I said. I felt a painful separating, as if there were gleaming threads of ectoplasm between us as we pulled away, no longer one. I wished in that moment that I could switch places with her, be her, take on her fear and anguish, her beauty and strength. She clutched my hand, quick, a squeeze, both our extremities cold as death. I squeezed back. Like a murderer I left, ducking out of the compartment on my cold bare feet, creeping down the coach and back to my bunk. Behind me the throbbing presence of the man with the red eyes, following me silently. I crawled back into my bunk thinking I might never stop shaking again, deep in my young bones. My friends in blissful sleep. Yamini awake, somewhere else, right there. Out the windows, electric lines slashing the dawn blue.

I never got the chance to ask her what actually happened. I wondered sometimes, how it had been possible. The man with the red eyes crouching by her berth, pulling off her blanket and shoving it into the corner of the bunk. Yamini, terrified, lashing out with all her strength, clutching the little totem of her Swiss Army knife. A spurt on her hands, across her T-shirt. The man's shocked, drunken tumble backward into his berth, leaving droplets like paan spit on the floor. The man with the red eyes lying in his bunk, watching Yamini and smiling, waiting for the opportunity to creep over to her. Yamini waiting in dread until those eyes lidded in drunken sleep, and creeping across quietly to sink her Swiss Army knife into his throat and pull it out before he could do the things his eyes promised, then rushing to the toilet to clean herself.

The man was discovered at dawn. His throat punctured, and a dark puddle of blood sloshing under his bunk. Rumor had it Yamini herself had raised the alarm, telling teachers about a bad smell from the man opposite, something leaking on the floor. Perhaps minutes after I left her bunk. It eventually made the Kolkata newspapers. Kolkata businessman found murdered on train to Siliguri. It was in the news that I read how the man's fellow passengers in the compartment heard the man thrashing in his bunk at night, and assumed it was something to do with his clear inebriation.

The murder was left unsolved, the killer assumed to be a vagrant or dacoit who'd snuck on at one of the nighttime stops, stabbed a random man in the neck, and got off at another stop to vanish into a vast country, maybe with some valuables taken from his victim. All the luggage was searched, but no suspicious weapons were found on the train. We were interviewed by the police at Siliguri, where we stayed in a cheap hotel, never reaching the Himalayan foothills because our school trip was canceled. We took a train back the day after, Yamini surrounded by chaperones this time, no students sharing compartments with strangers, a railway security guard stationed by the door and told to patrol all night.

No one in our class saw the body. No one but Yamini and me, not that anyone knew. The killing wound was hers alone to remember, though the blood from it was mine too. I barely remember my conversation with the police at the three-star hotel where we were all bussed to from the train station for our one night in Siliguri before the return trip. The inspectors sat in the banquet hall, at one of the tables covered in white cloths. All of us students and teachers were brought in and sat waiting to be interviewed at the other tables. When it was my turn, I said I hadn't seen and heard anything suspicious except the mud around the berth when I went to the toilet at night. I told them I thought the red was paan spit. I assumed Yamini said the same thing. When we all filed into the banquet hall, we saw her ushered out of there by two of our chaperoning teachers, who had their hands on her back. She caught my eyes so briefly I would have missed it if I hadn't looked at her the entire time. She looked ill, exhausted. I don't know, can't know, what she said with her eyes to me when they sought me out, our pupils black holes calling to each other across a cosmos, signals lost in vacuum. They must have interviewed her first, and alone, since she'd been opposite the corpse's bunk. If she broke down in tears or fumbled whatever lies she told them, it wasn't enough to have anyone see a small teenage girl as a killer. I thought of her Swiss Army knife and the torn shreds of her bloody T-shirt, lying on the tracks of the Indian railways, probably long salvaged by scavengers. When she walked out of that banquet hall, her ponytail neatly tied as ever, I could only look on in shocked admiration that she'd gotten away with it. That we had. I wanted to call out to her, tell her that I had meant it when I said that I'd dreamed the same thing as her on the train, that it wasn't a confused snatch of sleep talk. We had dreamed the same dream. We had approached the event horizon of violent death early in our lives, and it had warped us into ribbons twirling together in the void. We were one because of it. I wanted us to remain that way. I felt like weeping, sitting at that white-clothed table in that banquet hall with my other friends who suddenly seemed like ghosts, clutching our glasses of Coke and Fanta, fizzing orange and black. I wanted to follow Yamini, to supplicate myself before her, to never leave her side, to once again merge with her until her pain was mine, and mine hers.

Yamini never returned to our school. There was something of a scandal about the fact that she'd been given a berth alone on the train, and ended up sleeping next to an actual murder. There were rumors of a payout to her parents. That journey to and from Siliguri was the last time I saw her in person.

Years later, I looked her up on social media and found her. I didn't reach out. I was glad to see her, far away in some college in Canada, wrapped in layers of winter clothing on a snowy quad, smiling up at falling snow from under a thick woolen cap. Posing, clearly, for someone who cared enough to catch her in this moment of happiness behind the camera, be it illusory or real. When I checked again, her account was gone.

As I write this now on my laptop, about to delete it all, I am sitting on the bunk of a sleeper car, this one an AC two-tier and cleaner than the one we took to Siliguri more than two decades ago. There is a woman a decade younger than me in the berth across. College age, confident, shielded from the world and its errant eyes by headphones, an N95 face mask, and the glow of her phone. For all my studied indifference, I know the truth—that I want the woman to notice me, talk to me, make me feel less of a letch, less of a man, with her attention. I wonder if she will look to me at night, when the coach is silent except the music of the train, and darkness wells against the glass windows. I'll make sure to be on my side, back to her. I don't want to catch her eyes, and see the fear there. Or for her to see it in mine. Eye to eye, signals lost and corrupted.

I know that if I manage to fall asleep under the itchy blanket, through the noise of the train, I will dream again of a being in a train berth like this one, naked and alone, the coach empty and desolate. Out the window, I will spot Yamini, and I will pull the emergency stop cord. I will leap out of the slowing train, which recedes into infinity, no far rider visible pulling it. I will walk a desert of black dunes, different that the one we traveled so many years ago. This desert will have a horizon, and a dusky sky in which hangs a vast world so dark it burns the light that swirls into it like a drain. I will recognize this as the world city of no return that we saw when we were children, boundless in the illusion of a sphere. Perhaps the sky disappears and the desert becomes one with it when you're closer to it. Under that void hanging in the sky, I will follow in Yamini's footsteps, the dark matter of the sands under my soles glittering with the small jewels of stars. Farther away, the stars on the ground glow brighter and brighter, and on the horizon they seem like stations for the trains I can hear, cremation fires and far-off villages in which waiting souls gather, whether dreaming or dead I don't know. On the horizon is a thin tower of light, or a bridge, a straight line crossing the sky to intersect the darkness and emerge at its other pole to continue infinitely so it loops back down to the horizon behind me. A straight line and a circle, intersecting a circle that is not. Somewhere in the distance, the rumble and clatter of endless trains, their horns wailing across the blighted sky. Forever I will follow Yamini, longing to be one with her again, the redness of her sword gleaming in the distance. She will turn to look at me, ever at the horizon. Amid the howling black winds of her lashing hair, my eyes will meet her eyes, across infinity, and I will see that they glow with the unlight of failed stars. *Are you dreaming this right now*, I will ask her, *or are we dead?* She will not answer, walking ahead. My heart, wrapped in silken sleep, will beat so fast, like that of a woman in love.

MEMETO SANGRO

Paolo Bacigalupi

My name is Izio. I am a stilettotore.

I have slain so many men that I can no longer count their number, but perhaps they all await me in Scuro's Unseen Realms and will make their count known then.

I have been told that I am not a pleasant man, but that is neither the blood nor the wine. I am not some perfume maker, hiding the stink of shit. I am a stilettotore. I am the ugly end of ugly hatreds, the ugly tool born of ugly places.

A stiletto does not have to shine to spill blood.

It has only to be sharp.

I am very sharp, indeed.

I was born under the docks to a whore whose slit reeked like the catch that is dumped every day into barrels to make pescapesto. I do not remember my mother's face in joy or health or pride. I remember the boniness of her thighs, the slack folds of her belly and sagging tits. I remember the smell of her sex as she scrubbed after she lay with men. I remember sweat like jewels upon her split lip in Vesuna's summer heat.

Distinctly, I remember her death.

Her swollen face. Her shadowed sunken eyes. Her cheeks and lips puffy with blue blossoms in the flickering candlelight, sweating and panting as she tried to birth my sister, a slick bloody mass that made no cry as she issued from the torn maw between my mother's thighs. My sister fell like shit upon the floor. My sister died that night. My mother might have already been dead, even as she birthed, her body spasming, finishing the job even as her soul leaked out.

My father must have been some patron of my mother, but I have no knowledge of him. Matra Giulia said that in her youth my mother was beautiful, and I have been told that my own features match what people call appealing, so perhaps my father, too, was not as ugly as most of the men who frequented Quartiere Pescana, with their reek of sour wine, their stale sweat, their dirt and fish guts and blood unwashed, panting to fuck beneath the wharves.

Certainly, I have never had difficulty beckoning a woman when I desired but that, too, is neither the blood nor the wine.

Beautiful people are ugly within.

Ugly people are ugly within.

We are nothing but viscerasacci, clods of organs, bags of shit, and ropes of entrails.

I do not know who else was in the room with my dying mother as she birthed my dying sister, but I think someone must have been, for I was taken from there.

Or maybe I wandered the streets until someone found a use for me?

Childhood memories are as slippery as eels. I know that Matra Giulia fed me for a time and I cut fish for her, until I was old enough to be sold to Matra Desira, who whored me as she had whored my mother.

I remember little from this time. The men's belts mostly, or else their pantaloni discarded upon the creaking muddy floorboards as I gripped the bed and took their thrusts. I remember their hands upon my neck.

I distinctly remember the dagger one of them carried upon his belt.

I remember how its hilt beckoned me. Not a large thing. Probably used in his trade. A leather cutter or a pescatore or a rope weaver, I suppose, to have a sharp knife like that. I mostly remember that it felt good in my hand. As if it wanted to be there. My first friend.

When the man made me turn to suck him, I cut him.

Root and eggs. Serpent and grapes. Cock and balls.

I had already gutted many fish and slaughtered many chickens by that time. I had a knack for it. I could gentle a rooster in my arms and slice his head off, then let him run away, flapping and spurting blood. A man's rigid root is nothing against the neck of a chicken. It is much harder to stab through the spine of a serratine, which you must do quickly, or its fins will thrash and cut you. . . .

But ai, the blood, the blood.

And the noise!

The man stumbling about, howling like a dog, clutching his missing root, grabbing for me. And me, up on the woven rope bed, my back to the wall, that fescatolo pigfucker's writhing root held high, like Heios held his flaming brand high when he stole fire from Argo's forge.

The man clawed for me. He climbed up on the bed and pinned me against the wall. So much rage in his eyes. So much terror. His hot breath stank of sour wine. I let him pin me against the wall, let him claw for his precious root—and then I pushed his dagger into his belly.

In and out, in and out, in and out. . . .

I fucked his belly as he had fucked me and he stared at me with terror, for somehow, even as I murdered him, he could not comprehend that this small boy had slain him.

Matra Desira found me rifling his clothes for copper quattopezzi. She would have killed me then—if not for the murder, at least the mess—but I pointed my new dagger at her, and she stepped back.

Of course my name spread through Quartiere Pescana. A whore has not the right of memeto sangro. We whores are meant to be poked, not do the poking, and are never meant to seek a blood memory. My destiny was to be dumped in the salt marshes to bloat and rot and feed the razorgill, just as my mother had been.

But it was not to be.

Many people searched for me, but by then I was in the wind.

I joined a merchant caravan at the city gates, bound for Pagnanopol. I was poked by some. I poked some others. I made a little money.

I bought my first stiletto.

Years later, I went back to Vesuna and the Quartiere Pescana, thinking to pay back Matra Desira, to finish that memeto that had started not at me, nor my mother, but many mothers before . . . but by that time, someone else had poked her for me.

My name is Izio. And I have wandered far.

The priests of the catredanto claim that I have a soul that will either be gathered up to Amo or dragged to Scuro when I die, but for a soul to have a destination, is it not necessary to have a soul?

I watch others, the people of the many cities whose alleys I have stalked, and they seem full of something that I cannot name, but would like to steal, for there is an emptiness in me.

I see them laugh. I see them clasp hands. See them drink and kiss one another. See them growl and bark when angered. And I, too, do these things. I force my lips to take the shape of a smile, my brow to furrow in the ridges of anger . . . but it is a mask.

I feel nothing when I turn a man into a slumped sack of oozing guts in an alley. Nothing when I fuck a woman and she gazes up at me with those strange contortions of lust or fear or sadness or delight upon her features. I feel nothing when I win at cartalegge. I feel no sadness, nor regret. I do not think I will feel sadness even when I die. I will be eaten by dogs, much as so many of my victims have been. The dogs will get fat, as the Navolese like to say, and perhaps even those dogs will feel more than I.

When dogs wag their tails, they must feel something, I think.

My name is Izio. I have never failed to find a man, and never failed to finish him.

It was in Torre Amo that the offer came. We were both strangers there, neither of us comfortable in that sweltering miasma of a city with its swamps and the brackish Cascada Aro turned wide and somnolent as it flooded muddily into the Cerulea. That place of heat and sweat and biting sangrozi flies, with its women half clothed in the sheerest of laces and filmiest of linen, and its men with eyes glazed with the smoke of sweet black sinak, that terrible sticky stringy tar of leaf that makes men forget all.

Torre Amo. The last remnant of Imperix Amonese. Shattered columns and fallen domes. Great glittering marble blocks, half sunk in earth, cracked from buildings tumbled. Weed-choked streets and collapsed palazzi. Scattered carven arms and hands and feet and torsos of gods, strewn like bodies on an ancient battlefield, draped in verda robes of thickening grasses and accumulating soil—all except the heads—the heads stolen away by fortune hunters, those that were not smashed to dust by the rise of Amo's priesthood.

Torre Amo. A place of ruins and memory, of villages crouched within the larger city ruin, the remaining people clustered by the Aro or hunkering close to the great palazzi of the Nine Princes, leaving the rest of the city to the stalking shadows of dogs and wolves, to the grazing of deer and rabbits and goats, and the wingbeats of vultures and cauri birds picking at newly discarded bodies in the echoing weedy quadrazzi of old empire.

We two were strangers there.

He was of the Khur and I was of Vesuna, and yet we two were more alike in that shattered city than we were different, despite different hues of flesh and shapes of nose and wealth of dress and cousin mother tongues.

In the little shattered temple where we met, a goddess lay at our feet. Her head for a wonder was still half whole, but the eyes had been chopped out, and the mouth was a ragged shattered wound as well.

"The Amonese put jewels in the mouths of their gods," the Khuriani said.

I did not know if he thought this wise or foolish, frivolous or devout. Indeed I did not care. Some men when they come for murder, they take time to speak their desire. To see their foe paid well in pain. Others seethe to tell of their own hurt. As long as they paid, I let them find their own path.

"My daughter . . ." the Khuriani began, but then he trailed off.

He looked a proud man, but he was bent over as if he had taken a wound to the belly. His thin silk robes were open to the waist and his chest was smooth, though his forked beard was thick and shot with gray. He wore wealth on his fingers and around his neck, but the Cascada Aro's red mud clung to his toes from his climb to this hilltop temple just as it did mine, and he plucked at his forked black beard with worry. He spoke Lingua Amo with an accent thick as his land's honey, slow and difficult.

"My daughter. He took her off the street. People saw it done. He did not bother to hide that it was him. His men wore Venaius colors." He spat. "Princiia Venaius does not strike at Princiia Corino, because that would break the great peace. But to strike at me, who provides Corino with zetia and cumin, his kha spice and flowering pepper. . . ."

It made a certain sense. Few Khuriani came to Torre Amo except to sell their empire's spice to the city's Nine Princes. The princes did not like to fight one another directly, but ruining one another's profits was a game they enjoyed very much. And so the merchant's daughter had fallen to the game.

"Venaius thinks he can touch me and feel no touch in return," the merchant said. "He thinks because I am neither princiia nor archinomo that he can touch me and mine . . ." He trailed off, brooding, tugging his beard, staring down at the fallen goddess. There were stains upon one shattered arm, what might have been blood.

"They painted their gods," the merchant said.

I was startled by the turn. "The Venaius?"

"Nai. Of course not. The old Amonese. You people, you do not even know your own land."

I made a sour face. "This is not my land."

"Ci. You are off the hook. Your accent . . . maybe you are Vesunese so you think yourself different, but the Amonese raped their way up and down this peninsula and much of the world beyond. Even I likely have some of your dirty blood. But you are Amonese, of a surety. I see it in your eyes. And yet your gods, you have forgotten. Your history, you do not understand.

"We Khur, we have so many books that we have whole streets dedicated to them. We have more books written in Amonese Anciens than you whose land birthed that tongue. And so many others. Khusian. Lak. Wusti. Even the sigils of Xim. All side by side in our bazinalibri. And those are only the books written by foreigners! We have our own as well. The poetry of our mathematicians. Our diviners and truth finders. Our tetrascrivini. Vast wisdom, in every street. And yet your princii think they are great because they pocket a little gold from our spice trade. Because my emperor honors an ancient blood claim and gives you his dregs." He scowled darkly. "In Imperix Khur, even a child knows what colors to use for which god, whether ours or yours. And yet here in Torre Amo, you have forgotten nearly everything."

We stood regarding the toppled statue with its smear of blood.

It might have been paint.

The sun was sinking across the river, spilling gold and crimson. The shadows in the shattered temple were lengthening. A sangrozi bit my neck. It left a bloody smear on my fingers when I slapped it flat.

"I saw a man once," the merchant said at length, still staring at the fallen statue. "In Vaz. He strangled another without ever touching him. He reached for him, and the man stopped to breathe."

I looked up, puzzled. "That is not what I do."

"Nai. Of course not. But this man, who you will kill. He is very dangerous. I will give you a charm. It is a lucky thing."

"Luck is not something I desire," I said. "Sia Fortuna and I . . . We are not in the same business."

"Nai. You must listen to me in this. This little princiino of the Venaius is a dark creature. An akiz . . ." He brooded upon the fallen statue's hand. "The akiz . . . well, you maybe call them something like . . . demonus . . . golgozza, maybe?"

I laughed, incredulous, but he stilled me with a look.

"He is from the darkness below," the merchant insisted. "Golgozza is the only name you have, because your language is sad and simple, too basic and empty. Your people have lost all your wisdom. Call him akiz, and be warned." He spat, bitterly. "I would have entreated the Sag to do this deed, but their noble ways are not welcome here. You will have to do, but you will be vulnerable. You will need—you must stab him three times, and then you must cut out his heart and place it in his mouth. You must do this so that he devours himself, and does not try to eat you.

"He is akiz," the merchant said at my skeptical expression. "He is a dark creature."

"So I should place his heart in his mouth?"

"And stab him three times. Also, you will need a charm to bring you back safely from him."

I still could not discern if he was joking, but his lips made no smiling shape.

"I will do what you ask, but I do not need a charm," I said. But already the merchant was holding out to me a thing. It dangled from a beaded thong, a tiny pale thing. A bit of carved bone.

"A dog?"

Very small. Sharp of snout. Three amber eyes embedded.

The merchant nodded. "In my lands, ones like this guard the path to the afterlife. They herd the dead onward, and push back the living. In the high mountains we have similar, they guard sheep and herders from the great wolves."

"And they also have three eyes?"

"Do not jest. This one does the same for the dead and living." He shook it at me, holding it out. "You must wear her when you kill the man. She must be near, and she will guard you."

"She?"

"Of course! She could not be he!" And then he laughed, as though I had said something childish. "She will make sure the dead go where they belong."

He waited until I held out my wrist. He tied the trinket there, and then he gave me a sack of coin as well. "Count it."

I weighed the little sack with its leather braid. "It feels right."

"Count it. We must have no misunderstandings."

"I can always find you," I said.

For the first time he seemed to truly see me.

He shrank back.

My name is Izio. I am not a subtle man.

The man I hunted, this little princiino, he was nothing to me. Livo Arosciinto Venaius, he was called by others. Livo il Gaz, he called himself. Livo the Cat. A mere cousin of the Venaius archinomo, but rich enough and dangerous enough and preening enough to make a virtue of never forgetting slights. Small men like to hoard their grudges. They like to think that their unending hunger for revenge makes them strong. *The smaller the man, the longer the memory,* Matra Giulia used to say. Venaius was such a man, and so he could not resist to hurt those around Corino, not seeing that in his desire to continue a petty feud he had entered into a more serious one. But in any case, Venaius liked to be seen as strong. He very much liked to be seen.

I appreciated this about him.

Sometimes you will see a palanquin in the streets of Torre Amo, a number of slaves grunting under the weight of their master, their bodies sheened with sweat. The best palanquin runners come from the Issolae Nixosi, also called the Isles of Sorrows. There, men are taught to run at full pace with a bowl of water atop their heads, and if they spill a drop they are beaten with straps dipped in kepdis oil that causes boils to rise when it touches bare flesh, and if they spill three times they are put to death for they will never learn to run.

And then the same is done with teams.

And so these men learn to run.

These slaves are very expensive, but the Nine Princes and their scattered relations control the spices of the Khur. No expense is too extravagant to never be tumbled to dirt or cobbles. Their pride does not accept such humiliation.

Livo who called himself the Cat was not high in the ranks of the Venaius, but his slaves were still Nixosi.

Their oiled muscles rippled and shimmered under torchlight. His palanquin was plated in gold. The calloused feet of his runners padded gracefully down the darkened alley, accompanied by the heavier tread of his guards in their sandals, all of them returning late at night from his dice throwing. They made a very impressive entourage.

The lanterns of the outrunners swayed. The palanquin bearers padded through the weedy narrow way. I watched, idly toying with the little trinket dog the Khuriani had given me. The little luck charm I did not need.

The leading guards skidded and fell, crying out.

Pig fat and olive oil.

Unlucky for them.

The slaves reached the oily slick surface and fought for balance. They were superb. The palanquin rocked and tilted, but they kept their feet and their master kept his dignity—at least until the men I had hired dumped down fat and pitch and olive oil from the rooftops hot and liquid, and threw torches down after.

Flames roared up.

My quarry clawed from his burning palanquin, fleeing even as men burned all around him. He fled for the shelter of a doorway, beating at the flames, throwing off his smoldering robes, leaving behind men become pillars of fire, offerings to ancient Amonese gods, rising to the sky as black smoke.

Venaius shrank against the doorway, shouting at his burning guards to catch the assassins, to kill them all, to avenge him. Even as his voice squeaked with terror, he wished he could pay back those who insulted him so. Little men always want revenge.

I opened the door behind him.

He didn't have time to cry out as I dragged him through. I had been waiting there all along, watching the events through a hole I had cut in the door. Now I dragged my stiletto across Venaius's throat, separating tendons and arteries, sending blood gouting. . . .

I dumped him upon the flagstones. He was already dead, but I was mindful of my employer's preferences. I would not flee until the job was finished. I slammed the door closed and dropped the bar, blocking out those few guards who had not caught fire. Their sword pommels hammered upon the door.

I crouched beside Venaius. I pulled open his charred garments, exposing his chest. His men shouted for axes. Venaius gazed up at me, white-eyed. Was he dead? Did something dark stir behind those eyes? I drove my stiletto between his ribs, tickled his heart. One. Two. Three. He gasped. He arched. No more.

Suddenly, his mouth opened wide.

Wider . . .

His mouth opened as if there were no jaw or hinge. It became a cave. He reached up and seized me, dragging me toward that darkness. I tried to stop my plunge, I drove my dagger into his chest, searching for his heart again, I cut and stabbed and tried to get the thing out, to shove it into that terrible gaping maw. My blade caught a rib and stuck.

My hand slipped.

For the first time in my life, my blade failed me. The blood-slick stiletto slipped from my hand.

Venaius swallowed me entirely.

My name is Izio. Though I am dead, I still continue.

The creature that was Venaius haunts me. And I hunt him. I follow his trail over hills of ash as soft as feathers, across black gritty plains spangled with human teeth. I know that he has dragged me into Scuro's realms, and that I am finished—but still I pursue.

Just ahead of me, his footprints hollow the ash, the trail of his bony tail slithers as well. He has a tail. Of course he does. And fangs as long as daggers. But his neck still hangs open where I gave him a second smile.

If I sever the rest of his head, then I think my duty will be done.

Dune after dune, I climb. Then stagger down the far sides, raising the dust of the dead with every stumble, with every slip. Blackened bits of bone cut my bare feet. I am naked. Sometimes, I glimpse others in the distance, but whether they are people like me, or akiz like Venaius, I do not know. The trail before me is enough.

I will find this last one. This last one.

I am Izio. I do not rest, even though I am already dead. I continue, just as my mother did. Did she not birth my dead sister, though she herself had already gone slack in death? Perhaps this is the way of my people. We keep on, regardless. Not even death stops us.

I top a new dune. Below me, a wide river cuts the gray land, sinuous and blackly glittering, as if flowing with mica or diamonds. Upon its shore, Venaius crouches, drinking from its flow.

Eager to be finished, I plunge down the dune, tripping, stumbling, tumbling, coughing. Here, whole bones protrude from the slope: ribs and femurs, ilium and skulls, all of them charred and broken. I take up a thigh bone. A bludgeon.

Ahead of me the river flows. But it churns too slowly. Like mud . . . nai . . . it *undulates*. And as I approach I at last understand. A flowing, skittering, tumbling, clacking river of insects. A river of beetles, black carapaces glinting, mandibles snapping, their bellies bloated with blood. A great heaving flow, some clawing up as others are drowned beneath. A black living mass tumbling and churning, flowing thickly past.

Venaius crouches upon this shore of madness, scooping up beetles and shoveling them down his neck, pouring them into the wound that I created. I heft my bone club, thinking to smash his head to pulp, but as I do, a wailing draws my attention.

A raft floats into view, bobbing upon the churn of insects. It is crowded with people, but one I recognize. The beetles have been at work upon her. Her ribs are flayed open. Her skinny thighs are nearly gone. Her long bones, like the one I grip, gleam white where the beetles have feasted. Her face is tatters, but her eyes remain, staring with horror upon the creatures feasting upon her.

My mother.

Despite the years since I saw her die, I know her. And standing over her, another.

Matra Desira.

The woman who whored us both and who I never had opportunity to repay. As the raft draws closer I see now that she grips my mother's hair, indeed drags back her head. Her lips quest along my mother's cheek. But where she might kiss, instead she gnaws alongside the beetles, chewing into my mother just like the insects.

But Matra Desira, too, is set upon by others in the crowd of passengers. Two men are lashed tight to her. One man stabs Desira's breasts with a knife, the other saws at her buttocks. And as they do, she cries out, and yet still she bites and feeds once more upon my mother. But Desira's tormentors, too, are lashed to others on the raft. A man who rapes. A woman who stabs. A boy who strangles. And so it goes for all the passengers of the raft. Some I recognize, some I do not, but this vast and seething mass of lashed humanity . . . I know instinctively that all these people lived and died beneath the wharves of Quartiere Pescana in my youth.

And the noise of them!

Howling, screaming, begging, and moaning!

When one moves, all move.

When one wounds one, all wound all.

A hand that stabs a belly drives another to shove their face into another and that one cries out and is bitten or stabbed or raped or smothered or castrated or strangled or torn, and so they slowly proceed down the river, all lashed together, sawing back and forth in mutual torture like some mad flour mill grinding them all to pieces and indeed it is more horrifying than that, for now I see that there is no raft at all. They themselves—their lashed-together bodies—make up the craft entire, all of them sobbing and wounded, all of them screaming rage and ravaging others. The ropes that bind them creak and groan, biting into flesh. They all float together. A raft of human animals, a raft of misery.

"And now for you, stilettotore . . ."

In my distraction, Venaius has snuck close. His neck is mended. Ropes dangle from his hands. Creatures of Scuro accompany him, monsters with bodies all scavenged and stitched together, the heads of animals, the bodies of men, the rotten pelts of animals for skin, chicken legs and burned wings and goaty heads . . .

They, too, hold ropes.

I lash out with my bone club, but it shatters instantly. Venaius and his companions laugh. Nothing in Scuro's realm is a threat to them.

Quick as night they bind me.

Through the beetle flow they drag me. The raft of human suffering looms. I cry out in terror, for I see now, at last, what awaits me.

A man. My first kill.

He reaches out from the seething mass of bodies, straining for me, grinning with eagerness even as he groans under the rape of another man. He has a knife, my first knife, that knife that I used to unman him. He beckons me with it.

Venaius and the rest of his creatures shove me close, lash me to him. His sour wine breath gusts over me. His fingers fumble for my root.

I scream. I scream and scream until my voice is hoarse. This is a suffering of my own making, of all our making. Pain, delivered from one person to the next, to the next, to the next . . . Our pain binds us to one another, dooms us all to this seething mass of ruination and rage and retribution, consuming us as we consume one another . . .

And then I hear a howling.

A great howling.

Sharp teeth sink into my arm. Suddenly I am dragged from the mass.

Venaius and his demon friends howl in rage, but a blur of white tosses them aside. They fly and disappear like leaves in a whirlwind and then I am being dragged by a tempest, dragged and dragged through the beetle river, across the bone sands, up and down the ashy hills. Dragged faster and faster. Choking and coughing. My skin flaying, scouring, peeling . . . faster and faster . . . burning with heat, burning and burning—

I wake to flames.

I lie in the building where I effected Venaius's murder. Ashy smoke chokes the air. The roof beams burn. Dead Venaius lies beside me.

A tiny pup licks my face.

Her amber eyes gaze upon me with worry. She licks my face again. Her pale fur is smudged with soot, coated with it, in fact. I pull her close. Hug her squirming happy body to me. And as I do, a weight falls from me. All the weight of that heaving mass of terrible flesh, all those people torturing one another, endlessly, the weight I have always carried. . . .

It all falls away.

I gather the pup into my arms and stumble from the burning building.

Behind me, I leave my stiletto. I leave all my evils. I leave all my blood hungers, all my memeti sangri, justified or not. Matra Desira and Matra Giulia, who so callously sold me for their profit. The man whose root I severed so long ago. All the others like him I could never pay back. My mother, who brought me into this fetid, brutal life.

It all falls away.

They are in Scuro's realm, all of them bound together by their cruelties and broken souls, all still bent upon breaking one another. An endless raft of terror and sorrow and pain and revenge—but I am cut free.

I walk down the burning empty street. I step over the blackened corpses. I bury my face in the sooty fur of the pup who saved me, and I sob.

I sob for days.

I am Izio. I was once a stilettotore.

Now, I wander the ruins of Torre Amo, and I paint the remnants of the old gods. I do not carry a blade, whether rusty or bright.

You see my friend over there? She guards over me and she watches you.

She recognizes those who approach with darkness in their hearts.

Do not scoff. We both know you seek to hire me for murder.

Nai. I will not take your coin. I have seen the Unseen Realms. I have seen what waits there. I will not lash myself to that raft of suffering once again, and I urge you to find a different path as well. We reap a bitter harvest who inflict pain on others. I know this, for I have seen this, and I tell you clear—it never stops.

It never stops.

BLIND MONKEY

Daryl Gregory

The macaque didn't know what was going to happen next. This ignorance was a gift, the lab tech thought—for the monkey, yes, but also for him. He stroked the crown of her gray-brown head with his gloved hand, careful not to touch the back of her skull. He looked into her ruddy, old woman face. The eyes did not look back—the optic nerve had been severed two months before—but the two tiny cameras stitched into her forehead were still live, sending signals. Perhaps a few phosphenes fired deep in her visual cortex. Perhaps she registered a handful of bright pixels—the glint of his gold-rimmed glasses, or the bright tip of the needle—and knew he was there with her.

He was to first inject ketamine—the training manual was clear on this—to reduce anxiety. He wished he could inject a little into himself; he was gripping the syringe tightly, and his hand was trembling. His other hand moved down the animal's neck, to her chest, and found the small nub of the vascular access port. Thank God he didn't have to find a vein. He wasn't sure he'd be able to do that. He inserted the needle through the port's membrane, and pressed the plunger.

He watched as her breathing slowed. Three minutes. Five. This time at her side was an indulgence. He had a lot to do before his shift was over. Yet he stayed with her.

Soon she was asleep. The lab tech turned her head to see the back of her skull, where the X2 was implanted. The device was a couple inches in diameter, the size of a large bottle cap. Almost all of it was battery. The skin around the implant was red and puffy. The monkey had been clawing at it for the past two days, trying to pull it off—and out.

That would've been bad. Under the battery lay a sliver of a chip, from which dangled 128 impossibly thin wires, decorated with 2,048 electrodes, like the tiniest string of Christmas lights. These threads nestled into the visual cortex and spread into the temporal lobe, some stretching almost as far as the amygdala. Who knows what kind of damage the monkey could have done to herself if she were allowed to pull them free.

The lab tech delivered the second shot, three milliliters of highly concentrated sodium pentobarbital. It was a heavier dose than the protocols mandated. He didn't want her to linger. Her chest stopped moving within a minute. The cameras stitched onto her brow were still recording, wirelessly sending images to the X2. And the chip was still firing signals into the dead brain. He was not authorized to turn the device off.

"Good night, Gilda." He removed his glasses and the lenses seemed to stare back at him. He wiped a tear from the side of his nose. Breathed. It was his first month in the lab. His first sacrifice, ever. He was supposed to be an experienced veterinary tech, and it would be suspicious if they found him getting emotional.

The macaque's small body fit easily into the plastic bag. He carried her to the procedure room and placed her in the large refrigerator. Then he busied himself with his other subjects in the AHR—the Animal Housing Room. Most of his job involved feces and urine. He replaced the cedar mulch and pee pads, carried the garbage bags to the dumpster. The cages were twenty years old, with thin wire and fussy door latches. He made sure each water bottle was full and each food bin loaded, and he was careful to double-check the door locks. Then it was time for the nightly Health and Condition check. He picked up the electronic tablet they'd assigned him and began to visit each cage.

Now that Gilda was gone, there were fifteen rhesus macaques to care for—six post-op, and nine pre-op. Two of the subjects showed signs of infection. That meant extra electronic forms to fill out for both subjects. The amount of data they required him to collect seemed excessive, but he hadn't questioned his supervisor. This was capital *S* Science. He may be the most lowly employee on the org chart, but he'd do his part. This company, this project, would change people's lives.

At seven a.m. the lights went on in the offices behind the AHR doors. The lab tech knew who it must be. He waited a few minutes, then picked up his coffee cup and went through what he called the airlock—two sets of doors with a vestibule between them—that separated the AHR from the research area.

Dr. Martha Chou was at her desk, waking up her computer. Martha was always first in. She was only five years and four months older than him, but she already had a PhD, with several publications to her name. She was also one of the few scientists who looked him in the eye and talked to him like a human.

She asked him about his night. "Gilda's in the fridge," he said. "She went gentle."

Martha frowned. "Gilda?"

"G-2."

"I wouldn't name them," she said.

The lab tech heated with embarrassment. Martha waved off his apologies. "It's just that word's come down that there are a lot more animals coming," she said. "We're ramping up. You're going to be pretty busy."

"Really?" The news made him nervous, but also excited. They'd need him. "I hadn't heard."

"Alberto confirmed it in the general staff meeting yesterday."

"Alberto was here, in person?" He'd only seen their founder on company videos. And on the news. The lab tech understood why Alberto couldn't visit too often—he was one of the richest people on the planet, and this company was low on his list of priorities—which meant that the lab tech may never get another chance to meet him. "Nobody told me about the meeting," he said. "I would have come in for that."

"He was here just for a couple minutes," she said. Trying to make him feel better. "He wanted to tell us in person that they found our first human volunteer. Wait, let me . . ." She flipped through some papers on her desk and handed him a printout. It was the picture of a woman with salt-and-pepper hair and a warm smile. "Alberto promised her she'd see the face of her granddaughter in six months."

"Is that possible?" The lab tech had gotten the impression they were years from human subject testing.

"We're going to find out." He couldn't read her expression.

He stared at the printout. Martha told him to keep it.

"It is nice to have a face," the lab tech said. "Very motivating."

The volunteer's name was Carol Romine. The lab tech pinned her picture to the corkboard in his cubicle, on top of the OSHA safety flyers. In the picture Carol wore sunglasses, and a bright yellow sleeveless top. She was somewhere sunny, and the sky was bright blue. The beach maybe. She was fifty-six years old, and lost her vision in a fungal infection that had attacked her retinas. He looked at her smile several times a day.

Martha was right about the accelerated pace. Four macaques arrived from Georgia the next week, and three more the week after that. The AHR was nearly at capacity, two monkeys to a cage. The new arrivals were lively little guys, not exactly wild, not exactly tame. The protocol was to put them through three months of behavioral training before surgery. They had to become acclimated to frequent blood draws, learn to tolerate being strapped down into the MRI, get used to scientists poking at them. In one of the final steps, they were fitted with fake X2s—empty plastic discs, with no wires—that were stitched to their skulls.

An email informed the lab tech that the training period was being trimmed from twelve weeks to eight, but the training *hours* would remain the same, and his assistance would be required. This was new; until now the dayshift staff were responsible for all training. But the lab tech was assigned a few simple exercises. He'd put on heavy gloves, secure a leash to Henry's neck, and let him scamper up his shirt with his tiny hungry hands. When the exuberant Marty sat on the exam table without trying to jump away he rewarded him with raisins. He'd carry Junebug—sweet, timid Junebug—to the procedure room and let her get used to the alarming smells. Each time she stayed a minute longer, she received a dried apricot.

The pre-op macaques didn't know that these experiences were the last they'd see with their own eyes. They lived in the moment. Humans were the only animals that ruminated on disaster, imagining possible dooms. The lab tech worried constantly. Would his bosses find out he lied on his résumé?

Would they fire him? He'd finally found a job with purpose, and he worked with animals that loved him.

The pre-op animals did, anyway. The post-op subjects were another story. They were growing sour and wary. They often yawned, showing their teeth, a sign of anxiety. They twisted their heads back and forth, trying to scoop light into their tiny forehead cameras. When he leaned close to the cage they'd sense him—perhaps only his shadow?—and back into a corner, mouths agape.

Of course they were afraid. They were in pain, and lived in darkness.

As the number of subjects increased, the lab tech was forced to work overtime. Before he'd finished his assigned tasks it would be well into the morning and the building would be filling with scientists and programmers and other day-shift staff. He began to leave the AHR not through the back door by the loading dock, but through the airlock, into the research area. From there he took a meandering path to the front door. He passed the busy offices and cubicles, admiring the cryptic equations and diagrams on the whiteboards, gazing at printouts of scatterplots and MRI scans. In his domain it was all shit and piss and pus, a riot of bodily fluids and smells. But out here, all that messiness was rendered into clean data and bloodless math.

He had so many questions, but he was too nervous to talk to the scientists, except Martha. When she wasn't too busy she'd kindly give him a few minutes to answer his questions, which really boiled down to two questions: Was the X2 working, and was it worth it? He could only ask one of those questions.

Martha assured him that the X2 was definitely working. "I had my doubts about the new schedule," she told him one morning, "but I have to admit we've seen huge improvements in the model. You can't talk to anyone about this, okay?"

"I signed the NDA." The penalties for talking to outsiders about the project would bankrupt him for life.

"Right. Well, just look at this regression plot." Her computer monitor was as big and curved as a top-line gaming rig, and the screen was crowded with open apps. "That trend line is crazy."

He leaned close, not sure which window to look at. He grunted appreciatively.

"With every new version of the software we're getting better signal-matching," she said. "Edge detection, depth perception, contrast . . ." The X2 code was continually updated with the best results from the other subjects. The monkeys were learning from each other. Even when a macaque was sacrificed, the most successful code in its algorithm was forwarded to the other animals.

"I get that the X2 sends the video to the brain," he said, "but I don't understand how—" He stopped because she was shaking her head. He'd gotten something wrong. "I'm sorry," he said. "I should let you get back to work."

She put up a hand. "No, you should understand what we're doing. You're part of the team."

He was looking into her eyes when she said this. Emotions rushed through him—elation? Terror? His body couldn't sort through the feelings. He felt hollow and heavy at the same time.

"The chip's not sending video," Martha said. She didn't seem to notice that he'd been struck dumb. "It's *receiving* video from the cameras, sure. But it turns that complex data into a more manageable stream, turning full video into a, well, think of it as a line drawing. Just the brightest points and the sharpest edges. Then it sends that simplified data to the brain. The X2 doesn't give the animals *vision*, not like you'd think of it, but visual information. Does that make sense?"

The lab tech nodded, but his face must have betrayed his confusion, because she kept talking, kept explaining. He was both grateful and embarrassed.

"Say the cameras record the monkey looking out of its cage," she said. "The chip turns that into simple shapes. There's the rectangle of the cage wall, which is made up of a grid of squares, and then beyond the cage are a bunch of other shapes. We send that data to the neurons. Not just the ones in the visual cortex, but way past it, into the lateral nucleus, the basal ganglia . . ." He loved the excitement in her face. "The brain's job is to try to sort through the blast of data and figure out what to pay attention to. Is the rectangle important, or the squares, the blobs beyond the squares?"

This was the longest Martha had ever spoken to him. She told him of the team's long struggle to turn images into electrical charges, and then try to record that mental activity to verify that the monkeys were perceiving them.

They're reading their minds, he thought. Aloud he said, "It sounds impossible."

Martha smiled. "Just really, really difficult. The thing is, the pattern-matching algorithm will get better for later subjects. They'll learn from previous X2 installations, and that'll help every subject down the line, all the way to Carol Romine."

"She'll see what the dead have seen."

"What?"

"I just mean..." What did he mean? Why had he said that aloud? He was an idiot. "I'm just glad that their deaths will mean something."

"No, that's not—" She seemed upset, and he didn't know why. "The monkeys don't have to die."

"But—"

"Afterward, we'll remove the X2s—they're designed to be removed. Or we'll leave them in if they're helpful to the animals."

She doesn't know, he thought. She was a data scientist and got all her information from the Health and Condition reports. She knew the infection rates, could see the death count, and thought that told her everything she needed to know. The data people rarely went into the AHR anymore. They didn't want to reckon with wet reality.

"Helpful, yes," he said. "That's so great."

A week before, something had gone wrong during Henry's surgery. An edema had formed beside the implant, swelling the left side of his head, and he'd clawed at the X2 until it was bloody. The lab tech reported it, and the next morning the day staff operated again, and found that a piece of the X2 had broken off inside him. Bacterial infection had set in.

As always, it fell to the lab tech to sacrifice the animal. He moved Henry into the squeeze cage, so the monkey couldn't escape the needle, then injected the prescribed amount of ketamine. The lab tech didn't have time to wait for the drug to take effect; he had another subject to attend to. When he returned twenty minutes later, Henry lay on his back, his hands slowly pawing at the air in a swimming motion. The lab tech loaded the pentobarbital and the needle tapped one of the metal bars.

Henry turned his head at the sound. The twin cameras were like tiny black eyes, all pupil. The monkey screamed. The ketamine was wearing off, or had worn off completely. He pushed backward on feeble arms but there was nowhere to go.

The lab tech slid the needle between the bars, aiming for the access port on his chest, but Henry twisted sideways. Finally the lab tech put on his heavy gloves and opened the door. He put his hands on Henry's chest and held him down. The monkey's jaw worked, teeth trying to find purchase, failed. The cameras stared into the lab tech's face. The needle plunged into the port.

After, the lab tech went to his cubicle and sat with his back to the room. The monkeys yipped and barked in agitation. He gazed at the picture of Carol Romine. He'd been doing this a lot, lately. Her smile calmed him. In only a couple months now she'd see her granddaughter.

A few days later he received an email from Alberto. The subject line was "INNOVATE OR DIE"—an all-caps command. He began to panic, and then realized it was an all-staff email. They were to stop thinking like academics, Alberto said, and start thinking like developers in a start-up. Anybody who wasn't onboard should get out now.

The lab tech wanted to stay. He wanted to be an innovator.

He was supposed to eat in the AHR breakroom. Instead the lab tech took his lunch to the research area, where it was dark, and quiet, and clean. The scientists had been staying later and later, sometimes until midnight, but by the time mid-shift break came at three a.m. he had the place to himself. He was rarely hungry these days, but he forced himself to eat. He'd nibble at a protein bar, wash it down with the special filtered water they'd installed only in the research area. He'd find an unlocked computer and look at the latest data, read the reports.

He always checked Martha's desk first, and felt a thrill when she'd left her PC unlocked. That had been happening more and more lately. It was as if she wanted him to see the data. To stay informed. Be part of the team.

He began to fall in love with watching replay videos. A replay was when the scientists took a scene the cameras had recorded earlier—from that monkey's cameras, or any monkey's—and fed it through the X2 while the animal was in the MRI machine, and it would experience the scene as if it were wearing a full VR headset. It would respond—turning its head as far as the restraints allowed, even trying to reach for objects that weren't there.

The video was broken into multiple windows. One showed the monkey in the machine, another various stats from the X2, another a heat map of brain activity generated by the MRI. The most interesting window was the interpretive map, where the X2 made statistical guesses at what the subject was perceiving. It was like a primitive video game; bright, quivering line segments struggled to form shapes, like toothpicks being rearranged on a bar top. Squares, rectangles, rough circles. A flickering rectangle might be a cage door opening. A bright grid might be the examination table.

Some of these shapes increased activity beyond the visual cortex, into the amygdala. They weren't just visual events, but emotional ones. One event that reliably sent a flare through the emotion heat map were the twin polygons: pairs of vaguely circular shapes that appeared again and again, in different sizes—very small, suddenly very large. None of the scientists seemed to have made notes about the pairs. Maybe they weren't important after all, the lab tech thought. Maybe his own interest in the doubles, his own flare of emotion when he saw them, meant nothing either.

The behavioral training time was cut to four weeks. There was no more talk of squeezing the required training hours into those days. The all-staff emails started using words like *iteration*, *cadence*, *sprint*. Software development terms. They were sprinting now.

Animal subjects continued to arrive from Georgia, but the AHRs were running out of room for them. One night the lab tech came to work to find that his cubicle had been disassembled to make room for additional cages. He found Carol's picture in the trash. He retrieved it, smoothed it out, and taped it to a wall of the breakroom

Pre-op macaques were prepped as quickly as possible, sometimes three a week. They went into the procedure room and came back with tiny cameras stitched to brows and X2s screwed into the back of their skulls. Vascular access ports were installed in their chests like badges to signify their promotion. These modifications used to require three separate procedures, with days or weeks between them. Now they were all performed at once. It was more efficient.

A few days after Marty's surgery, the monkey became unable to move his left hand or leg. His feces was bloody. He became the lab tech's third sacrifice.

Then another monkey developed an issue; its implant became so loose that it jostled when the creature moved. Blood wept from the sides of the device, and when the animal sat down, its whole body trembled uncontrollably. The lab tech noted this on his table. The animal was designated Subject M-2, and that's how the lab tech thought of it. He couldn't remember when he'd stopped naming the animals. M-2, eventually, became his fourth sacrifice. A fifth, for Subject J-3, came a day later.

The reduced behavioral training time meant that some of the monkeys never learned to tolerate the enclosed space of the MRI. They fought their restraints, thrashed and bit and yowled. They had to be partially sedated when doing the replay experiments.

Behavior in the cages became more extreme. Some of the post-op subjects knocked their heads against the cage walls, over and over, like severely autistic children trying to soothe themselves. Aggression increased. Two different macaques shook their cage doors so fiercely that they sprang open. The first one's poor vision made it hesitant to leap onto the floor. But the second one jumped down, and scrambled erratically across the floor. The lab tech quickly pulled on his padded gloves and seized the animal from behind. The animal snapped at him and barked.

The lab tech began to feel that every post-op animal hated him. Often they stared blindly at him with their mouths agape, a macaque's most aggressive expression. When he moved his face too close to their cages, they screeched and banged the walls of the cage. He duly noted this in the Health and Condition reports.

He received an email from his supervisor, to stay late for a "morning chat." He was sure he was going to be fired. But the supervisor put a hand on the lab tech's shoulder and told him that the monkeys' behavior was actually a good sign—proof they were seeing him, that the X2s were working. His grin was meant to be reassuring. The grin faded. The lab tech was to restrict his report comments to the health of the subjects. "Listen, writing stuff like 'the monkeys hate me'—that's not helpful, okay? Leave your personal feelings out of it." The lab tech didn't understand—he was recording facts, not feelings—but said nothing.

Don't think like an academic, he told himself. Innovate or die.

The lab tech went to a hardware store on his own time and bought twenty bungee cords with his own money. He wrapped them around the cages of the most aggressive subjects. He didn't mention this in the Health and Condition reports, and neither did the day staff. No one removed the cords, though they made it more difficult to open the doors. They all understood.

He didn't put a cord on Junebug's cage. His sweet timid girl had somehow become the longest-lived macaque in the project. They continued to update her software, but she never seemed to see him through her cameras. She smelled him, though. He'd slide open her door and she'd lean forward so he could scratch the back of her neck. Fur had grown up around her X2, hiding it. Maybe Martha was right. They could let Junebug keep wearing the implant, for the rest of her life. The other monkeys wouldn't even know she was different.

The lab tech sat at Martha's desk, studying the replay videos. Shapes appeared and disappeared, combinations of line segments that suggested a three-dimensional world. Sometimes the screen would erupt in bright geometries. Sometimes everything would go black except for a block of rectangles that suggested a face, or perhaps a hand. The X2 was learning what was foreground, what was background. What to pay attention to.

The twins kept appearing. Many of them were hexagons, like pairs of stop signs. Once he noticed them he saw them everywhere: floating in the background behind a wall of squares, small and barely visible; then suddenly large, driving out other shapes. Several times, at the end of the feed, the twins filled the entire screen.

Looking for answers, he downloaded Martha Chou's research papers, going back to her grad school days. Sometimes he printed them and took them home to his apartment, a studio with small-paned windows. When he couldn't sleep, he'd sit on his bed reading and rereading them. He learned a lot about the visual cortex and other areas of the brain that participated in perception in mysterious ways. One of Martha's studies confirmed the existence of a subcortical pathway between the V2 area of the visual cortex and the amygdala—a superhighway between vision and emotion. What we saw affected our emotions, and what we felt affected what we paid attention to.

But there was nothing in her papers to explain the importance of paired shapes, and nothing in the replay notes. Had he noticed something no one else had? He felt like a janitor at the observatory who'd noticed a new star. Imagine Martha's surprise. The scientists would come by to thank him. Alberto would pump his hand—so lucky to have you! But he had to be sure. He loaded one of Marty's replays, one he'd watched before, and began to take notes.

"What are you doing?"

He jolted as if coming awake behind the wheel of a car. Martha! A nervous giggle escaped him.

"You scared me! Sorry!" He jumped up from her chair. Words tumbled out of him. Apologies, explanations, questions. How are you doing? What was she doing here at this time of night?

"I couldn't sleep," she said. "I decided I might as well work." She looked at her desk but did not sit down. Crumbs had fallen on her keyboard and on the surface of the desk. "Have you been eating here?"

"Yeah, no. I just—" He quickly brushed the crumbs into his palm and closed his fist over them. "I just wanted to see how we were doing."

She nodded slowly.

"Have you noticed the double shapes?"

"What?"

"In the feed. These twin polygons keep popping up, and I was wondering, because of your work on vision and emotion, if you considered—"

"You've read my research?"

"I wanted to ask you about the pathway that runs between the amygdala and the visual cortex through the, the . . ." He gestured at the side of his head.

"Superior colliculus," she said.

"Yes! That was so interesting to me, that superfast feedback loop? It makes so much sense, that link between what we see and what we feel, or maybe what we should pay *more* attention to? We have to focus, right, even if—like the tiger's face in the grass, evolution has, has . . ." He hated when he got tongue-tied. He needed her to know that he understood, really understood. Evolution made sure that vision and emotion were tightly linked. A threat is detected, and the human has to react—without *considering* the threat, *pondering* it—because those slow thinkers never passed on their genes. "I was thinking how the brain comes preloaded with these threat images, right? Like the movement of spiders, or . . ."

She was staring at him.

"I'm sorry," he said. "I'm wasting your time."

He expected her to say, *Of course not, tell me what you've seen in the data, we're all on the same team here, all hands on deck.* She said nothing.

"Yeah, I need to get back," he said. "It's getting kinda crazy back there." He hurried toward the airlock. When he reached the first set of doors he looked back, and Martha was still standing by her desk. Watching him.

The next night a printout was taped to the airlock doors that led out to the re- search area.

ANIMAL HOUSING TECH STAFF ARE RESTRICTED
TO AHRS, PROCEDURE ROOMS, AND BREAKROOM.
EXIT BY LOADING DOCK. NO EXCUSES.

The lab tech felt sick to his stomach. Martha had complained about him. Next thing, they'd fire him. He thought about quitting first. He pictured himself ripping down the printout and storming out. Kept picturing it, all night, as he cleaned the cages and refilled the food dispensers and filled out the Health and Condition forms. He pictured it the next night, too, and the next. Soon it was a soothing mental image, like the picture of Carol Romine. He could quit at any time, but he'd stay for her. They had to make the X2 work, because otherwise, what was all this suffering for? He was surrounded by pain. Swimming in death.

His termination notice never arrived. He gradually realized that they couldn't fire him because there was too much work to do, and his job was too awful for a new hire. Bacterial infections raged through the AHRs. Even some of the most promising subjects had to be put down. None of the day staff ever sacrificed an animal. They left that ugly work to him. One week there was a bad run, and he received three sacrifice orders in two nights. He did as he was told. He injected the ketamine, then the high dose of pentobarbital, and watched their faces as they died. Then he bagged their bodies stacked them in the refrigerator. He'd lost track of how many procedures he'd performed.

Alberto's six-month deadline passed. The all-staff emails talked about "exciting progress" without specifying details. They didn't mention the SEC investigation, the news stories about animal deaths at other company labs, the congressman threatening to subpoena Alberto. But the emails did frequently remind everyone of their NDAs. If anyone outside the company contacted them, they were to notify HR immediately.

It was so hard to sleep during the day. Light blasted through the blinds in his apartment, heating the room, and when evening came he was exhausted. Yet he forced himself to get up, eat something, and drive to work, as if these were behavioral training exercises, and he was his own handler. He no longer went into the research area to check the data for himself. He cleaned and fed and reported. He put down the animals they ordered him to. His body knew what to do, so his mind could sleep.

Time became slippery; the hours were long but the weeks seemed to melt into each other. New subjects appeared and were given as much training as his time allowed. X2s were installed. Software updates were rolled out. It seemed to him that the X2 was working. Almost all the macaques could clearly navigate their cages, and several could reach unerringly for treats. Many watched him as he passed, staring at him with gaping mouths, or banged on the cages. He thought about buying more bungee cords.

Junebug didn't need one. She sat in her cage and waited, quietly. One Tuesday, when a shipment of fresh treats came in, he opened her cage and offered her a dried apricot. She leaped toward his hand and bit down.

He shouted, yanked back his hand. Junebug leaped onto the floor and scampered away.

The meat of his palm was bleeding badly. He pressed a paper towel to the wound and went looking for Junebug. Turned a corner and she looked up at him, mouth open. "Hey, girl," he said, and took a step. She leaped onto another macaque's cage. Barks and yips filled the room.

He pulled on his heavy gloves. Stuffed more towels into the glove that covered his injured hand. It took him nearly twenty minutes to corner Junebug and push her into her cage.

He reported her escape and her demonstration of visual acuity without mentioning the bite. He didn't want her to get in trouble.

Eight weeks after Junebug's breakout, and twenty after Alberto's original dead-line, the lab tech received an email saying that Carol Romine had received the implant and was doing well. Alberto did an interview talking about what a huge leap forward this was. Right now Carol could see only the edges of some objects and distinguish brightness from shadow, but that was enough to let her navigate around furniture, find a door in a wall, reach for a water glass. There was no mention if she could recognize her granddaughter's face.

The lab tech wished he could talk to Martha about it. She was the only one at work who spoke to him like he had a brain, and the NDA made it impossible to speak to anyone outside of work. Only Alberto could talk about the things the project had accomplished. Or how they'd done it. He didn't understand why he didn't feel better about this milestone. Maybe because his job didn't change? Two weeks after Carol's implant, the influx of new test subjects slowed, but the rickety cages were still full.

There was one bright spot on the horizon: Carol Romine was coming. That Friday afternoon there'd be a "media event" that all staff were invited to, so Carol could thank them in person. The day before her visit he got a haircut. After his night shift, he went home, took a shower, and put on clothes that he'd never worn in the animal housing rooms. He went in through the front door.

The desks in the central research area had been pushed to the walls to make way for a stage. The floor was crowded. Many staff members had brought their families. Bright balloons printed with the company logo hovered overhead. He looked around for Martha Chou, and finally spotted her. She was standing beside a smiling Chinese man that he didn't recognize. Practically glued to his side. Was Martha married? In all their talks before he'd stopped going into the Research area, she'd never mentioned that to him. But then again, their relationship was based around work. Their conversations were about evolution, neuroscience, biology. Important things.

The room erupted in applause when Alberto and Carol entered. She was accompanied by her daughter, son-in-law, and six-year-old granddaughter—the famous granddaughter. Carol wore a little hat, something like a skipper's cap, and the large glasses that fed video to her X2 chip. She seemed frailer than her picture, but her smile was just as brilliant. She had a little trouble finding the microphone, but then she leaned close and thanked them. "You changed my life," she said. Then she took off her cap and half turned to show them the back of her head. Her hair was already growing over the X2. "Isn't she a beauty?" she said, and everyone cheered.

The lab tech's eyes blurred with tears. It was such a relief to have something good come out of this, after such a long time.

Alberto stepped up to the microphone. "One more thing," he said. Everyone laughed. "Monday morning we start developing the X3!" Everyone around the lab tech clapped and hooted. "In one year, two tops, anyone wearing one of our chips will have *better* than human vision."

The applause continued. The lab tech didn't believe artificial vision at that level was remotely possible, not within the decade. Did any of the scientists believe it? Maybe it didn't matter. The underlying message was clear: Alberto wasn't going to stop. Maybe there was no such thing as stopping.

Carol was helped down from the stage so she could greet the staff. She stood up front with her family, as if forming a receiving line at a wedding or a funeral, and the staff obediently formed a queue. The line moved slowly because Carol wanted to talk with everyone. The lab tech noticed that she kept tilting her head, as if trying to get more light to enter the video cameras.

He waited almost twenty minutes to reach the front of the line. He shook hands with Carol's daughter, then the son-in-law. The granddaughter was half hiding behind her father, one arm looped around his leg. "Are you one of the researchers?" the man asked the lab tech. Carol was talking with someone, so he was filling time.

"I take care of the monkeys," the lab tech said.

The granddaughter looked up at him in surprise. "You have monkeys?"

"Oh yes." He crouched down to her eye level. "I feed them, I clean their cages. I give them treats."

That excited her. "What kind of treats?"

"Lots of stuff. Fruit, nuts. One of my favorite monkeys, Junebug, she likes apricots. I just hold out my hand . . ." He extended his palm to the girl. She laughed and reached out as if there were something in his palm. "And zip! She just—"

Carol screamed.

The lab tech looked up—and Carol threw herself on top of him. He fell onto his back and she was straddling him, clawing at his face. His glasses went flying. He didn't understand what was happening. He raised his arms and she slammed her forehead into his nose. His head fell back and the woman bent close. He felt a bright pain on his cheek.

He shouted and twisted away from her. Arms grabbed him, hauled him sideways. Other people pulled Carol away from him.

Everyone was shouting. People scrambled away or surged forward. A chaos of moving limbs and shapes. He put a hand to cheek. It came away bloody. She'd bit him.

"What *was* that?" Carol said. She was only five feet from him. Her own glasses and been knocked off. Blood painted her chin. Her voice was full of terror. "*What was that?*"

The lab tech's supervisor and another man steered him out of the research room, into the airlock, then into the main AHR. Pushed him into a chair. They pummeled him with questions. What did he do? Did he touch the girl? Did he know what the fuck he'd done? Carol would want them to pull the X2, send them all back to square one, is that what he wanted?

"I didn't do anything." It was hard to look at their faces. His vision was blurred. "I don't know why she did that."

"Jesus Christ," his supervisor said. They were very angry with him, as if he had been the attacker. They seemed disgusted by his bleeding, and debated calling 911.

A female voice said, "I'm a doctor. Let me see him." It was Martha.

"I brought your glasses," she said. "Don't put them on yet, let me see the wound." She dabbed at his cheek with a napkin. Hissed in sympathy. "I'm going to need bandages." His supervisor sent the stranger to find the first-aid kit.

He stayed in his chair, looking down at his wire-rimmed glasses. The lenses were intact, but the bridge was bent. He gently twisted it back into true, until the two gold frames were staring back at him. Twin hexagons.

His hands stopped moving.

The stranger had returned with the first-aid kit. Martha sorted through the supplies with quick fingers, found what she needed first. "Close your eyes." The bite was very close to his left eye. She soaked the area with antiseptic. "When was your last tetanus booster?"

He couldn't answer. He was finding it hard to breathe. Martha touched his shoulder. "Hey. It's going to be okay."

"It's so obvious," he said. His voice was a whisper. She didn't seem to hear him. She was pressing a bandage to his cheek.

"They're all through the feed," he said. "You must have seen them too."

"What the fuck are you talking about?" his supervisor said.

"*Please*," Martha said to the man. Her voice was stern. "Could you give us some room?"

"Jesus Christ," the supervisor said, but he stepped back.

"It's all right," Martha said to the lab tech. "Hold still." She taped the bandage to his skin. Murmured something about stitches. The supervisor kept asking him, Can you drive? You don't need an ambulance, do you? The lab tech agreed that he didn't need an ambulance. He promised he'd seek medical attention.

The supervisor told him to leave by the rear exit. Martha walked with him to the door.

"Martha," he said. He kept his voice low so the supervisor couldn't overhear. "Look." He turned the glasses so she could see. "They know."

"Who knows?" she asked. "What are you talking about?"

"I always thought humans were the only animals who knew we were going to die. But what if we've taught them?"

Her brow furrowed.

"I'm the last thing they see," he explained. "All the subjects that come after, even Carol . . . they see what the dead have seen."

Martha opened the door and he grabbed her arm.

"They recognize me," he said. He looked into her face. "They know what I am."

He didn't seek medical attention. He went to his apartment. Sat on the bed for a long time. When the bite on his cheek began to sting, he took a couple of ibuprofens. He considered eating, but he wasn't hungry, and there wasn't anything in the apartment anyway. At his usual time, he got into his car and drove to work.

A dayshift staff member—Anthony? Aaron?—was in the AHR breakroom, getting an energy drink from the fridge. He was surprised to see the lab tech. "They told me you had the night off, because of the . . ." He tilted his head, a gesture that implied everything and said nothing. "That bandage looks a little bloody."

"I'm good," the lab tech said.

"You sure?"

"Enjoy your weekend."

The dayshift man left and the building quieted. The lab tech turned on his tablet, and made a zip file of the year's Health and Condition reports. Then he searched online for news stories about the company, picked the first reporter email he found, and clicked send. The data would be the start of a good story. He could make it better.

He walked into the AHR. It was quiet except for the hiss of the air filters, the creak and shuffle of the macaques. They watched him as he moved between the cages, their tiny hands gripping the wires. They gaped at him as he refilled the food bins, topped off their water jugs. Almost all the monkeys were post-op, their bodies decorated with plastic and metal. Their insect eyes tracked him.

Junebug's cage sat at the end of the row. She crouched in the corner, her face turning to follow him. "Hey there," he said softly. She was trembling. "Don't be afraid."

He reached for the door latch and she exploded toward him. Her body slammed into the door. It would have popped open if the bungee cord hadn't kept it shut. Her arms reached through the wires, tiny claws reaching for him.

He'd jerked back when she charged. A speedy, natural reaction. He took a breath, and then reached around the side of the cage to unhook one end of the cord. She wheeled and threw herself at his hand, teeth out.

"I know," he said. "I know."

He hooked the bungee cord to the door latch, then let the cord hang to the ground. Junebug watched him. He moved to the next cage in line, and repeated the procedure: first he unhooked the cord, then he attached it to the latch. And so he went down the line.

The animals grew more agitated. Their barks and hisses grew louder. They leaped in their cages, and clung to the walls, and threw clumps of cedar mulch.

"I know," he told them. "I know."

He moved down the center of the row, gathering up the cords in each fist, as if he were holding the reins for a team of horses. The other ends were hooked to the latches. Very carefully, he sat down in the middle of the aisle.

He knew what was going to happen next. The knowledge was a gift.

A MURDER HOUSE

Andy Duncan

On Christmas Day 1925, in Stokes County, North Carolina, a farmer named Charlie Lawson sent his oldest son, sixteen-year-old Arthur, to a neighboring farm toting a gift, a jar of still-hot red-eye gravy wrapped in a soap-scented, lemon-yellow dish towel. The towel kept the boy's fingers from burning, and the errand ensured one person's survival, if *survival* is the word.

Once Arthur was away, Charlie Lawson turned his 12-gauge shotgun on his daughter Carrie, age twelve; his daughter Maybelle, age seven; his wife, Fannie, age thirty-seven; his daughter Marie, age seventeen; his son James, age four; his son Raymond, age two; and his daughter Mary Lou, age four months; all listed here, for reasons of accuracy and fairness and common decency, in the order in which they were murdered—though the two youngest boys are, frankly, a toss-up, as they were huddled together, trying and failing to be quiet and good.

When he was done in the house forever, Charlie carried his 12-gauge out back, into the woods, and walked circles around a shortleaf pine for two hours and forty-eight minutes, until he heard the neighbors and the police and the dogs, and then he let them all know where he was by blowing his own head clear into Forsyth County. They say that the cold hard ground was so tramped down, you'd think Charlie Lawson's entire family had been walking around that pine tree with him, just to keep him company.

After the murders, Charlie Lawson's brother Marion needed money to keep up his place and Charlie's too, so Marion opened the murder house as a tourist attraction, ten cents a head and a nickel apiece for the little ones.

You really ought to go, to take the tour. What else is there to do in Stokes County in winter?

You go on a Sunday, which turns out to be a mistake. You get caught in the after-church crowd. Whole congregations are sitting in the Lawson yard on benches of planks and bricks, waiting their turn.

As people wait, many sing hymns. "Just a Closer Walk with Thee" is popular. Others swap murder theories.

"They say Charlie Lawson had a fight with some foreigner, a drifter, just a few days before, and that so-and-so come back and killed all of them."

"Ed, don't say so-and-so, and besides, that can't be right. What is Lawson supposed to have been doing all that time, while his family was being murdered one by one?"

"And over the course of forty-five minutes, the coroner said."

"And why wait to kill Lawson until all the neighbors were here? How'd the drifter expect to get away?"

"And how come they didn't catch him at the time? And how come they ain't caught him yet? No, Lyle, it don't make sense."

"It don't make any sense for a man to up and shoot his wife and babies on Christmas Day, neither. Of the two, I'd rather believe in the crazy foreigner, thank you very much."

"Well, my daughter is best friends with the cousin of the best friend of the oldest Lawson girl, and according to her—"

"According to which one?"

"Well, according to all of them, I guess, Marie confided to the friend just before Christmas that she was *with child*." The last two words are whispered but still carry a good twelve feet. "And no man on the premises but her *own father*."

"Lord have mercy."

"Now, Hilda, there ain't no evidence for that."

"Well, the coroner ought to have looked for some. If Marie was with child, that baby still would have been inside her, wouldn't it?"

"Hah. You obviously didn't see the body."

"Did *you*?"

"No, but my brother the deputy did. He said she was cut in half, nearly. There wouldn't be no baby left to find."

"Shot like that on purpose, I bet you."

"If y'all don't talk about something else, I'll be sick."

"Just think of that. Maybe Charlie killed seven of his children, then, not just six. If you count the one in the womb, I mean."

"Lord have mercy. Who wants a lemonade?"

When your number is called, you gather with two dozen others at the rope that has been tied across the porch steps. A Lawson cousin leads you inside, the men all taking off their hats. The house itself is nothing special. The bodies have long since been buried, of course—in a single grave, Charlie Lawson tumbled in with the rest. Tongues wagged about that, of course, but the family insisted, the extended family that is, and besides, what else would they have done with him? Hung him in the town square? So the bodies aren't there, and the messes inside the house have been cleaned up, the furniture straightened, the Christmas tree taken down when it turned brown and dropped needles and was declared a fire hazard.

"This house *ought* to burn," mutters an old woman jostling you from behind to peer into the next room. "This house is cursed," she continues. "It ought to be burned and salt sown where it stood. My land, I have a set of curtains just like those." That is how it goes, everyone remarking on how normal everything looks.

The Lawson cousin leading your tour, a rickety, sallow-faced girl, blandly states in a flat nasal voice where each body was found, minus the two found in the barn. "The boys were found here, beneath the stairs," she honks, her gesture coming several seconds too late, and later, "The baby was found here, in this crib." She has not a speck of showmanship, but the crowd is eating it up, and maybe showmanship is unnecessary in a murder house.

The last room entered is the kitchen, where the oldest girl was found. While the baby and the toddlers are the most pitiful cases, the death of the eldest girl seems to excite the most curiosity. A cynic would say Marie is the sex angle. "Here the eldest girl, Marie, was found," honks the cousin. "And here you see the very raisin cake that Marie baked on Christmas morning, that she pulled out of the oven not an hour before she died. This cake was never eaten."

This last remark is unnecessary, as the cake clearly has not even been sliced. It still sits on the cutting board next to the sink. The top of it is jumbled, though, for when the cousin isn't looking, people pluck raisins off the top and pocket them as souvenirs.

On the front porch again, the children are sent on into the yard to play, and the curious adults—all of you, really—are allowed to look at the only remaining bloodstains, the ones left by Fannie Lawson's body. "Here," the cousin intones, lifting an area rug to reveal a black-red smear. A woman swoons. Then the cousin offers prints of the Lawsons' last family photograph, taken two weeks before the end, for a nickel apiece. On the back of each photograph is the name and address and telephone number of the photography studio the Lawsons patronized, in case you, too, want to have a nice photo of your relatives taken before you murder them all.

You walk slowly through the yard, studying the faces in the photograph, wondering what has become of Arthur, wondering whether the boy has taken the tour. You look up from the photo to see that you have automatically gotten back in line, waiting to buy another ticket and take another number. You've walked in a circle, just like Charlie Lawson. Clearly you are not done with the murder house, and the murder house is not done with you.

You dream yourself onto a dirt road. On both sides are tobacco fields. You do not walk but instead move forward. You glide. You cannot control your progress. You cannot stop. You cannot slow down. You cannot turn around. You want to turn around. You look at the fields on both sides. You cannot control where you look. The harvest is over. The fields are gray and dead. A shotgun fires. You know the sound. The shotgun fires a second time. A murder of crows rises into the gray air. You want to flee the sound. You move toward the sound. You pick up speed. A tobacco barn is ahead. The shotgun fires a third time. You stop counting. You veer off the lane. You move closer to the barn. You want to be anywhere but the barn. You enter the barn. The harvest is over. The barn is dark and empty. The barn reeks of tobacco. On the floor is a carpet of leaves. The leaves make no noise. In the far corner lie two girls. Through the rough planks of the barn the sun patterns the girls in light and dark. You want to move no closer. You move closer. The black patterns on the girls are not only shadow. The wind moans. The wind stops. Black stains pattern their dresses. Black stains pattern the floor around them. The arms of the girls are folded across their chests. The left arm of the older girl does not line up. Look closer. It looks wrong. Look closer. The blast hit her in the shoulder. Her shoulder was damaged. In trying to fold the arm across afterward it was damaged again. The arm lies there. The wind moans. The wind stops. The face of the younger girl is black. The blast in the torso blackened her face. The face of the older girl is unmarked. She could be sleeping. Even after what you did to her arm. Look closer. Her eyes may not be closed. Not anymore. The wind moans. The wind stops. The moan is not the wind. The moan is coming from you. Wake Carrie up. Carrie is the big sister. Carrie needs to look out for Maybelle. How can Carrie look out for Maybelle if she is asleep. Wake up. Wake up. Her eyes open. She sees you. She says I love you Daddy.

You are in the dirt road. You are past the barn. The house is ahead. The house is in a grove of trees. You move closer to the house. Someone is on the porch to meet you. You are glad someone is there to meet you. You move closer. The shade feels good. The shade feels better than the sun. You move up the steps. You move across the black stain. The stain leads from the steps to where the woman waits for you. She waits for you beneath the porch swing. She lies in a black stain. Her arms are folded. She is a handsome woman. Everyone says this. They never say she is pretty. You try to pull away from the handsome woman. You struggle. You move closer. Look at the blackened midsection of her dress. Look at her face. Someone has closed her eyes. You have closed her eyes. Do not pull away. You cannot pull away. Her lips have drawn back. You can see her lower teeth. She is not smiling but you can see her teeth. The flies have found her. Behind you the screen door opens.

You move through the doorway. You move into the hallway. A smell is in the hallway. The hallway is dark and close. The smell is of apple cider and old meat and balsam fir. The flies are louder here. You move past the tree. You move past the presents. You move into the kitchen. The pretty one is in the kitchen. The pretty one lies beyond the table. Her arms are folded. The black stain is everywhere in the kitchen. The pretty one ran. You shot her in the back. She kept going. The pretty one had spirit. You shot her again. You cannot pull away. You move closer. It is right that you shot the pretty one twice. The fault is hers. The pretty one came to you. The pretty one planned her Christmas gift to you. The pretty one planned her Christmas gift to the family. The pretty one planned her holiday surprise. Now the pretty one has had a holiday surprise. From the waist down something is wrong with the pretty one. Top half and bottom half do not fit. The flies are loud. You are loud. You and the flies are moaning.

You move out of the kitchen. You want to leave the house. You move farther into the house. You move faster. You play hide-and-seek. You are It. It is looking for the boys. It asks Where are you James. It asks Where are you Raymond. You can't hide forever. Furniture has been overturned. Toys have been scattered. A fruit bowl is upside down. The fruit has rolled into the corners. You have found the cubbyhole. The cubbyhole is under the stairs. The door is ajar. The cubbyhole is dark. You open the door wider. The feet of the boys are lined up. The feet of the boys are lined up in the dark because It found them. It found them didn't you? Here in the dark they are hard to see. They are hard to tell apart, the boys. Your breath is loud in here. The cubbyhole is a dark close place. You must breathe. You cannot help breathing. You cannot live and yet you breathe. You must not live and yet you breathe. It is hard to breathe in the cubbyhole. You move out of the cubbyhole. You must find air to breathe. Your breath pulls you upstairs. The air you must breathe is upstairs. The air is in the nursery. The window curtains move. The window is open. The window lets in the air. The window lets in the flies. The flies have entered the nursery. You have entered the nursery. The toy over the crib moves. Seven angels hang in the air from strings. The angels move. The baby could watch the angels. The crib is dark. The crib is in shadow. The bars of the crib are stained. In the middle of the crib the baby moves. The baby does not move. The flies move.

You are out of the house. You do not know how. You do not know why. You know nothing. You move through the trees. You cannot breathe. You sob. You choke. Your face is wet. You place your hands over your face. You do not need to see to move. You move through the trees through the bushes through the thickets. You sob louder. You reach the clearing. Someone is alive in the clearing. You are there in the clearing. You see yourself walking in the clearing. Your back is to you. You catch up to yourself. Your face is in your hands. Your undershirt is black. Your trousers are black. Your hands are black. Black stains are everywhere. You will never be clean. Once the black was inside your family inside Fannie inside Carrie inside Maybelle inside James inside Raymond inside Mary Lou inside Marie pretty Marie and you let it all out. Now the black is everywhere. You can see it and smell it and grease your hands with it and make your hair tacky with it. The black is all over you. The black is also inside you. The black inside you wants to come out. The black needs to come out. See how funny your hair is. How funny your face must be. Look at your face. You try to see your face. You turn away. You do not want to be seen. You turn away again. You walk in a circle. You follow. You move closer. You walk in a circle and you follow behind. You are close so close. You are so close to yourself. You are close enough to smell yourself. To smell sweat and tobacco and worse. You both walk in a circle. You want to walk as close as you can. You are so close to yourself as you walk this tight black circle in the woods. Nothing ever will grow here. Nothing will grow again in this circle that you walk. You lower your hands. You turn. You look at yourself. Your eyes are gone. Your eyes are two holes. Your mouth opens. Your mouth is a third hole. The black hole moans. The black hole widens. The black hole widens for you.

WALK THE EARTH

Jeffrey Ford

Stu, taking a break from writing a story, was sitting on the patio beneath the spreading sycamore in his backyard. He existed now in a realm where new stories were pointless, looked down upon as a self-indulgence. There was to be only one story. Still, he couldn't help himself. There was a pink sunset, a breeze out of paradise, a Ziz martini in his right hand and a Mt. Horeb Filter in his left. Pretty much everybody smoked in heaven. Why not? His dog, Bidi, lay next to him on the concrete—a brindle pit bull he'd raised from a puppy back in life. On the day he'd crossed over, she was waiting for him inside the gate. She looked the same as when she'd left him on the other side.

That was Stu's first inkling that you didn't get a fresh body in heaven. It's not like you suffered from whatever disease or illness finally finished you off, but your stomach didn't shrink, muscles were still flabby, and that trick knee, bad back, bald head were yours. What would it have taken for the Almighty to just air brush off the wrinkles, but no, you were you. That was that. If you checked out in a car accident, something like that, they patched you up to a degree, at least enough to where your insides weren't falling out all over the streets of gold.

Bidi still had that ugly growth on her left back leg and would prefer a nap to fetching a stick, but the one difference now was she could talk. Stu saw her at the pearly gate and felt a deep sense of relief and joy. He'd have preferred his wife, Ivy, but she was still back in the world. It might be a decade or two before he saw her again. He petted the dog and held her to him. "Bidi," he said. "I missed you."

"Stooge," she said (it was what his wife and kids called him, and it brought instant tears). "How was your trip?" Her voice was as low and sweet as he'd always imagined. She'd been a dog who never barked.

"Life left me like a wave pulling back from the shore," he told her.

"Ever the poet. I put a good word in for you."

"Was it all those treats I doled out?"

"They didn't hurt."

Anyway, that evening on the patio, it was Bidi who, looking up, first saw the angel descending, all aflame, enormous wings flapping. "Shit," she said. "Here we go."

Stu tilted back his head and finished his martini as the seraphim came in for a landing next to the picnic table. Their flame went out and they stepped forward. "I'm Athenial, one of the twenty-eight angels of the Mansions of the Moon. I've been sent as a messenger by God."

"Pleased to meet you," he said and waved them over, sweeping his hand out toward an empty patio chair. "Martini?" he asked.

"Can't," said Athenial. "I'm on duty."

The angel did bum a smoke off Stu as the resplendent sun of paradise sank below the infinite horizon, and blossom-scented night rose around them. Athenial exhaled a big cloud of that thyme-scented Horeb exhaust and laid it out for him. The filmmaker George A. Romero was right—"When there's no more room in hell, the dead will walk the earth." As it turned out, same for heaven. While God sent out to a celestial Best Buy for a portable hard drive to ease the load of the old deus ex machina, some from both camps were to be put back on earth. It wasn't enough that the living would really notice, but it was just enough to open a sliver of space on the drive so things kept operating.

The angel was a beautiful creature—delicate features, and a voluminous head of deep blue curls like cushion springs. "You know, the boss always has to get Satan to fix the tech problems. Czar of Evil was the one behind the computer and all that AI bullshit. That takes some negotiations. So, maybe figure a week and a couple of days."

"What do I do once I get back over there?" asked Stu.

"You've got to lay low. We're sending you to a state where you didn't know anybody. I believe you're going to Thermopolis, Wyoming. All you have to do is get a room in the Best Western, order room service. Whatever you want, we've got the bill. Take a few day trips—visit the hot springs. There are some beautiful parks. Catch up on some reading. We give you a fat stack of cash. The only rule is you've got to do your damnedest to stay away from anybody you knew back when you were alive."

Bidi stood, shook herself, and ambled over to the angel. Sitting in front of them, she lifted her right paw and placed it gently on a robed knee. "Look," she said. "You should let me go with him. I could keep an eye on him, and it would be one less soul in heaven, albeit a dog soul."

"I don't know," said the angel. "I don't know if that hotel is pet-friendly." Athenial swayed back and forth in silence, as if weighing the request. "I guess I could arrange for that to be the case, though. Okay, fuck it. You can both go."

"When do we leave?" asked Stu and they were there. Checked in and everything. The two of them sprawled on the king mattress, the air-conditioning on high. "First order of business," he said. "Room service." Bidi looked over her shoulder and grumbled, "Get me a steak with a bone. Rare." He phoned in their order and then sat back and let the shock of being alive rush through him. In that brief fever, he envisioned how great his BLT and Coke would be.

"How does it feel to breathe again and prowl the earth?" he asked. In heaven there was no breathing. Some of you are going to wonder, "Well if they don't breathe in heaven, how can they smoke?" The answer is simple—it's heaven and if God wants things to work that shouldn't, what do you think is gonna happen?

"By this point, I'm well past surprised at the madness of existence," said Bidi and shook her head.

"It feels good to me," Stu told her. "I've got this giddy feeling in my chest. And I'm filled with enthusiasm for my lunch, which I haven't been in quite a while."

"Yeah," said Bidi, "the lunches in heaven don't cut it."

"Every day it's the same thing, a fucking caprese salad," said Stu. "I'm tired of it already. I'm on my way to infinity, here."

They'd thought of everything—clothes for him and a collar and leash for Bidi. After lunch he dressed up in a pair of mint-green Bermuda shorts and a matching T-shirt. He slipped into a pair of moccasins that seemed as if he'd been wearing them for ten years. The refrigerator was stocked with small cans of Ziz martini, on the dresser in front of the television there was a carton of Horebs and a small canister with the image of a frog on it jammed with fat joints.

"It's party time," he said to Bidi.

"Act your age," she said and laughed.

The instant the fresh air hit him, he was thrown for a loop and had to sit down on the bench right outside the hotel's main doors. To feel that fresh atmosphere hitting the back of his throat, percolating in his lungs, and then exhaling. That rhythmic exchange of air was like nothing in heaven. He had no notion that he'd been missing it until his return, and he realized from that moment forward he'd miss it forever.

Bidi saw Stu was crying and went over to him to rest a paw on his knee and lick his elbow. A woman walked by and caught him blubbering. He smiled at her and wiped his eyes. Bidi whispered, "I know what you're thinking." Another person came out of the hotel and they both shut up. When the gentleman had passed, Stu said, "What?"

"You're thinking about Ivy, aren't you?"

He nodded. "She's alive somewhere in this world. If I could meet her, she would talk to me. I could see how she's doing. Check up on the kids. You know, all that shit that slid out from under me when I went upstairs."

"Better not to meddle with that, right?" said Bidi.

"I don't know anything of the sort."

She growled quietly.

"I need to see her."

"You'll wind up in Lava Lake with a pitchfork in your ass."

"There'll never be another chance," he said, and behind his eyes he was swamped by a vision of Ivy. It was early morning, the sky was overcast, and the wind blew fallen leaves in waves across the shorn fields. Hair gone completely white and thicker glasses than he remembered, but the sight of her keen gaze and a private smile on her face broke his heart.

She was wearing her favorite green sweater, with a pink flannel nightgown underneath. On her feet were a pair of his old work boots, untied. She was back in the dying autumn garden, overgrown by weeds, all the drooping sunflower heads in a row. She held a basket and moved amid the chaos. From within the tumble of thistle, crabgrass, and knotweed, she retrieved giant perfect tomatoes and frying peppers.

Next thing he knew, Bidi was leading him back into the hotel. They took the elevator up, she having to remind him what button to push.

"Pathetic," she said.

Back in the room, he removed the pillows from their cases and loaded the empty sacs with what he called "supplies." One held the cans of Ziz, one the joints, and carton of Horebs. Another, he filled with clothes, and the last held a few cans of food for Bidi.

"You're down with this?" he said to her. "I don't see your tail wagging."

"Do I have a choice?"

"No, let's go."

They caught some side-eye from the receptionist behind the desk when traipsing through the lobby carrying hotel pillowcases. The dog food and the Ziz were tied together and draped over Bidi, like saddlebags on the back of a burro. Stu had found a pair of shades in the drawer where the Bible usually was and added them to his mint green look.

Out in front of the hotel again, he sat on the bench and Bidi lay at his feet. He lit a Horeb and they waited. Eventually a big white SUV pulled up and parked. A man and woman got out, followed by a boy and a girl. They each took a piece of luggage and went into the hotel, leaving the vehicle running.

"What do you think?" Stu said.

"That oughta do it," said the dog.

Stu helped Bidi into the front seat on the passenger side, lifting the full pillowcases off her back. Once she was strapped in, he ran around to the open back of the SUV and emptied it of three more large suitcases. Climbing in behind the wheel, he put the car in gear, and it was then that the man who'd previously been driving came out of the hotel. He gaped at what was happening and broke into a run. Stu hit the gas, and as they barely eluded him, Bidi powered down the window and told the guy, "Thanks." That stopped him dead in his tracks. A few minutes later they were on the highway heading for Ohio.

"Keep your eyes on the road," said Bidi while Stu dug around in a pillowcase at his feet.

"Okay, okay," he said and brought up the carton of Horebs. He deftly dug out a single pack, thumbnailed it open, and got one lit.

"Do you know where you're going?" asked Bidi.

"Home," he said. "We just take Route 80 pretty much all the way. When we get closer I'll get the car's GPS going." With that, he turned on the radio and the song "Dreamin' Man" by Neil Young came on. As they slid down the highway, he blew his smoke out the open window into the rushing stream and thought, "Heaven."

Neither of them gave a thought to trouble, the reexperience of life was too amazing. The cop put his siren on about a mile and a half earlier after Stu passed doing eighty-five in a sixty-five-mile-an-hour zone. They never heard his approach over the torqued-up din of Beverly Bremers's "Don't Say You Don't Remember." It was only when that tune ended that they finally heard it. By then the cop car was right behind theirs.

"It's a bust," said Stu. He pulled over and turned off the radio and the SUV.

"You've cat fucked us now," said Bidi.

Stu looked into the rearview mirror, saw the cop get out of his car and walk toward them.

"I'll do the talking," said Stu and the dog gave a grumble.

When the officer banged on the window for Stu to open up it was with the barrel of his gun. The window slid down.

"License and registration," came the command.

"Oh, damn," said Stu, "left them at home."

"Okay, you and the dog, out of the car. And make sure that dog is leashed or I'll put him down."

"It's a female," said Stu.

The cop leaned toward the window, pointing his gun inside the car. "Quit fucking around and get out."

Stu had a brief inclination to try to bribe the officer with half the fat stack. At the same time, Bidi was thinking, "I hope he doesn't try a bribe."

Before anybody could shoot, talk, or move, a head of blue curls and a gleaming smile poked itself into the front seat from between Stu and Bidi. A soothing voice said, "You're done here. Go home."

The cop withdrew the gun and backed away from the car. "Have a nice day now," he said and waved.

"Hit the gas," said Athenial.

Stu started up the SUV and pulled into traffic. Once he was settled in a lane, he looked into the back seat and saw blue satin, feathers, and a crown woven from red salvia, exuding an aroma of sage. "You two think you're so slick," said the angel.

"I'm hardly to blame," said Bidi.

"It doesn't matter, we're all going to be up for relocation to a warmer climate by the time this thing is over. I mean, God, they're omniscient. How'd you think they wouldn't see you doing exactly this—what you're doing right now?"

"God already knows?" asked Stu.

Athenial laughed, "Are you kidding? They knew this whole enterprise from word *go* to the grim finale, like last month some time. You can't put one over on the Almighty. I was supposed to cast the two of you into Lava Lake about five minutes ago."

"Shit, Lava Lake, I told you," said Bidi.

"Why are we still here?" said Stu. Taking a quick glance into the back seat and then concentrating again on the traffic.

Athenial leaned forward and put a hand on each of their shoulders. "I said, '*You* can't put one over on the Almighty,' but that doesn't mean I can't."

"You're going to help us?" asked the dog.

"Seems so," said the angel as they leaned back in silence. The trio drove on through the day and into the night, stopping twice for McDonald's and gas. Around midnight, having somehow lost Route 80 in the driving, Athenial called out, "Make a right up here onto that dirt road. We'll take a break." Stu guessed they were somewhere in Nebraska. The road led down into a thicket of Mulberry trees at the bottom of which a fleeting white form swept through the headlights and vanished. Stu hit the brakes, and then continued as the road led up and up to the level top of a hill of buffalo grass that spread out in every direction.

In an eyeblink, Stu and the angel were seated on camp chairs and Bidi lay between them. There was a small fire going and the angel roasted a hot dog on the end of a stick. Horebs and Ziz were in play. The sky above was resplendent with stars. A breeze blew, reminiscent of the one in Stu's vision of Ivy.

When Stu got his bearings, he asked Athenial, "Why did you help us?"

"To understand that, you need to understand my usual job. So, I'm one of the twenty-eight angels of the Mansions of the Moon."

"Right," said Stu.

"When I say that, I'm sure you're thinking of a huge old building with creaking stairways, a mahogany interior, chandeliers, inlaid floors, stained glass windows, situated on a crater estate in the Sea of Tranquility. A mansion. But the mansions of the moon are not real places, they're junctures in its 27.34 day orbit around the world when it is not in the aspect of some other zodiacal body. That means it isn't under any celestial influence and is termed 'void of course.' What we're talking about is not even a place, but a measure of time."

"The Almighty goes in for astrology?"

"Not exactly, but nothing's wasted. Everything has an iota of importance—every wrong turn, every bum notion." Athenial pulled the hot dog stick from the fire and waved it slowly around above their head.

"What does it have to do with you helping us?"

"Because I'm ostensibly a master of time. I've spent an eternity studying and coming to understand it just from my few hours a year in the seventh mansion. I've been slowing the movement of the moon, just a hair, on each orbit through, and saving that sliver of time to use on this journey. It was so minuscule each time, and there was so much bullshit going on everywhere—famine, wars, celestial arrangements, apocalyptic threats, and just the general decomposition of the universe—that God had more than enough to do without watching the watchers?"

"God's not onto us?" asked Bidi.

"Not as long as the time I've stolen from the universe holds out. It will cloak us until then. The Almighty is a manifestation of time and the only way to fool time is with time."

The angel brought the stick down to hover the hot dog in front of Bidi's snout. She snapped it off the point and downed it in five chews. "Appreciated," she said. Athenial nodded, and the stick was already back in the fire with another hot dog on the end of it.

"I believe you can," said Stu, "but why?"

"Because of the connection you have to this woman, Ivy. I could feel that energy from the moment I descended into your yard. I can see clearly when you envision her. There's nothing like it in heaven. Let's call it 'vegetable love,' it grows like a plant, in the physical world, sinking its roots ever deeper, its foliage opening, its blossom exploding over a significant period of human life. How long were you together before you checked out, forty-plus years? I need to be in the presence of that, if only for a brief while. And I've had all this time accrued to put to a deceptive use for a good situation like this."

"By 'brief while' you mean that no matter what we do, we're not getting away with this?" asked Bidi. Athenial shook their head, eyes closed in the admission. When she growled, "Lava Lake," the angel reached the stick down, offering a hot dog as consolation.

"It's been quite a while since last I saw her," said Stu. "I can't really remember how long. I see mostly glimpses of us together—a kiss, standing in the rain on the corner loaded down with groceries, waiting for the bus, falling asleep together on the couch in front of the television (in my mind it's always that movie with the giant ants that's playing), her making suet cakes for the birds in the kitchen, sitting on the porch having drinks at sunset, the summer fading. It's hard to capture and harder to hold on to."

"You want to see her, and I simply want to behold that meeting, so we both get what we want."

"What do you want, Bidi?" asked Stu.

"Another hot dog," she said.

Stu carried on, almost stream of consciousness, recalling for the group bits and pieces of his old life, like inspecting shards of a shattered plate. Bidi broke in a few times with an "I remember that," and only once did Athenial speak. Stu was describing how beautiful Ivy looked in a yellow sundress. It was a vision from way back when they spent their summer vacations at the New Jersey shore. The angel piped up with, "Yes, and she's wearing lemon perfume." Stu didn't even notice but blithered on. Bidi rolled onto her side and said, "Jesus."

The party broke up a little after midnight. Stu was loaded on Ziz and Bidi had consumed her last hot dog an hour earlier. Athenial insisted on driving, saying, "I'd like to get there some time this millennium." They bundled into the car, the dog in the back and Stu in the passenger seat.

"Belt up," said the angel, and the seat belts were secured with no one lifting a finger. Stu powered down his window and lit one of the joints from the frog tin. "Stones," said Athenial and pointed at the radio. On came "Beast of Burden." Instead of turning the SUV around and going in search of Route 80, the vehicle lifted off the ground like a helicopter and flew toward the stars.

The morning sun found them parked along the side of a country road in western Ohio. Stu opened his bleary eyes and groaned. "Great being back, but I forgot about the hangovers."

"That's a bitch," said Bidi who'd been awake for an hour, sitting next to the open back window, catching scents from the old homestead that was only a few hundred yards farther on around the bend. An end of summer breeze blew through the windows of the SUV from the yellowing soybean fields that stretched out everywhere for miles.

"I know where we are," said Stu. "My old place is right up here." He pointed at the windshield. "You remember it, Bidi," he asked.

"Yes."

"I propose reconnoitering the situation," said Athenial. "I'll make us all invisible, like ghosts, and we'll pass through the walls and check the scene? What do you think?"

"I'm down," said Stu.

"In," said Bidi.

"Now listen, Stu, you especially, you can't go shit face when you see your wife. You've got to keep it together. We're pretty much undetectable by Ivy, but not completely. She'll be able to pick up vibrations, a mood, a vague memory, especially if you're upset."

"But I am going to see her for real, aren't I?"

"Yes, eventually, but first we should see what's happening in her life."

"Like *A Christmas Carol*," said Stu.

They all got out of the car and walked along the side of the road. Ten yards into the journey, they vanished. Rounding the bend, they passed a white house with a red barn whose roof was eaten away by time. Beyond that and past a cornfield, Stu laid eyes on the old place. "When I lived there I used to only think about all the repairs that were needed and how run-down it was," he whispered. "It's a hundred and twenty years old. But seeing it now is like seeing the Taj Mahal. Beautiful roses in the gardens and that amazing wrap-around porch. The apple trees, the white oaks. How was I ever so lucky to live there?"

"All I can imagine," said Bidi, "is taking a nap in the heat of the midday sun on the hot driveway."

Athenial warned them to quiet down as they stepped on the property and walked across an open field to the porch steps. Up they went in a row, and then easy as a thought passed through the closed porch door and into the kitchen. The smell was so familiar to Stu and Bidi, stronger than any memory. The angel went off into the dining room, and the dog followed.

Stu spun around, taking in as much detail as possible. A lot was the same but there were additions, a few tchotchkes, a new set of chairs at the kitchen table, a new coffee maker, a vase of bright sunflowers, no doubt from the garden out back. He immediately noticed that the place was a lot neater. He left the kitchen down a long hallway and wound up at the foot of a set of stairs. Fifteen steps to the top, and even in his invisible form, he was winded. His first stop was the room where he wrote, his desk surrounded by books. He put his hand on the doorknob but hesitated to turn it.

"Say it's barren or turned into some other kind of room?" he asked himself. "Why shouldn't it be?" he said aloud, although inside he knew to discover it utterly changed would be a sword through his heart. He pictured himself beholding an empty space and curling up into a ball in the middle of its blankness. He opened the door, and the deep yellow aroma of old books punched him in the nose and misted his eyes. The entire glorious mess was exactly as it had been the day he'd departed. He sat down in his writing chair and lit up a Horeb, flicking his ashes into a hard candy tin from another century.

Upon leaving the office, he ran into Athenial in the upstairs hallway. They each had to turn to the side to pass. As they did, the angel said, "I can still feel the presence of you and Ivy living here together. The energy leaches out of the walls. There's still a lot of you left here."

"I guess that's good," said Stu.

"Where's your wife, though?" asked Athenial.

"How the hell do I know. She probably went out early to the store. What about Bidi?"

"She's downstairs. We discovered there's another dog here, a small stout one with a lot of hair and a pointy snout. The old girl's not so happy about it. She's calling it an interloper."

"Where are you going now?" asked Stu.

"That room you just came out of. I want to see your ridiculous paper collection."

"Thanks," said Stu who continued on down the hall to the bedroom and laid on his old bed for a few minutes. He hadn't felt so relaxed since he'd left the world. Eventually, he got up and went down to the basement, where Ivy had a small workshop in which she created her mosaics. There was a large piece on an easel. The colors were vibrant, red and orange flowers. He was surprised by the technical command of the materials and the generosity of the design. In comparing it to the work she'd done when he was alive, it seemed as if it'd been done by somebody else. He stood before it, entranced for a long while until Bidi came down the stairs and called, "Stu, a car just pulled in the driveway."

Each of the three took a corner of the kitchen and stood as still as statues. The angel put a finger to their lips as a warning not to give themselves away. They heard footsteps on the porch outside and then the door opened. In stepped Ivy. At first sight, Stu's knees buckled, and he almost went down on the floor. She passed within an arm's length of him, and he reached out but stopped at the last moment. There were tears in his eyes and a huge smile on his face. The little dog that had been following the three ghosts around the house all morning, barked and ran to greet the slight, white-haired woman.

Then the door opened wider, and in stepped an older man with a bald head, a pointy beard, and glasses, carrying two bundles of groceries. He walked past Stu on the way to the island counter and set the bags down. Bidi looked over at Athenial and then pointed her nose at her master. The angel took a look at Stu—mouth agape and eyes bulging, limbs trembling.

He almost exploded, but just then Ivy spoke, and the sound of her voice distracted him from the presence of her gentleman friend. She said, "Herb, wait for me out at the picnic table, I'll make some coffee." The visitor said, "Thanks," and left through the sliding glass doors to the patio. Athenial nodded once at Stu and put him in a state of paralysis. He knew that if he didn't, the gathering cry of *Who the fuck is that?* would reach a point of power where it might actually be audible in the world.

Before anything came of the situation, angel magic transported the three of them out to the front porch, the part farthest from the patio or kitchen. Athenial calmed Stu's thoughts and told him, "If you scream we're going to have to leave." Stu, all his faculties returned to him, nodded and put his hands together as if in prayer as a sign that he understood.

"Who the fuck was that?" he said in a restrained tone.

Athenial shrugged. "Could be a friend or a lover."

"She didn't even wait for the body to get cold," said Stu.

"Look, you don't realize it, but you've been gone for six years. That's nothing in eternity, but here, six years can be forever."

"He looks like such an asshole," said Stu.

Bidi said, "Calm down. Carrying on is pointless. You're fucking dead. If you want this to count for anything you need to be more contemplative. The days of screaming and exerting your will are gone forever." Stu turned and took a step away from his companions. Facing the wall, he lit up a Horeb and mumbled to himself for a while. While they waited, Bidi walked out onto the lawn beneath the trees and Athenial rolled up the sleeves of their robe and sat down on the porch railing.

An hour later, Bidi lay under the picnic table. Athenial made Stu sit next to Herb and the angel took a spot on the opposite bench with Ivy. The living were discussing some old movie they'd seen recently. Ivy laughed and Stu was mesmerized by her. He was convinced that Herb was a blithering know-it-all. He knew the names of all the character actors in the film and for each had to tell a piece of their bio. Athenial gave the conversation an eye roll and Stu smiled. The angel's voice sounded in his head. "This guy has never considered how short one's time in the world is."

"I hate to see Ivy this desperate for a friend," Stu signaled back in his thoughts. The conversation went on, and Ivy revealed the name of the movie and that it was the first time she'd seen it. Herb looked proud of himself for bringing this gem to her. The only problem was that Stu remembered having seen that very movie in a theater with Ivy on their second or third date. Eventually, she said, "Well, come on downstairs into the workshop and check out my flowers."

"Can't wait," said Herb and Stu thought, "I just want to kick him in the nuts." Athenial prevented the dead husband from following the couple.

"Leave them to themselves," the angel said. "Get ready to meet her face-to-face. As soon as Professor Whatnot leaves, I'm going to reveal you to her. If you don't control your emotions, though, you're going to give us away. The time cloak already has cracks in it from your nitwittery."

"You don't know what it's like."

"That's what I'm here to find out."

Athenial set Stu up at the picnic table with a couple of cans of Ziz they found in their voluminous sleeves. "I'll be back in a few minutes," said the angel. "I have to find the perfect spot for the meeting to take place. I'm going to look around. You two stay here."

As the angel walked off, a voice came up through the table. "Stu," said Bidi. "There's something not right about this. If you physically confront Ivy, where she can see and touch you even though she knows you've been dead for quite a while, you're going to ruin whatever years of life she has left. You're going to step all over that unpredictability that can make it sing or sting. In the past couple of days, I've seen how precious each minute is."

"But I love her," said Stu.

"Prove it."

Athenial summoned them, and they appeared behind the white garage that lay at the end of the long driveway. "Look sharp," said the angel. "We're going to do this. I have it on good authority that Herb will be leaving in a minute."

"They've been in there a long time together," said Stu.

"He's checking her flowers," said Athenial and laughed.

"What's that supposed to mean?"

"Listen, Stu, you need to get past it and get your shit together. What is about to happen here has never happened before in the history of heaven or earth. It's bigger than the rebel angels storming heaven, bigger than the inception of Satan's dominion. This is where the rubber meets the road. Do you understand?"

"I guess so," said Stu.

"Welcome to Lava Lake," said Bidi.

"Keep your eyes on that apple tree way across the yard. You see it?" The angel raised their arm above their head and waited for the sleeve to fall back. Then they pointed. "She's going to appear there in a moment. I've set a trap for her. Beneath that tree there lies a perfectly preserved dead cardinal, bright red as the sun of hell. Her favorite bird. She will discover it and study it, and all the time she does her back will be to us. Stu, you walk slowly and quietly up behind her. Don't say her name until you're there. I want to see her face when she turns around and sees you're back."

A minute later, Ivy came into view. She'd obviously seen the dead cardinal at a distance as she was walking on a beeline for the apple tree. They heard her say, "Oh no."

The angel tapped Stu on the back and said, "It's all you."

Stu's mouth was dry, his legs were weak, and his hands trembled. He couldn't fathom how quickly they'd come to this point in the story. So much had flown by. There were echoes in his head and moths in his heart, but he stepped forward in her direction. He moved silently, slowly, like in a dream, but somebody else's. Images of his life with her flashed behind his eyes. And beneath all that, he wondered what the angel meant by, "It's all you."

When Stu had covered exactly half the distance to Ivy, Bidi sat up and loosed a bark upon the world composed of all the barks she never barked in life. The sound and vibration of it split both the day and Athenial's time cloak that hid them from the Almighty. There was some rumbling above, the sky broke open. Pieces of shattered blue and clouds fell like snow. An enormous hand swept down like a rushing ocean wave and gathered up the three conspirators. The wreckage vanished instantly.

The sound of the wind howling drew Ivy's attention from the beautiful bird. She turned and faced the sudden gale, surveying the yard and the harvested cornfields beyond. Yellow leaves fell around her. When all was still again, she closed her eyes, listened more intently, and said, "Stu?"

Unfortunately, Stu and Bidi were on the red eye of the damned, traveling to Lava Lake. Everything happened so quickly, their judgment, their sentence, God's rebuke. The Almighty said, "You could have undone creation with that little stunt." Stu tried to say they had no idea, but the words changed in his mouth and came forth, "We're asses." They were each given a bottle of water for the trip, the last they would have for eternity. Athenial was somewhere separated from them and sent to a more angelic punishment.

A problem occurred when they reached the shores of a bubbling, burning body of liquid as large as an ocean. The din of sinners screaming as their flesh sloughed off in the molten wavelets was a suffocating wave in itself. The sand was searing hot. The demon guiding them to their fate was halted by a larger demon, who spoke through his single eye, "These turds have been reassigned." His lids moved like lips. "Get them the fuck out of here."

As it turned out, there were still too many dead in Hell, so they were sent to Purgatory and wound up on a snowy mountain side, in a realm of perpetual darkness. They were shown to a small cabin with none of the amenities Stu had in his place on Damascus Road, in the suburbs of Celestial City. There was a wood stove, one lantern, two beds of straw, and an empty cupboard.

Leaving the door to the frigid outside open, their demon escort showed them around the place with a flame he flicked into being at the end of his thumb. "Cozy," they said. "OK, there's a gun in the closet over there. It will always be loaded. You and the mutt are destined now to hunt Gutlatch. You'll know them when you see them, they're out in the woods behind this place, vicious little entities—some say a cross between a badger and a shrew. Lose a leg to one and you'll be hobbling around up here in the dark. You don't get a new one. Try not to get lost in the woods when you go hunting, it's full of God's and Satan's nightmares. The only thing to eat here is smoked Gutlach, so you better get good at your jobs. It's been decided you'll be here for at least a couple of eternities. After that, they might let you back in upstairs. The demon said, "Enjoy," and turned to ashes. A gust blew in the door and took him.

Stu grabbed the rifle from the closet, lit the lantern, which immediately popped into flame with a simple turn of a key. Bidi took the flame and led the way. Her master followed, freezing in his mint green Bermuda shorts and T. Snow came in over the edges of his comfortable moccasins. As they headed for the tree line of the woods, three shades darker than the ambient darkness, Stu said, "I can't believe you betrayed me."

Bidi grunted and spoke from the side of her mouth since she clenched the lantern handle. "You've got plenty of time now to come to understand that I was doing you a favor."

"I was only steps from her," he said, and then they passed in among the twisted, barren forms. Something leaped and Stu fired. The creature fell into their pool of light. It scrabbled in a kind of death seizure, all sharp hair, Sabre-tooth canines, and hideous claws as tortured in their shapes as the branches above. As it wheezed out its life, the sound was identical to that of the sinners in Lava Lake. They killed a few more that first hunt and dragged them to the cabin. Prepared, smoked for hours, and sliced thin, they were chewy, and had a strong taste of mildew and rot.

Days, weeks, months, decades, centuries went by, and the stranded pair made do with the tribulations of Purgatory. Stu fashioned some hunting garb from the coarse hides of the beasts, sewed them up with intestine and used a paw bone needle. Bidi became an expert hunter, and the Gutlatch told mythic stories about her fierce nature. The one grace that Purgatory had that Hell didn't was that sinners doing time there got to lie down and sleep a few hours now and then.

Stu finally forgave Bidi, although he didn't understand how she'd "done him a favor," but he loved her, and anger, hate, malice was too heavy a load to carry into the darker woods, through the deep snow. When they were done for the day, they'd light the wood stove with branches from the forest floor, the dog would curl up at Stu's feet. He sat in a chair he'd made from stones and tell her a story he was writing in his head.

So on and so on and so on and so on . . . etc., until, during the middle of a raging blizzard that had enshrouded the mountain and trapped Stu and Bidi inside for what seemed a week, there came a knocking on the door.

"Oh, shit, here we go," said the dog.

Stu got up but was afraid to answer it. The pounding continued, stopped and then resumed with more vigor. He stood there like a statue. "Wake up," said Bidi. Her master moved, reached the door, and opened it. The wind blew it back and tore the handle out of Stu's grip. In the doorway stood a short figure dressed in a bear skin coat with an enormous hood and boots made of the same. In its mittened hand it held a tall walking stick. The hood dropped back and revealed a face obscured by a scarf and large, dark goggles.

Stu took a step backward, but at the same time noticed a head of white hair as the stranger leaned back to drop the stick in the snow. Bidi's tail was wagging before the scarf was undone. The goggles came off, and there was Ivy, a smile on her face. "Found you," she said. Stu laughed and wept at the same time. He went to her, and they embraced, kissing, and rubbing their hands along each other's bodies to be sure what was happening was really happening. Bidi ran in circles around them.

When all finally calmed down, including the blizzard outside, they sat on the floor in a circle and Ivy told how she came to them. "I was in heaven, and one day I met a wingless angel, named Athenial. It seems he was being punished for some great crime. I was sitting on a bench in Celestial City park, resting from my wanderings in search of you. They came over and sat next to me and whispered, 'Look straight ahead like I'm not engaging you.' I did as they said. 'You're Ivy, if I'm not mistaken and you are searching for your husband who has passed on some time before you.'"

Stu said, "Athenial," and he and Bidi laughed.

"He told me where you were and how to get here. Instructed me on how to find the tunnel that links Heaven to Purgatory. It took me . . . a century? two? to find you. I was damned if I was going to give up."

Stu shook his head at the enormity of her sacrifice, but then said, "What about Herb?"

Bid growled and said, "Jesus."

"Oh my, Bidi can talk," said Ivy.

"Love you," said the dog.

"Who's Herb," asked Ivy.

"Never mind," said Stu.

"Athenial said he had a message for you. He said, 'Whatever you do, tell that dopey husband of yours that every soul's afterlife exists in their own image."

Soon after, the moon appeared in the sky along with a sea of stars, the mountain weather slowly changed, white leaves grew on the trees in the forest, and one day the sun appeared and brought daylight. Ivy had instructed their kids that when she died and was to be buried, she was to be dressed in her garden clothes. "It won't do to put on airs for Death," was how she explained it. They honored her wish, even though a lot of people at the wake thought it odd. There, on the mountain, she found seeds in the pockets of her overalls from countless Springs and Summers spent in the world. With them, she planted a garden that grew in size as the seasons fell away. Bidi napped in the sun and gentle breeze. Stu worked on a story he hoped might not be pointless.

TIME IS A LIQUID

Kelly Robson

Elaine was the only accredited western hemisphere guide in her neighborhood who wasn't committed to other gigs, so when they won a contract to usher a V-V-VIP around the continents, she couldn't refuse the job. She tried, though.

"My chickens haven't settled in yet. Can you get someone else?"

"There isn't anyone else. If we don't take it, they'll offer the contract to another hood."

The neighborhood prez gave her a neon-bright smile. A year back, when Elaine had moved in, the prez had been a vivacious eighteen-year-old just stepping into the job. Since then, she'd blossomed into a talented micromanager, with the ability to be everywhere, all the time.

"Yeah, okay, but with everything going on, I haven't even thought about renewing my license. I'm pretty sure it's expired."

"It's not. I checked." The prez held two pinched fingers in front of Elaine's nose. "We're *this* close to funding the rec center. Your fee will put us over the top."

"But my chickens—"

"I'll take care of them. I'm amazing with chickens."

"Fine." The flinty look in the prez's eyes told Elaine this was a losing battle. "I guess I don't have a choice."

"Nope. Show me the girls and I'll get out of your hair."

The hens raced frantically around the yard. A dozen black Australorps and two dozen Canadian Bresse, seven months old, feathers glossy with health, and eating like hogs but refusing to lay. They spent half of every day running around like something was chasing them, and the other half scratching up dirt like they were being paid by the gram. Elaine was new to raising hens—it'd been Monica and Lu-bon's job back in the day—but she was pretty sure the new coop was the problem. A half-timbered hulk printed out of scavenged plastic feedstock, like a child's idea of a historical farm building.

"I think they hate this thing even more than I do." Elaine gave the coop's hempcrete foundation a half-hearted kick. "That's why they won't lay."

"Nope," said the prez. "Anik and Pleasance have the same design and their hens are happy."

Elaine pointed out the hose, drinkers, and light timers, and swung open the feed shed door. A bag of mixed grit had split open in the night, burying her scoops and buckets under a heavy layer of sand and crushed oyster shell.

Elaine's gut clenched at the sight of all that spilled rock. She rounded on the prez.

"I really don't think I can—"

"I'll have them laying like champs before you get home," the prez promised. She gave Elaine a playful punch on the shoulder, and trotted off down the lane to strong-arm someone else.

Elaine lugged a bucket of compost to the half-built raised beds that would be her new garden, if she ever got it built. She'd piled up walls of scavenged bricks and ripped them down a half dozen times, certain anything she built would collapse into a pile of rubble.

That evening, while the neighbors down the lane filled the night with thrumming music and trills of laughter, she fired the tourism broker's request onto her studio wall.

She didn't recognize the V-V-VIP's species at first glance, but it didn't matter. She'd guided hundreds of aliens, and they all wanted the same thing—to ogle a species that engulfed food with their bodies and based entire cultures on the practice of murdering each other. Humans were disgusting, but oh so exotic, and a trip to Earth was picturesque and cheap.

Guides were supposed to make aliens feel welcome, keep them safe and fed, show them the sights, and most especially to make friends with them. Answering their questions was usually the biggest challenge. Translator apps smoothed over perceptual, cognitive, and cultural differences, and if the gaps were simply unbridgeable, provided dialogue out of whole fiction. She was never sure if she'd ever really talked with an alien or just exchanged lies with their translator. It made the whole job disorienting. If she thought about it too much, she got vertigo.

But fine, if she was doing this, she was doing it. The V-V-VIP had chosen a name (Frank) and pronouns (he/him). He wanted a four-day tour of multiple violent death sites in North and South America, following on from a similar tour of East Asia. Not an unusual request, given humanity's reputation, but a weird way to phrase it. Or maybe not? She's been out of the game for more than a year. Her entire reality had changed.

Multiple violent death sites. Okay. She pulled up a list of the bloodiest massacres in the hemisphere, cherry-picked a bunch, and fired an itinerary to the tourism broker for approval. Then she went back to cleaning squeegees and rearranging her studio. She sketched and doodled, mulling over the fine details of her next run of T-shirts. Stacked and unstacked bricks. Checked the chickens for parasites and worried over their feeding schedule. In her old life, she would have complained to her family about alien tourists and their fascination with the human ways of death, and they all would have had a good laugh over it. Instead, she kept herself distracted by busywork until she had to leave.

The prez showed up to walk her to the hopper station.

"Thanks for doing this," she said. "I know things have been rough."

"You just want to make sure I don't flake," Elaine said.

"That too." The prez gave her a bright, encouraging smile.

On the hops to Cambodia, she looked up details on the V-V-VIP's species. He wasn't an individual as much as the fishlike host to a symbiotic community, which was standard; the vast majority of aliens were symbiotes. Completely aquatic, he'd be traveling inside a floating life support carapace, and that meant he'd be highly mobile. It'd be easy for him to get away from her. She'd have to stay alert. Just four days. She could do it.

When she got to the handoff spot in Phnom Penh, the East Asia guide was dragging Frank behind her, her long hair gleaming in the sun like glass. The alien was asleep, practically snoring. His carapace was filled with clear liquid, and provided a hand's breadth of space between his body and the edges. It flexed with the gentle movements of his tail.

"I wore him right out," said Chantrea. "He wanted death? I gave him death. In abundance."

"Did he say why he made that the focus of his tour?" Elaine asked. "Is there something specific he wants?"

"Dunno. He keeps giving me some nonsense about time being a liquid."

"Sounds like his translator is getting creative."

"No kidding." Chantrea giggled, and her hair rippled over her shoulders like a cape. "Let me know how it goes? He's a nice guy. You'll have fun."

On the way to São Paulo, Elaine took the opportunity to sketch the sleeping alien. Long, smooth tubular body, skin a silky cobalt blue. Six sets of long, finny fingers drifting gently along his flanks. Huge head on a mobile neck, chin quivering in slumber. A unique shape, but page after page, her sketches made him look generic, a cross between a swordfish and a barracuda, but with a whippy tail. She couldn't capture the essentials that made his figure uncannily, undeniably alien. She could have asked Lee for advice, once upon a time.

The alien woke an hour out of São Paulo.

"Hello," he said. "I'm Frank."

"I'm Elaine," she replied. "How are you doing? Are you comfortable? Do you feel rested?"

"Yes, I'm fine." He stretched out his neck and swung his head around her, as if examining her scent. "Do you have a present for me?"

"You bet." She unfolded the T-shirt on her lap and held it out like a flag. "This is a traditional garment, with an original graphic design. I make these myself. I'm a screen printer."

"That's a type of artisan and that's printed language, I think. What does it say?"

"Welcome to Upper Canada, Land of the Bland."

"Is that a self-deprecating joke? And a rhyme?" She nodded. "It's beautiful. I like it a lot. Thank you."

Elaine warmed to the praise, then reminded herself it was meaningless. He could have said anything from, *Your primitive handicrafts are so quaint*, to *I will be sure to dispose of it in your nearest traditional landfill.* Or—more likely—simply nothing at all. *It's beautiful. I like it a lot?* Not a chance.

But Frank wanted to wear it, so when they landed in São Paulo, she helped him pull the T-shirt over his carapace. Its short sleeves flapped as they boarded the bullet-shaped private hopper. Elaine should have made small talk on the way to Iquique, asked him questions, got to know him, but her guide skills were buried six feet under. Luckily, Frank didn't seem to mind. He dozed, occasionally stretching out to examine the air around her.

On landing, she helped Frank navigate the narrow hatchway. She followed him into the open, determined to start doing a good job.

"Iquique is the site of the Santa María School massacre of 1907," she began, and then the surrounding mountains loomed into view.

She ran back to the hopper and slammed the hatch behind her, shaking, nearly gasping. She sunk to her knees and clutched her skull. Of course there'd be mountains. Half of South America was mountains. She'd have to edit the itinerary. Was Cuevo mountainous? No, but it had gorges and ravines, deep ones. Mountains in Cajamarca. And Lima. Big ones.

An hour later, Frank nudged the hatch open with his tail. The T-shirt was speckled with dirt.

"I just had to work out some details with the local tourism authorities," she lied. "Just a few small changes to the itinerary. Did you have a good look around Iquique?"

"Yes, extremely interesting."

"Next stop is the Eleventh Parallel Massacre site in Cinta Larga."

Rain lashed the trees as they landed. When Elaine stepped out of the hopper, she sank shin-deep in red mud.

"I can't do this," she said, gripping the edge of the hatch.

"That's fine. There's no need for you to get wet." He slipped out into the rain. "I am content to explore on my own. Please feel free to commune with your ghosts."

"My what?" she asked, but Frank was already drifting away. She climbed back inside, and after wiping off the mud with a towel, she filed a ticket with the suppliers of Frank's translation app. *Please clarify this conversational exchange.*

Priya would tell her to get her head in the game. No excuse to leave Frank alone to encounter the locals with no explanation or support, no matter how agreeable he was being. If she lost the contract, the prez would cling to her ears for months. Okay. Elaine dug her rain gear out of her bag, slid on the boots, shrugged the poncho over her head. She squelched out into the mud but didn't get far before a falling tree branch sent her scurrying back inside.

The problem was, she hadn't eaten all day. That's what Venetta would say. She'd feel calmer once she had a good, hot meal.

When Frank returned to the hopper, she peeled the wet T-shirt off him, and strapped him in for the hop to Baía do Arraial.

"Did you enjoy Cinta Larga?" she asked.

"It was somewhat alarming. I witnessed a wading bird being caught and eaten by an aquatic reptile. Poor thing."

"I'm sorry, Frank. I won't let you go out alone anymore."

At a beachside bistro overlooking the turquoise sea, Elaine ordered a nutritional pack for Frank and a bowl of coconut shrimp for herself. A good guide would have it pureed and decanted into a sippy cup to minimize distress to the guests, like all the other guides in the restaurant were doing, but she needed comfort and a shrimp milkshake wouldn't do it.

"Are you emotionally upset?" asked Frank.

She stared into her bowl for a moment, then steeled herself to look into his glistening eye patches. From the front, his head was bottle-shaped. Wide skull narrowing to a bulbous chin organ, quivering and sensitive.

"That's not the kind of question I usually get from guests."

"Oh no? What do they ask?"

"They want to know if I've ever cannibalized my own kind. They're disappointed when I say no." She lifted a shrimp. "This is animal protein. Does it bother you, Frank?"

"Not at all."

"Are you sure?"

"Go ahead. You must be hungry."

The flesh of the shrimp parted under her teeth, the sauce zesty and perfectly seasoned. Lee would love it.

"Is it good?" Frank asked.

"Yeah. We can't get anything like this at home." Frank was really going easy on her; she should make an effort. "Shrimp and humans diverged hundreds of millions of years ago, you know. We're really not related at all."

"I understand."

"Not everyone does. See that pair?" she nodded at two elongated, caterpillar-ish aliens with feed bags pulled over their antennae, sitting at a nearby table with their guide, a young man with bouncy dreadlocks. "They're watching my every bite. Like I'm an animal in a zoo."

"How rude we tourists are."

"That's okay. Humans can be rude right back." She took a big bite and chewed loudly. The caterpillars recoiled. Their guide glared at her. He took a big sip of his meal through a straw, demonstrating proper guide behavior. Elaine ignored him. She took the wet T-shirt out of her bag and draped it over a chair to dry in the sun.

"Qual é o seu problema?" the guide whispered at Elaine as he escorted his guests off the terrace. *What's wrong with you?*

Good question. She finished her meal in small bites, chewing politely, mouth closed. Before boarding the hopper, she ran to the local pharmacy, bought a pack of beta-blocker patches, and slapped one on each wrist.

By the time they got to Canudos, she was feeling much better.

"This was the site of a vicious massacre of more than twenty-five thousand farmers and villagers by the Brazilian army," Elaine began, but by now Frank was used to exploring on his own. He drifted away, exploring the depths of the flowery meadow.

Elaine captured a clip of Frank floating diagonally across the grass, face down in the dirt, long tail whipping the air. She sent it to Chantrea with the message, *Happy as a clam.*

So cute, the Cambodian guide replied. *Frankie just loves a killing field.*

Tourists are freaks, Elaine said, and they exchanged a battery of laughing emojis. Chantrea sent a flirty selfie—herself in a market, wearing a hat-like cloud of swarm-entities who could very well be mistaken for gnats. Elaine had guided many swarms over the years. They were pleasant, even lovely, once you got used to being surrounded by a chorus of musical buzzing.

She watched Frank explore the meadow, then they hopped to Tenochtitlan. Huge mountains all around, but the beta-blockers seemed to be working.

"That is Tláloc," she said, pointing out the peaks as if to prove they didn't bother her. "Chichinautzin, Ajusco, and Pelado."

"Very nice," said Frank.

They walked around the Sacred Precinct tracking down massacre sites until Frank admitted he was tired. She led him to their hotel suite overlooking the Templo Mayor and got him settled in with a fresh nutrition pack.

"Do you want to stay in for the night?" she asked, doing her best impersonation of an attentive guide.

"Yes, I want to rest." He looked exhausted, his skin mottled with white patches.

"Do you want me to stay with you?"

"No, please feel free to commune with your ghosts."

Oh right, the ghosts. She checked her support ticket. It provided several alternate translations for the statement, ranging from unhelpful to alarming:

Stay with your thoughts.

Meditate on mortality.

Visit with your dead.

Think about your departed loved ones.

As if she ever did anything else.

She said goodbye to Frank and ran off to find her favorite bar. She'd brought her family there, a few years back, and they'd all gotten looped on tequila and charcoal-grilled lamb. A local spot, no tourists, but a lot of returning expats who'd come back home to explore their ancestral habitat. Expats were weird about food. They took tentative nibbles, as if the meat was going to bite back.

Two of the expats were old and ailing, as evidenced by their various prostheses—eyeglasses, canes, floaters, med patches leeched to their wrists, little oxygen tubes snaking into their nostrils. Maybe they'd come home to die? Couldn't be, because they looked cheery, laughing with their friends, and she couldn't imagine how they could possibly be happy with death on the near horizon, stalking them and everyone they knew.

The bartender cut her off after four shots of tequila. She ordered a Michelada and some buttery escamoles, and managed to not cry into the bowl. When she returned to the suite, Frank was lounging on the wide terrace, gazing at the Templo Mayor under moonlight. His skin rippled with white hair.

"What's wrong with you?" she asked. "Are you supposed to be furry? You used to be bald."

"Oh." He curved his neck in an arc, looking back at his own body. "These are the symbiotic partners that reside in my skin. They clean detrimental compounds from my body. None of us are single entities, you know. Not even humans, though you generally refuse to acknowledge your symbionts. It's one of the oddest things about you, apart from your obsession with death."

"Obsession with death," she echoed. *Excuse me, who traveled a zillion light-years to survey multiple violent death sites?* But come on, she told herself. You can be a good guide, even if you're drunk. Be solicitous. Be kind. "Did you have a good day today?" she asked. "Did you see anything interesting?"

"Many things. Earth is full of ghosts."

She snorted. "Your translator needs a swift kick in the soft parts." So much for being a good guide.

"I don't understand." His head swung, and his fur—no, his *worms*—rippled.

"There's nothing to understand, Frank. We're both worn out. We need to rest."

She shut herself into her room and fell face down on the bed. She clawed the pillows into a rough nest and curled up, the ceiling spinning overhead.

The problem with death, she thought, was that it turned human beings into gaps in reality. Individuals who took up time, space, and attention suddenly became inexplicable, unfillable, gaping voids. And what can anyone do with a void but howl into it?

In the gloom of the morning, a message from Chantrea: **Ping me right away.**

Flirty selfie, and now an urgent message? She's interested in you, that's what Monica would say. Make an effort.

Elaine showered, slapped some color into her cheeks, and tried to do something about her hair. Shaggy and wet was sexy, right? Whatever. It would have to do. Not like she could ask Frank to give her a trim around the edges.

She arranged herself casually on the bed, and when Chantrea answered, flashing lights lit her hair like fireworks in a midnight sky. Shadowed figures lurched in the background, and a driving drumbeat forced its way through the audio filters.

"Hey," Chantrea shouted, her voice raspy. "I just want you to know I looked you up. Sorry. I couldn't resist."

"That's okay," Elaine replied automatically.

"No, it's a total invasion of privacy. I shouldn't have done it." Someone leaned over and draped themselves across Chantrea's shoulders. She shrugged them off.

"Yeah, well . . ." Elaine ventured. Some kind of noise was called for, and it was the best she could do.

"I'm really sorry about your family. Losing five people all at once, holy shit. And like that, too? Is it true they couldn't even retrieve the bodies?"

"Chantrea, are you stoned?"

"What? No. A little drunk, I guess?"

"You're going to feel really shitty about this in the morning. I've got to go."

"No, wait. I need you to know how sorry I am about what happened."

"I got it. Saying goodbye now."

Elaine shoved her face in a pillow. When she opened her mouth to scream, it came out as a moan. She kicked the mattress and blocked Chantrea on all channels.

Frank drifted out of his room, dragging the T-shirt with his tail. His skin was smooth and blue again, with no hint of the carpet of worms, but the liquid inside the carapace looked a bit murky.

"Good morning," she said, determined to be professional and stay that way. "Are you feeling comfortable? If the carapace is irritating, I can book you into a spa. You could stretch out, have a nice swim."

"No, I'd like to stay with you, Elaine. Your company is very interesting."

"That's sweet, Frank. I'll try to do better today."

"No special effort needs to be made."

She helped him connect the nutritional pack to the valve on the side of his carapace. A faint scrim of iridescent fluid seeped into the liquid and swirled around his fins. Pores opened on his flanks, and inside, little white threads squirmed. She backed off, fast. Made a hurried excuse and hid in her bathroom until her skin stopped crawling.

When she came out, Frank was still toying with the T-shirt, flipping it around with his tail.

"Do you want to wear that again today?" She tried to sound cheery. "I can help you put it on."

When she pulled it over his head, she noticed the mud on the neck and sleeves.

"It's a bit dirty. I should have put it through a hygiene cycle last night. Do you want a new one? I saw some nice Nahua designs in the street market."

"No, I like this one because you made it."

"You're a charmer, Frank."

"That's a compliment, I think? Thank you."

A quick hop north to Guaymas, a city clustered around bays and headlands, with hills lounging on the horizon. The gleaming, arc-shaped residential towers provided sweeping ocean views, and the locals were happy, tanned, and making maximum use of the coves and beaches. She thought Frank might appreciate the scenery, but he didn't give the views more than a cursory look before they hopped a short distance to Mazocoba.

"More than five hundred people of the Yaqui nation were massacred here in January of 1900," she said, as they ventured onto the fragrant scrubland.

Frank put his face to the dirt. "The history is a bit obscure."

"Do you want to move on to the next stop on our itinerary?"

"No, I'm happy to explore. There will be moisture somewhere. Or you could pour some, maybe?"

"Do you mean dump some water on the ground?"

"Yes, you could give it a try if you liked."

She trotted to the hopper and came back with a cold bottle sweating in her hand. She wiped the condensation on the leg of her shorts, and cracked the seal.

"What, just anywhere?"

"Under this plant, I think." Frank pointed with his tail.

She poured the water over the roots of a large scrub sage, and Frank dove in, chin quivering. He stayed like that for a long while, tail whipping like a cat. Elaine found some shade under an old maul oak. She watched the alien drift over the landscape, pushing his face into the dirt under one bush, then another, returning each time to the scrub sage. When he floated back to her, she could swear he was smacking his nonexistent lips.

"Happy?" she asked.

He contemplated the question for a moment. "*Happy* wouldn't be the word. Intrigued, perhaps. Intellectually engaged."

"By the dirt?"

"By the ambient ghosts. Though they are much smaller here, because of the dryness of the air and soil."

"That doesn't make sense. Does your translator want to give that another try?"

"Is *ghost* not the right word?"

"Ghosts don't exist." She led him back to the hopper. "Listen, do you want me to adjust our itinerary to skip over arid and semi-arid locations? We're supposed to hit some big massacre sites in New Mexico, but the monsoon is late this year so it's pretty dry. We could skip it and go straight to Goliad."

"That sounds fine. Wherever you want to go."

"It's not about me, Frank. You came all this way. It's my job to make sure you get what you came for. Right?"

"Right."

He dropped behind her. She turned, expecting to see him nose-deep in the dirt, but he was following close, eyespots huge and sunken. She'd nearly gotten used to regarding Frank as a friendly fish, almost a cartoon animal, and then he had to go do something creepy and break the illusion.

"I guess it would help," she said, strapping him into his seat in the hopper, "if I knew exactly what your goals are. The broker said you wanted to visit multiple violent death sites."

"Yes," he said. "Chantrea and I visited many. And now you and I are visiting some."

"Why exactly do you want to do that?"

"Because time is a liquid."

She strapped herself in. As the hopper rose, she tried again.

"Lots of tourists are interested in Earth's history of open violence. It makes sense, because most species are symbiotic colonies instead of individuals. You don't die as much as move from one state to another, so you think killing and death is exciting and dramatic. Of course," she qualified, "it's dramatic to us, too."

"All this is true."

"In your world, nobody is ever really gone. They're just a little less immediate."

"Yes, that's true, too. Their essence lingers."

"Nobody you've ever known has died." Her voice rose; she couldn't help it. "Do you know how lucky you are, Frank?"

"Lucky?"

Calm down. Be professional.

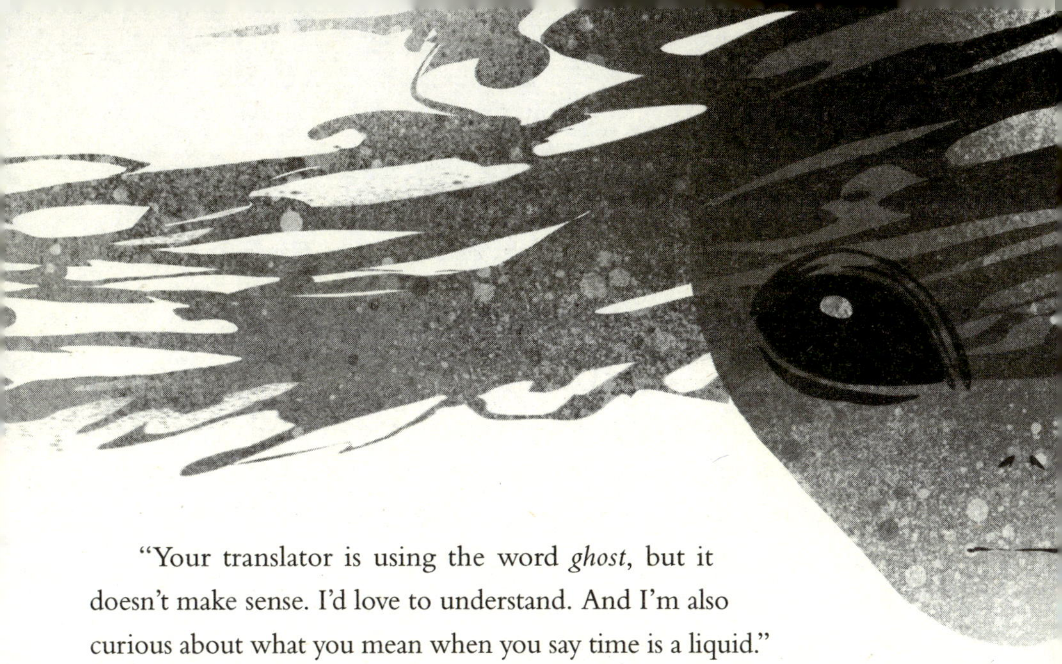

"Your translator is using the word *ghost*, but it doesn't make sense. I'd love to understand. And I'm also curious about what you mean when you say time is a liquid."

"I'll try to think of a way to clarify," said Frank.

They dropped into Goliad, a town populated by crumbling cemeteries and the overgrown husks of concrete foundations crouching under a canopy of oak trees. A few new houses dotted the landscape, cows and chickens browsing in the yards. She pulled up her notes, ready to give Frank the tour, but he didn't care. He was in his own world, mooching around in the dirt.

As soon as she got home, she'd cancel her guide license. She was too sensitive, too labile. The prez wouldn't like giving up the potential income stream, but that was just too bad. If she couldn't even get her chickens to lay, she had no business taking responsibility for alien tourists.

Rain had fallen recently in Goliad. Frank found a nice wet spot and lowered himself into the mud. Elaine sat on a patch of buffalo grass and watched him wallow.

"This is nice," said Frank, stirring the mud with his tail. "How much do you know about my world?"

"I know it's aquatic, but that's it." Elaine folded her arms across her chest. "I've been thinking, Frank. We should get you another guide. Someone who'll do a better job. I can find you a replacement."

"No. Don't do that. I like being with you." He writhed, stirring the mud, deepening the wallow. His carapace shed mud in runnels, and the T-shirt was getting filthy. "When you live in a liquid world, time moves differently. Evidence of things that are happening travel in the currents, and when it reaches you, it's all immediate. The off-gassing of an algae bloom might be half a world away but when it reaches your senses it's happening now."

"You swim in a world of sensory information," said Elaine. "So do we."

"I suppose. But humans perceive so little, it's hard to even fathom. I'm not trying to be rude. It must be very relaxing."

"Relaxing." Elaine repeated. She picked at the edge of the beta-blocker patch, watched it pulling at her skin. "Not really. So when you say time is a liquid, what do you mean?"

"Our perception of time is not linear as you perceive it, but flows back and forth according to the information contained in the liquid matrix."

"But not forward. You can't know the future."

"Not exactly. But one can make predictions with reasonable accuracy if one is perceptive enough."

"You can predict natural disasters? Like a landslip. An avalanche?"

"Certainly. But so could you."

"No, I can't." Elaine climbed to her feet. *I've got to get out of here before I punch him in the chin.* She kicked at a rock and sent it skidding into Frank's wallow. She stomped away.

"Is that true that you cannot?"

"Nobody can," she shouted over her shoulder.

She paced down the lane until she found a yard full of chickens. A few stark white leghorns in a sea of flashy wyandottes, their feathers mottled copper and white.

The screen door banged, and an old woman stepped onto her porch.

"Can I help you?" she asked.

"I've got three dozen young hens, and I can't get them to lay," said Elaine. "Any tips?"

"You got a good warm coop?" Elaine nodded. "They getting enough light?"

"All that. No parasites. Lots of good feed and room to roam."

"Your fault then. Fix yourself first, and the hens will lay."

"Okay." That's what Elaine got for asking advice from strangers.

"What? You thought I'd tell you to spill blood under a full moon or some such?"

"No. Really. I appreciate your time," Elaine said.

"Okay, but I think you have a bigger problem than some lazy hens. You've got a . . ." The woman circled her hands as if trying to pull words from the air. "You got . . . some kind of monster behind you."

Elaine turned. Frank was nuzzling the air behind her shoulders, his eyespots hugely dilated. Mud dripped from his T-shirt.

"Hello," he said. "I've been counting how many people died on this land."

"Okay then. Enjoy." The old woman retreated into her house, banging the screen door behind her.

Elaine led him away. "Frank," she said softly. "You can't go freaking out the locals."

"Did I not greet that person politely?"

"We don't go around mentioning death all the time."

"Why not? Is death not humanity's most salient characteristic?"

"It's not . . ." Elaine sighed. "Yes, I guess it is. But we don't talk about it, okay?"

"Okay."

She helped him back inside the hopper, then left him waiting while she paced around outside. She had to make a decision. She could stay on the itinerary, get the job done, and then forget all about him. That would be smart. But it wasn't what he wanted, was it? Not with all his comments about ghosts, about being able to predict the future. She was the worst kind of guide, and he'd been nothing but tolerant and kind. That meant he wanted something from her, didn't he? And maybe she wanted something from him, too.

She wiped the itinerary clean. Savannah, Charleston, and Gettysburg weren't going anywhere; they could wait. She told the hopper to head north to Kananaskis, to the pile of rock that used to be Loder Peak, now sitting at the bottom of the Bow River valley.

"Can you tell me something?" Elaine pulled the safety strap tight across Frank's torso. Mud from the T-shirt smeared the hopper bulkhead and safety couch. She should have taken it off him before strapping him in, but she had bigger things to think about. "What exactly do you experience when you grub around in the dirt?"

"Comfort," said Frank. "I feel comforted. I didn't expect travel to be so difficult."

"Difficult in what way? Intellectually? Emotionally? Or is it just hard to be somewhere so different from home?"

"All those things, but it's the information deprivation that's most difficult to bear."

"And sniffing dirt helps with that?"

"Sniffing? Like with a human nose? You're being glib, I think, Elaine? I'm trying to answer your questions."

"Yes, sorry. Go on. Please."

"I don't understand how you humans bear your existence." The translator kept a measured, calm tone, as if commenting on the weather. "You barely understand what is happening in the moment, much less the past. And the future is especially mysterious. You perceive little and know nothing. How do you not go mad?"

"We do go mad," said Elaine.

"Clearly. So, to answer your question, when I put myself in the soil, especially when the soil is wet, I can see all the information it carries. I can see who has trod the land, and especially who died there, because part of their being remains in the soil."

"You see dead people."

"I perceive beings with all my hundreds of senses, in a level of detail you would characterize as visual."

"What do you see, exactly?"

"My translator assures me that any human would call them ghosts. Perhaps spirits, but that word is less exact."

The hopper landed in Kananaskis. Elaine snapped open her safety harness and wrenched herself out of her seat.

"Ghosts," she said. "Okay. Fine. Prove it."

She released Frank's harness and swung open the hatch, stepping aside and flinging her arms wide, inviting him to lead the way outside. He swung his head back and forth, regarding her with eyespots now shrunken and dull. His chin bulb quivered.

"I don't believe I need to prove anything to you, Elaine," he said softly. "But I will enjoy investigating this terrain." He glided through the hatch.

Elaine paced back and forth in the tiny hopper cabin, slapping her palms on the headrests. She hadn't been anywhere near Kananaskis since the disaster, had done everything she could to avoid it, and she didn't have to go outside now. She could just wait until Frank had had his sniff, then take him somewhere for a nice, warm nutrition pack. She didn't even have to question him about what he might or might not have seen, but if so, she could do it gently and appropriately.

She punched a headrest hard, bruising her knuckles, then slammed her body through the hatch and out onto the rubble.

If she aimed her gaze high, the view was familiar, unchanged. Green forested slopes topped by gray-blue crags cupped the valley. The summer haze put the mountains into soft focus, as if they were just a static backdrop. As if they couldn't come tumbling down at any moment. As if each one of those cliffs wasn't a potential killer, about to come loose from gravity and crush everything.

As if it hadn't already happened.

The evidence was at her feet. Sedimentary stone in boulders, slabs, and plates, ripped apart and crumpled together like the cards of fate. Jagged rocks, skull-sized and fist-sized. Gravel and sand washed into crannies by a year of rain and snow. Rock powder so fine it could choke the breath out of a pair of lungs. And all that debris, tons and tons of it, piled atop her home, her people, her family. Monica, Lee, Lu-bon, Priya, Venetta.

Halfway down the slope, Frank sniffed at a clump of fireweed poking out from under a boulder.

"What do you see, Frank?" Elaine shouted.

"It's a bit obscure," he replied.

She grabbed an armful of water bottles from the hopper. The debris shifted underfoot as she leaped recklessly from one slab to another.

"Let me add some water," she said.

"You could try that."

She poured a bottle over the fireweed. The water splattered around the blooms, forming a corona of wet rock. Frank investigated the plant, then drifted toward a slab canted up against a boulder like a discarded toy.

"Stay uphill from those big ones," she called. "Don't get under them. They could shift."

"Yes, I understand," he replied.

Another clump of fireweed, here. A tiny buffaloberry, there. Frank nosed around the massive slab, then drifted to a clump of detached turf. It lay on a slope, as if tossed by a giant. It could be from her own yard; the family hens might have been pecking at it when the world turned to rubble.

"Anything, Frank?" she called.

"There isn't much to see."

"Let's try the river, then." She pointed east, where the rerouted Bow River skirted the landslide.

"If you like."

By the time she caught up with Frank among the toppled trees and scattered rock, he'd already had a leisurely wallow in the fresh river water. The Texas mud had left stains on the T-shirt. A branch of wild rose clung to his sleeve.

"What do you think, Frank?"

"This water is extremely clear."

"Is that good?"

"It doesn't hold much information, but it's refreshing."

"What about . . ." She had to make herself say it. "Ghosts. Are you finding any ghosts?"

"No, there are no ghosts here. Much of the rock was below ground until recently. The soil will take a long time to develop."

"You said you can see into the past."

"When there's soil to hold the information, yes."

"You're just making excuses." She called for the hopper. It rose from its spot high above, hovered for a moment, then slowly landed beside them "All right, let's get a move on."

Elaine strapped him into his couch, roughly, then curled up in her seat. She cradled her head in her arms as the hopper sped toward the Atlantic coast. Savannah would be wet and humid. He'd enjoy playing around in the mud, pretending to be all-knowing, all-seeing. Whatever. She could finish the job, keep it professional. No problem.

When they dropped into Savannah's harborside park, she yanked his straps open and nearly pushed him out the hatch.

"Are you angry?" Frank asked.

"No. It's my job to take you places. We're back on our itinerary."

"But clearly you're angry. Why is that?"

She didn't owe him the truth; she didn't owe anyone the truth, not anyone in the world. But if she kept it to herself, she'd burst.

"I'm pissed off because I don't believe you, Frank," she said. "I think you're lying to me about ghosts. Manipulating me."

He nodded his monstrous head. His eyespots gleamed in the sun.

"That's amusing," he said, "because I don't believe you, either. Humans cannot be as oblivious as you claim. It's simply impossible."

"Okay," she snapped. "I guess we both hate each other after all."

"Nothing of the kind. We simply don't trust each other. Which is natural, because we don't know each other. However, it's also ridiculous, because I can clearly perceive the truth and have no reason to lie. Nor do you have any reason to lie to me. Therefore there's no logical reason for you to deny it."

"Deny what?"

"You don't have to keep insisting that ghosts aren't real."

"But they're not."

"How can you say that? They've been with you from the very first moment we met."

"With me?"

"You have ghosts, Elaine. Five ghosts. Here they are." He glided around her, nodding at the air. "Venetta. Monica. Lee. Priya. Lu-bon. They are your family, are they not?"

Elaine stalked away, stiffly.

"Fuck you, Frank," she shouted.

"I can see them so clearly." He pursued her, following close behind.

"You're a liar." If she hadn't been so furious, she might have laughed. "You looked me up, didn't you?"

"They're with you. Watching you, caring for you." He raced ahead, blocking her path, his bottle-shaped head nodding, chin quivering. "They intercede when you need help. Don't you know that? They love you."

"Nobody loves me."

"You truly don't see them, Elaine?" he asked. "Very truly and sincerely?"

"Truly. Sincerely." Elaine flung her arms wide. "I'm absolutely, utterly alone."

Frank backed away from her, his eyespots wide.

"Poor you," he said. "Poor you."

THE DEAD-END PARTY

Cadwell Turnbull

We'd heard about the party during our last cross-country trip on the southern edge of the United States. At the time we were passing through Arizona and stopped into a service station to stock up on junk food—Brit had developed a dangerous obsession with hot sour cream and onion chips, the ones with Lebron's smiling profile on the front—and inside were two women grabbing handfuls of Red Bull from the ice box and dropping them into several blue shopping baskets already overloaded with Monster Energy drinks.

They smiled and waved at us, and one of them, the one with dirty-blond hair and a large nose ring hooped through her columella, said, "You just missed it."

"Missed what?" I asked.

They looked at each other. The other one said, "How do you not know about this yet?"

Brit and Reina and I shared a glance of our own. The two women were white, and our crew was various shades of brown. The answer seemed obvious to us.

"Could you tell us?" I asked.

A look of pity passed the women's faces. "You poor things," said the one with the nose ring, and I tried not to be offended by the use of the word *things*. Finally, she said, "The Dead-End Party." Then they explained what it was.

It might've been the second go-round (our crew called them "loops"), or maybe the third one—the women couldn't remember when they'd found out about it. Anyway, they'd been going to the party for three years now, and even this they were unsure about (which we understood, of course). This year, they said, was the craziest one yet: RV races through the desert, and battle royale brawls, all-day raves on any drug you could imagine, tons of drinking (they were still drunk, they admitted) and, yes, of course . . . lots of sex.

The one with the nose ring looked at me and smiled.

I glanced at Reina. "Where are you going now?" I asked.

Nose Ring said, "Wherever the road takes us."

And we were the same, cutting our way through this more-deserted patch of Americana until we found something worth stopping for. This was the way many of us spent our time, those who didn't settle down in one place: drifting uselessly, moving forward until an obstruction forced us to stop.

"Want to start a caravan?" I asked my group.

Reina said, "I could use a shower."

Brit said, "I think we should call it for the day and find a motel."

It was a little after noon.

Nose Ring: "We got a spot a few miles down the road."

My companions looked uncomfortable, so I cut my losses. "Maybe we can catch you at the next Dead-End Party?"

They both shrugged. Nose Ring said, "Maybe." The other one began hauling their catch of energy drinks out the door. Nose Ring passed her phone to me, and I passed mine and we exchanged numbers.

We gathered our junk food as the women continued to carry even more drinks to their SUV. They were gone by the time we came out to fill up our tank.

I'd forgotten all about it until the same time the next year when I received a text from "Kat Arizona" with a set of coordinates. I had to rack my brain for a solid five minutes to make the connection.

At that time, our crew (now four) were up north, near Chicago.

We weren't doing anything, just wandering again, passing the time with arbitrary adventures. By this time Reina had become a different person: less moody, more prone to risk-taking. She was the one to say we should go.

We pointed our car southwest, doing a hundred on the freeway. No cops would stop us, so we weaved through lanes, passing all the phantom cars with no people inside. Come by this stretch of highway the exact time the following year and the same cars would be there, completing the same circuit, going nowhere they hadn't gone before.

We were different. The world was on loop, not us.

We did see one other person during the drive. In Kansas we abandoned our banged-up Tesla at a Walmart. We waited for a ghost SUV to pull to a stop before we rushed the vehicle. I commandeered the wheel, feeling the phantom force of other hands give to the primacy of mine, and just as we were pulling out, we spotted a guy idling in the parking lot, smoking and nodding his head to music we couldn't hear. We did not like the look of him, so we were quick to get out of there.

It took two days for us to make our way to Arizona, driving through the night, ignoring the universe's call for us to sleep.

Brit hadn't slept for days and looked no more tired than the rest of us. "It's just programming," she said. "I let it run in the background until it tires itself out. Get it? Okay, fine."

"Well," Jed said, "the feral unicorn upstairs made me sleepy so I'm going to embrace her will."

We'd had more than our share of philosophical conversations by this point about the nature of our current circumstances, whether real or simulation, heaven, hell or purgatory, an alien experiment, that sort of thing, but on this particular week Jed's theory was that mythological creatures were taking their revenge on humanity for all past slights, real or imagined, and we were their lab rats, the pilot program for future incomprehensible tortures.

On the night before we made it to the Dead-End Party, we finally decided to stop because Brit desperately wanted a shower. We found an inn down a winding road nearby, dropped our junk in front of the biggest rooms we could find, then went back downstairs to scour for a master key. The inn was well-kept, which was a relief to us (we'd gotten stuck in some bad places on the road) and well-lit, driving out the darkness of the surrounding forest. It was likely the expensive kind of travel accommodations, the kind for people with at least some disposable income, a "get away from the city for a few nights" type of bed-and-breakfast. We played coy with details like this, all of us dead-folk, calling everything a "nearby motel" or a "place to crash." No dead person, if they could help it, would choose to stay in a motel. That was the last option if everyone was too tired to find a nicer place. Chains were fine; they were easy to locate on the sides of highways. But the real prizes were the small inns and bed-and-breakfasts that served great food and had nice clean rooms and bedding. For the dead, money was no option, so the culture had developed organically: if you're going to sleep on the road, sleep somewhere nice.

The bedding in the rooms was nice indeed. I'd dropped my stuff off in my room for the night and had come back to pass the time in Brit's room. Then Reina came by after her shower. Jed made some burgers in the kitchen and brought them up. We spent the next couple hours with a movie playing as we talked about the next day of driving.

There was no one there but us, which would've made the place creepy if it was just me. But with the group I was able to feel relaxed, the sounds of doors opening and closing (the phantom actions of the living) forming a staccato backdrop to our aimless chatter.

"What do you want to do when you get there?" Brit was asking.

I didn't want to admit that what I really wanted to do was find Kat. So far, my romantic life, post-dying, had been uneventful. But I wasn't about to say that out loud.

"I don't know," I said. "It'll be cool just to hang out in the desert for a few days. Just camp out under the stars or whatever."

Reina shrugged. "I've never camped before."

"Seriously?" I said, and hearing the judgment in my tone, corrected myself. "I've only been a handful of times. It's all right, I guess."

And this was true. Those times when I went camping, I'd gone with white friends. Friends from college or after college. Professional friends in my income bracket. Reina worked multiple jobs, lived paycheck to paycheck when she was alive, which meant she had no need to go into the woods and sit around in nature, didn't have friends who did that sort of thing. Who had the time? Plus, she didn't have a lot of white friends that talked her into hiking and camping and shit. Not saying Black people don't camp. Just saying I've only met a handful off the top of my head that did it as a personal interest and not socially. Only because they'd been invited.

And it wasn't that I had wealthy friends either. I'd say most people I hung out with when I was alive were middle class, worked long hours, had tons of millennial guilt about calling off. Or they were gig-folk, like me, who didn't make a ton of money but had enough disposable income to have adult getaways they saved up for (getaways that had to be polled because everyone was super busy).

Reina didn't seem to take offense to my unintentional jibe. "Hey," she said, eyes lighting up, "don't we need stuff for that sort of thing? Camping out, I mean."

We all looked at each other, actually bewildered. Jed said, "Wow, we're bad at this. We should stop tomorrow and pick up some camping stuff."

"Like what?" Brit asked.

Silence.

Reina was the first to laugh. The expression on all our faces.

"Doesn't matter anyway," said Jed. "We can just pick up anything we want."

A slasher film was playing on the television. A recent one, and as far as we knew, all the actors in it were still alive, even though they were pretending to die on-screen.

A thought I had often: What was so-and-so doing on the living side? What kind of music, or movies, or books, or comics were they making or involved in? Who was getting married, who had divorced? I'd play out all sorts of scenarios in my head. Of people I knew, sure, but mostly of people I didn't know. The strangers whose art I consumed.

The door to Brit's suite opened and closed, interrupting my thoughts. No one was there, but we'd seen it so many times, we only glanced that way before returning to the movie in front of us.

"Hey, any of you remember *Happy Death Day*?" I asked, trying to sound casual.

Brit and Jed nodded. Reina did not. This time I restrained myself.

It was Jed that said: "Well, we'll have to watch it. Required material considering the situation we find ourselves in."

"Okay," Reina said, but she didn't seem excited in the least.

We'd long ago covered the classic loop movies and episodes of TV shows, but every once in a while, we'd remember another example. Truthfully, I'd thought about *Happy Death Day* my first year on the loop (I had lists of such things) but didn't bring it up before because I was always bringing up movies, or books, or music, or some other pop culture artifact and had gotten the memo that the casual habit was annoying to Reina, who was opposite to me in this regard (and many other regards), having been too busy living her life to waste it consuming media. I was busy too, but a great chunk of my busyness was professionalizing the consumption of media. I'd worked myself to death as a content writer and media critic. How pointless it seemed now. And yet, all I wanted to do, even now, even dead, was make lists.

After a while, the slasher movie ended. One sole survivor, the rest living out their afterlives in some fictional shadow reality: like us.

We were all tired and called it for the night, disappearing back to our individual luxury suites. I collapsed on my bed and sleep took me instantly. My dream was a boss battle between Jason Voorhees, Michael Myers, and the Bayfield Babyface Killer where they all managed to kill each other and found themselves in an afterlife occupied exclusively by other slasher villains. And *me*, which, you might not be surprised to learn, encouraged a competition among the serial killers to see who could kill me first. Not fun. Not fun at all.

"I've been thinking," Jed said from the back seat, about an hour from our desti-nation.

Brit, also in the back seat, and me driving, locked eyes. "Here we go," we said, our practiced routine. In the front seat of the vehicle, this one a 2021 Honda CRV, Reina continued her vigil of the increasingly barren landscape.

"Is it Dead-End Party or Dead End-Party?" Jed asked. "I mean I get the joke of the first instance. A play on the typical use of dead-end, but I think the latter is more fitting. Like a party to celebrate the end of a loop. The Dead's End-Party."

"The first one," Brit said. "The second option takes too much explaining. And besides, this isn't the end of a loop. That would make more sense if it happened on New Year's Eve."

"You're taking the question too literally," Jed said. "I meant: Wouldn't the second option be better?"

"Define *better*."

"And where in the world would you host the New Year's Dead End-Party anyway? It's not like the end of the year happens everywhere at the same time."

"Tokyo," Brit said. "Easy."

"You're doing this on purpose."

"Doing what?"

"You know."

"I don't. What am I doing?"

"Look at your face, Brit."

"How can I look at my face? Oh, here's an actually interesting question: How does the loop happen? All at once or by time zone?"

"It's an expression, Brit. See what I mean. You're—wait . . . that *is* an interesting question."

I tuned out the rest of the conversation but kept thinking about the two versions of "dead end." I actually liked a third option best. Dead End Party. Each word standing alone. A party for the dead, but celebrating the end, whatever that meant for each person. The end of their lives. The end of being alive. The end of who they were, in anticipation of who they could become on this side. Whatever interpretation of ending, it held a promise of a beginning of something else since we were all still there to celebrate it. I liked that idea a lot.

When we finally arrived at the desert, it seemed like we were late, not because of time of day, but the sheer number of vehicles already there. RVs and trucks and vans and buses (some retrofitted into mobile domiciles) were littered across the stretch of cracked earth like some rich kid's discarded toys. At the center of the spread of vehicles was a haphazardly constructed town: blow-up castles, sky dancers waving in the wind, structures cobbled together out of plywood, more than a few cookie-cutter cottages and other small buildings than must've been hauled in by big wheelers (and, sure enough, the perpetrators were still there among the mess of vehicles). Among all that human stuff—people. Thousands. More than I'd seen in one place since I'd died. My mouth was open as I took it in. How had I missed this? How had we all missed this?

Brit was first out of the vehicle, dropping down with a shout of glee. Jed was out second.

Reina looked at me and I could see the excitement, the wonder, but also the fear. She was asking me with her eyes if we were sure we wanted to do this. Anything could happen here. I gave her a reassuring smile. We were dead anyway. Dead with nothing better to do. We got out.

A man ran past me stark naked, his back muscles flexing with each pump of his legs, butt cheeks jiggling fearlessly. He disappeared behind a row of cars, his shouts blending with the other noise around us.

"Come on," Reina said, and I followed.

Brit and Jed had already fallen in with all the people. I got on my tiptoes to look for them but gave up. We'd find them eventually.

Reina and I weaved between the parked vehicles. A van on my right rocked suspiciously and I kept myself from looking. Music played loud from inside, leaking out from a cracked window, adding to the current of noise. Reina reached for my hand and pulled me forward. She was moving fast, brushing past bodies recklessly, as much as that could be said here, in this place. We stumbled into a fenced-off area (the "fence" being a circle of badly nailed together plywood). Inside was a fairground, or a paltry attempt at one—about a dozen manmade structures where one could play fair games. I imagined the effort of someone finding these fair rejects and hauling them across country, across a desert, to plant them here just so that people could stumble drunkenly from one game to the next, trying and failing to win.

There was the dart balloon game, the one where you throw darts at a wall covered in rows of half-blown-up balloons, only these balloons were all the way blown up (why not be fair in a looped world where there was enough stuff for billions of people and only millions to use it).

Reina and I took rounds throwing darts at the balloons. The guy standing there with an expression of boredom handed us random prizes after every round no matter how well we did: stress balls, yo-yos, a tennis racket, a calculator, two e-readers, a yoga mat, an iPad, and (of course) teddy bears.

After we were done, he asked, "You think you're going to use any of that stuff?"

Reina shrugged. I looked at the two e-readers on the pile next to my feet. "I'd like to keep the e-readers." I glanced at the pile again. "And the stress ball."

The man didn't look at me. "Cool."

We handed him back the other items and carried on.

We found Jed and Brit in the line for the bumper cars. There were a dozen cars on the round track and a lot of tantalizing screaming and laughter from the people driving full speed into each other. Jed and Brit were at the front of the line, but there were not a lot of people around. We walked right up to them, me giving an apologetic smile to the people behind me (a group of five, so busy talking to each other, none acknowledged us).

A bell rang and all but four people left their bumper cars where they'd come to rest.

With our crew and the group of five behind us, there weren't enough bumper cars to go around.

"Hey!" Jed said. "Didn't you hear the bell?"

The four remainers glared back.

One, a trucker's cap shadowing his eyes, said, "Fuck you, man."

Jed, turning a little red in the face: "Why don't you come over here and say that again."

I'd already started to panic, but Brit and Reina were cool as steel.

The four remainers got out of their bumper cars as one; it looked almost coordinated, like a stereotypical gang from a nineties movie. There were three men and one woman.

Brit was first to respond, jumping over the low barrier and onto the track, shifting into a battle stance. Dust kicked up around her and the image of her powering up like an anime character leaped to my mind. Something you should know about Brit: When she was alive, she was a martial arts hobbyist. Now, with an abundance of time on her hands, she had become the real deal.

Our nemeses faltered just a bit, sharing a glance, but then one of them, Trucker Cap, stepped forward.

Reina and Jed jumped the barrier as well. I followed behind them apprehensively. Everything had quieted down. The group behind us had stopped their conversation, staring on at the promise of violence.

Without another warning, Trucker Cap ran at Brit, throwing a punch.

And Brit sidestepped the wild swing. Calmly, she watched the guy fly past her, stumbling into the low barrier. He made to turn, but Brit was already airborne. She landed a roundhouse kick to the back of his head, and with a yelp he tumbled over the barrier, dust flying up around him. Brit then spun to the other three—who slid to a stop before her, more dust everywhere—and smiled dementedly, hands clenched into fists.

Reina came up to stand next to Brit.

Jed got into a fighting stance of his own now, and said, "Your choice."

The girl of the group was the first to come to her senses. She pulled the arm of one of the other guys and he yielded to her influence. The other followed, all of them giving Brit a wide berth.

It was over that quickly. Anticlimactic, but I was grateful. I released the breath I was holding.

I know how this must seem, but it wasn't like we got into fights all the time. This was actually only our second. We'd been participants of a bar brawl a year back. Brit and Jed had fared well. But Reina and I had gotten the shit kicked out of us—Reina because she refused to back down from a dude twice her size, and me because I thought I could swoop in and save her from said dude. In the end Brit had to save us both.

I'd been traumatized from the experience (it took two weeks for my front tooth to grow back). Apparently, I was the only one. But this would be far from the last time we had to defend ourselves in the afterlife. As you might imagine, in a big lawless world filled with people who can't die (again), defending yourself would become a prerequisite of existence.

The nineties Villain Squad retrieved Trucker Cap from off the ground—he'd wisely stayed where he fell—and scrambled away.

Brit didn't look back at them. She just walked out to the center and dropped down into Trucker Cap's bumper car. Once we'd all found our own cars, the five behind us included, there were still three left over. No one entered to occupy them. The bell rang and we enjoyed twenty minutes of sweaty bliss in the sweltering sun, me squinting the entire time so that the dust we were kicking up didn't assault my eyes.

When the bell rang again, we relinquished our bumper cars to the half dozen people waiting in line.

That night was bonfires, scattered at the edges of the temporary civilization the Dead-End Party creators had made. I say *creators* but it was unclear all through that first day if there were any creators of the party or any real planning involved. Like I said, everything looked like it had been hauled out there at the last minute, a potluck of debauchery. So far I hadn't witnessed much debauchery though, so maybe just a potluck of "bring your own junk so we can have a big desert party."

Why here though? Why not some stadium in one of the big cities with the right facilities and no sports team to use it? Why not a mall, or a hotel with a convention center? Why not anywhere else?

Here's what I think: It was a spiritual exodus, an attempt to be close to whatever had trapped us in this looped world. We wanted to catch a glimpse of greater cosmic forces, be one with God, air our grievances, dance with oblivion. Or we were trying to re-create Burning Man.

The night sky was beautiful in the desert. It felt like every star in existence was visible above, like the hand of the divine had dipped their brush in white paint and, with a flick of the wrist, splashed it against a black canvas. The rare sight of clouds were little wisps in the sky, thin as cigarette smoke.

We'd set down with one group at a bonfire, and were welcomed with beers and ciders, and savory scones that were made, we were told, from weed butter and "mushrooms!"—the woman said the word, with all its ambiguities, like she was shouting back any questions, and so we didn't ask, only ate them, though I was careful not to eat too much at once.

There around the fire: Emily (the mushroom woman) in overalls and a sports bra; Jos, a lean shirtless man who could've been the naked man I'd seen when I first arrived, but I wasn't sure; Tony and Tom, who looked very young and were definitely lovers; Cynthia, a very beautiful but also severe Black woman with long locs, hooped earrings, and a serpent tattoo wrapping around her neck; and Jed, Brit, and myself, Reina having wandered off at some point (this was still the early loops, where people could go off by themselves and no one would worry).

By this time, I'd looked everywhere for Kat and had not found her. A text I'd sent to her phone remained unread.

So, I'd settled into the evening with the people before me. I'd only eaten a small bite of the scone still in my hand, pacing myself. I had, however, drunk quite a bit of the cider in my other hand, and a series of beers and mixed drinks in solo cups, and some more ciders, and at least one hard seltzer over the course of the day. I'd spaced them out with time and water so that I would maintain a buzz. But at some point, I had stumbled into something beyond a buzz, not drunk yet but getting there.

"You think there are other planets out there like this one? Dead aliens looking up at their sky, thinking about us?"

This from Jed. And who else would it be?

"Why would they think about humans?" Brit said. "They've never met us."

Jed glared at her.

But our new friends didn't just barely tolerate Jed's question; it launched a full-on debate.

"I think they have their own empty universe," Emily said.

"That's wasteful," said Cynthia. "To make a whole universe and just put a handful of people on one rock?"

"That's what happened here though, right?" asked Emily. "Only people who died in 2025, trapped in the year 2025? How is that not wasteful?"

Cynthia shrugged. "I suppose the world of the living wasn't particularly less wasteful. Def should've been more aliens, given all that space."

"But we all agree though, right?" Jed said. "Dead aliens are out there."

Cynthia wrinkled her nose. "Yeah, I think so. Who knows, there might be a planet full of dead aliens. Some world-ending calamity. Only their civilization continued on this side."

This got them all animated, thinking of the possible ways those aliens could've died: asteroids, pandemics, exploding stars. They wondered, in the case of the exploding star, if the aliens got to see it every year, see that star explode. And what happened after that? Did the loop just reset?

"What if the dead aliens had space travel?" Jed asked. "You think they might try to travel to see us?"

"Not us specifically," Tony said, "but maybe they're visiting some other dead aliens as we speak."

"Conquering other dead alien home planets," Tom said, grinning.

Tony punched Tom on the arm and they both laughed.

All of us around that fire looked so youthful. Even Cynthia and Jos presented as being in their early forties. But just like the possibility of teeth growing back, the world granted other changes over time. The process was gradual though. Slow metamorphosis, transformation by inches, each of us still making our way toward some ideal, if that could ever be reached.

Jos looked at me, his pecs bulging. "What you think, Trevor? Think there are dead aliens out there?"

"Well," I said, trying to buy time. Truth was, I'd somehow crossed the threshold into drunk *and* high territory during the course of the conversation and my brain was eating itself. Undesirable thoughts. Not about aliens, but about my last year alive. How I could've done things differently and maybe be alive right now. Eventually, after probably too much time, I said, "I

believed in aliens on the other side. I guess I don't see any harm in believing in dead aliens. I don't think they're coming here though. And if they did, not for another million years."

I could tell by the look on their faces that I'd said something terrible. Each one of them had latched on to my words and found something there that terrified the absolute shit out of them.

"Another million years," Jos repeated.

I got it then, and the implications sobered me up a little. A million years from now, when those hypothetical aliens showed up, we'd all still be here waiting for them. And who would we be by then, having spent a million years trapped in this pocket dimension? Where we can't age or die, not really. Nothing to do but what we're doing now. I'd be done reading and watching and listening to everything I could get my hands on. We'd likely have nothing left to do but sit there, eating our thumbs. And the aliens would arrive to a planet of lunatics, eating our thumbs to pass the time, and waiting for our thumbs to grow back to do it all over again.

"Well," Cynthia said, "I need to take a walk." And she got up, stalking back toward the lights of the Dead-End Village.

The rest of us remained quiet, the chatter of neighboring bonfires and the ghostly echo of distant K-pop filling the silence. Until Jed asked: "If there was another year you'd want to live in, which death year would it be?"

This was enough to divert everyone's thoughts back to the moment.

I decided I needed a walk as well.

"One of the World War II years," I heard someone say as I left the group.

I didn't walk toward the lights, choosing instead to wander farther into the darkness.

I walked past all those islands of bonfires, the indistinct masses huddled around flickering flames. Everything was swimming together, orange tendrils and inky darknesses. A few times people called out to me, asking me if I wanted to sit with them, or "What's your story, man?" or "How did you die?" (said while laughing, because he knew you don't ask that shit), or "You got any drugs?" I kept shaking my head and kept walking, until only the desert was in front of me. There wasn't much to look at other than dirt and piles of rock in the deepening black. I kept on, passing a couple having sex, and then, peering at their shadows for a while, realized it was three people, not two. I sped up before they noticed me.

I saw the silhouette of someone leaning against a rock in the distance. Something felt familiar about the silhouette. I approached tentatively.

Reina looked up and also recognized me, and I imagined myself standing above her, backlit by distant bonfires and stars overhead, like a visitor from another world.

"You got sick of people, too?" she asked.

I sat down next to her, leaning against the same rock she leaned on. "Yeah," I said. "Jed had them talking about space-faring undead aliens."

We both laughed, her likely picturing it, me remembering it. It was the Jed-est thing imaginable.

"I don't know," she said, after the laughing died. "I try not to think about anything other than what is in front of me. Thinking too much in a place like this leads to ruin."

I told her about what I'd said about a million years and how everyone got really quiet.

"That's exactly what I mean," she said.

"I'm terrified of the idea of being here a million years," I said. "But I am scared of not being here even more. Dying and never waking up."

Reina shrugged. "It couldn't be so bad. Going to sleep and not waking up. *Nothing* isn't scary. The thought of it, maybe. But actual *nothing*? Sounds great to me, anyway."

"But it wouldn't be great either. Just empty. That doesn't freak you out?"

"Two choices, Trev. *Everything* forever. Or *nothing* forever. With the latter choice, at least you had something for a while. Followed by infinite rest." She shrugged. "Not so bad."

I got quiet. She wasn't wrong, but I still would choose the everything for a minute more if I could choose it. If there was a button right in front of me asking if I'd prefer one more minute, I'd press it. I'd press it for a million years, for sure.

Our shoulders were touching, which is why I felt her lean into me, resting her head on mine. She let out a sigh like she was tired and had just found somewhere to sleep.

Something terrible had happened to Reina. Unlike the rest of us, she hadn't even hinted at how she died. I couldn't help but think that experience had something to do with her stance on eternal life.

"What?" Reina asked.

"Nothing."

"Always keeping things to yourself."

I thought, *I'm not the only one.* I said, "This place. Something made it for us. God or something."

"So that's where you land on the great mystery," she said—no question in her tone, all disappointment. "God made this place for the dead to live. A separate purgatory for each year of dead."

"What would you like this place to be then?"

Reina lifted her head off my shoulder. In the dark she was looking into my face. Perhaps she could see me, but from my vantage her face swirled, throbbed. "All options are bad. If it is God, that's the worst."

"Why?"

"Because look around. God had nothing better to do for us, nothing better to offer us. So he, or she, or they, or it, stuck us . . . *here.* To keep ourselves company. Work it out on our own. Even in death, our divine creator doesn't give a shit. Absentee parent for all occasions."

"I don't know," I said. "Maybe we're here for just a little while. Maybe we have to work something out. In stories about time loops it's all about working things out, fixing something so you can move on."

"Move on where?"

"I don't know. I suppose, if you ascribe to the purgatory idea, then—"

Reina leaned in and kissed me. The leaning in was fast, urgent, but the kiss itself was soft, and she didn't remove her lips right away; she pressed them to mine, cupping my face with both hands, then pulled away, keeping her hands where they were. "Shut up, Trev. For the love of all things holy, just shut up."

I nodded.

"You're a better kisser than you were in high school," Reina said.

I laughed nervously. When we dated in high school Reina was the first girl I'd ever kissed. After we'd parted ways, I had many other experiences. But of course, that first time had stayed with me.

How surreal. To have died in the same year. To find each other again here of all places.

"You're as good as I remember," I said, and this time I was the one to initiate. As we kissed, I felt myself both in my body and as a cloud floating over myself, ready to burst. We kept going for what felt like hours, and then we rested on each other, our faces to that beautiful, star-specked sky.

And I imagined the large hand of an absentee god, reaching its brush into a pool of pure creation. Readying itself to lift that hand, that brush heavy with creation, readying itself to smear that creation onto some other canvas, make another attempt at the elusive project called heaven. Maybe our creator was the one working things out. Maybe it was trying to get everything just right and we had to wait, and this was where you went to wait: a slice of time made infinite.

"What are you thinking about?"

I shook my head, a little dizzy. "I'm high as fuck," I said.

Reina laughed to herself, amused by some secret joke. "Sure."

ANGELS OF THE WATERS

Elizabeth Bear

We were both of us dead at the outset, but Johnny Backus remained a good deal more mobile than me. He was also a good deal older, because by the time I awakened (dead and immobile) in 1876, Johnny Backus was already a vampire.

A vampire like Varney, or Carmilla.

Oh, Carmilla. How my former self would have loved to have played her on the stage—the ageless temptress, and the tender young maidens whom she seduced, adored, and slew. I would have shocked Boston far more than I ever did in trousers roles!

When I awakened in my cold new body, Johnny awaited me.

He'd felt something change in his city. He'd felt my bronze limbs imbued with some anima, some essence from the death of the woman my creator had modeled me upon. My other self had been the sculptor's lover. Because Johnny felt what changed in his city as if feeling what had changed in his body, he'd noticed me awakening and come to see. He stood across the winter-drained basin of the fountain that footed me, snow about his booted feet, the moonlight shining on him.

"Welcome to New York, stranger," he said. "Do you have a name?"

"No," I said. Then, "I was Charlotte. I've been here before. This isn't heaven."

"Maybe it's purgatory." He mantled his arms. "But one thing is for certain. You are an angel now."

I strained against the confines of my immobile metal body. I could not twitch a finger.

My new acquaintance said. "I'm Johnny Backus. This is my town."

Johnny soon became a friend of mine.

Johnny built this city. His city.

For two hundred years, he built it.

I was one of the things he built. Or not *me*, exactly. He didn't cast my bronze. But he worked on the mortar of Bethesda Terrace, the iron bones holding the gorgeous tile ceilings aloft.

I couldn't see the tiles in the dark of the February night from my pedestal above the rubbish-strewn fountain. But I remembered them well, from when my Emma and I had come here for the statue's unveiling.

For my unveiling.

The *Angel of the Waters*, they called me. I was built to celebrate the pure water that flowed into the city after the Croton Aqueduct was opened.

You've gotten used to clean water. You've forgotten it is a treasure. But it's not a given, and through neglect you can lose it.

Love is like that too. If you are wise you don't dare take it for granted.

Emma, who cast my form, called me after the Angel of Bethesda, who blessed the water and made it pure. Her name came to encompass the whole of the terrace surrounding and overlooking me. Over which I spread my wings in benediction.

Water is the source and the enemy of civilization. It circulates through the city. It flows like blood through mains and up to towers. It is the font of life. Nothing is inhabitable without water.

But dirty water carries disease and breeds mosquitoes. There were outbreaks, before the clean water was brought, plague seasons of yellow fever and cholera and typhoid.

Water eats away the city's metal bones. It is the enemy of brick and marble and when burning fuel taints it, it washes acid across facades and softens the lines of hand-hewn gargoyles, the decorated downspouts and leafy-haired Green Men.

It showers from beneath my feet, and I bless it.

It's lonely being an angel, especially a bronze one. But I bear witness, and I endure.

As for Johnny—Johnny came to New York just before the brutal days of the Dead Rabbits, the Shirt Tails, and the Bowery Boys, of the Roach Guards and the Atlantic Guards. He laid brick and riveted steel in churches and in Central Park, hucked rivets through the rise of the New York World Building and the Flatiron. He built brownstones and tenements and the cast-iron facade buildings of SoHo until the invention of the high-speed elevator. A hundred years after he first set foot here, he walked the high iron of the Chrysler Building and the Empire State. He raised the Twin Towers and saw them fall, and his hands helped shape One World Trade Center in their place.

His hands touched it all.

To say "aching bones" is a cliché, but there's a truth in it. The bones are the center of everything. They hold it up and hold it together. And the bones of the city are steel.

Johnny talked to his buildings. And his buildings talked back to him. He had no breath of his own, so he sang in their steel bones and they sang, in turn, in his.

He had many friends. I think he knew everybody in New York City. I had . . . only him.

He came and told me about it. And I heard the music, and I also sang back to him.

Once I had a famous voice, my contralto celebrated for its depth. I performed Lady MacBeth for Abraham Lincoln, but was well-known for my breeches roles. The envy of many a male Shakespearean, I played both Hamlet and Romeo.

That was less of a scandal in my time than you might imagine. I found my scandals elsewhere, in my choice of lovers and the salons I kept. You can get away with nearly anything if you have money.

Even being a (gasp) Lesbian.

I knew Johnny wasn't mortal from the first, because he could talk to me. Because he was waiting for me when I awakened, and because he told me stories about his city, the work of his hands. He came and visited me often, and he didn't try to hide what he was. He didn't pretend to be anything other than a vampire.

Dracula wasn't even a glimmer in Bram Stoker's imagination when I woke in Central Park, frozen solid but unable to feel the chill. It would not be published for yet another twenty-one years.

But *Carmilla, Carmilla* was au courant and all the rage. It had been published the year before I died and no respectable woman would be caught reading such a piece of trash, such a penny dreadful. My circle—my beloved Emma's circle—of course, we daughters of Lesbos, we artists and sculptresses and actresses and playwrights, *we* bought every copy we could get our hands on, and passed them from one to another.

I was already dying when my darling Emma read it to me, making of it a welcome distraction from the pain of the cancer eating me away. Emma had given up her work to nurse me. The *Angel of the Waters* would be her final piece, and her most famous.

And it would bring me, irony of ironies, to meet a real vampire.

Real vampires, and the vampires of legend, are not much like the ones the children in the park dress up as and play at being. Carmilla and Dracula and Varney had no difficulty going out in the sunlight.

Neither did Johnny, who walked abroad at all hours with assurance.

That was good, because I had no one else to talk to.

Plenty to watch, plenty to see—tourists and street performers, breakups and proposals, runaway children and the make-believe vampires and Shakespeare in the Park. (I could have done better.) In the long fullness of time there were film productions, and I was sorry I had not lived to see the results.

Often, at first, I would see my own dear Emma. For the six years she lived after my passing, she returned to her native New York.

How I yearned after her. How I wished . . . how I wished I could reach across the water and touch that beloved face. How I wished I could speak to her.

But statues and most of the dead are silent. Perforce. And though she grew more feeble and knew her time was upon her, I could not give her the comfort she had given me.

People moved around her, a woman of a certain age in her black coat who stood regarding the *Angel of the Waters*. It was strange to know that not one of them recognized her. That not one of them knew her as the source and begetter of this monument.

I wished I could tell her that I was here. That I loved her as ever. That some magic in my creation and her devotion had linked my two selves together, the one that died and the one she made.

Forever? Was I trapped here without my Emma, while Emma went on to her final reward? Could I escape the statue then?

It was not long before Emma came no more to regard me and I was even more alone. I had hoped when she passed she might join me. But perhaps she had been ready to move on.

Perhaps I wasn't.

Perhaps Johnny needed me.

A statue can move no more than it can speak. It wasn't so bad in the summers, in the daytime, when my terrace filled with children dancing from the surfeit of life running quick through their bodies, with lovers arm in arm, with stately older couples promenading. But at night, in the winter, my tiny demesne was empty and still. Even though Johnny came to visit—I think now that he was relieved to find someone who would not leave him, as everyone must leave immortals—there were many nights when I was on my own from the bitter sunset to the chill sunrise.

So I dreamed the years away.

There was once an apartment in Rome where the women artists gathered. There were once the salons, the parties, the suppers and dinners, the beautiful and brilliant women I loved and lost and whose creative genius I promoted in a man's world.

From the genius of the arts, to the Genius of the Terrace.

It suited.

There was Emma. Always Emma. My dear wife, though no church would sanctify us. It's true that I used my connections to help her get commissions. But her brilliance is proved by the fact that her art is still celebrated. That I am still celebrated. And if she hadn't been a woman, she wouldn't have needed my interference to succeed.

When I tired of those memories, I could review my life on the stage. So many triumphs.

They say you cannot live in the past. But you can die there. In fact, once you are dead there is only the past to consider.

What did Johnny and I talk about? Oh, pretty much the same things I dreamed on, for my part. For his—he had a thousand stories, each one more roughneck and improbable than the last. He had come from upstate. He was half-Mohawk, and he said his people had a tradition of ironwork. I imagined he must have helped originate that tradition, but he didn't elaborate and I didn't ask.

Neither of us questioned the other. I didn't want to know whether he kept a coffin half full of blood and native earth somewhere in the city. I didn't want to know how he fed himself, and whether he dined on the blood of innocents.

Call it cowardice if you will.

That's what it was.

Instead of asking questions, we told stories. In sixty-odd years, he had collected some real lally-cooler anecdotes. By the time his second century rolled around, he could have held a stage with Sam Clemens. And I told him of the people I saw moving through the park, their loves and quarrels and (eventually) their cell phone conversations. And their regrettable fashion choices, also.

When we ran out of stories, we sang.

Most of the city could not hear it. They heard at first the rumble of horse carts and the cries of drovers, the answering rumble of the subway and the calls of conductors. As time went on the horse carts gave way to the blare of automobile traffic, the shouts of pedestrians. The people of New York heard the drum of rain and the whistle of wind between tall buildings.

They did not hear Johnny's voice pulsing, sublimated, through every one of those things.

We sang through first one century, then through much of another one.

They did not hear the echoes change when the city began to drown.

It was slow at first; a storm flooding basement apartments, a hurricane inundating certain subway lines. But then it became a constant battle. I could feel the water seeping into the city's basements, eroding New York's bones.

"Is the city sinking?" I asked Johnny, on one of his visits. We didn't need to be close to talk now—we could hear each other through the metal of the city from Brooklyn—where Johnny sometimes visited his many-time great descendants—to Staten Island, Queens, and the Bronx. But he still came to see me. To talk face-to-face.

"No," he said, in a voice thick with grief. "The sea is rising. But the outcome is the same."

I learned about global warming and climate change because Johnny painstakingly explained them to me. It wasn't hard to grasp. Even in my day, we knew that coal smoke was bad for lungs, buildings, and the atmosphere.

Soon some streets were under water on a sunny day, if the tide was pulling. Salt chewed the footings of the skyscrapers. Some of the subways couldn't always run.

People began leaving. First a trickle. Then, proverbially, that other thing.

It was the second storm in a summer, I think, that broke him. The first one we endured—the drownings, the flooded tunnels. An undermined building collapsed below Tenth Street. The city picked itself up, toweled itself off. It carried out the dead and started raking up the litter.

But we were barely on our feet when a storm broke over us again.

And anyone who could leave, did leave. A flood predicated upon that other flood.

"Will it be like Pompeii?" I asked Johnny. "A city frozen in time?"

I knew the answer, but I wanted him to tell me anyway. "It won't," he said. "Nothing I've built can outlast this much water."

"Don't leave me," I said, hearing the despair in his voice. Hearing the despair in mine.

Johnny did not answer.

It's not easy for a vampire to die by suicide, but Johnny managed. I don't know how he did it—perhaps he drank some poison, or stepped in front of one of the last few running trains. Perhaps he died—died a second time?—by drowning. That would have amused him bitterly.

But I knew when it happened, because I felt him in the city. I felt him in its metal bones, the way I felt myself in the statue. His second death was no more permanent than the first.

He was in the emptying city, the dying city. Like me, become a restless part of the thing he helped create.

And he was singing.

Now the people heard us. Now the remnant population, those without money or resources, those too stubborn to go—now they heard the song. Johnny's song, and my song. It rang through the steel sounding boards of the massive towers, which could not stand for long unmaintained. It echoed down the empty, windy streets, and it begged those who remained to leave, leave while they still could.

To leave before the rising waters claimed them.

Some did. I think our constant yammering annoyed them into going as much as anything. Some stayed, and another storm washed over them. Three, in one summer. More of the survivors limped away, any way they could.

Soon the city will be empty. Soon the city will be awash in the Atlantic that I crossed so many times.

I had money when I was alive. Money, social power, the ability to live as I liked even when society didn't like how I lived. Now I was the remnant guardian of these folk who had no power—no power and no place to go.

Life's—and death's—little ironies.

When the city drowns for good, will Johnny's ghost drown with it? When the metal hearts of his buildings rust and rot, when their foundations soften and they fall, will his spirit be freed finally to go on to whatever rest it deserves?

Or will his voice ring forever through the empty, fishless reefs and canyons of what was once an inhabited world?

I don't know. I won't be there, because before the end, before the dirty salt water reached me, people came to take me away. They moved me to a new place, to a park in the mountains.

Upstate, where Johnny came from. A canal at my left hand, and a highway at my right. Looking back the way I came.

Fewer people come here. I've become a different sort of memorial, an Angel of different Waters. A monument not to cleanliness and life but to a rising tide and a disaster still ongoing. Nobody wants to think about it, and there isn't a lot of foot traffic here. I am lonely.

I guess I won't be free of this statue for a long time. Bronze is a durable metal. I can't hear Johnny anymore, but I miss him. Even though we are still, at a remove, part of the same system. Two Angels of the Waters.

Would that I had the puissance to bless all the seas and make them calm and pure once more. To save Johnny from the bones of his city. But I am just a statue, long dead, only an observer.

I can't even return to the empty city where I left my friend, singing, watching the rising water.

LIFE GOES ON

K. J. Parker

I'd rather be alive and slave to a poor man,
A dirt-poor man, scratching a living,
Than be king and Kaiser of the glorious dead
—Homer, *Odyssey*

"Purely a matter of form," said the bishop, "but I'll need you to run through the catechism for me, and then we can dot the *I*s and cross the *T*s and the job's yours. Now, then."

Hell, I thought. But I started off in a nice, clear voice, "I believe in the Father almighty, maker of heaven and earth," while the bishop smiled pleasantly at me and allowed his attention to wander. But then we got to the bit about the resurrection of the dead and the life everlasting, and I had to stop.

"Go on," the bishop said. "Would you like a copy of the text?"

"No thanks," I said. "But the next bit— It's awkward."

"Excuse me?"

"Sorry," I said. "But I don't think I can say that. About the resurrection and so on."

He was looking at me as if I'd just farted during the elevation of the host. "Why on earth not?"

"Well," I said. "It's not that I don't believe in them, I do. Well, actually, it's more than belief, I *know*. But the way it's worded makes it sound like the resurrection from the dead and the life everlasting are a good thing, and I happen to know, they aren't."

"My son—"

"I'm from Hjortsriverdale," I explained.

He went white as a sheet. "Oh," he said.

Another job I didn't get, understandably enough. I have a degree in theology from the Studium and a doctorate from the College of Divinity, but every time I apply for something, even being a curate in some godforsaken slum in Poor Town, it's always the same. The place I come from gets mentioned and then that's it; thanks but no thanks, goodbye, please close the door when you leave.

Not that I blame anyone. I wouldn't hire a Hjortsriverdale man to empty chamber pots, let alone take charge of the spiritual well-being of believers. It's been fifteen years since I last saw the Old Country, except in nightmares, but the stigma follows me wherever I go, like a sausage maker's dog. And you can see why.

Just in case you can't, let me explain. Hjortsriverdale is a slab of moorland, mountainside and bog about fifty miles north of Svansvik, extending up as far as Jarlsey, the bit that juts out into the Bitter Sea. It's cold and wet, with eighteen-hour nights from late autumn until the middle of what we laughingly call spring. Nothing grows up there apart from leeks, onions, and a unique variety of coarse-leaf bitter grass that only our special breed of sheep can eat. There aren't any trees, because some fools cut them all down for charcoal five hundred years ago. People on the coast go fishing, but they don't always come back, because the storms break on the headland and the currents in the channel are murder. We have a tradition of making the finest swords, axes, and spears money can buy, forge-welded out of tiny lumps of a unique kind of bog iron you only get up our way. Unfortunately, Hjortsriverdale folk also have a tradition of using these excellent weapons on each other at every possible opportunity. That and a keen sense of family honor mean that any man who reaches thirty-five is either a master swordsman, unnaturally lucky, or both.

But so what? There are loads of horrible places in the world, and men and women who manage to get out of them alive are, generally speaking, accepted in civilized society as soon as they lose the accent. Not us. No, we have something special that doesn't occur anywhere else on earth. Lucky, lucky us.

In Hjortsriverdale, dead people don't necessarily stay dead. It's a matter of debate whether it's something that runs in families, or whether it's particularly obstreperous and antisocial individuals who die violently—a moot point, actually. There are only about twenty extended families in the Dale, hopelessly intermarried, and all of them, men and women, are jerks from birth, and see above for premature violent death. Are you getting the impression, by the way, that I don't care a great deal for my native land? How very perceptive of you.

We call them walkers, and the phenomenon is depressingly common. It starts when a dead man digs his way out of the mound he's been buried under and goes back to the district where he used to live, usually but not always at night. Walkers can cover extraordinary distances in a few hours, and when they get there, they slaughter sheep and cattle, smash up barns, climb up on the roofs of houses, and jump up and down until they break the roof-tree—spiteful and mischievous, like really unpleasant kids, only they're as strong as bears and there's absolutely nothing you can do about them, unless you're one of the once-in-a-generation heroes who has the special knack (and to be honest with you, I've never met one and I don't think they exist). More often than not they play their tricks on the farm where they used to live, but not always. They tend not to kill men and women unless provoked, but provocation in this context can mean anything you like, including simply being there; there are no rules with walkers, and just because they didn't rip your head off last week and last night doesn't mean they won't do it tomorrow, if that's what they feel like.

Received wisdom says that if you dig a walker up and burn it to cold ashes, that'll put a stop to it. Unfortunately, that's simply untrue. They always come back, sooner or later, and being interfered with tends to make them mad. It's true that sometimes they go dormant, maybe for twenty years or so, and they're territorial, so mostly you only get one per district, and the Dale is a very big place. When you simply can't hack it anymore, you have the option to pack up and move and start again somewhere else, which is fine until your uncle or your cousin or your nephew dies and suddenly you're jerked awake in the middle of the night by squawking chickens and the sound of splintering wood. Then you assess the damage and make a carefully considered decision: Does the aggravation justify the disruption and misery of moving on, or do you just grin and bear it, for now, until someone gets killed?

That's Hjortsriverdale, my own, my native land. I managed to get out when I was sixteen, purely and simply because back then I had a beautiful singing voice, and His Grace the archbishop (our absentee landlord) needed tenors who could reliably sustain the D above middle C in the Procopian "Gloria." I was able to parlay that into a scholarship at the Studium, and my thesis on the Einhardian Heresy would've earned me a doctorate if I'd turned up for the viva with horns and a tail; but after that I was outside the system and into the real world, where your origins are never the stated reason for not giving you the job, but after a while you start to see a pattern. So these days I grind along tutoring the stupid sons of rich people, choral work when I can get it, and copying manuscripts of the scriptures for the bookseller in Hoof Alley, who charges an extra five gulden for a psalter if it's been copied by an ordained priest. On one level it's a kind of living death, but you can trust me on this, it's better than being in Hjortsriverdale.

Go back? I don't think so. Mind you, if I were to go back, the forty-six gulden I keep in a sock in a place I have no intention of telling you about would be enough to set me up nicely for life. Actual silver money goes a long way in the Dale. For instance, I could buy Einarsvatn, including the big house and the barns and the six cottages, or Laxarness, which is good enough grazing for raising horses, or even Reginsfjall, with its own salmon stream, quarry and private cove for mackerel fishing. Fine properties, all of them, except that each one comes with a sitting tenant.

"You're him, aren't you?" she said. "The Hjortsdale man."

"Hjortsriverdale," I said. "What about it?"

I'm not usually surly to strangers, especially well-dressed middle-aged women who arrive on my doorstep in a carriage. Quite the opposite; any hint of money tends to lead to me laying on the smarm just a trifle too thick, which is off-putting and I really shouldn't do it, but I do. But the woman showed up when I was on my way out, already late for tutoring the Escheburg kid, and a certain place name always brushes my fur the wrong way. Fortunately, she didn't seem to have noticed.

"I'm a scholar," she announced. "I'm writing a book about death."

"You don't say," I said. "Now you'll excuse me, I'm late for—"

"I need to find out," she said, "if there's anything beyond death, or whether it's truly the end. My husband," she added, in what I assume was a non sequitur, "is the city prefect. Maybe you know him."

"Not really. Seen his head on the coins, of course. Sorry, but I really do have to—"

"My husband," she said, "fully supports me in my research. Including with money. I'm prepared to pay well."

All right, she had me. I reined myself in, like a skittish horse. "Splendid," I said. "What for?"

She frowned. Clearly I was a bit slow on the uptake. "I need a guide," she said, "to escort me round Hjortsriverdale, so I can find out the truth about the undead. I firmly believe that they hold the key to unraveling the greatest mystery of all."

And now she'd lost me again. "Ah," I said. "Sorry, no can do. If it means going back there, that's really not an option. Of course, I'd be happy to answer any questions you may have, for a moderate—"

"Oh no, we have to go there. I need to experience the place for myself. To my mind the key question is, what makes Hjortsriverdale so special? Once we know that, we can start to unravel the mystery, and hopefully that'll lead us to the true secret of life and death."

"I can't go back to Hjortsriverdale," I said. "I killed a man there. If I go back, they'll hang me."

(Untrue, needless to say. It'd be an exaggeration to say I'm the only Hjortsriverdaler of my age who hasn't ever killed a man, but not an outrageous one. Of course, I left when I was quite young.)

"You've been living in the city for sixteen years, according to the census, so you've been away a long time. I'm sure anything like that will have been forgotten by now."

"Don't you believe it," I said. "Long memories where I come from. The moment I set foot across the border, I'm a dead man."

"That's unfortunate," she said. "Because it's come to the attention of my husband's office that for the past six years you've been practicing as a minister of religion without a sponsor, which is a breach of both civil and canon law. As I'm sure you know, the penalty for that is five years in the galleys. Such a shame you have nowhere to go to avoid the wrath of the law. Of course, men have been known to survive five years in the galleys, it's not a guaranteed death sentence."

I looked at her with great respect, one chiseler to another. The usual, as opposed to maximum, penalty for practicing without a sponsor is a reprimand and a twenty-gulden fine. But she was the wife of the city prefect, and somehow I could see that the prefect might be willing to back her up on this, even to the extent of bending the law a little, if it meant she'd be going away for a long time, and possibly not coming back.

"You have no idea," I said, "the lengths I'm prepared to go to in the interests of scholarship. Fine, I'll do it. But right now I've simply got to rush off, because I'm already late for the Escheburgs and they hate to be kept waiting."

"The duchess is a personal friend of mine. I'll make your excuses for you."

Damn, I thought. A dreamer and a lunatic, my new patron, but clearly no fool. Needless to say, I hadn't been planning on keeping my appointment with the duchess and her obnoxious son. "All right," I said, "here's the deal. If I do this idiotic thing and we both make it back alive, I want a parish. A proper parish with a house and a decent stipend, the West End, not Poor Town. And a readership at the university, with tenure. And a hundred gulden."

She gazed at me for a moment. "Well," she said, "that certainly proves you're from Hjortsriverdale, not that it was ever in any doubt. Very well. I'll talk to my husband."

"I want it in writing."

She sighed. "What a tiresome little man you are. Yes, if you insist, in writing. Though I can't guarantee the readership. The faculty have this quaint notion that permanent appointments should be on merit. But I'll see what I can do."

Now then, this life-and-death business.

I am, as noted above, a priest. I have a piece of vellum, fifteen inches by ten, that tells the world I'm qualified to act as an intermediary between God and man and interpret the scriptures (but not, inside the city limits, without a sponsor); so I can tell you, authoritatively and definitively, what's going to happen to you when you die, depending on whether you've been naughty or nice, once all relevant mitigating factors have been taken into account.

I don't believe a word of it, needless to say. I used to, when I was a kid in Hjortsriverdale. But then I went away to be trained for the ministry, and that involved reading the scriptures—gospels, epistles, prophets, the whole nine yards—and I challenge anybody to read the whole of scripture and come out the other side with his belief in God unshaken. The more I learned about the faith, the crazier it all seemed, until the point came when the scales fell from my eyes and I realized it's all drivel. There is no God. There can't possibly be. It's all made up, to fool people.

By the time I attained this moment of clarity I was irrevocably committed to earning my living as a priest; embarrassing, but as far as I can tell, by no means unusual. Ah well. You don't have to believe in something in order to argue eloquently and intelligently on its behalf—ask any lawyer—and as soon as I'd accepted it as a fascinating mental exercise, nothing more, I had no trouble reasoning passionately about the Stauracian heresy and the dual procession of the Holy Ghost; in fact, it allowed me a degree of flexibility in argument denied to those unfortunates who happen to believe in what they're saying. Not a handicap, therefore. If anything, the opposite.

So; I believe that when you die, that's it. The fire goes out, the flesh stiffens and seizes up, all the knowledge and memories and experiences that make up a person drift away like smoke on the wind, nothing's left except carrion. There is no eternal life, nice or nasty. Which stands to reason, doesn't it? Nothing could possibly last *forever*. And the thought of living *forever*, even in the nice place with sherbet and houris promised to the fire-worshippers of Sashan, is so unspeakably horrible, if you stop and think about it, that if I truly believed, I'd never be able to get to sleep again.

Except, of course, that I know for a fact that it's possible, and it happens; the resurrection of the dead and the life everlasting. But only in Hjortsriverdale. Which is the main reason I left home.

Say what you like about the Lady Eudoxia—that was her name, by the way— she wasn't slow with a gulden, not when her own comfort was in issue. A covered coach with actual springs from the city to Beloisa, where she'd chartered a ship—a full-sized cog, not some pimped-out fishing-boat; decent food, a steward waiting at table and a cabin of my own, with a bed, and pillows. Then nine days up the coast to Barsness; nine days I greatly enjoyed, because she was sick as a dog the entire way and never stirred from her cabin, whereas I sat on deck, enjoying the fresh air and reading Hildebrand of Bissen on the immortality of the soul, a copy of which I'd liberated from her luggage.

When my mind started to wander, as it always does when I'm reading

Hildebrand, I considered Eudoxia, wife of the city prefect. I couldn't honestly say I liked the woman, but she'd put her bony finger on what was, for me, the crux of the whole life-and-death business. Furthermore, she was prepared to get up off her fundament and go somewhere extremely nasty to find out the truth. Fair play to her, that was class. And (said the horrid little voice in my head that gets me in so much trouble sometimes) the man who went with her and assisted her in her quest must inevitably come in for some of the blaze of reflected glory, when she wrote her book and overturned nine centuries of received wisdom, and that wouldn't exactly hurt his chances when it came to getting a decent job. Indeed, since Eudoxia was a woman, and every priest and tenured academic from Antolbia to the Bitter Sea knows that the ladies (bless them) are incapable of thinking about anything more significant than hemlines and cushion covers, chances were that everybody would assume that I was the one who really did the work and probably wrote the book, and Lady Eudoxia's involvement was limited to paying out money and making a feeble attempt to steal the credit. Probably, they'd whisper behind their hands in chapter and at high table, she never really left the city at all.

Well, it's a stupid world, and one of these days I simply must get around to doing something about it. Meanwhile, maybe going home wouldn't be such unmitigated torture after all. Being there would be, of course, but maybe it's worth going somewhere horrible and doing and suffering horrible things if you come out of it set up for life. Or maybe not.

We landed at Barsness, where a carriage was waiting for us; a genuine carriage, with a roof and windows. I have no idea how such a thing came to be there, whether she'd had it shipped in specially or whether someone realized he'd got one stashed away in a barn, and dragged it out and filled in where the rats had gnawed it with sawdust mixed with glue. But it was a carriage, with springs and seats padded with horsehair, a driver and six milk-white horses, and she barely noticed it as she hopped in and plonked herself down, leaving me to load the luggage.

She didn't draw breath all the way from Barsness to Ketilsheath. She explained to me in detail exactly what was wrong with the accepted theory of general mortality as set out by Copinus in the *Meditations* and refined and perfected by seventeen generations of the world's finest minds. "It's all nonsense, of course," she said, looking past me out of the window. "It's all based on a fatuous analogy, the caterpillar and the butterfly, which is a purely intuitive and emotional connection with no foundation in science. Now if any of them had actually studied caterpillars, as I have—"

I wasn't really listening, no more than she was really talking to me with intent to communicate, but I guess we were both following the same train of thought. In the Copinian model, the mortal body is the caterpillar, the immortal soul is the butterfly, and death is the point of emergence from the cocoon. Nominally that's heresy, since Holy Mother Church insists on the resurrection of the body, and we're all condemned to spend the rest of eternity wearing the same arms and legs and cauliflower ears and unsatisfactory noses we were born with—which means that in the hereafter, the pretty ones will still be the prettiest, and the toad-faces and the fish-faces (like me) will still have to win friends and influence people by virtue of our kind natures and good works, instead of being adored on sight by everyone we meet. I don't know what that says about God, except that He has a nasty sense of humor; the point being, nobody in the Church really believes in any of that guff anymore, though nobody actually says so out loud.

I believe it, of course, as a fact of life, in Hjortsriverdale. And so, apparently, did the Lady Eudoxia. "Whereas," she was saying, when I started listening to her again, "the Permian horse moth retains the same basic coloring in both the caterpillar and moth stages, and if you look really closely, the shape of the mandibles remains essentially unchanged post-metamorphosis, proving that there's real continuity between the two stages—"

The urge to point out that moths are moths and people are people came and went, like a pang of indigestion, and I went on sitting there until we reached Ketilsheath, shortly before nightfall.

Ketilsheath is and isn't Hjortsriverdale. On a map, if there is such a thing, it would be inside the boundary line, and it's owned by the archbishop, like two thirds of the Dale. But it's a proper town, with houses and a street and a church and an inn, the only one in the Dale, and very few Dalesmen have ever been there. The shopkeepers and the landlord of the inn are off-comers, catering to the wool-merchants and other southerners who come to Ketilsheath to buy the few miserable things the Dale produces that outsiders might possibly want. When we arrived, the only other guests at the inn were buyers.

One of them was in the dye business—wild bilberries grow all over the Dale, and they make a cheap blue dye, not colorfast, popular with contractors who supply clothes and blankets to prisons and the Imperial Navy. It takes a family of six all day to pick enough bilberries to fill a two-gallon basket, for which the buyer pays a shilling, the price of a small jar of pickled walnuts back in the city. The other buyer was after swords.

"You don't know of any, do you?" he asked me hopefully. "Named swords especially, my customers go crazy for names, provided there's a provenance."

"You're new to this, aren't you?"

"Well . . ."

"Because if you'd ever been here before," I told him, "you'd know that no Dalesman would sell a family sword to an outsider, not for a thousand gulden. But if he suspected you had a thousand gulden on you, or even ten, he'd follow you back to the inn, wait till nightfall, climb in through the window, and cut your throat for it. And you're an offcomer and far from home, so who the hell will care?"

"Oh," he said.

"No," I told him. "What you want to do is go to Reginsvatn or somewhere there's a smith, and show him three gulden, and ask him to make you something that looks like an ancient Hjortsriverdale family sword, which he'll cheerfully do, and swear to you on a stack of breviaries that he dug it out of Angantyr's burial mound with his own hands. Then you piss off back down south and sell it for two hundred to some clown, and then if you've got any sense you never come back. Capisce?"

"Yup. Thanks."

"What you don't want to do," I couldn't help adding, "is so much as lay a finger on a genuine family sword, because all of them have the most eye-watering curses on them, guaranteeing bad luck and a violent death to anybody who touches them, and for some reason these curses do actually work. Trust me, they do. We had one in our family, and nobody who even went near the ghastly thing lived to be twenty-five. In the end we buried it with my great-uncle Kari, and with any luck it's just flakes of rust by now. Just saying, that's all."

"Noted."

I left him to his beer and headed for the stairs that led to the loft that constitutes the guest rooms at the Ketilsheath inn. She was waiting for me. "Who was that man you were talking to?" she said.

"Oh, just some idiot who thought he could make money buying up antique swords and selling them to collectors."

"I heard what you said to him."

"Ah, right. So wh—?"

"I need to know more about these magic swords," she said, inaccurately, in my opinion. "Tell me about them."

We were standing at the top of the stairs. It was a narrow landing, and someone might want to come past at any moment. "There's not a lot to tell," I said. "They're swords. I gather they're pretty good. They keep their edge and they're well-balanced and so on, broad fullers, optimum edge geometry, distal taper in both planes, sweet spot nicely on the forte, center of balance about a handspan from the hilt. I really don't know all the technical stuff like a real Dalesman would. But they're tools for killing people."

"You told that man they carry curses, and the curses work."

"Yup. It's true. The fact is, they're a menace. You really don't want to inherit one, unless you're some kind of lunatic. Of course, lots and lots of people in these parts are just that. So we tend to bury them with their owners if we possibly can. And then, of course, some nutjob from the next farm but one down the valley comes along and digs them up, and they really don't appreciate that, but some people never learn. They're typical Hjortsriverdale; mysterious, unique and a total pain in the arse."

"I want one."

Oh for crying out loud, I didn't say. "No," I said, "you don't, because the only way you'll get one is to dig it up, and shortly after that you'll die."

"That remains to be seen."

"Don't," I said, "please. It's just not worth it. Trust me."

"Tell me exactly," she said, "how they're connected to the living dead. I feel sure there must be a connection."

"Oh, there is. If you're the kind of headbanger who goes out of his way to acquire one, it's practically a certainty that you're going to walk after you die, though whether it's cause and effect or the other way round I just don't know. Furthermore, if you're buried with one and someone comes along and pinches it, I can more or less guarantee you'll wake up and go and get it back. So yes, they're connected. A bit like falling out of a high window is connected to breaking your neck."

"Thank you. Now, we'll need a pickax and a shovel. Can we buy them here?"

I didn't have to die. I had (I reflected as I lay awake, gazing at the roof beams) a choice. I could get up quietly, steal some coins from her purse as she snored, steal a horse, and go home. Stealing is against the law but nobody minds much in Hjortsriverdale except for the person stolen from, who won't rest until he's killed you; by the time she woke up I'd be miles away, and there were no authorities for her to go whining to. Knowing her, she'd persevere in her quest after I'd gone, and very soon after that she'd be dead. And with her would die my chances of a good job and a comfortable life. Whereas if I stayed—

If I stayed, I was a dead man. Walkers don't just kill you, they annihilate you. Their signature move is to put a hand over the top of your head and squeeze, until the skull is crushed and the soft stuff inside comes squirting out like egg yolk. But first they break all your bones—all of them—and once you're dead they tear you in two or four pieces for good measure. They're unbelievably strong, like wind or floodwater, or tree roots, and nothing can harm them. Well, almost nothing. A genuine certified hero with a magic sword, maybe, if you believe the stories, which I don't. That, incidentally—you can see why I didn't mention it to her—is why we tolerate the family swords, in spite of the horrible baggage that comes with them. A really special sword, so the stories (see above) say, can cut the hide of a walker, if used by a very special man. Hence all the aggravation and carnage and death, on the off chance that the legends are true. And if you'd lived in Hjortsriverdale like I have, you'll understand that the off chance makes it worthwhile.

So—to get back to my internal debate—go; there's nothing stopping you, and if you don't, you're dead. Dead, what's more, in Hjortsriverdale, the last place on earth I wanted to die. Three guesses why.

There are walkers in our family, like in all the other families in the Dale. Now I don't fit the typical walker profile in terms of character and circumstance, but you just don't know. Being killed by one of those things would be bad enough. Turning into one of them—

The resurrection of the dead and the life everlasting. Oh shit.

So I waited till I could hear her snoring through the partition, got up, put my trousers and shirt on, and crept into the passage. I figured I'd only steal what I genuinely needed—five gulden, say, or maybe ten to be on the safe side. She could afford it. She was loaded. I felt for the door latch and found it—

There's this trope, in all the stories. It's pitch dark, inside or outdoors, and the genuine certified hero is asleep. He wakes up, and a shaft of moonlight breaks through the cloud or slants in through a window, and lights up the walker. Some of the storytellers I listened to as a kid made a really big deal of it, enough to scare you sleepless for a month.

A shaft of moonlight slanted in, therefore, through the skylight, and I saw him. Not the first walker I'd ever set eyes on, but I'd never been that close before. He had the light behind him so I couldn't see his face clearly, but he was big—seven feet, maybe seven six; they grow after death, God knows how—and his skin was tight, like the skin of a berry, and the color of a ripe bilberry, somewhere between black and a very deep dark purplish blue; the color of bruises. There wasn't a single hair on him and no fingernails or toenails. He was leaning against the wall, like you do when you're dog-tired, with his left hand supporting his head. He was watching me.

They do that, apparently. They're very patient. If you don't make a move, neither do they; and in some of the stories, the hero survives by staying absolutely dead still, until the sun comes up and the walker slouches away. Oh, and he had sad eyes, like a cow or an old dog. Very sad eyes.

At this point in the story, the hero grabs his magic sword and either he wins or he doesn't. I, of course, had no magic sword. But in some versions of the story, they talk first. I can talk. In fact, it's probably my best, or only, thing.

"Hello," I said. "Nice evening."

I'd been in the city too long. I'd forgotten. Dalesmen are country people. In the country, you don't talk to anyone, even your father, unless you've got something to say. He looked at me, but he didn't move.

"Who are you?" I said.

Worse and worse. You don't ask people who they are in the Dale, because you know, because everybody's known everybody else all their lives. I was making a real mess of it. "Go home," he said.

It was a deep voice, and very soft, with the Dale accent, so it came out something like *Gaw whoam*. "I am home," I said. "Worse luck."

"You're Tyrving's boy, from Eyvindsvatn."

"Yup."

"Left to be a scholar and sing in a choir."

"That's me."

"Go back where you come from. You're not wanted here."

Something warm and wet was trickling down my leg. I hated myself. "All right."

"You can't have it. Go home."

"I don't want it. Whatever it is."

And then (as always happens in the stories) a cloud covered the moon and it was pitch dark; and walkers can see in the dark, the way you and I can't. And in the stories he'd have killed me, there and then, no messing. But he didn't.

"Has he gone?"

"Shut *up*," I hissed, because if he was still there, he'd kill her too if he knew she was awake. Then I heard the appalling sound of a tinderbox, and a light flared off to one side. It filled the corridor. He'd gone.

"What a shame," she said. "He was talking. We could have learned so much."

I'm a peaceful man and a man (on paper) of God, but I'd clenched my fist to smash her face in before I managed to get myself under control. "You lunatic," I yelled at her. "You could've got us both—"

"He knew who you were. That's promising."

"For God's sake—"

"What was *it*? 'You can't have it,' he said. What was he talking about?"

"Shut up," I said, "and listen to me. You have no idea how lucky we are. By rights he should've killed us both. That's what they do. They hardly ever talk, and they never ever back off. Anyway, that's it. We're leaving."

"I'm guessing," she said, "it's the sword. You said there was one in your family. You said it was buried in someone's grave."

"I couldn't give a—"

"Pull yourself together," she said. "I appreciate that you've had a frightening experience, but you're being ridiculous. We most certainly can't give up now. This is precisely what I need. If I can talk to that man, and ask him what it means to be immortal, to have gone through death and come back— Don't you want to know? You must do."

"No."

"Don't be—"

"No," I repeated. "I don't want to find out what it's like to die, and I really don't want to find out what it's like to come back. As one of those. You stay here if you want to. First thing in the morning, I'm out of here."

Her face tightened. "If you leave," she said, "you won't get a penny from me."

I couldn't even be bothered to reply.

I don't know how I managed to fall asleep, but I did, and daylight was leaking through the shutters when I woke up. But it wasn't the light that woke me, it was the screaming.

I was out of bed and in the corridor before I realized I was moving. Something about the racket they were making rang a bell. I'd heard it before, when I was a kid, the day we woke up and found my mother, killed by a walker. There's a special sort of, what's the word, timbre, owing no doubt to the unique blend of terror, horror, and hatred that only walkers and their deeds can inspire.

The doorway of her room was blocked; people trying to get in, people with their hands clamped over their mouths trying to get out. I sidled through somehow and saw the mess.

He'd crushed her skull. It was now roughly flat and the size of a missal or a fancy book of hours. Also he'd pulled off her arms and smashed her legs and quartered her, and her guts were on the outside, in strings, like sausages. There were two women in the room having hysterics, and a man I recognized as the hostler, crouching in the corner with his head between his knees. Also the landlord, counting out coins from her purse. He looked up at me.

"Shilling fourpence," he said. "Six for the room, ten for the damage. All right?"

At which moment it dawned on me that, for legal purposes, in Hjortsriverdale, I was her next of kin, and all the money in her purse was therefore mine. "Sure," I heard myself say. All that money . . .

"You still want the shovel?"

Shovel; to bury her, presumably. Well, the least I could do, since she'd left me a fortune. "Yes," I said. "And a pick and a cart for a few days. Sixpence?"

He looked at me. "Already paid for."

Of course. She'd arranged for the tools, because we were going to go up on the moor and dig up a sword out of a walker's barrow. "That's all right, then," I said. "Where do I find them?"

"In the barn."

And that was that. For threepence the sutler and the potboy gathered up the bits and loaded them into the cart for me. An extra three farthings got me an old blanket, to keep the flies off. "Otherwise," the landlord said (a born salesman), "they'll be buzzing up a storm by the time you get up on the moor."

There's a complex etiquette about where you bury strangers in Hjortsriverdale. Understandable; you don't know where they've been, more to the point you don't know if you'll be seeing them again. And it may look like a desolate wilderness (mostly because it is a desolate wilderness) but every square inch of the Dale belongs to somebody. The moor is our livelihood, our property, our inheritance, the way we make our living. You can't just go around burying people. It causes offense.

Our place—I hadn't given a thought to it in years. Presumably my family still lived there; at Ohtarsvatn, between Hrappsdal and Laxmoor. My father, my three brothers; presumably my two sisters were married and long gone. Or maybe some of them were dead, or all of them, and the tenancy had been handed over to somebody else. No idea. But I decided I was entitled to bury my dead at Ohtarsvatn; besides, if I snuck in nice and quiet, nobody would ever know I'd been there.

Also; let's face it, I'm lazy. Digging was never my thing. But at Ohtarsvatn, where the Lax marks our eastern boundary, there's a bit of a waterfall, where salmon leap in the season. And behind the waterfall, eaten away by the flow of the river, is a cave. In winter it floods, but in summer it's dry. You could stick a body, or bits of a body, in there and no digging needed, and no telltale mound of disturbed earth to show what you'd been up to. Also, there's an idiotic legend that the fey folk live in the cave, when it's not flooded out. She'd like that.

Why, you ask, were you prepared to go to all the trouble of burying her, when you didn't like her much and it'd mean staying in the Dale until the job was done? Ah, but you don't know the Dale. If I'd tried to sneak off leaving her unburied, they'd have lynched me, I wouldn't have got six hundred yards. Also, I guess it's ingrained, from childhood. In the Dale, you don't leave a body unburied. Killing people is fine, we all do that, but not burying them is frowned upon. In fact, it's the worst thing you can do. I considered it—for all of three seconds—and realized I couldn't do it. Old habits die hard, like everything else in that godforsaken place.

So, another fourpence for bread and cheese for six days—we dearly love gouging off-comers in the Dale—and off I went. Call it a sentimental journey; across Laxmoor and the Chains till I hit the river, then following it up through Eastdale. Last time I'd been that way was when I rode south with the priest, leaving home forever and ever. It hadn't changed much, or at all. The keynote of the Dale is immutability. It looks now like it did a thousand years ago, and how it'll look in a thousand years' time. Nobody builds new houses, or barns or smithies or sheds. Nobody takes in moor for plowland, because every square inch that can be plowed already has been. The Dale is essentially timeless, as you'd expect from the Land of the Dead, where time has no meaning.

On the third day I saw a cairn of stones on a hilltop and knew I was home. The cairn was a futile attempt to keep my great-uncle Geir from getting out, so that lot over there was Geirsdale; nominally part of our spread, but nobody in his right mind would ever go there, or allow his sheep to stray onto it. Across from Geir's Barrow is Two Gates, where there's a slab bridge over the Lax. I crossed there and headed up the hill, and on the other side was Myri, where the cave was.

I looked up, and reined in the horses. On Myri Nap there was a new barrow, with a cairn. Not all that new, because the sides of the barrow were grassed in, but it hadn't been there last time I was there. Well, somebody's died, big deal. People die. My father, or one of my brothers; I wasn't sure how I felt about that. Like I cared about my family. I'd turned my back on them, and never expected to see or hear about them ever again. It stood to reason they'd die sooner or later. But I never liked them, so why give a damn?

Of course we still pay rent on Geirsdale, even though we can't use it; two shillings a year to the archbishop, to the greater glory of God. Life goes on, in spite of the unfairnesses and the inconveniences. I looked up at the sky. If I got a move on, I could stash the bits of Eudoxia in the cave and be back down the combe to Laugar by nightfall. This place was none of my business anymore, and the land wasn't my land, and the dead body in the bed of the cart was no kin of mine, even though I'd inherited her money.

Life goes on isn't an optimistic sentiment in Hjortsriverdale. Quite the opposite.

The cave was still there, and so was the sheep track leading to it. I peered in, and something moved in the darkness, got up off the floor, and lunged at me. I got out of the way just in time to let it pass me; a fat old ewe, woken out of sleep by the sudden advent of a monster.

It took me six trips to and fro to shift the remains of my employer, and my shirt and trousers were ruined. The climb up to the cave was steeper than I remembered, or maybe I was a bit older and tubbier, who knows? Consequently, after I'd fetched in the last load (a leg and half a pelvis), I sat down on the floor to catch my breath, and to hell with the company. It was around noon, and I wasn't wearing a hat. It never gets properly hot in the Dale, not by city standards, but perhaps I was beginning to get reacclimatized. Anyway, I was hot and sweaty, and the cave was cool and dark. I'll just close my eyes for two minutes, I told myself.

I woke up because an animal nearby was making a hell of a racket. I stuck my head out of the cave, and saw the carthorse. It was flat on the ground, missing its head, and every bone in its body looked like it had been broken.

He was sitting on the cart, what was left of it; he'd snapped the boom and smashed in two of the wheels, so it slanted at an angle. He was cradling the horse's head in his lap. I must've been asleep for quite a while, because it was just starting to get dark. He looked up at me and grinned.

"You killed her," I said.

"Hello, son," said my father. "Yup, I killed her."

"And now you're going to kill me."

"Reckon so. I told you, you can't have it."

It? What, for crying out loud? "I don't want it."

"Sure you do, or why did you come here?"

Oh, surely not. I nipped back inside the cave. In the wall, on the dark side, someone had driven in a nail; and from the nail hung a sword belt, with a sword in a scabbard. I recognized it. No surprise there; it had hung on a nail on the wall of our house for all the time I was growing up.

My father, let me point out, was a cantankerous sort of man, even by Dale stan-dards. When he was fourteen he killed his cousin Bjarni (I forget why). When he inherited Ohtarsvatn, aged twenty-two, he had a falling-out with our neighbors, my second cousin Hrapp and his two sons, over some hay. So one night my dad and a couple of farmhands went over to Hrapp's place, nailed the doors and the windows shut, and set light to the thatch, with Hrapp and his family inside. That led to a certain degree of unpleasantness, in which my father eventually prevailed—thanks, according to him, to our family sword, the Woodpecker. He fought many duels with the Woodpecker and survived many ambushes, and never so much as a scratch on him. It's not natural, people used to say, and no good would come of it. Of course, in the Dale they say that about pretty much everything.

Oh well, I remember thinking. Nothing more dramatic or profound than that; just disappointment, that it was all over and I really didn't have anything to show for it, but not really unhappy to be rid of a burden. I hadn't enjoyed my life, I realized, and going to sleep forever and ever wouldn't be so bad. "Eternal annihilation, blot me out!" yells the hero of one of Saloninus's plays, at a crucial moment; sure, I thought, me for some of that, but lose the melodrama. Serves me right for coming home and taking money that didn't belong to me.

He got up off the cart and walked slowly, stiffly toward the cave. He'd cut me off from any escape route, but I wasn't going to bolt in any event. Walkers are faster than deer when they want to be. "Well, go on," he said. "Run inside and get it."

What? Oh, that. "I told you," I said, "I don't want it."

He laughed. "Thought you could sneak up here and pinch it," he said. "Rob your own father."

"Just get it over with, will you, please?"

He stopped. "I told you to fetch it," he said. My father never liked to be crossed. He'd give me an order. From time to time, I disobeyed. He'd give me a clout that made my head spin, then repeat the order; and so on, until I did as I was told. Moral: Obey the first time and spare yourself the pain. I was a slow learner, but I got there eventually.

"Fine," I said, and went in and lifted the sword belt off the nail. I drew the sword, not looking at it, and went back outside. "Happy?"

He looked at the sword, then at me. He looked at me as if he'd caught me in bed with his wife. I put the sword down on the grass and stepped back.

"Pick it up," he said.

"All right. But first, you've got to tell me two things. Straight answers, no bullshit. All right?"

He glared at me. "Get on, then," he said.

"What's it like," I said. "Dying?"

He took a moment. "Like falling asleep and then you wake up."

"And?"

"That's it."

"All right, then," I said. "What's it like, being dead?"

"Cold," he said. "You can't get warm nohow. But it's not so bad after a while."

I looked at him. My father wasn't a very nice man, but he was no liar. Break your neck as soon as look at you, people used to say about him, but he always tells the truth. "That's all?"

"Pretty much."

"No God?" I asked. "No angels, no blinding white light, no lake of fire, no scales of justice? No feeling of floating in the air looking down at the world?"

"You always were a gabby bugger. No, nothing like that." He grinned. "Don't take my word for it, see for yourself."

I stooped and picked up the sword. "Fine," I said. "Only don't—"

And then he was on me, and his massive paw hit the side of my head, and I went sprawling. Blood pumped out of my nose and into my mouth, and I spat it out and got up. I was still holding the stupid sword. My father always did hit hard, though he judged it well enough that he never did anything permanent.

He came again. I tried to sidestep (like he'd tried to teach me, when I was six) but he anticipated and hit me again. I felt a rib crack, but this time I was still on my feet. He had that angry look I knew so well. He was going to keep hitting me until I did what I was supposed to do. "What?" I said, through a mouthful of blood.

He hit me again, and that was another rib. Like I said, I'm a slow learner, because it was only then that I figured it out. He wanted me to fight.

"Have I got to?"

He drew back his fist. I swung at him with the sword. I caught him on the neck. His eyes rolled back, and then he fell over.

They always come back, everybody knows that. But if you cut off the head and lay it between the knees, then scrabble together a pyre of dead heather and thorn branches and burn the body to cold ashes, you can buy anything up to twenty years of peace and quiet before you have to deal with the problem again. Or so they say.

Twenty years of what? Sleep, hopefully. I'd hate to be a handful of ash for twenty years.

I was lucky. I had plenty of wood from the smashed-up cart, and I'd inherited the Lady Eudoxia's city-made state-of-the-art tinderbox. He took an age to get going, but then he burned like he was soaked in lamp oil, so hot that I had to stand back ten yards so as not to frizzle my eyebrows. Well, I thought, at least he'll be warm, for a little bit.

At least we're all warm, for a little bit, and then it gets cold and stays that way, but you get used to it, apparently. That, I guess, is what Eudoxia came to Hjortsriverdale to find out, though it would've been nice if she'd lived to write her book. A short book, and I don't suppose anybody would've believed her. But it doesn't really matter in the long term, does it?

I really, really wanted to throw the sword Woodpecker into the Lax river, but instead I brought it home with me, and now it hangs on my wall, incongruous in the study of a tenured professor of theology. From which you'll gather that I came out of it all right. The city prefect insisted on honoring his late wife's agreement with me—shortly after, he married a coalmonger's daughter twenty years his junior—and now I'm pretty well set up, with everything I ever wanted.

Including faith, or at least belief in something, only I never really wanted that. I shall live the rest of my life in the sure and certain terror of the resurrection from the dead and the life everlasting—because as we know, it runs in families and tends to happen to violent people who do bad things; and what can be worse than killing your own father?

I get offers for the sword, silly money, from collectors, but I'm not selling. I'm pretty comfortable these days. If ever I'm strapped for cash, then maybe. Or maybe not. We'll see.

Life goes on.

WAIT

Cassandra Khaw

The black dog arrived at Antigone's stoop about an hour before daybreak and laid there until dawn bled its syrupy golden light over its dark pelt. It stretched languidly in the heat, pleased, it seemed, to have a moment for itself. While it was a psychopomp first, it was still an animal second and even if it wasn't alive in the traditional sense, more analogy than flesh, it was alive enough to relish being warm. The small things mattered.

Antigone opened the door as the dog rolled onto its back, tongue lolling out of its mouth, the red muscle garish against the dark of its coat, and at the sight of the beast, the witch let out a sigh.

"Shit," she said.

The dog's ears pricked in her direction.

She stared appraisingly at it for another minute, taking occasional sips from the bone-yellow mug of tea she held in a hand. It wasn't the first time she'd seen the dog; it wouldn't be the last either. By and large, her bloodline was unburdened with blessings. According to their records, there were generations who'd escaped with nothing more than an affinity for herbalism: Antigone envied their quiet existences. She, much to her chagrin, was like her mother and her sisters; they always knew when their deaths were coming. Antigone's grandmother had known her end was arriving six months before it came to the hospital's front door. There'd been baying each night, which she met with a pinch-mouthed frustration, the cancer having lapped what sentimentality she had left from her bones. *Like I don't know it's there,* she'd rasp, scowling out the window at her death, a small black terrier who Antigone had thought of as polite. And perhaps, it was. When Antigone's grandmother finally died, it hadn't been the gasping miserable death she had envisioned: no, she'd gone in her sleep, gentle as a whisper.

Despite this, Antigone's mother had taken no chances. Her death arrived on a crystalline morning ten years later: it was a massive beast, an amber-eyed cane corso whose hulking frame belied its calm manner. At the sight of it, she had gone inside, freed the revolver she kept in her desk, and wrote several extensive letters to Antigone, most detailing the logistics of accessing her estate and one explaining, in frank but compassionate terms, that she regretted leaving her daughter but wasn't about to take her chances with a death as potentially monstrous as that. Then she shot herself with the same precision that had permeated her life. Antigone had been twenty-eight, old enough to be unflustered by the funerary arrangements that followed but young enough still to feel betrayed in a nebulous way.

And now she was forty, with her death laid outside her door, a mug of tea cooling in her right hand.

"Well," said Antigone. "I suppose you might as well come inside."

To her surprise, Antigone found some comfort in how quickly her death made itself at home on her couch, draping itself over a corner. Its pelt had a refractive quality, she realized, a grackle-like iridescence that made it slightly less real. It was quiet too, which she did not anticipate. Antigone had expected the thing to gnaw open the cushions, to chew apart the tassels of her throw pillows, to autopsy the massive knitted merino blanket her last boyfriend had abandoned along with their relationship. Instead, it just stared at her with doting patience.

"It doesn't seem like it's planning to leave any time soon," said Antigone.

She could almost hear her sister shrug. It'd been several years since the two had met in person. Lisa loved the desert more than she did anything else in the world, something Antigone had found as comprehensible as their mother's suicide but alien as the whole thing was, she understood just because she found something unpalatable, it didn't mean everyone else would share a similar aversion.

Or something like that.

"Death and taxes are the only two constants in the world."

Antigone had to laugh. Her death thumped its tail against a pillow, and there was weight to the noise she hadn't expected either.

"But why is it here *now*? I suppose—"

"Not for a long time yet," said her sister firmly. "You know that."

This wasn't untrue. It wasn't the whole of it but neither was it untrue. Antigone and her sister had spent a year reviewing the possibilities, anticipating them, the many routes to their waiting deaths, and while Antigone had stopped before she could verify any specifics, she knew it'd be a long time before her end came.

And yet here it was.

"If that's true," said Antigone. "Why is it here?"

"Maybe, it just wanted to remind you it's waiting."

After that, their conversation turned to banalities: Antigone's garden, her nephew's fourth birthday and how he had demanded skulls from the guests, the speed with which autumn had arrived, how climate change colored the foliage early, musings about retirement, Antigone's plan for adopting kittens, her sister's aspirations of owning a parrot.

"It'd probably outlive us all," said Antigone. "And then it'd just be alone, an immortal flying toddler with claws and a bad temper."

Her sister had laughed. Antigone had tried to do the same only for the sound to wither as she recalled again what sat on her couch, staring at her like it had all the time in the world. They said their *I love you*s shortly after that, promising to call, knowing they'd forget, and Antigone hung up on her sister. The silence opened like a mouth. It was evening now, somehow, the sun puddling like melted butter on her living room floor. Her death was still there, watchful.

"What do you want?"

It kept staring.

"If you're not here to take me away, what are you doing?"

In answer, it let out a thin impatient whine, pouring from the couch onto the carpet. For some reason, its pelt ate the evening light: it was a negative space, a hole cut into the universe in the shape of the dog. Or would be if not for its amber eyes.

"Go away," tried Antigone.

Her death whined again and would not.

Over the next few weeks, Antigone would discover, much to her relief, that while her death would eat bacon from her hand, it didn't have an actual digestive system, per se. There was no need to walk it around her neighborhood although some days, she would, anyway, discovering in the process an odd pleasure in its company.

From a young age, Antigone had been told to make peace with the idea she was going to die one day, something she worked hard to do.

What she didn't expect was making friends with it.

Which was not to say she didn't try getting rid of it, anyway. A month passed and it became clear her death had no intention of leaving. She tried twice to abandon it in a different town. When that failed, Antigone attempted leaving it in the woods upstate. She went home to find it on her stoop, looking almost reproachful as her car entered the driveway, its eyes like headlights in the near-dark. After that, she gave up, allowing it to come and go however it pleased. It even accompanied her to the grocery occasionally, eliciting compliments from passersby, who inevitably commented on how well-behaved Antigone's dog was, how civil, and how intelligent. *Aren't you a cat person, though?* They'd sometimes add with furrowed expressions and Antigone would—lightly!—shrug. *Things change,* she told them.

Because of this, Antigone was almost unsurprised when she woke up one morning, panicked, not at the notion that her death had made itself comfortable in her home but the fact there was nothing she could do to elide it from her life. As surely as she lived, she would die one day. This was the bargain. This had always been the bargain. Just like how all love was paid for with grief. For forty years and change, the idea had invoked neither animosity nor fear: it simply was. If anything, she'd found it propulsive, motivation to pursue her research past the limits of her daily endurance.

Now, she was afraid.

Not of death itself. Not of its agent. (It was hard to be terrorized by something whose belly she knew to be velveteen in texture, and who only snored when it remembered that sleep was a part of being alive.) Not even of the decline that preceded a death of old age. Antigone did not look forward to the senescence, of course. The aesthetics of it appalled her. Though she wasn't particularly vain, she was repulsed by how time would crepe and mottle her skin, desiccating her features. One day, a stranger would inhabit her reflection and there would be a reckoning when that time came. But she wasn't afraid of that.

What frightened Antigone was the lack of choice.

There was no opting out. Dying would happen, sooner or later, and her death would lead her to whatever waited on the other side—or eat her, bones and all. It'd never been clear what happened after death came to take the women of Antigone's family, and she'd never thought to ask. This latter was a revelation that thinned her breath to gasps.

Her death woke from its customary place at the foot of her bed, ears swiveling in her direction.

"Fuck you," said Antigone.

It whined.

And she thought of her mother then and her chill resolve, how she had not waited, how she absolved her children of any need to dissuade her from her decision, how she'd simply done what she deemed necessary, practical to her last breath. Dead was still dead but Antigone's mother had at least been the one to choose the moment. At the thought, Antigone's breathing eased and her death crept up so it could nuzzle its brow under her clammy palm. Distantly, she registered the worry in its expression, its panting anxiety. But Antigone could not think past the idea that if her mother had a choice, so did she. It was a small and terrible comfort, far from what she wanted but it was better than nothing, right? Certainly, her mother had seemed to think so.

Antigone's death pawed at her hand but she paid it no mind, thinking for the first time, with a tenderness she did not expect, of the rope and the bullet, the water and all the ways a person could simply, quietly, unfussily disappear.

"Forty is a good run," said Antigone over coffee the next day, fingers finding her death's soft ears as it laid its head on her thighs. It was a mistake, she decided, announcing her intent but provisions had to be made for the garden and the

enormous orange cat who haunted it. There was the question of the house too, the paraphernalia she kept, her books; God, someone had to deal with the books, Antigone didn't trust them to behave without supervision.

And there was her sister too.

Someone had to tell her.

"Forty isn't enough," said Antigone's oldest friend, who was all of seven years her senior. Vera swore up and down she lacked a talent for anything but baking, but Antigone knew better as did the dead in the graveyard, who all knew her friend by name. "Forty is barely getting started—"

"Forty is arguably dead center of an average lifespan. If you factor in—"

"Your grandmother lived to be ninety-three."

"My mother barely made it to fifty-two," countered Antigone, sipping at her mocha. In theory, it was a coffee drink. In reality, it was the owner's excuse to melt a prodigious amount of chocolate into a cup and then temper it with a slick of espresso, with cinnamon, with cardamom, with more spice that Antigone suspected the usual clientele was used to. Though she understood that dead meant never aching for a single damn thing again, she nonetheless felt a pang at the idea she'd never be able to see what else the café owner might devise.

"She shot herself," said Vera, who could be counted on to be ruthlessly unsentimental. Most days, the woman wore her hair in the most severe buns. Today, the white strands fell loose, a fleecy cloud around purple-shawled shoulders. "She doesn't count."

"You know, you could learn some tact," said Antigone, unable to repress a smile.

"I will if you promise you won't do anything stupid."

Antigone's smile faltered.

"At least promise you'll give it a week," said Vera, expression losing its combativeness and, for the first time, Antigone could see the old woman her friend was aspiring to be: straight-backed, magnificent as the redwoods of her home state. "Sit on this for a week."

"Vera—"

"A week."

"I don't know. I—"

"*Please.*"

The *please* brought Antigone up short. The Vera she knew was too proud to beg anyone for anything so it meant something to have her friend on her metaphorical knees like this, voice ragged, face raw.

"If I decide I want to do it in a week, what then?"

"Then," said Vera, the muscles of her jaw rippling. "Well, we'll see."

"I'm not going to change my mind."

"Tell me that in a week."

"Fine." Antigone's death raised its satin-eyed head from her thigh and she patted it absently, like there was no difference between it and a normal dog.

Vera sighed then.

"Well," she said. "Let's see what their specials are then. I'm buying. While you're still here, you might as well live."

The news continued to seep through her circles. Antigone stopped answering her phone after an old lover called, sobbing to ask if she needed help getting committed to psychiatric care, if it'd been his error, the burden of their relationship that led to her snapping like this. It took Antigone an hour to subdue her ex's misery and for the rest of the day, all she could stomach was sitting with her death on the porch, relieved that there was, in fact, an end to all this and no risk of spending an eternity weighted down by someone else's secondhand grief while suffocating on her own.

In the end, she decided on the water.

Drowning wasn't a painless end but there was something appealing about the thought of her constituent parts entering the river, feeding what was there, returning, in some way, what she took in life.

When Antigone had told her death this, it had only stared at her and she had the impression she'd disappointed it somehow.

He was there at the river the day Antigone had chosen to die, the late evening bloodying the black of his clothes: as tall as she remembered him, if a little grayer at the temples, a little less human that he once was, skin stretching awkwardly over bones she was sure he'd borrowed from a previous life. He looked up from his book as she neared the water, the light glinting along gold-rimmed glass.

"Tiggy?" he said, laughingly, and then cleared his throat, standing. His shadow dragged over the shore like a wing. "You're too much of a grown woman to be called Tiggy any longer. Antigone, darling, it's been a long time. What are you doing here?"

She considered lying but that seemed puerile somehow, even cowardly.

"I'm planning to drown myself."

He stared at her without comment for a moment and then said.

"Why?"

"Because forty years seemed like it was enough," said Antigone, looking down to where her death stood beside her, its expression pensive. "It was a good run."

Antigone swallowed, said again, "It was a good run."

"Is it because of him?" he said when it was clear Antigone could manage no more, crouching before Antigone's death, a hand extended. The latter nuzzled his knuckles, tail beginning to wag. "I think he'd have waited."

"He'd have waited my whole life, I'm sure," said Antigone when she could trust herself to speak again. "Which I suppose was forty years. A good run."

"Yes."

She could never remember his name, something that had amused him dreadfully when they'd been younger: it wasn't that Antigone did not try her best. It was just that the words that would reel from a human mind even one predisposed toward the weird. His name was one of them. Antigone had once wondered if she could assign him a moniker she could use, but that seemed anathema.

"What are you doing here?"

He cocked his head, the motion birdlike.

"I don't know." He stood again. "It seemed like a lovely day to read by the water, I suppose."

"Or to die," said Antigone, regretting the words as soon as they left her mouth: they seemed spiteful and he'd done nothing to merit that kind of petulance from her. "Sorry."

"Don't be," he said, settling on a polished stone again. "Sit with me?"

The slow-moving water was a featureless obsidian; a trick of the light, Antigone was sure, but something about its lack of texture made it seem particularly uninviting.

"Sure," said Antigone, doing as told, seating herself beside him. Her death laid itself over her feet, head turned up to them both like they were twin suns in the sky.

"Tell me what I've missed."

Heat seemed to ripple from his frame.

"Well," said Antigone with a bitter half laugh. "There's the fact I want to—"

He shook his head. "No, not that. Tell me what you've been up to, what you've done, about your mother's garden, and the cat, and everything else."

"Why does it matter? None of it is very memorable."

"But it is *you*," he said. "And when you're gone, I'd like to have something to hold."

"Even if it is just something stupid and banal."

"All of life is stupid and banal."

"Tell me about it," said Antigone, laughing despite everything else and the sun broke from behind the clouds, casting its warmth over her face. She glanced at the water and thought to herself, *The cold could wait.*

"Tell me about your tomatoes," he said when her laughter had subsided.

The cold could wait, Antigone thought again. Her death too, it seemed from its languid posture, its bottomless amber gaze: it appeared to be enjoying the sun too, rolling onto its back so that more of its belly was slathered by the golden light. And so deprived of excuses, she began to talk of her tomatoes, then of roses, then of everything else: of cake and the way the autumn light seemed almost thick enough to paint with, of good coffee and bad movies, every small strange thing that comprised a life.

Night had slunk across the sky when Antigone's stomach let out a gurgle.

"I've kept you," said her companion, barely more than an ink sketch, an impression of personhood in the dim. "I'm sorry. My curiosity absolutely gets the better of me, at times. Will you be going now?"

Antigone considered this.

"Tomorrow, maybe. You reminded me that there were still things to do. And besides," she said, offering a hand. "It'll wait."

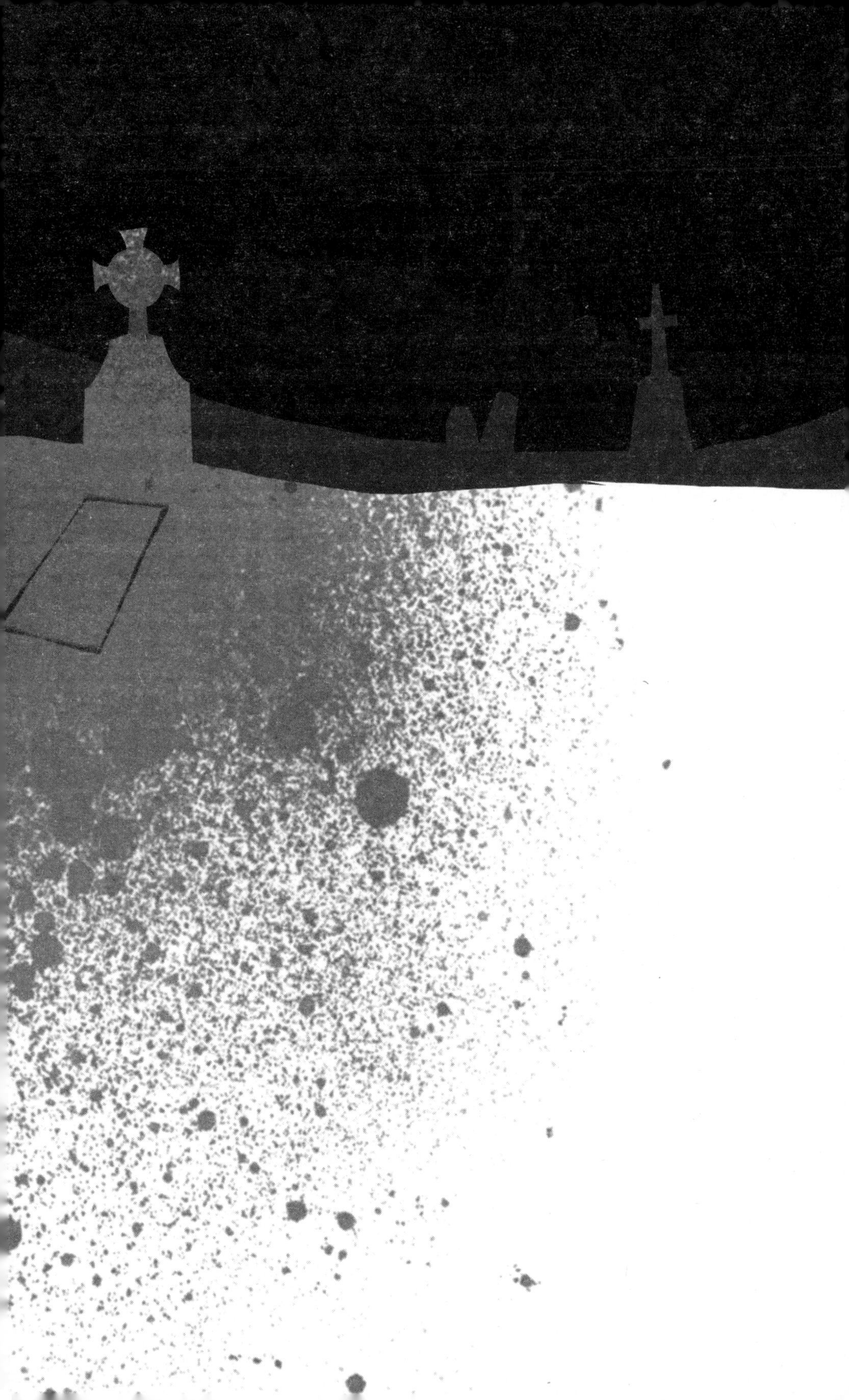

A SHOVEL, A ROPE, AND A BOTTLE OF WHISKEY

Samantha Mills

Arthur Sullivan lowers himself into the chair. His anxiety, quite frankly, is through the roof.

The woman sitting opposite him asks, "Have you done this before?"

"Many times."

"But not recently," she guesses.

"No," he says softly. "Not recently."

"Is there someone in particular you are thinking about?"

There is a tense pause while Arthur fights his instinct to stand, to storm out, to denounce this entire endeavor. Then he says, "Yes. I had a friend."

It began over a pint. Arthur and Joseph had crawled straight from the cotton mill to the saloon, their muscles cramped, their clothing covered in dust, their heads still aching from the stench of gaslight. They lamented the low pay, the ire of their supervisor, the drudgery and grime of daily life, same as every other night. Neither of them had come to this city expecting to end up like this, but it's where they'd ended up nonetheless.

It was Arthur who floated the idea of another line of work, equally dirty but paying far better. He'd been chewing on the idea for months, unwilling to do it alone and uncertain if Joseph, the more God-fearing of the two of them, would do it with him.

When he thought his friend appropriately lubricated for inappropriate plans, Arthur murmured, "I hear there's a doctor at Jefferson Medical buying bodies for twenty-five dollars apiece." Arthur, presently making a dollar a day, could not shake the figure from his mind.

But Joseph nearly choked on his drink for another reason. "Bodies?" he repeated. "Did you say *bodies*?"

Arthur shushed him, looking around, but there was nobody sitting adjacent. "I mean exactly what I said. There's students there that need more than they can get, and they'll pay for them."

Joseph was scandalized, but he didn't storm off. "What do *you* know about medical school?"

Arthur's brow furrowed. It occurred to him that he should keep some details to himself. He said, "I know a man, that's all. You think you're the only person I know?"

"It's Charlie Davis, isn't it?"

Arthur gaped, too surprised to lie. "How'd you figure that?" he demanded.

"Well, he's in here all the time and he's the only one I see pulling you aside. I thought he was a whiskey man."

"He's a deliveryman," Arthur corrected. "Sometimes that's whiskey."

"Well, whatever he does, why isn't he doing—" Joseph caught himself and lowered his voice, leaning over his cup. "You know what I mean. Why isn't he doing it then?"

"He's a deliveryman, like I said! You want to hear how this works or not?"

Joseph did not, at first. But he was younger, lonelier, and less certain of himself than he liked to believe. And twenty-five dollars for an evening's work was hard to pass up, once that number got fixed in your head.

Here's what a pair of enterprising young resurrection men needed to rob graves in 1882: a shovel, a rope, and a bottle of whiskey.

The shovel was for digging straight down at the head of the grave and smashing open the top of the coffin. There was no need to expose the whole thing—the weight of the dirt held the rest in place while the lid cracked.

The rope was for hauling the corpse out, looped snug around the neck or under the armpits.

The whiskey was for steadying their nerves.

With a bit of practice, the whole operation could be accomplished in less than half an hour—a relief for an anxious lookout. The bigger concern was selecting the right grave. Medical students had no use for corpses that had already turned halfway to sludge. This meant keeping an eye on death notices in the newspaper, lurking near the cemetery for signs of a funeral, or, if they'd really gotten themselves established, paying the mortuary men for inside information.

The fresher the better.

If stock came in faster than the local medical college could use it, that was just as well. The deliveryman could fold the body into a barrel, fill the remaining space with whiskey, and pop it on a train to the next university town. The body was sold, the whiskey was sold, and everyone was happy (except, perhaps, the folks drinking the whiskey).

"I want you to place your hands upon the table," says the woman sitting across from Arthur.

"Like this?"

"Yes, that's fine. Would you like to tell me what happened?"

"Not particularly. Is that a problem?" He is belligerent, an old habit difficult to break, but she isn't fazed. She says, "Close your eyes and think about your friend."

They'd met on the train into Philadelphia. Arthur, twenty, had already been on his own for years and felt rather worldly. Joseph, eighteen, had just left home and assuredly did not. They bonded over their love of variety shows (though Joseph didn't like the bawdy ones) and liquor (though Joseph abstained on Sundays). Arthur promised to keep an eye out for him, and felt a swelling pride at the gesture that he assumed elder brothers must have felt.

They found work together, and housing together, and spent their evenings drinking together, and then they started digging up dead bodies together.

It wasn't long before Arthur and Joseph were resurrecting on the regular, but they weren't as well-off as they'd hoped. Charlie Davis took a hefty delivery fee, even though they suspected he was lying about what he was being paid by the anatomist to begin with. It was still more money for fewer hours than the textile industry, and they'd moved out of the cramped row house behind the mill.

But the work was filthy. It was wearying. There were sights and smells that neither of them would ever forget. The only way to inure themselves against it was to quit calling their cargo *bodies* and start calling them *things*. The things for Charlie. The things for Jefferson Medical.

Joseph was struggling, Arthur could see it. He was quieter, less quick to laugh.

"They're just things," Arthur kept telling him. "Nothing's left behind when they go."

And Joseph always muttered, "It's not what's left behind that bothers me." It was the ever after that weighed on Joseph. Crimes on earth punished after death. He spent every Sunday at Mass shaking with worry over the fate of his eternal soul.

Arthur didn't believe in all that. He'd been born on the precipice of the Civil War and toddled his way through the worst of it. He'd grown up surrounded by a community in mourning, parents without children, children without parents, betrothals broken by the grave. Even those who'd survived did so with physical wounds and distant minds. They were quick to anger and to drink. Joseph had grown up in the same stew, but where he found reassurance in the almighty, Arthur rejected it entirely.

Arthur was one of the orphans, his mother felled in the act of birthing him and his father on the shore of Totopotomoy Creek. Arthur Sr., a Union soldier in the 118th Pennsylvania Regiment, left the world in 1864 and took all of his parents' love with him. Mary and Frederick Sullivan had lavished affection on their oldest son, but that affection didn't transfer to the toddler he left in their care.

That might have been the end of it, a story simply told: Arthur raised in the shadow of the dead, a cold childhood turned to a cold adolescence, a move to a new city and a brief stint as a grave robber until his only friend convinced him of the error of his ways.

But Frederick and Mary had never managed to let their loss go. They were hollowed out by grief, halfway to the grave themselves, and like many of their contemporaries, they became fixed on the idea of talking to their son again.

Arthur didn't like to think about those years, but he'd seen all he needed to see. There was nothing waiting for them in the end but a bed of bones, and all that mattered between now and then was the comfort accrued along the way.

"I think I'm done," Joseph whispered.

They'd gone after a double burial, a husband and wife. It should have been an easy haul, but it was early December and the ground was growing hard. They fought the cold and dug all the way down only to find iron caskets. Somebody in the family had deep pocketbooks.

Joseph wanted to go home, but Arthur was bullheaded, intent on getting paid. He dragged Joseph down to the potter's field. It was easier digging there—the dirt hardly packed, the coffins thin, the unclaimed bodies of the city's poor and indigent largely left unguarded. But because of that, it was a popular destination for resurrectionists.

The result was predictable. Hours of drudgery to find already-emptied coffins, or worse: putrid corpses too far gone for the anatomist's lab.

They stumbled away from the last one, the scent unbearable, the sight of writhing maggots enough to make even Arthur's gorge rise, and that was when Joseph made his trembling pronouncement. "I think I'm done."

"It was one bad night," Arthur said, still bent with his hands on his knees.

"They're all bad nights," Joseph retorted. "This is bad work, Arthur."

Arthur didn't want to have this conversation. "We have to get Charlie his cart back," he said. "Get some sleep and regroup in a couple days."

But there was more bad news when they got back to Charlie. He stopped them at his door with a copy of the *Philadelphia Press* clutched in one fist. "Sorry, boys, deliveries are on pause," he said. "We can talk after this dies down."

Arthur took the paper and squinted at the headline. GRAVEYARD GHOULS ARRESTED WITH A CARGO OF CORPSES. The editor and a team of reporters had spent months staking out Lebanon Cemetery, a Black burial ground, to track the plundering of the newly dead. They'd apprehended a trio of grave robbers with a wagon headed for Jefferson Medical College, the bodies of four men and two women in the back. The neighborhood was in an uproar.

Arthur swore. "We have nothing to do with them!"

"But my employer does," Charlie said. "And if he's not paying me, I'm not paying you."

Joseph was scuffling his shoes. "Let's go, Arthur. This is a sign."

"This isn't a sign. This is a setback. Charlie, you know we need that money!" Arthur wasn't proud of how he acted then: spitting mad and a poor example for Joseph, who looked up to him in all things. Later he'd look back on this moment and boil in his own regret. They'd made their extra cash and they hadn't got caught. They could have walked away. But the money was too good and the thought of downgrading back to the mill and their mold-infested room in the back was too rotten.

Maybe he was really trying to help, or maybe he knew where it would lead them, but one way or the other, Charlie said, "Damn it all, Arthur, calm down! Listen, if you're serious about pressing on, there *is* another buyer in town. He's not with the college, but he pays just as well. Sometimes better."

"Well, why didn't you say so!" Arthur crowed. "Count us in, Charlie. We can grab the cart from you again tomorrow—"

"*No*," Charlie said firmly, and to Arthur's surprise the man made the sign of the cross right then and there. "I won't have anything to do with it. You want to make a deal with that devil, you go to him direct."

Arthur refuses to close his eyes.

"You're skeptical," the woman observes.

"Of course I am." Arthur expects it to come out angrily, but instead his throat is choked with tears.

"And why is that?"

Because there were numerous ways that a medium could bilk her grieving clients, and Arthur Sullivan had seen them all. He was eight years old when his grandparents dragged him to his first séance. They'd been skeptical of Spiritualism before the war, but afterward they and millions like them began to wonder, longingly, if there was something to it.

The Fox sisters, whose miraculous dealings with the beyond had sparked the movement, were no longer touring as a trio in 1867. Leah was in New York; Maggie had converted to Catholicism after her husband's untimely death; but Kate was more active than ever, and according to the newspaper her talents had expanded to heights heretofore unseen.

Mary and Frederick could not resist. They leaped upon her next appearance in Pennsylvania, and they dragged their frightened ward into a dark room packed with other grieving hopefuls. He sat there, shaking, while the room filled with the rappings of ghosts. He watched as Kate spoke one message aloud while simultaneously scrawling another on paper. He watched an old man snatch up the paper, crying, "It's John! It's John!" while his own grandparents asked, "And what about Arthur? Is Arthur here?" and young Arthur Jr. cried at the sound of his own name in association with the dead.

They got a single message that day—*It was good of you to take the boy*—and they were enraptured. Kate Fox moved on to the next stop in her tour, but the Sullivans found more practitioners. Over the next several years, young Arthur saw tables shake and lift from the floor. He heard knockings and saw women fall into ecstatic trances. He saw messages appear on school slates and the back of men's jackets. His grandmother sat for a spirit photo with William Mumler, and he produced an image of Mary with the ghostly overlay of a man who could have been anyone's dead father. In 1869, Mumler was charged with fraud, but Mary Sullivan refused to take their photo off the mantle, and a couple years later when word got out that Mary Todd Lincoln had also sat for him, his grandmother whispered fiercely, "I knew it was real."

And all the while it was Arthur who felt like the real ghost, a half-forgotten shade wandering a house of perpetual mourning, and when he told his grandfather what he really thought—that they were frauds, they were all frauds, there was nothing on the other side—he was answered with a beating.

Arthur was twenty-three years old now, and he had spent every one of those years surviving to the next. He fled his grandparents when he was fifteen, and he worked his way across the state, celebrating every mile between himself and that house of perpetual mourning, and when he found his life once again revolving around the dead, it was reassuring this time because it confirmed, night after night, that the dead were still and gone. His father had never whispered to him through the mouth of a young woman, nor rapped vague messages of affection from beneath a séance table.

So when Charlie Davis gave him the address of a devil in that cold winter of 1882, Arthur did not feel even one solitary hair raise upon his neck. He didn't believe in devils or ghosts or eternal repercussions. A job was a job, and a well-paying job was best of all.

When Arthur does not answer, the woman says, "I am here to help you, if you'll let me."

When Arthur still does not answer, the woman says, "That is why you came, isn't it? You have a question, and this is the only way to get your answer."

Arthur closes his eyes.

The devil's name was Filippo Rossi. His family was from Piedmont, textile mer-chants who emigrated overseas before the Risorgimento. He was the last-surviving bearer of his name. Reclusive and strange. There was not much else that Arthur and Joseph could glean from his neighbors, no matter how many drinks they bought.

He lived in a two-and-a-half-story mansion with three porches and four stone chimneys, located at the end of a long, tree-lined dirt road.

Arthur and Joseph had scrubbed up for their unsolicited call, but they still looked unbearably shabby on that well-manicured front step. A servant opened the front door and was ready to turn them away until Arthur said, "Charlie Davis sent us."

And then it was a long wait outside, stamping their feet against the chill, until they were shown into a parlor so tidy and refined they didn't dare sit on the furniture.

"This man's no doctor," Joseph whispered.

"Could be," Arthur said.

They fell silent when Filippo Rossi entered the room. He was an older man, his hair gone to gray and the lines of his face set deep. His frame was narrow; his suit well-tailored; his glasses round.

He came straight to the point. "I thought Charles would never work for me again."

Arthur said, "Charlie's not the one offering to work for you."

"I see." Rossi had a speculative gleam in his eye—a look Arthur would come to recognize over the following months as the gleam of discovery. He gestured for them to sit.

They danced around it a bit, neither side wanting to be the first to mention grave robbing for fear there had been a comically dark misunderstanding, until Joseph blurted, "What do you want those things for, anyway? Are you a doctor?"

"I am a scientist," Rossi said. Calmly, as though it were the most ordinary thing in the world, he added, "I am investigating the tethers between the body and the soul."

Arthur barked a laugh. He couldn't help it. "What are you doing that for?" He didn't notice the way Joseph froze at his side.

Rossi spread his hands. "I believe that by more firmly anchoring the soul, we can keep the grievously injured alive long enough for surgeons to complete their work. As things stand now, the person who lays down in the operating theater is just as likely to die as they are to be cured. The pain is shocking to the system—so shocking, the soul prematurely untethers, convinced that violent death is upon it."

Arthur could have pressed him further on this outrageousness. He could have asked why Rossi was not practicing this technique in the operating theater (the obvious answer: no self-respecting surgeon would allow him access), or how on earth the man thought he could observe the soul, tethered or not. But Arthur fixed on another hitch instead.

"What good does a dead body do?"

Rossi smiled. "I do not need you to believe me. I only need you to bring me the materials of my research, and in exchange I will pay you fifty dollars apiece."

"Well, that's all you had to say!" Arthur turned to clap Joseph on the back, but Joseph was pensive. It was an easy moment to dismiss. Joseph was always pensive. When they left the mansion, instructions duly memorized, Arthur was walking on air.

These were Filippo Rossi's requirements:

The body could not be embalmed. It could not be beheaded, nor any of its limbs recently amputated. It could be disinterred, if necessary, though Rossi urged them to pursue leads anywhere a body might be unclaimed—the poorhouses, the asylum, the prison, the docks. Whatever the means of acquisition, one factor remained: under no circumstances could the body be more than six days dead.

The fresher the better.

And suddenly, Joseph was a willing participant again. More than willing. He was going out of his way to scope out new mortuary contacts, he was tracking death notices in the papers, he was spending free afternoons at the saloon nearest the Hospital for the Insane, trying to cozy up to the staff.

It was the money, Arthur assumed. One night's work and they were already flush with more cash than either of them had ever seen in one place. They could afford separate rooms, buy whatever they liked, they could open accounts with the bank.

But it wasn't the money. It was Rossi. Over the next two months, Joseph lingered longer and longer after each delivery. Arthur would be standing outside, literally itching to go wash off the stench of death, and Joseph was dawdling in Rossi's workroom, helping set out tools and asking questions.

"Why are you humoring that man?" Arthur finally snapped. It was February, the ground was hard beneath a layer of snow, and they were walking the grimiest alleys of Philadelphia before dawn, in case there had been any deaths in the night.

Joseph shook his head. "You don't get it, Arthur."

"I get that he's rich. I get that he's delusional."

Joseph stopped walking. His jaw was set hard, his shoulders set even harder. He said, "Rossi's a genius."

"Come on now—"

"He's a genius!" Joseph insisted. "He's really done it. He's proven the existence of the soul. I've *seen* it."

"You have *not*."

Joseph's voice trembled. "There's a force that lingers around the body after death. It stays up to a week, Mr. Rossi said, before it learns how to move on. It's the *soul*, Arthur. There's an anchor point when we're alive, located under here"—he prodded Arthur on the sternum—"and he's working on a way to coax it back after it's come untethered. I saw it with my own eyes."

Arthur physically recoiled from this. His ears were ringing and his body broke out in a sweat. He was eight again, being dragged from séance to séance, being told, *Your father is in this room, don't you sense your father, don't you care about your father?*

"It's a lie!" he barked. "Whatever he showed you in that room, it's parlor tricks, mirrors and lights. This is just a job, easy money from an old fool."

"You don't believe in anything," Joseph accused. "You never have."

At that point, Arthur began to shout and couldn't stop. He said things he couldn't unsay, blasphemous and full of fury. It had never come between them before—Joseph's weekly Mass and Arthur's steadfast avoidance of anything of the sort—but now a terrible explosion brewed.

Joseph stormed away. Arthur wouldn't see him again till spring.

"You have regrets."

"Yes."

"Shame."

"Yes."

"You have something you wish to ask your friend."

Arthur showed up at Rossi's doorstep three days later, cooled down and ready to put the fight behind him. But this time the servant shook his head and offered a ludicrously thick envelope of cash. An insulting amount. *Go to hell and don't mention this to anybody* money. Arthur took most of it to the bank. He used the rest to get drunk.

It was another week before his pride let him seek out Joseph. He knocked repeatedly. "Joseph, wake up. We have to talk. You've made yourself clear." And then, more desperately, "Please, open the door."

He trekked to the back of the house, prepared to plead his case through the damn window, but one look made it clear: Joseph's room was vacated.

Arthur was out of a job, and he'd lost his only friend.

The following month was a blur of drinking and sleeping and complaining to anyone who would listen. The years that Arthur Sullivan had spent burning with loneliness far outweighed the years he had spent with Joseph, but in the end, it only took a brief taste of companionship to spoil him for good.

Arthur grieved. Arthur pulled himself back together. He found a new job cleaning at the hospital—another world in perpetual proximity to death, but this time some of the bodies got up and walked away. Things weren't great, but they were better.

And then Joseph came back.

It was nearly sunset. When Arthur saw the dark figure at his door, he tensed, ready for his head to be bashed or some forgotten bill to be called in, but it was Joseph huddled in a dark coat.

"I should have come sooner," Joseph managed to say, and then he burst into tears right there on the step.

Arthur ushered him inside. He'd scarcely got his coat off when Joseph blurted, "I'm a murderer."

It spilled out of him in a tearful babble: the way the work had escalated, the way Rossi kept pressing him to find fresher bodies, younger, fitter, less damaged, more ideal. Rossi's experiments had been ticking closer and closer to his real pursuit, anchoring the spirit *before* death, and that was the natural next step, was it not? To implement Rossi's methods upon a living body and observe the effects?

"He is so close," Joseph kept repeating. "I was in the room this time, I saw the anchor take hold, he really is on the verge of a breakthrough—"

Arthur, aghast, struggled to keep his tone level. "What did you do?"

"I found someone," Joseph whispered. "I found a man in the street. His leg was all gangrene. I said I was taking him to a doctor. And then that wasn't the end of it. It had nearly worked, so we tried again. I found a—a girl. An indigent."

"Oh, Joseph," Arthur said.

"I'm going to hell," Joseph wept. "The soul is real and mine is headed for torment. You've got to believe me, Arthur, he's going to succeed. He's going to save so many lives. And I don't know which is the worse sin: the things I've done to help him, or the fact that I'm too weak to see it through to the end."

Arthur was shaking. He pulled Joseph forward in an embrace.

He said, "This is all my fault, Joseph. I should never have talked you into this. I should never have taken you to that house. This is over, do you hear me? No more bodies. No more fetching anything for Filippo Rossi. Charlie was right. We have to stay away from that man."

He did not try to argue over the reality or charlatanry of the situation again, though later he would wish he'd tried. He only begged his friend to stay the night, clear his head, and tomorrow they would make a plan. No more bodies. No more Filippo Rossi.

But Joseph only latched on to part of what he'd said. His tears slowed. He relaxed against Arthur's chest. Almost sleepily, he agreed, "No more bodies."

Abruptly, Arthur says, "I never believed in any of this. My grandparents did. I think it was the only thing they believed in."

"Are you hoping to hear from them today?" she asks, with commendable tact.

For the first time all evening, he almost laughs. "God, no."

Arthur awoke in the dark of night, alone.

He had liquored Joseph up and put him to bed, and then he'd slept a few uneasy hours in the chair. His back ached. His mouth was sour. It took a minute to realize: Joseph had fled, and he'd left a note on the pillow:

Thanks for everything, Arthur.

"You damn fool," Arthur whispered, but it wasn't Joseph he was damning. Arthur was the fool—for getting his friend into this mess, for thinking he could assuage the other boy's conscience with a few fumbling words, for thinking it was safe to fall asleep.

Joseph had always been the better of the two of them. When he did wrong, he atoned. An eye for an eye.

Arthur fled across town with his heart in his throat. When he reached the house at the end of the lane, sweaty and breathing hard in the dark of predawn, he did not knock. He circled the property until he found an unlatched window and climbed inside. The halls were dark, the servants gone home for the night. He ran to Rossi's workroom.

Rossi looked up, eyes wide and full of tears behind his glasses. His hands were slick with blood. Joseph lay on the dissection table, half covered by a sheet. His face was slack. An incision ran down his chest.

"Murderer!" Arthur cried. He ran to the table. He didn't know what to do with his hands—hold the wound shut or pull up the sheet or slap Joseph on the cheeks or launch himself directly at the man who had done this—

Rossi backed away, bloody hand upraised and still holding a scalpel. "Joseph volunteered himself," he said quickly. "He wants me to succeed. Look. Look right here—"

Arthur watched the last breath leave Joseph's body.

"Do you feel it, Arthur?"

He hesitates. Had the room gotten colder? Was the light a bit dimmer?

Rossi slumped. Not horrified. Not stricken. Only disappointed. His voice sounded far away. "I am very sorry. He was a good man. Selfless. I promise that this won't be in vain."

Arthur snapped back into focus. "He's dead," he said.

"And I am sorry, as I said. But didn't you see, there on his chest—?"

Arthur recoiled. "I saw nothing!" he shouted. "What you're doing here—it's—it's monstrous!"

Rossi shook his head, like Arthur was the one who didn't understand. "How many of our boys died in the mud because they could not get attention in time? How many of them succumbed to illness? To shattered limbs? How many died under the knife of the field surgeon trying to save them? I am going to end of all that, Arthur. I can fix this."

And Arthur realized he was standing in front of another grief-stricken parent. Another old man so fixated on his past hurt that he couldn't see himself propagating worse in the present.

Arthur placed his hands, trembling, on the body of his friend. All of his carefully constructed self-defense measures melted away. He could not see it as a thing. He said, "Joseph killed people so you could play at giving life. Don't you understand what you did to him? I'm ending this. I'm going to tell everyone."

It was Rossi who rushed forward, scalpel hand outstretched.

It was Rossi who turned it into a fight.

Arthur's ears pop. He could swear he feels a breeze across his face, although the windows are closed. He cannot help himself. He opens his eyes again. The woman's face is relaxed, dreamy.

She says, "Hello, Arthur."

Here is what a grief-stricken, former resurrection man needed to conceal a mur- der in 1883: a shovel, a rope, and a bottle of whiskey.

The shovel was for digging a hole in the garden, a task made easier by the softer soil and the digger's extensive experience.

The rope was for tying the body into a manageable bundle of sheets, the better for dragging it to its grave without leaving any mess in the hall.

The whiskey was for steadying his nerves.

The whiskey was for pouring over the cuts on his knuckles.

The whiskey was for getting blackout drunk and dulling the memory as rapidly as possible, because there was a light around Joseph's body when he died. There was a light, and it was concentrated at the incision on his chest, there were tendrils hooked in as though they were struggling to hold on to something there, an anchor point beneath the sternum just like Joseph said, there was a genuine undeniable light with a hint of a face, and if that was true maybe all of it was true, and if all of it was true then Arthur wasn't just a murderer—he'd killed the man who might have cured death.

The whiskey wasn't enough.

In a small room, at a plain table, sitting across from a woman attempting to channel the ghost of his only friend, Arthur whispers, "Is there life after death?"

"Undoubtedly," she says.

He swallows hard. He chooses to believe it. He asks, "Is there suffering?"

SINKING ALL THE WHILE

Premee Mohamed

1.

We didn't kill him. He fell—sometimes people die of a fall—it's known—we are accustomed to blame but we are not to blame. Perhaps he was dead already. We don't know. It's not our fault. We can't tell.

It is true that we embraced him as he sank, and we pulled on his soft rich clothing, yes, that's true. We pulled him—not down! toward!—in a direction toward the center of things, you know the one. Deep inside. People have this silly idea about directions, the way to cut up the world, north south east west up down. They forget away and toward (the center).

You cannot cut water; we think he still tried. The scabbard on his belt was empty. His hand clutched a knife. He sank slowly toward the center.

How we held him! Like a lover, entered him, tenderly, sweetly, in silence, not wishing to be too forward (not a direction). His juices meeting our juices. Blood of the city: rainwater and pisswater and the oozings of trash, offal on Butcher Street, fishsplash from the docks, slopwater from the wooden buckets of charwomen scrubbing out the houses of their masters, yes, and the backwash of the river, the king tides of the faraway sea, all flow into our right-angled veins.

Thick dirty stuff we are. Gurgle of our limbless body over his—or you could say infinite limbs—however you want to count it—then the fish lipping and kissing him, then the efforts to slide deep into him (efforts of the eels: how they do love a warm body even losing its warmth in our embrace). Toothless fish we are/we contain. Eels we are/we contain. They cannot chew the resilient flesh of him who fell and sank.

Toward—toward—bubbles from the lungs, tinged pink as dawn in the deepdark murkymuck of us. Sweet salt bubbles. A shapeless mass sinking, velvet and gold and the moonlight shimmering in the rubbish-cluttered skin of us. The body cooling—becoming one with us—thank you for this gift. The fish will eat well.

Protesting our innocence. We know not the moment of death. It is of no concern to those who feed from it (as you know).

2.

In the name of all those holy and invisible spirits without name who supervise and guide our work, this inquisition is completed today the Fifteenth Vrish in the Year of the Two Columns of Granite.

I, Tituli Ched, serve as coroner, and the signatures of the jury testify to the accuracy of this inquisition as well as my good reputation as a servant of the Quing's Bench of Justice.

The deceased person is one Bartram Tellman, aged fifty-three, former member of the Royal Society of Wizards and alumnus of Lyshrod-Uat College of Encantation (conferral of degree in Year of the Smoke-Feathered Sparrowhawk).

The body was retrieved from the waters of the canal directly adjacent to the deceased's domicile. The body was submerged entirely and no portion of it remained above the water.

The individual who espied the body at approximately four a.m. and alerted Private Constable Kalef of the Royal Cloaksmen was one Matthias Trag, aged sixteen, occupation given as "baker's boy."

Investigation has determined that Mr. Trag is a boy of ordinary repute and his employer (Bonfer Mill & Bakery) confirms that the boy's primary duties are delivery and supply management, thus he is accustomed to being out at the hour and it is reasonable to accept that he was not intent upon nefarious business. His employer confirms also under oath that the boy has never involved himself with criminal matters in civil or royal courts nor has any church ever found him to be guilty or suspected of blasphemy or other crimes against the divine regardless of personal faith.

I must confirm that the Royal Society of Wizards was contacted through the normal offices and has declined to participate in this investigation. The letter of regret is attached to the back of this inquisition. However as per the Statutes of Holbrook in the Year of the Moon Thread Circle, no practitioner or educator of magic may be compelled to participate in any inquisitio regularis.

The deceased appeared to be drowned. The lungs were filled with water. No bruises or marks were found upon his person that seemed candidates to contribute to the death. However, bruises and marks were found upon his person.

(Official figure of autopsy attached to the back of this inquisition.)

The housekeeper of the deceased, one Mrs. Shirley Lindi, was questioned. She reported that she exited the domicile as normal (seven p.m.), leaving the deceased alone, as he has required her to do every night of her tenure of employment (two years, three months). She reported that she did not possess keys to the doors and stairs allowing access to the second or third floors of the house, which are normally locked and can only be accessed by the deceased, and all her duties occur on the main floor.

No keys to the second or third floor were found upon her person, in her domicile (searched by PC Kalef), or in the domicile of the deceased nor upon the body of the deceased. The doors leading to the stairwells were locked and the locks had to be forced to allow investigation. The housekeeper is not assumed to be responsible at this time.

Permission was not granted to my personnel for lock-off and dredging of the canal for the keys, assuming they were upon the person of the deceased at the time of death.

Due to the open window on the third floor of the deceased's domicile and the location of the body it is the conclusion of myself and this jury of thirteen men and women of local residence and good repute (attached &c) that the death was caused by accidental or self-directed falling and was neither magical nor criminal in nature.

No finding of deodand as relates to blame of the canal.

Tituli Ched, Coroner.

3.

When I came for this one I rode my second-best mount, as one wears one's second-best dress to a dull but necessary ceremony. And the fox of black and silver knew it, and he was not offended (as my best would have been, the white horse) nor resigned (as my third often is, the golden crow), but swore to work harder: "I will be the best one day," he said.

I did not tell him that the rankings never change.

We cantered over the border-river, its thick blood soaking the rags of my uniform. Then the distance broke and we were in the land of the living, a shock of smells and noises, lights and sights and the pressure of real air. A moment later the pressure of water, riding into the gelatinous contents of a canal built of cemented black stone. Moonlight penetrated a handsbreadth into the stuff, like a layer of milk atop the jelly.

Inside, clearly visible to eyes such as ours, hung the dying man. I suspected the wind had been knocked out of him when he hit the water, and he had gasped reflexively, as usually happens to the unprepared. Still it would be some time before I could carry him away. It is surprising (not to everyone) how long a human being can extend that final breath.

His movements were spasmodic, twitching without purpose. Lobster-like. Even his clothing, mottled brown and gold velvet, like a lobster. As if he belonged there in the canal. Had been raised there. One hand had locked around the hilt of a dagger, so small as to be decorative; to stab your foe you'd have to be close enough for them to bite you in return. Expensive and impractical, like the rest of him. The shoes, the watch chain, the scabbard. His belly lapping a little over the velvet breeches he had been too vain or too stubborn to simply have tailored for the extra flesh. Even though he could afford it.

The soul emerged at its time, a sphere (why always a sphere?) of soft greenish light, no stronger than the moonlight above us. With my left hand I took it; with my right I covered my left, enclosing it. A cold brightness. Taste of lightning. The fox waited under me, patient as only my steeds can be patient, bubbles gathering in the dense fur of his nape.

"It can't be," the man whined. "It is a trick, an illusion. Let me out, monster! Torturer!"

I am not the torturer; I only deliver souls to the torturers. He had no way of knowing that, of course. One only dies once. I opened my hands and the sphere bloomed into a loose cloud of light, dim and shapeless. Fish swam through it all unheeding.

"It can't be," the man said again. "I am too young to die! I have not even fifty years! Why are you here? Did one of my enemies send you? An assassin? Was it the bloody Society? Eh? Answer me, servant of your darker master!"

I paused, considering the cruelty of various responses. He was upset to have died; I was quite used to that. People weep out of self-pity for their own death. Sometimes they are grateful. Sometimes they are, like, this, confused, and angry about their confusion, because they have lived a life in which they may not have always been right but they heard no dissent. At any rate it could not harm either of us to correct his misperception. "I am not a servant," I said. "I am she whom you first recognized."

He snarled. "In every reliable piece of documentation, you are a man. Riding a white horse. Do you take me for a fool, you vile impostor?"

"I have a white horse. I can look like a man when I like. Are you satisfied now?"

"No!"

"It is of no account," I told him. "And I have not come to satisfy you, at any rate; I am your escort to another place." I held out once more my left hand, and recaptured the mean orb of his soul.

"My house," he wailed from within my fingers. "My furniture, my carpets! I had them imported from Rakatlor—my chandelier of real crystal! My gold . . ."

"You can carry none of that where we are going," I replied. "Only what you had within you: your learning, your memory. Your love and your grief."

"Oh, sod all that! And my two bloody—lazy—*ugly* daughters—gods help us, if the gods are real, I can say that now, can't I? They cannot harm me now for disbelief! Ha! Those two poxy whores, ungrateful for the roof I kept over their head, the food I placed in their mouths, always putting on airs . . . *Respect your elders!*" he shouted. "And they never did! Oh, I was betrayed long before this . . . this most foul murder . . ."

His voice died into a low burbling, as if he still had a body and it was still trying to speak through the water of the canal. He was telling a story—one the humans called a myth, but I knew was true, for I had been there—about a brave lion (back when animals could speak), seduced and then traduced by a snake, the most beautiful snake in all the world, the lion dying in a ditch, in undignified agony, receiving, he said, his just reward for trusting the untrustworthy.

"And you are the lion," I said when he fell silent.

"Of course I'm the lion, you stupid bitch. Why do you think I told the story?"

"I do not know," I said. "I was being polite. Dead people tell me many things. Sometimes they do not know why they are telling them."

"They are idiots then," the man sniffed. "I *always* know why I say the things I say. And I never take it back! Never! That is for cowards and fools and dotards who cannot remember. Oh, what the world has lost—irreparably—irrevocably—by losing me . . ."

I knew what was coming next, and I touched my heels to the flanks of my fox, pointing him the way we had come. "You cannot go back," I said.

"You could bring me back. Turn it around—this dog—and just—"

"I do not take orders from the dead," I said. "Let me tell you a story now, Bartram Tellman. When I came for your great-great-grandfather Wolstan the Gray, he had been stabbed from behind by one of the bandits who had raided his village. He had been fighting the raiders for nearly five hours bearing only a bent sword and part of a cabinet door as a shield. The bandit used an estelm—long and thin—and it pierced the old man's liver clean through. He bled out on the floor near the fire and I came to him at his appointed time and waited with him until his soul was released.

"And when he could speak again—free of his body and the pain, the dizziness, the dark of his eyes, the woodsmoke in his lungs—he did not whine about the bandits nor his mortal wound, nor the destruction of his house, the theft of his horses, the burning of his fields. He said, *The twins—perhaps you are not vouchsafed to tell me, lady—but please, if you can, where are they? Do they live?* For he had fought to distract the bandits long enough to let his daughter slip away into the forest with his grandchildren Felusi and Erisa. Who then became your grandfather and grand-uncle."

The dead man grunted, fell blessedly silent, and I thanked the gods (for they do exist, and we speak sometimes). Yet his silence was not in shame, for I could still feel the spikes and barbs of his anger stabbing my palms.

And I wondered why I had said that, any of that, because I do not often speak to my charges as I take them to their journey's end. There is no point, for one. I cannot change their minds. I can hurt them or offer them comfort or hope with my information, and I cannot control what they will receive from my words.

Wolstan the Gray? I did tell him where the children were, and that they lived; I had not come to collect their souls that night, nor that of their grim and courageous mother. They raced through the forest like wraiths, into the black valleys where even the bandits do not go. They survived there for a fortnight, living on wits and luck, before the pass cleared and they climbed through and into the neighboring land of Verquea, where their distant kin took them in. And there were many times in the lives of all three that I arrived with the expectation that I would be needed very soon, and yet I departed empty-handed, for it was not their time. Always this family has mazed and charmed me. Till now.

At least the man did not speak again as we crossed the border. I did not grieve for him or for what I had said. I have learned much from humans, but not that; not yet.

4.

Do you know what they do when they *expel* you from the Royal Society of Puckered Assholes? Oh, they use the word on purpose, you're meant to feel like you're a child, you're being punished. Not as if you're a grown man who pays thirty—*thirty! thirty!*—gold crescents a year to belong to their little club, to have the letters after your name as if they mean anything.

They have a whole—are you listening to me? I don't care *what* you are, you ugly little shit, horns this way, *listen*. They have a whole ceremony! It's like defrocking a bloody priest! May as well ritually hex you like they're a coven of filthy witches squatting in the countryside and fucking the billy goats, that's how they sound. Exactly like that.

A man recovers from a slap in the face pretty quick—always prided myself on that—but a wizard is no ordinary man, so yes, it took me a bloody minute, all right? It took me a minute. There's proportionality to consider, there's the stature of the insult, which was *significant*, and the stature of the insulted, which I may say myself—get back here, I'm not done!

So yes, I was drinking, all right? The insult. To drink is a man's prerogative, if he is a real man. And to drink whatever he likes, whatever he can afford, and I could afford *anything I wanted* while I was alive, let's be clear. A *good* drink, seacoal brandy and a spoonful of bittersip, so it looked like an angry storm in my crystal goblet, and . . .

I had a few goblets, I remember that, and . . . I remember shouting for the servant, what's her name, because I was hungry, and then I remembered that she'd gone home, the lazy bitch, she went *home*, she *abandoned* me, and I had forgotten that was the night I intended to tell her where things really stand between a man of my stature—I mean, my status—my *standing in the community* and as one of the people who, you know, really run things in the city—and her, who licks the floors for pennies, and by the gods if she didn't start acting right when I laid hands on her we'd see how far she could stretch those pennies in the future.

Except I wasn't planning to word it that way. Got to use simpler words for the lower classes so they understand you. Mere proximity to my books and scrolls and wisdom and degrees doesn't have an effect if they can't bloody read.

No, I don't *care* that you can't read either, I am starting to suspect that you are some kind of imp or demon and what use do you have here for literature? Stop interrupting me.

And I don't remember hitting the water, though I suppose that's the only place to go, the walkway on that side of the house is hardly a pace across, two fat women couldn't walk abreast. I remember, of course, fighting the canal fish that attacked me—horrible things they are, just as rumored, you can't see them because they change color to match the water, so it's said, and I knew then that it was true.

Luckily I had my sword with me, for I never go without it now (they may say I cannot call myself *wizard* but they cannot tell me I am not *nobility* and permitted to be armed with whatever I like at all times). So even as the life was draining from my body—even as the assassin's shove succeeded—I was still defending it, by the gods, because that is what a man must do. Their huge stripy bodies, like the tigers of the water! And teeth the size of cinder blocks! You'd almost not believe they could live in the canals of the city, that's the size of 'em. And with my dying thought I wanted to give one to the servant to cook for me . . . a kingly dish that is, a whole fish with the head on. That way you know it's really the fish you paid for and not some other creature foisted off on a stupid woman in the marketplace . . .

Ye gods, and I only hired her because I *am* a soft man at heart, and she reminded me of my two hideous, slatternly daughters—Judeth and what's the other one, her bloody mother named her, can't recall the whole thing, Pip she used to call her. Horse-fart ugly the both of them, hair like a wet mop, and all those years I hurled money at them—tutors—governesses—charm lecturers, etiquette instructors, bloody *elocution advisers*, what did they care?

Turned their backs on me, moved out of the house, hardly ever visit. Me, their father, who slaved to raise 'em after my wife fucked off, when I could have given them away or sold them, and I *told* them that, me, they never visit. Ingrates! Probably out offering their goods to half the city. Split it up by the river: half north, half south. Imagine that, the insult to the family name—selling *their* bodies, that belong to *me*, their bloody *father*, the reason they *exist*. I hope they changed their names for business, is all. That's what I hope.

You know, one of them did visit the other day though—can't remember—the dog barked like he's supposed to, mangy brute, and then he stopped, and I got my staff, gods be damned if I'm going to "obey" the Society of Assholes—but it was just her. Wanted to "talk" to me about something, probably try to fleece me out of her inheritance early. Well, joke's on her, there isn't going to *be* an inheritance, not with the fines I've got to pay the Assholes after they found out about the accounting of the—

—I said *get back here*, you hairy little weasel's bollock, I'm not finished!

5.

He always made a great show of his atheism—he was not any mere "man without faith," but a denier of the gods, the very concept of them, the premise and the need. I suppose he would find it infuriating that he is now held in the dead-room of a church. Then again, in life he found many things infuriating.

The coroner's office removed his clothing for the examination, as they do for all unwitnessed deaths—it said so in their report. The items have been returned to next of kin, all proper and correct, but I have no wish to touch the linen sack. Slumped on a table several paces away, it still smells of canal water—that peculiar stench of vegetable and animal. I will wait until Philippa gets here, and then we will decide what to do with it. If she does not come, I will take it away and burn it back at the shop.

Someone has put the shroud over his body, draping it loosely from chest to knee. They will not sew him into it until we give permission. He is marked here and there with a livid bruise or scrape, as vulnerable as a sleeping child. The windows allow a gray and shadowless light to fall upon him.

The priest is watching me, his face a mask of sympathy: *Poor girl. Poor girl, looking upon her dead father—poor little orphan.* And I could tell him the truth, but I don't want to talk to him, and I don't want his pity, and I just want this to be over.

Cold cross drafts fill the room. I hug my arms as I approach the stone table and look down at the familiar face I hate. Hated? No, hate. Slack and loose now, not taut with anger, distorted with screaming. No breath fouled with drink or vomit. I have not seen him for a year or so, I think, but even in so short a time he has lost more of his hair. What remains is mottled and thready, like nettle-stock before it is spun. And the hands I hated, hate, are hidden under the shroud.

I feel . . . there are too many words for it. I don't feel as I expected to feel. For fifteen years he was our whole world, the sun in the sky—the sun that nourishes, he said, but the sun can burn, too. The sun can kill. Now in the darkness of his absence I feel as if I am seeing the world for the first time. A different world, not the one he illuminated.

The feeling reminds me of, gods forgive me, a few weeks when I was . . . I think eight years old, and the new neighbors moved in, and we did not know them or what they were doing but we had mice in our house for the first time, and then rats. And a particularly enormous rat got in one night when Philippa and I were alone, and our old dog fought it, and was bitten and fell ill and died, and the rat escaped.

And our father laughed at us. Laughed at our fear and our weeping over the poor dog, and then his mockery turned to rage, and he said he would slap our eyes shut (and he did). But we still feared the rat. And one day, a colleague of his came to the house to drop off a scroll, and she spotted the thing and cried "Ugh!" and killed it with a single word of power . . . the relief was overwhelming, monumental. It blotted out all thought and language. My sister and I could not speak even to thank the wizard. And when the stunning blow of our deliverance wore off, when sense returned to us, we both realized the same thing. But we did not ask our father, ever, why he had not killed the rat himself.

So it comes back to me. Relief to see the body for myself: overwhelming relief. He will never touch me again, never violate me again. Never, never, never; it cannot be done. Other men may. Other men probably will. But not him. There have been other rats in the world, but never another nemesis.

I wonder what the priest thinks my face is telling him. I wonder if he thinks these tears are for the corpse. They are for me, little Judeth, me when I was too small and young to fight, and too frightened of the consequences to try. I told Philippa later that year, if I have my years right. She was almost eleven, and I had thought . . . I don't know. We were alone, as we so often were, and folding sheets and towels, and blood—it mostly comes out, if you're careful. But often a ghost remains, a thin brown outline around the removed stain. And I said . . .

. . . Well, never mind. I had thought to commiserate with her, thinking that he was doing the same thing to her in her chamber as he was in mine. I had thought we suffered alone in silence and shame and I was tired of suffering but I was also tired of *alone*. And she was shocked, so shocked. She dropped the basket, and our clean sheets tumbled onto the hearth.

"We'll have to rewash them," I said, numb. "Quickly."

"He's never done that to me," she said. "Never."

I believed her back then. What did I know? I did not think she denied it for any other reason than that it was true: It was only me he came to on those nights. Her reaction convinced me wholly. What else could surprise her so?

But now I wonder, looking down at the body, at the small, fresh marks of a fight or a scuffle . . . what if Philippa made a decision that day? What if she (gods spare her and bless her) held it in and held it in and held it in and then one night (Monday night) she crept back to the house, and found him drinking, and pushed him out of the window? If she plotted her revenge on my behalf until she could make it look like this—an entirely predictable accident?

I hope so. I damn myself by saying so. But I ache with hope—I feel it within myself like a cramp.

I wanted to do it so often. Every single day, until the day I left. And after I left, maybe every other day.

When I lived at the house—that soft, gilded prison!—I wore myself out thinking of ways to do it. But I will confess now, in silence, to myself or to the corpse, that it was not lack of opportunity that stopped me. It was cowardice. It was the fear of it going wrong, of him surviving, of what he'd do to me.

My best chance came a year or two after Philippa left. He did not want to hire a housekeeper, insisting that while I still lived at home, I would serve just as well. So I prepared our meals and beverages . . . and then I became apprenticed to one of the apothecaries in town, and I learned about the poisons that could kill at once, or over long periods of time, or mimic something else.

And I remember settling on one that caused a swift deterioration of the liver, because his drink-sodden liver would be more susceptible to it, and it therefore would look even more like a natural death. Kesom root, from very far away. A smell of something sharp, like burning hair, in the black powder: a perfume of hope.

I went so far as to steal enough to do it—about twenty grains in a tiny clay vial. Brought it home. Stared at his food that night: at the tray I had prepared (bread, beer, a perfectly dark beef soup with black mushrooms).

Couldn't do it.

I wanted him to die but I didn't want to kill him. I wanted *someone* to kill him (desperately) and I dreamed of it as often as I dreamed of doing it myself, but I didn't want it to be me. I suppose I wanted the hand of some god. The gaze of some god.

And now I am weeping, sincerely and hotly, and drying my face on my sleeve. No tears for him—the lecherous, covetous, cruel charlatan. Tears for the blood I am forced to share with him. Tears of freedom, of release. Of rest, for the first time in my life, from the work of trudging through the world with him chained to me. Tears to wash the world in which I now live. The beautiful world. Or the world I can now see to be beautiful.

Footsteps scrape behind me; I turn, blinking to focus. The priest, a royal cloaksman, and Philippa, looking wan but well, dressed in a spring-green woolen gown. Wagging next to her our father's dog, Dux, his leash loose on her wrist.

6.

It rained. I heard it from the place where I sleep, in the room where the Broom-woman works and sings, washes and cooks all day.

In my sleep there was no rain. I smelled and saw people like me, and a few cats too, local boys, and we were running over the grassy hills of the painting in the hall—flat from every angle but they had height if you ran fast enough—and we must rescue someone, a fair maiden with bright eyes and a long curling black-and-white coat, whose master had locked her in a tower...

Sleeping, I saw a strange thing, a silveryblack person much like me and also much like a cat, with small paws and a pointed snout. He ran with us for a little while, carrying something on his back I could only smell, and could not see.

Then I woke with a start, because the Broom-woman was getting ready to go, and I stood up to make sure she knew I was awake. Then she did go, and the fire was low and safe, so I lay down again in my place near it.

But I did not sleep again, because I had to be awake to think about the small-pawed thing I had seen in my dream. How strange it had smelled! How familiar, and yet I could not remember the word either in my own tongue nor that of the cats or the mice or the rats or the birds or the Men or the Women.

The door opened again in the darkness and I rose roaring as I knew I must and then I stopped, because my mouth filled with water, and my heart woke from a deep sleep and romped in my ribs, hurting them, for it was one of the Girls, the First Girl. She bent to me, held my face in her cold soft hands, the sweet smell of her. She said my name, Girl I love, Girl I have not seen for so long only my nose remembered.

Master swayed downstairs, holding a light; a smell of poison breathed from him, his face and his clothes, and I worried, but he and First Girl spoke, and they went upstairs again.

No one called me. I did not hear the short, sharp sound they use for me. But I am so rarely allowed upstairs—I was overcome, as if I were a puppy, with the need to see and smell it, and I followed quietly behind First Girl. Bare stone the stairs. Downstairs is all rugs.

They began quietly to speak. Then loudly, then First Girl snapped out an arm—so fast! I believed she was going to hit my Master but she struck something else instead, on the table next to him, and there was a bright noise as it hit the floor, and my whole head filled with the reek of it. Poison, something sweet, something rich, already on his breath. I backed away from it, trying to clear my head.

He roared like me. I heard no words in it. From his hip he took something small, no longer than his finger, like a flame, and I was dazzled.

First Girl roared back, her voice high and pure. First Girl was not afraid. My Master brandished the flame: I know I saw it. It did not smell like burning. First Girl spun, her clothing flying out, and she went down the stairs and I followed her, and I think she still did not see me. Then she went back outside, the opened door admitting a sweet breath of rain, as if a cloud had blown inside. She slammed it shut.

I could not stop thinking about the poison. Something else, too—the word I wanted was up there. I did not want to lick the liquid (though my mouth again filled with water, thinking about it) but I wanted to sniff it again. Then I hoped I could stop myself from licking it. Important to have restraint. Not a puppy any longer—puppy days long past.

Back upstairs, marveling at it, uncertain. Claws loud with my steps. In the room I had so rarely entered, the smell of the poison on the floor growing stronger by the minute, wetting the stone so that it was as dark as the night sky, a sky filled with intensely near stars. My Master picked his way past these, shouting and weeping. His nose watered. His feet were in light coverings, not shoes. He left behind two small dots of blood as he walked through the stars and the wet. Still he swung the flame in his hand. Still he spoke to no one, loudly.

Did he see me?

I do not think he did. Because as he stumbled to the window and opened it—breathed deep—then vanished—I do not think he would have wanted me to be the first to know that Men could fly.

7.

Judeth watches me, her face wet, wary, not twisted with grief. I suppose I should not expect it to be. I always come to things expecting too much.

I drop the leash and let Dux run to her as best he can—he is old, his black fur graying at the muzzle, and he is thin besides. Father probably was not feeding him, counting on his housekeeper to do it, and she probably was too run off her feet to take care of both of them.

We stand beside the body, listening to Dux's happy, panting breath. The corpse looks . . . well, drowned, I suppose, is the most accurate thing to say about it. In my most recent memory of him, the night before last, he was crimson with drink and rage, so angry I thought for a moment, hazed in the brandy fumes, that he was physically *expanding*—like a frog.

I look down at our fingertips on the gray stone table, a handspan apart, no two sets of hands ever more different in the world. Judeth's are roughened from her work, spotted with dyes and strange substances, flecked here and there with burns and scars. Mine are powerful, knotted, and yet silky from the constant immersion at the dairy.

"I've been accepted to St. Algomir's," I say quietly.

She gasps, and even flinches—I know how she feels. I did the same when I received my letter. To be accepted into any program of wizardry is a stroke of luck, but to get into the most prestigious in the entire quingdom, to be the one out of the ten thousand applicants for each spot, that is fortune and terror nearly unheard of.

Eventually she manages, in a stiffly formal tone, "Congratulations, Philippa. I suppose it's a terrible shame that Father missed the news."

"I went to see him," I tell her. "On Monday. To tell him." The room is darkening around me the way it did when the constable knocked on my door to give me the news. Or no, because that had not been so bad. More the way it did when I read the report of the coroner, stating the time the body had been discovered.

Judeth stares up at me, stunned, trying to put the pieces together, just as I did. "*You* were there? When?"

"Around ten o'clock." And I tell her the rest, quietly, so the priests cannot overhear: housekeeper gone, Dux waking him up, the fight, the knife.

I leave out the last thing, because I am not sure of it anyway, and it was already dark, and you see things in the moonlight—perhaps, perhaps not, something in motion as I walked down the street and glanced back at the house. Perhaps, perhaps not the sound of something hitting the water. But things are allowed to move. And people throw things into the canal all the time. Probably I saw nothing. So she doesn't need to hear it.

"I thought maybe," she finally says, and chokes on the rest, even reaching for her throat. Before I can stop myself I take her shoulder, turn her to one side, open three of the buttons on the high neck of her gown. Her breath does not ease. "I thought you . . ."

I shake my head. Her eyes fill with tears again, and she turns from me, and at last her own pain slices through the strange cold heavy coat I seem to have worn for so many sleepless hours. She stifles her thick sobs exactly the way she did when we were children, before she learned to hold even that inside, to compress it into a piece of coal, dull and inert. I know why she weeps.

"I'm sorry," I whisper. "He was alive when I left. But . . . I'm sorry for more than that. I'm sorry for everything. For not calling on you, for not going to the shop. I thought it might be . . ." I struggle against the hardness in my own throat, lodged there like a stone. I hope the dead are really as dead as we're taught, and his spirit can hear none of this, even if the gods can. "I thought you wouldn't want to see me. Be reminded of home, of family. Because our family was never . . . I mean, all I ever felt in that house was hunger to get out."

She nods, though I think she's not really listening. I have disappointed her again, even though the outcome is the same, just as the old days. I didn't believe her; she left anyway. It made no difference. The only difference my belief would have made would have been here, now, today.

"It's all right," she finally says. "We've all missed our chances. You, me. Him. It doesn't matter."

"He didn't leave a will," I tell her. "We checked, when they let me in the house again to get Dux. Just a lot of books, scrolls, artifacts, and spelled knickknacks. Goodness only knows if any of it's valuable. We inherit whatever's left after the Society gets repaid."

"Well, that's all right," she says, and manages a laugh at last, thin and croaking. "No skin off my nose; I haven't seen a penny off him since I left."

"We might not see one now he's gone, either," I say, and turn to her, and wait for her to turn back to me. It takes a long time; it looks like it hurts. "Come with me," I tell her. "My scholarship is enough for us both—or you can find work at one of their apothecaries. We'll take Dux. Nothing is holding us here."

She stares up at me, her mouth trembling—ready to laugh at herself for believing me, ready to make herself the butt of the joke before I can. Not this time, I want to tell her. Never again.

"I think I'd better say yes, Pip," she finally whispers. "If only because he would hate it so much. But I suppose it doesn't matter, now he's freed us."

"*We* did that, not him. We did that when we left. Nothing to do with him. Alive or not."

She bends and recovers Dux's leash, and hesitates only for a moment when I hold out my hand to her. Then she takes it, squeezing hard with her icy fingers, and we return to the doorway. We must let the priest know that we have said our goodbyes and no more need be done.

BECOMING FOSSILS

Darcie Little Badger

Vita stood on the edge of Lake Coraline, which resembled a fresh crater on the moon. From her vantage point, she could discern a tangle of green leaves and brown branches in the center of the dead lake. Otherwise, the earth supported little life aside from tufts of purslane that grew from cracks in the ground. The weeds crunched under Vita's hiking boots as she walked into the natural depression, heading toward an oasis of fruiting mulberry trees that—by all accounts—shouldn't exist.

Mid-hike, Vita plugged a lipstick-sized mic into her visor, activated the audiovisual recording function, and began to talk.

"I knew the lake before its waters vanished, when it was a round glittering of blue in the woods behind Merry Heights Apartments. My childhood home of Victor, Iowa, was constructed over an extinct seabed, slabs of fossil-rich limestone frosted by soil. Wherever water flowed, I found the bead-like fragments of crinoid stems, the honeycomb print of brain coral, and ridged shells in the exposed white rock. So I wasn't surprised when—while building castles in the mud of Lake Coraline—I wrapped my fingers around a flat chip of limestone with a horn-shaped lump. First, I dunked the rock in the shallows, like an otter cleaning its food, to rinse away the coat of muck. Then, I called my older brother, Mark. 'Hey,' I shouted. 'Look!' I was jumping at the bit, so excited to share my exquisite piece of ancient history."

Whatever happened to that fossil, the one that started it all?

"Mark's head—imagine a boy with drooping black curls and skin tanned dark under the piercing sun—popped out of the water about thirty feet away. AR visors weren't waterproof in the forties, so his eyes were bare and bright. My poor brother had been saddled with babysitting duty, which meant he'd dragged me to Lake Coraline, where he could swim laps. The public pool was too crowded in the summertime, and he had to stay in practice for the high school swimming team.

"I said, 'A horn coral! It's perfect!' and then brandished the fossil, as if holding a jewel. Its delicate ridges were inked by mud. Not chipped or anything! It seemed impossible that brutal eternity hadn't damaged the fossil."

Vita paused, unsatisfied. The podcast leaned into drama, but "brutal eternity" was a little extreme. The fossil had been moldering in the ground for four hundred million years.

"Scratch everything after 'Not chipped or anything,'" she corrected. In the distance, the mulberry trees seemed no closer. Vita continued.

"Mark front-crawled to the bank. His powerful kicks clouded the water. 'Let me see,' he said. After ambling ashore, my brother took the fossil and turned it over in his hands. 'That's a good one,' he assessed. 'Keep it. Be careful, though . . .'

"I asked, 'Why?' And I wondered: Is there a law against stealing fossils from the woods? At the Devonian Gorge in Iowa City, you can't remove any trace of the prehistoric ocean.

"Mark explained, 'There's fishhooks in the ground.' He returned the horn coral, adding, 'and bodies.'

"At nine years old, I was already too mature for my brother's attempts to scare me, but he hadn't caught on yet. Endearing, really. So I pretended to believe him, leaned forward like a confidante and whispered, 'What bodies?'

"'Victims,' he replied. 'Where do you think criminals dump their evidence, Vita?' He pointed at the lake with his lips, pursing them slightly and turning toward the water. My brother said, 'There's probably hundreds of skulls in the mud, becoming fossils.'"

A tan skink raced across Vita's path. It was the first living creature she'd seen in the craterous depression. Even the gnats, which had engulfed her on the hike to Lake Coraline, were gone. She'd have to recall that ominous detail for the podcast. *The lizard and I were the only two creatures in the lake,* she brainstormed. *Even the biting flies, starving for sweat, wouldn't follow me. What did nature know?*

"Next came my favorite part of playing scared," Vita continued. "I lost my concerned expression, grinned back at him, and crowed, 'They aren't dumped here, dumbass.' A term of endearment between siblings, really. As my brother watched, I poked the ground. 'The bodies are thrown in the deep water. You know. Where you swim.'

"Mark's own smile only sharpened. 'Oh yeah?' Smug bastard. Sorry, Mom. He turned his lips toward the tree line, the oaks and maples that abruptly stopped growing forty feet upslope, as if repelled by Lake Coraline. 'Can't you remember? The water used to be there.' He stood, shrugged tension from his shoulders and shook out his arms. Droplets of water and mud splattered on my forehead; I wiped them off with a loud, 'Ugh.'

"'You're digging in the deep end,' Mark said. And with that, my brother returned to his laps.

"He was right. The lake was shrinking.

"And I'd been wrong. He could still scare me."

Although Vita spent her childhood in a world of unlimited tap water, by age nine, she'd already sensed the early stages of the thirst crisis. There'd been her parents' endless complaints about the utility bills, the rationing, the conservation lessons in school. And there'd been the day her best friend, Aimee, cried during recess because "Mommy says we're all going to die."

Then, change happened quickly. The world of her youth seemed like a dream.

Into her mic, Vita said, "Over the years, the waters of Lake Coraline retreated, revealing fresh chips of ancient limestone containing trilobites bent into crescents; fanned shells; flattened sea lilies with their arms splayed, as if pressed within a book; branching and brain coral. Tourists in khaki pants who carried clacking sacks full of fossils gathered to mine the banks of Lake Coraline. It was a weird bonanza; in Iowa, it normally takes a great force—such as catastrophic flooding—to unearth such a high concentration of Devonian fossils. In Lake Coraline, they seemed to be bubbling up, but—and correct me if I'm wrong—limestone slabs are heavy, so that explanation seems impossible.

"I was present during the lake's greatest discovery. Picture this: me, age seventeen, sorting fossil shells when a tourist shrieked, 'Look!' I turned and saw a yellow-haired woman with an ancient visor, maybe third gen, its frame as bulky as welding goggles. In one hand, she carried a garden shovel; with her other hand, she pointed into a knee-deep, grave-wide hole.

"*She found a human skull,* I thought. It made sense, right? In the history of the lake, somebody must've sunk and never reemerged. Spurred by a macabre desire to witness the discovery, I pushed through the gathering crowd to stand on the edge of the pit."

A clipped, high beep rang from Vita's AR visor. Motion detected. Without pausing the recording, she activated the zoom function and scanned the thicket of mulberry trees. "AV, where is movement?" she ordered, and a pink dot appeared on the screen. Zooming farther, she saw a man standing between two trees, his arms slack, his visor looking back at her. He wore a green jumpsuit, which could be an official uniform. Was he guarding Lake Coraline? Did people still visit for the fossils? Surely not. All the limestone was covered by packed dust, and there were no visitors or scientists in sight.

A stranger hides among the mulberries, Vita mentally narrated. *What does he want? Is it the same thing I want? Answers?* She waved. The man raised a hand in acknowledgment. Then, he ducked out of sight.

"The bottom of the hole," Vita continued speaking, "was a shelf of limestone full of oddly shaped brown fossils that resembled puzzle pieces, as if a large stone eggshell—or skull—had cracked and scattered its shards across the ground. Among the puzzle pieces, the woman had uncovered a thick ring, about two inches wide. It resembled a stone iris, which wasn't too far from the truth. Using my visor's visual search function, I identified the structure as a fossilized scleral ring.

"The tourist had uncovered pieces of a Devonian giant, the massive Dunkleosteus. The biggest fish of its time. Imagine a hungry-hungry-hippo mouth with a crushing bite. The armored fish was an apex predator in the warm prehistoric sea.

"After that day, Lake Coraline closed to the public. Sometimes, when I wasn't studying for college exams or visiting friends in Iowa City, I climbed to the apartment roof to watch the paleontologists work. The glittering blue waters were no longer visible from my home.

"Lake Coraline vanished during the great collapse. By that point, my voice was my livelihood, so I moved west to escape the dust. Mark stayed with my parents, all of them holed up in Merry Heights, which had expanded to include a solar dome with a general goods shop and a spigot connected to the Midwest hydration pipeline.

"I largely forgot about Lake Coraline," Vita concluded, "until my brother called two years ago. 'Hey, sis,' he said, 'the water's coming back.' Had to be. Lush mulberry trees were growing in the deepest part of the crater bowl. He sent photos. Said there were scientists looking for water, with no good news. And yet, the mulberry thicket was spreading. Mark sent me photos. He even tasted the berries, which were foul and had no seeds. 'They're a weird breed,' he speculated."

If so, they were a breed of mulberry that could survive in an arid crater. Vita wanted to visit them before the site closed a second time, biologists gathering samples and hoping for a miracle fruit. In a rare show of material generosity, her producer had paid for the shuttle to Iowa. "If there's something special about those plants," he'd said, "you can turn this into an investigative season."

"And if they're just mulberries?" she'd asked, never one to count her chickens before they hatched.

"It's still a mystery, Vita," he'd reassured her. "And we'll have the scoop."

"How do they grow so green?" she narrated, now approaching the thicket, which resembled a single blob of dense, green-leaved branches, rather than a dozen separate trees. Within the tangle were clusters of deep purple and red berries; some were so ripe, they oozed dark juice. "I'm here."

Vita cut the audio recording. *Fruit the color of bruises,* she thought, extending a hand to pluck a ripe mulberry from its branch. *They taste of . . .*

She took a bite but immediately spat it out. Once, Vita poured salt instead of sugar into her coffee. That's what the berry tasted like: saline and vaguely bitter, with no trace of sweetness.

"They'll make you sick," said the jumpsuit man, who rounded the thicket. His AR visor was shaped like a pair of wraparound sport sunglasses, complete with mirrored glass. A fabric badge on his chest read: M. H. SECURITY.

"What are they?" Vita now questioned whether the trees were actually mulberry, although her quick image search returned a 100 percent match for the species *Morus rubra.*

The man, who was in his midtwenties, a full generation younger than Vita, shrugged. "Something gross."

"Is that why you're here?" she asked. "To stop people from eating poison?"

"Nah, all that'd take is a sign. I'm here because freaks keep breaking the law in this valley, and my employer"—he tilted his head toward the distant Merry Heights Apartments—"is fed up. So. Why are *you* here?"

If she said the wrong thing, he might kick her out before she gathered samples. A student botanist from the University of Iowa had agreed to analyze the mulberries for a modest fee. "Just visiting family," she said. "They live in here—"

He crossed his arms. "Name and apartment number?"

"Roswell, N-1709."

For a moment, the guard stood stiffly and quietly, no doubt comparing her information to a list of tenants. Then, he thrust his hands into his pockets and leaned back. "You're taking a walk, then?"

"That's right." Her inner podcaster, always looking for a story, added, "Is it safe? If there's a lot of crime, maybe I should leave."

"Just people dumping stuff." He patted a stun gun at his hip. "I'm on the job. Did you bring a respirator?"

She shook her head: no.

"Better hurry, then. There's a thick wind coming from the south."

That'd be dust from the earth or haze from the city; either way, she didn't want to breathe it. After thanking the guard, Vita made a quick loop around the thicket, and once she stood on the far side, she extracted a pair of glass vials from her tote bag. The leaves were unpleasantly rough and fibrous between her fingers, but Vita plucked several off their twigs and filled a vial with green samples. In the other vial, Vita deposited an assortment of berries ranging from nearly black to pale red. Then, she resumed recording.

"As I approached the trees, a gentleman from M. H. Security stopped me. He's employed by the residential hub that owns the land. People have been using the dead lake as a garbage dump . . ." Was that what the guard had said? Quickly, she rewound her footage and rewatched their exchange in AR. The first-person video played on a rectangular box that hovered in the top right of Vita's vision, and their dialogue chirped through speakers in the black temple hook.

Odd. He'd never specified garbage. What else would people leave here, though?

Again, she remembered the conversation with her brother. Criminals dumped bodies in Lake Coraline, he'd claimed. Maybe once upon a time, before the waters vanished. There'd be no point anymore. You'd have to dig a grave in the dust and limestone; you'd have to operate without cover, since the forest had shriveled away, reduced to an army of desiccated stumps.

Sweat beaded on her chest and temples; a drop slid down her lip, and she licked it. The mulberry had been saltier.

"Inedible fruit," she said. "It's a bitter discovery. A bittersweet discovery. A bitter reality. Hmm." She'd tweak the wording later.

Suddenly, a force resisted her steps, pressed on her shoulders and against her chest. Vita inhaled deeply, but the breath felt shallow, doing little to satisfy her thirst for oxygen. Her chest seized, and she coughed. What was happening? The winds hadn't picked up; if anything, the air had gone completely still.

She tilted her head back and grasped at her throat. Wisps of light—like the sun reflecting off ripples and filtering through deep water—danced overhead. Vita felt the instinct to kick and swim up, as if she'd find breathable air above her head. Instead, she jumped: rising, but too slowly. Vita was on the verge of fainting, gray spots spreading across her vision, when the pressure simply disappeared. She landed on her hands and knees and sucked in a deep breath. The air chased her wooziness away, left her trembling with near-death adrenaline.

For a moment, it'd felt like she'd been floating.

Vita scrambled upright, pulled her collar over her nose, and ran upslope. She didn't see smog or dust, but she'd nearly choked on something. Perhaps it was an invisible threat, a heavy toxic gas that had settled in the depression. Once she safely passed the crater's edge, Vita paused, turned, and searched for the guard. He was nowhere in sight.

Just in case, she'd warn the Merry Heights superintendent; there was something wrong in the old lakebed.

The Merry Heights Residential Biome resembled a dome-capped stadium connected to a blocky tower. The apartment windows were numerous, deep-set, and highly reflective. There were no balconies anymore. As Vita jogged toward the guest entrance, she gazed at the glinting tower and wondered if anyone looked back at her. "I feel watched," she narrated. "Scrutinized. Recognized."

By pulling a lever, she unsealed the airtight outer door of the apartment building, wrenched it open, and stepped into the box-shaped, drab intake room. After sealing herself inside, Vita slumped wearily against the wall. She rubbed a hand across her brow, which was slick with sweat.

In a couple seconds, the security cam AI identified Vita, the inner door automatically unlocked, and she entered the small ground-floor lobby. Still worried about the guard, Vita pressed a red help button on the wall. After a few seconds, a perfunctory voice asked, "Managerial office. How can I be of service?" The speakers were hidden somewhere overhead, perhaps embedded within a drab off-white ceiling tile.

"I was taking a walk near the trees," she said. No need to clarify which trees, since the forest was gone. "For a moment, I couldn't breathe. The air felt like cement in my lungs; I choked and nearly fainted. Could you check on the guard?"

"Of course."

"Thank you."

Again, the response was a clipped, "Of course."

Satisfied that she'd done her civic duty, Vita turned to the elevator and pressed the up button. The silver doors parted, and she stepped into the boxy space. "It seems like the rumors are correct," she narrated as she ascended to floor seventeen. "There's something odd about the dead lake. Dangerous, even. But what?"

Before she could answer that question, the elevator dinged, and its doors slid open. Her brother, Mark, stood in the hall, holding a plate of their mother's "kitchen sink" cookies, whose recipe changed based on the available ingredients. Mark had become gaunt over the years, just like Vita. "Did you say something?" he asked.

Vita hadn't expected to see him; Mark lived in the western building, cohabitating with a group of ten other singles. They pooled incomes to rent the upper penthouse and lived in enviable luxury. Vita's brother worked in marketing, although she didn't know what that entailed, just that it was generally more impressive than "podcast host and part-time stockroom worker."

"I'm investigating Coraline," she said.

"Oh, yeah. Mulberry land. That place is spooky." He lingered in the hallway, clearly eager to scare her, as if nothing had changed between them in twenty-five years. Vita raised her eyebrow. "You know that for a fact?"

"Ask anyone here," he said. "Lately, we've all had inexplicable experiences."

"For the record," she urged, "what's yours?"

"My succulent died," he said, "during the last tap restriction."

"When was that?"

"May, and it lasted three weeks. We were down to two liters of water a day. No showers, obviously. I smelled like a skunk by the end of it; at one point, I nearly bathed myself in dust like a sparrow."

"Ugh."

"I know, right? Anyway, the cactus barely survived. Its paddles turned yellow, and its stem withered. So Benny—you know my friend Benny, the finance guy?—he said I should try planting it where the mulberries grow. What do you know? The cactus bounced back. Resurrected, almost. Now, that's what everyone in the apartment does when our houseplants are thirsty. We put them in the center of the crater. It usually helps."

"How do you explain that?"

He shrugged. "Damned if I know. But the place is getting a reputation for miracles. You aren't the only visitor we've had lately. Why do you think there's security now?"

"Trespassers?"

"Bingo." Mark grabbed a cookie off the top of the pile and took a large bite. Crumbs snowed onto the threadbare blue carpet. "Strange people, Vita."

"Well, they might be on to something," she insisted. "Are you sure it's not a miracle?"

Her brother pressed the up button embedded in the wall. With a ding, the elevator doors opened. "Guess that's what you're here to find out," he said. "It's good to see you again, little sister."

She nodded. "Glad to be home."

That night Vita sat at a desk in front of the window in her parents' guest room and reviewed her recording. She'd transferred the audiovisual data to her laptop and converted her chatter into a written transcript. Methodically, Vita deleted the rubbish until she was left with about seven minutes of usable dialogue. She felt like Dr. Frankenstein, stitching together a story from different fragments of her ramblings.

The hook was interesting enough, but there were still too many unanswered questions. Maybe, come sunrise, she could track down the security guard for an interview. He'd know more about the trespassers and their goals. Maybe even have a freaky story of his own.

Satisfied with her work, she dimmed the lights. The nearly full moon shone through the window. Contemplatively, Vita peered outside.

Beyond the field of stumps, Lake Coraline glinted in the moonlight. For a moment, Vita thought its waters had returned, but no. That was impossible. She must be looking at a mirage, the air shimmering like ripples. Quickly, she grabbed her visor from the desktop and started recording. The video captured the illusion.

There had to be a scientific explanation for the mulberries, for Mark's resurrected plant. For the fossils bubbling to the surface as Coraline died. For Vita's near-death experience, when she'd felt trapped within deep water. For the silvery, spectral ripples.

Lakes couldn't become ghosts.

While using the zoom function, Vita noticed a figure standing on the edge of the glistening depression. It was too dark outside, the person too distant, for her to see many details. However, she did make out a large bundle in the figure's arms.

"A body," Vita thought. And just as quickly, she corrected, "It could be anything." However, her brother's stories haunted her. If the lake could resurrect plants, why not humans, too? Is that what the trespassers believed? Were they carrying their dead to the lake? Burying people near the mulberry roots?

There was just one way to find out.

After slipping into her hiking boots and grabbing an emergency respirator (just in case), Vita quietly left the dark apartment and entered the elevator, which whirred and thunked ominously as she descended to the ground floor. She passed through the empty lobby and out the set of doors. The air felt cool and dry against her face, different from the nightly mist she remembered from childhood.

Ground crunching underfoot, she wove through the eerie graveyard of stumps. *Eerie graveyard.* That'd be a suitably melodramatic line in her podcast, but she was reluctant to narrate her journey, as if afraid to be noticed.

Wasn't that the goal?

By the time Vita reached the edge of the lakebed, the figure was already halfway to the mulberry trees. Up close, Vita couldn't see the mirage. Instead, the crater and dusty landscape had a lunar quality, made her feel like an astronaut on Earth. After fastening her bulky respirator over her mouth, Vita pushed forward. She moved quickly, racing her better judgment. *It's safe,* Vita reassured herself. If there'd been toxic gas in Lake Coraline, the higher-ups would've issued an emergency notice. Plus, the stranger was doing fine. They could be her canary in a coal mine.

What a terrible thought.

As she entered the deeper crater, Vita vividly remembered her struggle to breathe, the way she'd felt a great pressure on her body.

She had to warn them: Get out of Lake Coraline.

"Excuse me!" she called, her voice muffled by the mask. "Hello?"

In the distance, the shadowy figure paused. Still cradling the bundle, they turned and looked her way. She couldn't see their face; it was covered in either shadows or dark fabric.

"I'm a reporter!" Vita shouted, just in case they mistook her for security. "I need—"

The figure ran.

"Shit." She hesitated, unsure whether to pursue them.

In that moment, Vita felt a familiar change in pressure, a weight enveloping her body. Despite the respirator, when she tried to breathe, her lungs seized. Ahead, the stranger thrashed in slow-motion, their clothes expanding fluidly around them. Then, the world dimmed, and Vita felt her feet leave the ground.

Chest aching, she floated in the memory of Lake Coraline. If Vita didn't escape, she'd suffocate; so she kicked her legs and swam up. One meter, two, three. Five meters high, and her head finally broke the surface of the dead lake. She sucked in desperate gasps of air, bobbing.

How long would Lake Coraline manifest this time? A few seconds? Minutes? Impossible to guess. There weren't textbooks on supernatural landforms. It might be the first of its kind. In any case, Vita was trapped. If the ghostly waters disappeared, she'd fall and—at best—break her legs. But she couldn't dive closer to the ground. They'd rule her death "by asphyxiation" and close the books without a second thought.

When they were young, how did Mark swim quickly? He'd windmill his arms and kick. So Vita did the same, her movements clumsy but desperately quick. There were no audible splashes, the only sound her labored breaths, but she felt cold droplets against her face as she pressed ahead. Vita squeezed her eyes shut, afraid to see the ground far below. Any moment, she could plummet and land pancake-flat against the hard-packed dirt.

It happened in a heartbeat: liquid became air. Her stomach lurched as she dropped.

"Fortunately, I'd reached shallower waters," Vita said; she sat within her make-shift recording studio, a closet coated with black foam. A studio mic was positioned against her lips. "There were no broken bones, but the impact winded me, made me claw at my chest, unable to scream. When I regained my breath, I sprinted to safety and collapsed over the stump of an old oak tree, with its rings against my cheek. Wide rings near the center, when the years were fruitful. Narrow rings near the edge. Barely any growth. And then none, never again. I wanted to cut down the mulberry trees, search for rot within their heartwood, but that'd involve returning to the lake, and I'll never make that mistake again. I don't know if the stranger survived. There were no reports of their death. However, after that night, access to the crater was strictly limited.

"When I share my video of the incident, you must trust that it's not doctored. Don't visit the lake to check; it's off-limits now, surrounded by an electric fence. My brother says that people still try to break through. Some of them are sick. Other carry bags of seeds, as if the lakebed might become an orchard or golden cornfield. I pity them. A ghost cannot heal us. A ghost cannot nourish our crops. The mulberries grow without seeds, are nothing but salt within purple skin."

Vita looked down. In her hand, she held a fossil shaped like a horn.

It resembled an empty cornucopia.

"That much is certain," she concluded.

SEVEN BELLS

Garth Nix

It was not immediately obvious that the village of Shrifby was located on an island bordered by two arms of the river Dynwell. Neither watercourse was wide, though both were very deep and fast-flowing, and the southern branch was overgrown with alders and silver birch that grew tall and fell toward each other, so the river ran for miles under a continuous green arch. A traveler coming from the south might cross the bridge without even realizing a river ran underneath, particularly if they were hard of hearing or unobservant.

The northern arm of the river was more evident, as a weir had been built to raise the water level for the mill and there was the rush of water from pool to millrace and back to the river again. But very few travelers ever left the village in that direction. The road did not even continue north of Shrifby, instead circling the village green before turning back on itself like a serpent eating its own tail. There was an old ford downstream from the mill, and a track northward beyond, but it was not kept up and was unsuitable for wheeled vehicles of any kind.

The reason no one went farther in that direction was because Shrifby was the northernmost village of Ancelstierre, only twenty-two miles south of the Wall and the Old Kingdom beyond. Its continued existence was entirely due to its sheltering, swift rivers, barriers against the Dead and other things that might come when the wind blew from the north. The local inhabitants knew the value of fast running water, stout stone walls, and heavy oaken doors and shutters, and incomers who lived there long enough would come to know this too, and to accept things that they had once believed mere superstition.

Visitors, unless their coming coincided with some terrifying incursion from beyond the Wall (which they managed to survive) did not think there was anything unusual about Shrifby other than its distance from civilization and its backwardness. Few noticed the total absence of telegraph or electrical posts and lines, or the unusual stone bell tower, presuming it to be a relic of some distant, long-ago time of war.

A quaint and picturesque village, living in the past, the only curiosity about it was the prohibited military zone beyond, which most southerners presumed to be a typical army land grab for their exercises and firing ranges and so forth, perhaps secret testing of things forbidden by international treaty, like the newly invented machine guns or constantly more terrifying explosives. That would explain the generally low, but constant casualty rate from what was, at this time, known as the Northern Military Area. Always more dead than wounded, and numerous cases of nervous breakdown. Obviously caused by experimental weapons and exercises gone wrong. But only those officers without connections or influence, and second-rate units, were sent to the forts dotted through the area. So the losses were acceptable. No further explanation was wanted, ignorance was to be preferred.

Benjamin Minoy came to Shrifby as just such an ignorant southerner. A huge, barrel-chested seafarer, clad as he nearly always was in a massive brass-buttoned peacoat so dark blue it was almost black, lighter blue woolen trousers and boots, and a ship's officer cap balanced on his blocky head. His white stubbled hair was razored close, in contrast to his impressive mustache and beard, both of which still retained some glimmer of red among the white.

His hands, which were large and powerful, were mottled with faded, ancient, and immovable stains of oil and grease and scars from long-healed burns, because Benjamin Minoy was a ship's engineer. Though he had long been a *chief* engineer, most recently of the *Seacliff*, the fastest and biggest transoceanic liner ever built. Despite leading a crew of more than two hundred engineers, machinists, and stokers, not a day went by he didn't get his hands on some machinery, big or small.

"The axel, this side, it needs some grease," he instructed the driver of the donkey cart that had conveyed him from the railway station at Bain. "Kenton's Number Five, I'd recommend. And the rubber on the tires, it's mortal perished. You should have changed them long since, and then I'd not have felt every bump and stone on the road, and you would not be lacking a gratuity."

"A what?" asked the driver, a young lad of twenty-five or so, who Benjamin suspected was playing the yokel for his own amusement.

"A tip," he replied. "Now, which is the doctor's house? I know it faces the green."

"The new doctor or the old doctor?" asked the driver, the blade of grass he was chewing moving up and down as he spoke.

"Dr. Minoy. My elder sister."

The driver sat up straighter and spat out the grass.

"You're Dr. Minoy's brother?" he asked, the yokel impression sloughed off like an old, loose-fitting coat. "You should have said!"

"I see it makes a difference," replied Benjamin dryly. "I am Benjamin Minoy. My sister is the *old* doctor, I take it?"

"Yes, sir. Retired two years back, and we have Dr. Lejean now. But Dr. Minoy still does . . . some things. She delivered me, you know! I was a breech birth and like to kill mother and myself, but Dr. Minoy saw us right! Most anyone over two and under fifty here and for twenty miles or more was delivered by your sister, sir. And lives saved a thousand other ways as well. Why, Fredric at the Two Rivers, he must have broken every bone in his body, twice or more, he's always falling down the cellar steps, and Dr. Minoy fixes him up every time!"

"I was aware she has a considerable reputation as a midwife *and* surgeon," said Benjamin. He smiled as he recalled his distant youth. "Even as a child she helped our neighbor birth her twins, and certainly she was forever cleaning up my scratches and soothing my bruises and burns with an ointment she made herself. Better than anything I've had since, I'll warrant. But which is her house? I am weary from travel, after the train from Corvere, and the journey here from Bain. I wasn't joking about your tires and the axel, you know."

"I know, sir, I know. It is a mortal problem, the tires wear so here, and the grease itself decays. *You* know, sir."

Benjamin raised an eyebrow. He had no idea what the driver was getting at. He let the question slip away as the man went on to point at the largest and most distinguished-looking home of all those facing the green, a house of mellow, pale pink bricks, three or four hundred years old, with crow-stepped gables, mullioned windows, and a slate roof. Two stories, or perhaps two and a half, with a long attic above. Noticeably, the lower windows had very heavy shutters, though they were open now, and there was a curious kind of birdcage portico of stout iron bars with a gate, which had to be passed through before being confronted with the heavy, iron-studded oak front door, which looked rather like it had once belonged to a castle.

"I'll bring your luggage, sir," said the driver, clicking his tongue at the donkey as they pulled up next to the house. It immediately stopped, and edged diagonally across so it could stretch out its neck and snatch up some luxuriant grass from the border of the village green. This broad expanse was a charming example of its kind, though Benjamin was surprised to see an open drain at its center, cutting it in half, rather than the more traditional pond. A deep drain, it looked, though not so wide a grown person couldn't jump over it.

His sister's house was bordered by an ornamental timber fence, with a narrow front garden, entirely put to lawn, though the neighbors on either side favored more labor-intensive flowers. Benjamin opened the gate, approved the lack of squealing, and trod heavily up the stone flagstone path to the strange birdcage barbican or outwork. There was a ring and chain next to the gate, a painted tin label said VISITORS. PULL CHAIN.

Benjamin did so, noting that the chain was fastened to a rope on a pulley that ran across above his head, through the bars of the birdcage, over to the front door, where it connected with a spring-loaded knocker. He heard the knocker thump upon the door, confirming that it was indeed a massive slab of oak and iron. For good measure, he pulled the ring two more times, enjoying the booming sound and the well-oiled mechanism.

"Yes, yes, I'm coming," said a muffled voice from behind the massive oak door. "You needn't swing on the knocker!"

The door opened to reveal a tall, angular lady of some eighty years, though unstooped and spry. She wore a dark gold scarf to contain her flyaway white hair, and gardening overalls of her own design, of brown sailcloth, the hint of a white silk blouse underneath visible at wrists and neck. Rather eccentrically, at least to some, she had a scabbarded dagger on her brown leather belt.

"Hello, Allie," said the engineer, rather bashfully for so large a man.

"Benjamin!"

"Thought I'd surprise you," said Benjamin. "Always said I'd come and visit, didn't I?"

"You certainly have surprised me," said Allison Minoy. "And as for saying you'd visit, after fifty . . . no . . . fifty-five years, I'd given up any hope of seeing you here!"

"Now, now, we saw each other in Corvere no more than a dozen years ago," said Benjamin. "At my Minna's funeral."

"Fifteen years ago," corrected Allison, shaking her head. Benjamin looked momentarily abashed, but it was the expression of a small boy caught out in some minor misdeed, not of a man who'd forgotten how long ago his wife had died. "But as I no longer go south and you have never, never, come to the north, I had indeed given up hope! But why are we wrangling on the doorstep? Come in, come in! Ned will bring your things."

Benjamin looked back to see Ned struggling to lift his massive sea chest down from the cart, and he had two other bags to come as well.

"I'd better assist the lad," he said. "He's not timbered up to the weight."

"I'm surprised you're still traveling about with that old box," said Allison. "Surely something lighter would make more sense, at your age."

"My age!" scoffed Benjamin. "I may not see three score and ten again, but I can stand an engine room watch or lug about an itty-bitty little trunk. And I can give you six years, sister!"

The itty-bitty trunk in question was three feet long, two feet deep and wide, made from oak, and had brass-bound corners and fittings. Ned had managed to slide it out of the back of the cart on to the ground, but had got no farther. Benjamin strode over, set the trunk on its end, then heaved it up on to his shoulder. Turning about he carried it into the house, calling over his shoulder.

"Bring my other bags, will you?"

"Yes, sir!" called out Ned, relieved to not be burdened with the trunk.

"In here!" called out Allison. "You can have the blue room. Very fitting for a sailor."

Benjamin followed her voice, along the hall, past two doors on the left and one on the right, lowering the trunk to maneuver it through the open doorway of the next room on the right. This was a pleasant bedroom, wallpapered in light blue, dominated by a massive four-poster bed of some antiquity. Two tall windows looked out to a strip of garden and the neighbor's house beyond, heavy shutters opened back, the bar to close them leaning against the wall. Both shutters and bar also would look entirely at home in a castle.

"Is the weather so bad here you need such shutters?" asked Benjamin.

"Not the weather," said Allison. "And it's more of a precaution, so long as the rivers run. I've never talked to you about the unusual nature of this place, have I?"

"No," said Benjamin. "And I admit to some curiosity. That's part of why I've come. But first things first."

He set the trunk down, and gathered his sister into a hug, lifting her heels from the ground. She laughed and kissed him lightly on the forehead, and he released her.

"I remember when you were first old enough to do that," she said. "Twelve, and enormous, and needing an extra dinner every day."

"You've grown lighter," said Benjamin. He patted his imposing stomach, which resonated like a taut drum. "And I try not to eat that extra dinner these days."

"You must be sharp set now though," said Allison. "Did you come from Bain?"

"From Corvere yesterday," said Benjamin. "The sleeper overnight to Bain and then a few hours waiting, till your lad here came to pick up packages and I inveigled him to carry me amongst them. I did have breakfast at the station, but luncheon escaped me, and I'll admit I am ready to eat whatever you might have handy."

"Cook is only in five days, and not today," said Alice. "But she's left a cold rabbit pie, and salad stuff from my garden, and seed cake after, and I've a keg from the Two Rivers, they make a fine beer, or wine from Roger's cellar if you prefer, there's still plenty of his favorite Martenelle laid down."

"I was sorry to hear about Roger," said Benjamin. "He was a good man."

"He was," said Allison. She looked aside for a moment, as if she might see her late husband coming along the hall. He had died six months previously, in his sleep, having reached the age of ninety-one in good health. "Your wreath arrived only two days after the funeral. That's not so bad for these parts."

Benjamin grunted, a sound that Allison immediately understood to mean that this was not good enough for him, but he did not wish to make more of it with his sister, while also promising dire retribution on the carriers who were supposed to have got the wreath there on time.

Ned came in and set the bags down. He hesitated for a moment, then clearly remembered Benjamin's point about the tip, and went to leave.

"Hold on, hold on," said Benjamin. He took a coin from his waistcoat pocket, a gold half-ancient, and handed it over. "Given as Allie saw to your birth, I can forgive a squeaky axel and worn-out tires."

"Thank you, sir!" exclaimed Ned. He practically skipped out, along the hallway, pausing only briefly to carefully shut the front door.

"Generous as ever," said Allison. "Come, let's get you food and drink. And you can tell me why you've come now, after all this time. I can see the cogs turning behind your eyes, Ben."

"Well, you always could," said Benjamin, following her along to the kitchen, a large room that was obviously the heart of the house, warm, expansive and most lived in. Unlike any modern kitchen, it had a small, covered well at one end. "But nothing conspiratorial is going on! Ideas, perhaps. I've bought the old house back, Allie. Treecircle, and the land about, all that grandmother owned."

"And our parents lost," said Allison. She poured hot water from the big kettle on the stove into a bowl, added cold water, and handed Benjamin a towel. While he washed, she went over to the well, knelt down, pushed the cover aside and reached down to a ledge to lift out a pie dish covered with a white linen cloth. "But why? It's too far from the sea for you, surely?"

"I'm retiring, at last," said Benjamin, selecting the chair at the kitchen table he thought most likely to withstand his weight. "Or rather, they're making me retire, come the end of the year. And Cleomine, my youngest—"

"I know who Cleo is," scoffed Allison. "She writes to me. A little more frequently than you do, though I can't fail you as a correspondent, at least. Beer or wine?"

"Beer, please," said Benjamin meekly.

She put the pie on the table, and bustled about getting cutlery and crockery, and salad from a basket also hanging in the well, and filled a jug of beer from the keg on the bench.

"Cleo and the little ones needed somewhere to live, after her Paston was lost at sea, and then Henri and Iseult have moved in as well; Henri's taken over Langham's practice in town, he's doing well, and likely their youngest will join the firm and live at Treecircle too. There's plenty of room, and it makes the place more lively and interesting. But there's still someone missing."

"Who?" asked Allison, expertly carving the pie with a surgeon's scalpel. They both knew her question was unnecessary, but Benjamin played along.

"You, of course," said Benjamin. "That's why I've come. To ask you to live with us all, with the family. In our old house, which I have brought up to date. Electric light throughout, one of those newfangled electric cold cupboards, everything!"

He didn't need to look at the well, or the unlit paraffin lamps on the table and sideboard to indicate he felt he was offering a significant improvement on Allison's way of life.

"It's true we don't have electricity," said Allison, dishing up his meal and pouring his beer in swift, economic movements. "It was tried for a time, by one of the newcomers, who had a hydroelectric plant in the river. But it simply doesn't work consistently here."

"You're avoiding the subject," said Benjamin, though his professional interest was stirred. "I expect it was wired wrong. Is the plant still there?"

"No, it isn't," said Allison. "And no, I'm afraid I won't come and live with you down south, Benjamin. Eat your pie."

She sat down opposite him and poured herself a glass of beer, modest in comparison to the silver tankard she had given her brother.

"Why won't you?" asked Benjamin. "You've retired too. The boy, Ned, told me."

"I still have some responsibilities here," she said. "Connected with the reasons I cannot go too far south. What do you know of the Old Kingdom beyond the Wall, Benjamin?"

"Kind of a nature reserve ain't it, by international treaty?" answered Benjamin. "I do know the seas are treacherous in the extreme. Forbidden waters. Massive gales and a mast-high swell, even worse than the Smasher, the northerly that comes down the west coast. Year-round, it's said."

He refreshed himself from his tankard, wiped his mouth and added, "Biggest blank space on the maps, that's for sure, in this hemisphere at least. Always surprising no one has charted the coasts. I daresay they will soonish. A well-found, modern steamship, a screw vessel, none of your paddle wheelers, it could—"

"The Old Kingdom is *not* a nature reserve," interrupted Allison. She hesitated, and drank a little more beer herself. "This is going to be very hard for you to accept, Benjamin. But I'm going to tell you anyway. The Wall is a divide, and the Old Kingdom on the other side is effectively another world. A world where magic works, and all your modern machines, your steam engines and electric cold rooms and the like, do not. And here, so close to the Wall and the Old Kingdom beyond, we are also affected, though not to such extremes, and not always."

Benjamin set his tankard down slowly, picked up his fork, put a piece of pie in his mouth, and chewed very deliberately.

"Well?"

"I'm thinking," he said, picking up another forkful of pie. "I think best when I'm not hungry."

He continued his comprehensive chewing, washed the last remnants down with another drink, and sighed.

"I can see you believe what you're telling me," he said. "But Allie, we live in a new age. It isn't like when we were children. Electric light has banished darkness and the things we imagined lay in it. Steam has let us go against wind and tide. Bridges span previously uncrossable—"

"I've told you the absolute truth," said Allison crossly. "It isn't childish imagination. I didn't believe myself, when I first came here with Roger, all those decades ago. But he knew, and he taught me. He gave me my Charter mark. Look!"

She tore the scarf from her head and pointed to a brand on her forehead, a small tattoo or painted symbol that to Benjamin's eyes was a daub of luminous paint of some kind, or glue and glitter. It shimmered, reflecting the daylight that shone down through the tall, unshuttered kitchen windows. Some trick of its painting made the mark seem to shift and move, even change color. It was a clever illusion.

"What's that?" he asked uneasily. He had tattoos himself, all seafarers did, but not on his face, and he was shocked to see one on his sister.

"A Charter mark," said Allison. "It's my connection to the magic of the Old Kingdom. One of the magics, at least. And because of that connection, I find it difficult to go too far south, too far from the Wall. And because . . . Charter magic is the only thing keeping me alive."

"What!"

"My heart is fading on me, Benjamin," said Allison, reaching over to grip his wrists. Her fingers were strong, her grip tight. "Worn out. Charter magic keeps it to a steady rhythm, not any modern medicine. And as I said, I have responsibilities here, and I need to stay alive to see to them."

Benjamin shook his head slowly, and looked at the mark on his sister's forehead again.

"How is that done?" he asked. "The shimmering effect?"

"It isn't a trick," said Allison. She looked him straight in the eyes, so like her own. Dark brown, clever eyes that could see to the heart of things. She touched the mark with her forefinger and it grew brighter, and trailing that light, she drew another mark in the air above the table, and then another, and the two hung there, a brilliant tracery of brightness. She gestured and they moved together, and faded away, but as they did so the scent of orange blossom filled the air.

"A simple spell," she said. "A favorite. You loved the orangery at Tree-circle, I remember, just as I did. Oranges do not grow here, but I can have their scent."

Benjamin stared.

"I don't understand," he said, after more than a minute's silence.

"You don't need to understand," said Allison. "Only accept . . . and tell me why you have really to come to see me, after so long."

Benjamin nostrils flared as he drew in the orange scent once more. It lingered strongly, as if they did indeed stand among the orange trees of their old family home.

"I wanted to see you," he began, falteringly. "I did think you might come south, to join the family. But also . . . they tell me I'm sick, Allie. Something growing in my lungs. A darkness, small now, but spreading. There's this new-fangled thing they call X-rays—"

"I know about X-rays," interrupted Allison. "I read the literature. I keep up. They'd be no use here, photographic plates and prints go dark as soon as the wind comes from the north. How long have they given you?"

"Six months to a year," said Benjamin. "I have little trouble now, a cough from time to time. But it will grow far worse, they tell me."

"I'd best take a look at you then," said Allison, all businesslike. She pushed her chair back and stood up. "Come down to the surgery."

"That's not what . . . that isn't why I came," said Benjamin, not moving. "I saw three of the most eminent doctors in Corvere, they all agreed—"

"And likely I will too," said Allison. "But not without examining you first. And while X-rays do not work here, there are Charter magic spells that will let me see what lies beneath your skin. It's possible I can help you, though some things are beyond magic, as well as medicine. Come on."

Half an hour later, Benjamin sat up from the examination table, swung his legs over the side, and reached for his shirt. The examination with stethoscope and tapping he had experienced before, but Allison's use of magic had been confronting. He had felt no pain, but the sensation of gentle fingertips under his skin, moving and pressing, made him feel fey and peculiar, and once when he had dared to open his eyes—kept shut against the strangeness—Allison's face had been obscured behind a shifting ribbon made up of dozens of moving, glowing marks that left trails of light behind them, weaving together to appear almost a physical blindfold, one that rather than blocking her sight allowed her to see deep beneath his skin.

"I'm sorry, Benjamin," said Allison abruptly, before he had even pushed a button through, his shirt open at the front. "The cancer is not only in your lungs, but also in your blood. It is beyond my healing, or of any Charter mage. I doubt you will have three months. I had hoped, arrogantly I suppose, that my magic—"

Benjamin took her hand in his own massive paw.

"Now then, sister," he said. "I knew the case before. I have had my three score and ten, and four more years besides, most of it well spent. And now I have seen you again. I can go back south and likely pass away in our old orangery, pushed there in a bath chair and bothered by my children or grandchildren wishing to fetch me something, or plump up my pillows or the like."

"I hope you will stay a few days, at the least," said Allison quietly. "It would be good to talk. I know so little of your life, really, despite all the letters."

"And I know even less of yours, it seems," said Benjamin. He smiled. "Since you left all this magic stuff out of *your* letters. But I think we must leave any talking for the morrow. I am quite tired."

"As am I," said Allison. "Charter magic exacts its toll. I trust you will sleep well, Benjamin. Cook will be back early, so breakfast will be better than dinner!"

Breakfast was indeed sumptuous. Allie might not grow oranges, but she obtained them from somewhere, and made them into an excellent marmalade. Her cook, who preferred to be addressed as such rather than by her own name, which she refused to offer with a shy glance at Allie to confirm that she was allowed to do so, was a dab hand at bacon and eggs and mushrooms and toast, served piping hot on heated plates.

"Cook hates her given names, both of them," whispered Allie, when the servant had left the room to collect eggs from the coop in the rear garden. "I've sworn never to use either."

"She is well-named as Cook," rumbled Benjamin. He drank deeply from his mug of tea, while Allie sipped from her more genteel cup, the saucer on the table.

"Shall I show you around the village this morning?" asked Allie. There was a twinkle in her eye as she added, "Between the rivers, as we say, and we can end up at the pub for early luncheon?"

"Hmmm—" Benjamin began to express a definite interest in that proposed itinerary, but he was interrupted by the boom of the knocker on the front door, immediately repeated several times, in frantic haste.

"One of my responsibilities, no doubt," said Allison, sweeping from the room, her hand resting in a very determined fashion on the hilt of her dagger. Benjamin hesitated, grabbed the remainder of his toast, shoved it in his mouth, and followed.

A panting, panicked messenger gripped the bars of the portico. A young, flour-stained woman in miller's whites. She started talking before Allison even had the front door open.

"Doctor! Doctor! You need to come quick!"

"Yes, Gwen. Take a breath, hold it for a count of three and tell me what's happened. Slowly."

The young woman took a breath, coughed it out with some saliva, choked on that, then somehow managed to get another breath down and hold it for three seconds. Benjamin noted that his sister had not moved from the front door, and had not opened the barred gate of her little barbican.

"Alf Jerrow's dead! He was digging out the downstream bed—the sluice gate's shut, the millstream's dry—and he found something . . . a box . . . and Chester told him to leave it alone, but he didn't, he opened it, and something inside killed him just like that—"

"And Chester?"

"He was scared, he climbed out when Alf was hitting the chains with his pick, he said he felt something bad—"

"The box was chained?"

"With silver chain, thick as a finger! Alf said it must mean the box was full of treasure!"

"Where is Chester now?"

"He's at the mill, but he's sick, he keeps throwing up!"

"Gas perhaps," suggested Benjamin. "Some underground pocket—"

"No," said Allison. "Gwen, run to the tower and sound the bell. Do *not* go back to the mill. I'll get my things and be there in a few minutes."

"Will Chester be all right?" sobbed Gwen.

"Probably," said Allison. "Go! Go!"

She turned to her brother, edging past him.

"You stay here, Ben. Keep the door and the gate closed."

"I'm coming with you," he said, following her up the hallway. He gripped her elbow, gently enough, but still holding her back. "I don't know what you think is happening but—"

"Something you haven't experienced and won't understand," snapped Allison. She shook him loose, opened a tall cupboard near the front door, and took out not the expected doctor's bag, but a scabbarded longsword on a baldric, which she slipped over her shoulder, settling the weapon at her side. "Silver chains . . . they would only be used to keep something in. Something best never let out. Stay here!"

Benjamin stared at her for a moment, incredulity battling with his usual acceptance of her wisdom. The latter won out, and he turned away to dash into the blue room. Opening his smallest bag, he took a revolver from it, snapped it open and quickly loaded it. But quick as he was, by the time

he came out again, Allison was already shutting the front door behind her. It took him thirty seconds to get that open again, and more than a minute to do the same for the barred gate. For a moment he thought he'd lost track of his sister as he looked up and down the road. Then he saw her walking briskly across the green, already on the other side of the drain.

"Hi, Allie!" he roared. "I'm coming with you!"

He lumbered over the grass, rolling as much as running, as if there were a shifting deck under his size fifteen feet. As he ran, he heard the toll of a deep bell from the tower behind him, followed only seconds later by distant shouts of alarm and shrill cries of "Get inside!" The bell kept booming, it sounded as if the girl, Gwen, was swinging on the rope like a monkey. He saw someone out of the corner of his eye rush around the front of their house and run inside, and he heard the clatter of shutters and doors slamming shut from other houses nearby.

Benjamin carefully jumped the ditch, grunted as his knees complained, and noted the drain was stone-lined and even deeper than he'd thought, with water running very swiftly through it. Beyond it the green slanted down toward the northern arm of the river, and he saw the mill, the waterwheel stopped, the millrace dry, and the weir behind it.

Allison had slowed down and was very cautiously approaching the downstream section of the millrace, where the water would usually rush back to join the river. She looked behind as Benjamin came puffing up.

"Stay back, Ben! Stay back, please!"

He had already slowed. There was a strange smell in the air, akin to the hot metal reek of overstressed bearings about to seize, which he knew well, but there was something else in it, something he didn't recognize, but instinctively feared.

There was also a sound, or maybe only a vibration, something felt as much as heard. It ran through Benjamin from nose to heel, a tremor that made his teeth and every joint suddenly ache, so much that he went down on one knee and took in several, juddering, pain-ridden breaths.

Allison was drawing in the air, her motions swift and sure. Benjamin stared as golden light fell from her fingers and hung in front of her. She sketched a kind of symbol, and then another, and another, and he gasped as she spoke and yet another symbol came from her mouth, brilliant even in the afternoon sun, the brightest of all the marks. It joined the others, and Allison reached out and pulled them together and they became a net of shifting lights, tiny rainbows blinking into brief life all around as she swung the net behind her head and cast it down into the millstream.

The awful vibration ceased, and the smell of hot metal ebbed, the light breeze taking whatever remained away. Benjamin staggered to his feet, but he did not move closer. The revolver hung limply in his hand.

"That will hold back the Free Magic," said Allison dryly. "For a little while."

"Uh, good," said Benjamin slowly. He put the revolver through his belt, and took another breath, very deep, before walking closer, as cautiously as he'd ever approached some mighty engine about to throw a piston, or a boiler with a stuck safety valve.

There was a dead man at the bottom of the millstream, face down in one of the remnant puddles. His rough clothes, heavy, hobnailed boots, the shovel and pick near him, and a ribbon of excavation a foot deeper than the rest of the stream, indicated he'd been engaged in deepening the watercourse. There was a chest in the hole, part of it still buried, but the silver chains around it had been broken and thrown apart, the lock forced, and the lid thrown back.

The net of shimmering marks lay over what was inside, wrapping them close, but it was still easy to see what they were.

"Handbells?" asked Benjamin. "What on earth . . ."

There were seven bells in the chest. The smallest was only a little larger than Benjamin's thumb, the handle a little less; and then they ranged up to the largest, which was the size of his closed fist, the handle half as long as his forearm. They were made of silver, or at least a silvery metal, he thought, and had handles of ebony or some other very dark, dense wood. Six were set in deep velvet cushioning, designed to keep them silent. One, in the middle, had been lifted out and lay athwart the others.

"A necromancer's bells," said Allison. The warning bell in the village tower tolled as she spoke, as if to lend extra emphasis to her words.

"A . . . a necromancer? But, but that's . . . you mean like in those gothic stories mother loved?" asked Benjamin. "Someone who reanimates dead people, to serve their evil purposes?"

"In essence, yes," said Allison. "These must have been buried here long ago, the chest specially made, bound in silver chain, buried under swift running water. But now, one of the bells has sounded. That's what killed Alf Jerrow. And others will die because of these bells, or wish they had. They are necromantic tools, used to raise and control the Dead."

Benjamin opened his mouth to say something to reject this assertion, but he swallowed the words. He'd felt and heard the strange vibration, he'd smelled the smell that was not like anything in his long experience of working with metal. He'd seen her work her magic. He was afraid, and he was afraid what his sister spoke of was absolutely true.

The tower bell clanged out its warning again behind him. Gwen was tiring, or someone else had taken over and was ringing it more regularly, in slower time, thirty seconds between each clamoring call.

"The net will not hold that freed bell long," said Allison, almost speaking to herself. "The bells have names, and each its own powers. But I do not know them, nor which one has rung, or what it can do. I do know they will all seek to sound, that is their nature. And the voice of the one that killed Alf will have been heard far off, perhaps even on the other side of the Wall."

"What... what can we do?" asked Benjamin. "Can you make another... another golden net?"

"Not easily," said Allison. She wiped her forehead, letting her fingers rest on the Charter mark there for a few seconds. "There is no other Charter mage in the village. It will take too long to send to Bain, or Wyverley College . . . or the closest fort. No one can possibly get here before nightfall. No one helpful, that is . . ."

"I don't understand," said Benjamin. He didn't like the mention of *before nightfall* and instinctively looked at the sun. There were probably six hours of daylight left.

"Think of these bells as a very, very dangerous weapon," said Allison. "They must not fall into the wrong hands. But I am afraid that is exactly who will have heard the bell and come looking, and there is no help to be had anywhere close at hand."

Allison pointed down at the middle-sized bell that had been taken from its velvet lined enclosure.

"We have to make sure they all stay silent, and . . . get them away from here. Running water will hold back the Dead, but not a necromancer, nor any living allies they might have."

"I'll put that one back in its spot," said Benjamin, and took a step forward, only to stop as Allison slapped her hand against his chest.

"No! No! We mustn't touch them. They want to be used, to be rung, and you have no defense against them. Nor do I have the strength. We must silence them first, close the chest, rewrap the chain, before we can move it. But I don't know how . . . ah . . ."

She stood back up, coughed and held her side, clearly in pain.

"I'll have to try to make another net—"

"No!" said Benjamin. "If running water is helpful, I can open the sluice—"

"It won't be enough," said Allison. "Not now. I'll have to take them away. But silenced, somehow."

The engineer stared down at the chest, measuring by eye how deep the bells were set, how high the rim, the padding inside the lid of the chest. He looked back at the mill. "There's flour in the mill?"

"Yes, of course. But why?"

"We can pour flour down into the chest, with a little water, to make a thick mixture," said Benjamin hurriedly. "With the lid shut the sludge will still the bells, and that one out of position will be choked, and should slide back into place. I might need help to lift the chest out—"

"No, no help. Not unless we absolutely must," interrupted Allison. She looked at her brother, her expression both fierce and sad. "I am so sorry, you came today of all days. But you are here, and I do not want to risk anyone else. Let's get the flour, quickly! It may work."

"I'll go," began Benjamin, but Allison was already walking fast toward the mill. He lumbered after her, looking back over his shoulder several times, though he didn't know what he feared to see.

"The miller won't answer you," said Allison, as they crossed the courtyard. She headed to the front door of the two-story stone house next to the timber-built mill. The house was entirely shut up, heavy shutters closed on both floors. "No one will, not a stranger, while the warning bell sounds. Knock on the door, will you? I need to catch my breath."

She had a hand to her left side again, and was hunching over, taking slow, deliberate breaths. Benjamin knocked on the door, urgently, and was about to call out when he remembered what Allison had said. She saw him realize, and smiled, before straightening up to speak. She had to wait a moment, as the tower bell boomed out again.

"Jenny! It's Dr. Minoy! I need a sack of flour. Throw one down from an upper window, but don't come out!"

"Jenny is the miller," she said to Benjamin. "Mother of Gwen and Chester."

"The dead man is their father?"

"No, no, Alf does . . . did . . . odd jobs around the village. Ah, the window there."

A second-story shutter edged open, pushed by a muscular arm, followed by the flour-splashed face of a woman of forty or so, who looked down at them with both alarm and suspicion, the latter evidently directed at Benjamin.

"Doctor! Can you come in and see Chester? He's stopped throwing up but he's awful pale—"

"Not yet," called back Allison. "It isn't safe to come out or for me to go in. Keep your door barred. This is my brother, Benjamin. We need a sack of flour *urgently*."

"Two sacks," said Benjamin. "If they're quarter-weight bags."

"Yes, of course, I'll . . . I'll get them," replied Jenny. She pulled the shutter closed after her, and they heard the iron hooks on the inside clang into place.

"Will Chester be all right?" asked Benjamin softly.

"Probably," whispered Allison. "Given he ran away before Alf opened the chest, and he isn't already dead."

She straightened up to her full height and stretched backward, still massaging the ribs on her left side.

"And you?" asked Benjamin.

"I'll survive," said Allison. "I ran too fast across the green, that's all."

Benjamin nodded, not convinced.

"We'll need that bucket as well," said Allison, pointing to a bucket by the side of the horse trough in the courtyard. "I'll bring it, while you carry the flour. You can manage two sacks?"

"Of course," said Benjamin, with a sniff. He regretted doing so, as he caught a slight whiff of the hot metal stench again, and with it came a faint nausea, a feeling of instability through his entire body.

"My net must be close to dissolution," said Allison anxiously. She cupped her hands and called up, "Hurry, Jenny! Hurry!"

The shutter came flying open, with a sack close behind. It landed only a few feet from Benjamin with a thud and a puff of flour, but the strong sack-cloth held. Rather than picking it up, he stepped away, just in time, as the second sack came plummeting down even closer to where he'd been standing.

"Thanks!" called out Allison. She was already heading for the bucket. Benjamin picked up one sack and settled it on his left hip, before picking up the other. They were heavy, close to thirty pounds each, but he managed well enough, while thinking that even a few years past he would not have felt it to be an effort.

Allison grabbed a broom as they left the courtyard and hurried over the weedy verge to the millstream. The awful smell was getting stronger again, and Benjamin found himself puffing while also trying not to breathe through his nose, not that it made any difference, the smell seemed to get in anyway. Bile rose in his throat and he coughed and staggered as they reached the edge. He half lowered, half dropped the sacks, but didn't hesitate, drawing out his clasp knife and cutting the tops of both, one hand clasped across his mouth and nose to try and keep back the racking coughs.

"Pour the flour in!" called out Allison. She threw down the bucket several yards away from the chest, scrambled down the bank after it, and started scooping up water from one of the bigger puddles.

Benjamin lifted a sack and started pouring flour into the chest, but a cough exploded out of him and blew flour everywhere, and he had to kneel down, his legs suddenly unsteady.

"More!" shouted Allison. She threw water from the bucket, still not getting closer than a few feet to the chest.

Benjamin grabbed the second sack and upended it straight down, his head averted. The corrosive odor seemed to rise straight up from the chest, an unseen cloud of something awful, and he couldn't stop coughing, a cough that brought up vomit, but he tightened his mouth and held the sick back and kept the sack in place until all the flour was gone, before he rolled away and had to let it all out.

"It's full up!" Allison called. "The broom! Ben! Use the broom to shut the lid!"

He crawled back again, eyes slitted, mouth clenched though the acrid vomit returned, threatening to come up and out his nose. He reached about blindly till his hand closed on the broom handle. He brought it around and down, made contact with the chest and pushed hard. He heard the lid slam shut, and with it came an immediate lessening of the hot metal stench, the insidious plucking at his bones and joints, the barely restrained fear in his guts. He rolled away again, got up to his hands and knees, and threw up again.

After a minute, the heaving stopped. He looked around and saw Allison climb out of the millstream. She had mud and flour slurry all over her, and looked no less worried than she had before.

"I've wrapped the chain around again," she said. "But it isn't fastened. We need to do that and get the chest out and moved."

"Moved . . . where?" asked Benjamin. He had to turn his head and spit out between the words. He'd never felt so bad, so quickly. It was even worse than excesses with rum back in his cadet years, or the tropical fevers he'd suffered in his years on various ships in the Equatorial Arc.

"Fort Janne, I think," said Allison. "There should be some Scouts there—Charter mages like me—and ordinary soldiers may be of some help. It is closer to the Wall . . . but I can't think of anywhere else. They should have message-hawks, we can send one to get help from the Abhorsen."

"The what?"

"The who," said Allison. "The Abhorsen is . . . hard to explain. Someone who sets things to rights. She can deal with any necromancer who might come for these bells."

"And what are message-hawks?"

"Somewhat like carrier pigeons, one can take a message across the Wall to the Abhorsen. She is a person of great authority over there, in the Old Kingdom. But she will cross to deal with anything necromantic here, this close to the Wall. She saved me from a necromancer once, about twenty years ago. Now, how do we reconnect the chain?"

"Overlap it and bind the crossed links through with a cord," said Benjamin. He got to his feet, wiped his face with his sleeve, and took out a long length of heavy black cord. "Spare bootlace. That should do the trick. I'll—"

Allison took the bootlace from him. He was surprised that his fingers seemed to have little grip.

"No, I'll do it," she said. "Best you don't get too close until the lid is completely shut. I am a little more armored against the effects of Free Magic."

Benjamin opened his mouth to ask what Free Magic was, but shut it again, swallowed unpleasantly, almost retched again, and stuck to talking about immediate practicalities.

"We'd best lash a rope about the chest as well," said Benjamin. "How far is this Fort Janne?"

"Twenty miles, nor-nor-east," said Allison. She climbed back down into the millstream, the bootlace in her mouth. She mumbled up to him, "Or close enough. It is situated a little less than a mile from the Wall."

"We'll need young Ned's donkey, to carry the chest any distance," said Benjamin.

"Yes, we can get it later. There'll be rope at the mill. Look in the shed by the courtyard, call the miller if you need to. Don't let them come out. We still need to hurry."

Benjamin obediently lurched away, forcing himself into a run. He was so tired, ridiculously so. Worse than after a double watch in an engine room, with all the heat and hammering din, the rise and fall and roll of the ship. How could it be worse? It was eerily quiet here now, save for the warning bell, its interval greater now. Whoever was ringing it was also growing tired.

He found the shed, and there was a coil of rope hanging from a hook in the wall. It was rotten, and fell apart under his hand. But there was also a braided leather lunging rein, not in perfect condition but still strong, and at least thirty feet long. He took it off the wall and hurried back, panting and trembling. He almost fell once, but managed to keep his footing.

"Bring it down," said Allie, looking up at him. He saw that she had shifted the chest out of the streambed, and lifted one end up onto the heap of spoil from the digging. The silver chain was back in place, the overlapping ends neatly frapped together with his bootlace. Flour mixture oozed out all around the lid.

"How did you shift it?" he asked, as he clambered down. He was thankful the hot metal smell was gone, only a faint trace remaining, like the hint of smoke from a distant fire.

"It isn't heavy," said Allison. "The timber is only a veneer. I'd guess it's made of several layers of bone, laminated together, with thin silver sheets between. Get that rope around."

"Aye, aye!" snapped Benjamin. He put a loop around the exposed end of the chest, drew it tight, and then began to put several lashings around the chest to keep it tightly closed.

"You haven't forgotten your knots and ropework," said Allison.

"You don't forget the way I learned," said Benjamin, as he tied off the rein, though he thought to himself he was far too slow. His clumsiness would have earned a rope-end across his back on the infamous training ship *All One Argosy*, a leaky, verminous square-rigger known to its cadet crew as the *All One Agony*. "That'll hold. Shall I lift it out?"

"Wait a moment," said Allison. She climbed up the bank. Benjamin watched her crouch and slowly turn her head, carefully gazing in all directions.

"What are you looking for? Surely, no one . . . nothing drawn by that bell could be here so soon? Wouldn't they have to come from across the Wall?"

"We live in a hinterland," said Allison. "There are people and other things, who only look like people, who hide out on this side. They generally lie low, and don't attract trouble, not wishing to take risks for no reward. But now, there is a potential reward. You can bring the chest up."

Benjamin nodded and bent to lift the chest, overcoming the fear he felt even to touch it. But the wood felt like wood under his fingers, the silver chain that brushed his stomach just a chain. It was much lighter than it looked, as Allison had said. He had no difficulty raising it above his head, up on to the bank. He climbed after it, brushing mud and flour mixture more into his trousers and coat than off it.

"Take this," said Allison, lifting the baldric off her head and handing over her sword. "I'll fetch Ned's donkey and a few other things. Let no one approach the chest. Absolutely no one."

"I understand," said Benjamin. The baldric was too short to go over his chest, the pommel of the sword would be under his armpit if he even managed it, so he simply held the scabbarded sword and followed his sister's example, slowly turning to keep an eye out in all directions.

The next fifteen minutes were among the strangest he had ever known. He was very tired, his joints hurt, he couldn't quite get his breath, and he was more apprehensive than he had ever been. The warning bell kept up its mournful toll, but apart from that, it was eerily silent. No birds called, there was no sound from the houses, the pub, the road. Every time the warning bell rang, he jumped and looked at the tower. The sun flashed from the bell as it swung back down. But he was glad of the sun and conscious night would come all too soon.

Allison came back, luring the donkey on with carrots. The animal was not keen to come close to the chest, and tried to eat the carrot and turn away, but Allison kept it coming on. There was a pad on its back, the chest could be lashed on the left side: there was a big water bottle and several sacks on the right, which Benjamin hoped contained food. He knew he could not stomach anything now, but he trusted he would be able to later.

The donkey did not want the chest strapped on its back, but Allison fed it carrots and stroked its nose, so after a few kicks and bucks, the animal allowed it. Benjamin checked the straps for the third time, picked up Allison's sword, and gave it back to her. She shrugged the baldric on, and eased the sword in its scabbard, making sure it would draw easily.

"Do you remember the donkey rides at the seaside?" asked Allison over her shoulder, as she led the donkey away, Benjamin walking beside it. "I think we stopped going to Felamene when I was ten, so you would have been very small."

"I have a faint recollection," answered Benjamin, frowning. He did have a memory of a pebbled beach, playing in the wash of the waves, watching a puppet show . . . and maybe a donkey ride.

"I wanted to be one of the donkey handlers," said Allison. "Better late than never."

They splashed across the ford, and started along the northward track. Though the river's edge was well forested, it was more open farther on, the alders and silver birch replaced by grand oaks, not too close together. Benjamin started to hear birdcalls again, and there were rustlings in the undergrowth, which at first alarmed him, before he recognized it as the work of squirrels and rabbits.

"It's pretty here," he said.

"It is," agreed Allison. She sighed. "But fair country can hide foul danger."

Ben nodded. Coincidentally, the bell tolled behind them as his chin dipped.

"How long will they keep that up?" he asked. "The warning bell."

"Till nightfall," answered Allison. "No one will come out now until tomorrow, and the sun fully risen."

She paused, then added, "I am so sorry you've been caught up in this, Ben."

"I'm not," said Benjamin. "Better I was here."

"We might be able to get to the fort before nightfall, if we push," said Allison. "Are you up to it?"

"Of course," said Benjamin, though he was not at all sure. He was strong, but shipboard life did not lend itself to long walks, and he already felt weak and washed out. "What about you?"

"Oh, I'll make it," said Allison. Benjamin heard the grim determination in her voice, and hoped he'd had something of that in his own reply.

Grim determination was not enough. They made good time for a while, following the remnant path, with Benjamin checking the sun to make sure they were headed at least mostly northward. But they could not keep it up, and once the sun had set, the way became even more difficult. At last they had to stop, both of them exhausted and the night too dark to continue. There was a sliver of a moon, and some few, scattered stars, but neither shed sufficient light for travel.

"I'll gather some sticks for a fire," said Benjamin, after they found a sheltered dip between a great stone and an oak, which had fallen to a forty-five-degree angle but kept growing, its roots arching up to form a natural grotto with the stone.

"No fire, we don't want any attention," said Allison. "Lift the chest down. There's bread and cheese in the bag, and water in the bottle. I'll hobble the donkey."

Benjamin undid his knots, and lifted the chest from the donkey's back. He sniffed as he did so, not because the hot metal stench had come again but because it smelled yeasty, as if the flour mixture inside the chest was becoming dough. The donkey sniffed too, when he set the chest down against the exposed roots of the oak, but quickly turned away, shuffling over to drink water Allison poured in a natural bowl of oak roots, and then to nibble at the undergrowth around them.

"We will go on at dawn, or before, if there is enough light," said Allison. "I'll take the first watch. We'll have to estimate the time from the moon."

"Nay, my watch is a marine chronometer," said Benjamin. "Almost brand-new, and luminous and all."

He took the vaunted timepiece from his waistcoat, and stared at the face. Though the hands and chapters did indeed glow in the dark, the watch had stopped hours ago.

"Bless me! That's never happened!"

"Machine-made things do not fare well close to Free Magic," whispered Allison. She settled down with her back against the great stone, her sword by her side, hilt near her hand. "An older watch might have fared better. Rest now. I'll wake you in four hours."

"No," said Benjamin decisively. "You must be far more tired, you have done much more. And I am used to standing night watches. You rest."

"Take my sword," said Allison. She drew it partly out of the scabbard, and touched the blade. Light spilled from the metal, bright Charter marks rising to her touch. "Keep it sheathed unless you absolutely need the light. Wake me in four hours."

"I will," said Benjamin.

But he didn't. For the first time in his seventy-two years, sixty of them at sea, he fell asleep on watch. One moment he was standing up, suppressing a yawn, the next he was swimming back up to consciousness, aching all over, with a particularly sharp pain in his shoulder, which came from Allison prodding him.

"Wake up!" she whispered, not for the first time.

There was more light than before, though it took him a few seconds to realize it was already dawn, soft light filling the sky though the sun was not yet visible.

"What!" he gasped, sitting up. "Allie! I'm sorry. I can't believe I fell asleep . . ."

"I should have realized," said Allison. "Exposure to Free Magic. Your body would *have* to rest, you did very well to get so far. Perhaps it is just as well. I only woke myself a few minutes ago, and well . . . we are still alive."

Benjamin nodded. Cool air brushed his face, and he turned his head, instinctively sniffing.

"The wind has come up," he said. "From the north."

"Yes. It isn't natural," said Allison.

"What?"

"Both Charter magic and Free Magic can be used to work the weather," answered Allison. "The north wind is beneficial to both magics, and for creatures to cross the Wall. We have to go on at once, we must get the bells to the fort."

Benjamin struggled to his feet.

"I, ah, have to p . . . urinate," he said. "I'll just be a moment, then I'll load up the chest."

"Get on with p-urinating then," said Allison, much as she had spoken to a four-year-old Benjamin when she was twelve, and in most respects, acting as a parent.

Benjamin did his business, wiped his hands on the damp undergrowth and then his trousers, repressed an urge to display the fact he had done so to his sister, fumbled around for the chest, and got it strapped on to the donkey.

He was surprised to find he was not hungry, he had no appetite at all. Allison did not mention breakfast, instead urging them to go on immediately, and he did not miss it.

Even with the growing daylight it was not easy to keep heading north. Several times they had to retrace their steps, finding themselves off the track, blocked by brambles and deadfall. Though Benjamin and Allison pushed themselves, they could not move fast, their bodies slow to recover the indignities of the past day and night. Several times they had to pause and rest, and each time moved on slower than before. To add to their difficulties, the ground began to rise, a slight incline that was enough to be felt by them both.

"There are no hills close to the Wall, not as such," said Allison. "But I recall a low ridge, not directly north of Shrifby . . . we must have veered more to the northeast."

"I'd say so. We have gone more than twenty miles, by my reckoning," agreed Benjamin. "Two or three miles, at the least."

"But the ground ahead slants a little down," said Allison, as much in encouragement to herself as her brother. "If we head more west, we will find the fort."

They talked quietly as they walked, mostly of their time together as children. Their feckless parents had little to do with them, and they had no other siblings. For many years it had effectively just been the two of them in their own little world, a golden age in many ways for both. That had ended first when Allison won a scholarship to university, beginning her career as a doctor, swiftly followed by Benjamin being packed off to become a merchant navy cadet, his parents unwilling to assume the responsibility for a young boy so long shouldered by his sister.

They laughed a little at shared memories of the many temporary nannies and tutors; at their parents' vanities, failings, and self-pity; at the most famous antics of beloved pets, always gone too soon. Benjamin did not remark on Allison's skin becoming gray, now very evident in the morning light, nor the blueish tinge around her lips. Allison, for her part, did not comment on his cough, or the stilted movement of his knees, and his occasional sharp intake of breath when surprised by sudden pains.

The north wind grew stronger as they struggled on, never veering. At last they came to an area of new growth, old oaks giving way to an expanse of young ash trees and saplings, and beyond they saw a cleared area.

"The army clear-fells for half a mile around each fort. We're almost there," said Allison, relief in her voice. She picked up the pace a little, Benjamin wincing as he caught up.

Beyond the new growth was a broad clearing, the land still slightly sloping down. Down toward a circular, stone fort, of a standard design named after its architect. It wasn't very large, no more than hundred feet in diameter and forty feet high, but its embrasures held half a dozen cannon, and room for a half company of soldiery inside.

"A Craddock fort!" exclaimed Benjamin. "I didn't know they built any here at home. Seen plenty of them brooding on harbor mouths and river entrances in the Sunder Sea and the Southern Arc."

"There are a dozen forts, or more, opposite the Wall," said Allison slowly.

She wasn't looking at the fort, instead staring due north. Benjamin shifted his attention from the promised objective, the sight of which had filled him with intense relief, and followed her gaze.

He hadn't properly noticed the Wall, possibly because his mind had shied away from paying it attention. But a mile or so northward, there it was, a modest stone wall, perhaps twenty feet high, running from west to east as far as he could see. An ancient wall, but in perfect condition, it followed the terrain, gently curving as needed, rising up and along a low hill before continuing along.

The wall looked ordinary enough. That wasn't what Benjamin's brain couldn't process. There was another sun in the sky on the other side, a noonday sun, much higher and brighter than the sun he could feel on the back of his neck. He turned around to look at the sun on his side. It was still only halfway to its peak. He looked back across the Wall again, at the impossible other sun.

"The . . . the sun . . ." he blabbered. "Another sun!"

"Time is out of joint between here and there," said Allison. "The seasons too. It is already summer in the Old Kingdom."

Benjamin shook his head like an angry bear woken mid-hibernation.

"You never told me," he mumbled. "How . . . I don't . . ."

"It isn't something you can be told in a letter, or even in person, far away," said Allison. "Like Charter magic, you have to see it for yourself. Come on. The sooner we get to the fort, the sooner you can rest."

"We can rest," said Benjamin, gripping her shoulder lightly.

"Yes," agreed Allison. "I admit I am very tired. But not much longer now."

She had hardly spoken the last word when a bright, white spark flashed between donkey and Benjamin and speared straight through Allison. She fell into his arms. He stared aghast at the smoking, coin-sized hole a few inches above her heart, her sailcloth overalls burned and blackened around it. There was no blood.

The hot metal reek was back, but it did not come from the bells in the chest. The donkey was already running away with them, braying in terror.

"Don't let them take the bells, Bennie," whispered Allie. "Bennie . . ."

A pinkish froth burbled from her mouth, her head fell back, and she went limp in his arms. He knew she was dead. No one could survive such a hole in their chest, so close to the heart.

Benjamin turned around, tucking Allison's body under one arm. He saw three figures advancing out of the oaks behind him. A tall, emaciated man of uncertain age, in riding clothes and polished boots, holding a long, white stick that it took him a moment to process was two human thigh bones joined with a dark iron ring to make a staff. On either side of him were thickset younger men, dressed as grooms. They each carried a rifle, the newly invented bolt-action repeaters that could fire five shots without reloading.

Benjamin drew his revolver and fired at the thin man, aiming for his chest. He instinctively knew the grinning, sunken-eyed man had done whatever it was that had killed Allison, that the bone staff was a weapon, as he instinctively knew this enemy was not entirely human. There was wrongness about his face, his movements . . . and the stench of hot metal came from him, or the staff in his hand.

Click. Click. Click. Click. Click.

The trigger moved. The hammer rose and fell. The five shot cylinder rotated. But the revolver did not fire.

Benjamin dropped the weapon and lowered Allison's body to the ground, ignoring the stabbing pain in his back and knees from the too-sudden movement. He gripped Allison's sword and stood back up, unsheathing it in the process. Sobbing with grief and anger, he stepped forward to be met by another white-hot flash that flew through the air, straight at him. But the sword leaped in his hand without his conscious direction, and parried the missile. Benjamin was blinded for a moment by the flash, but only a moment. He growled, set his shoulders, and began to run, straight toward the enemy.

"Kill him," said the emaciated man. His voice was wrong too, as if his throat was cavernous enough to cause an echo. "Your rifles won't work. Club him down. He won't know how to use that sword."

The two younger men reversed their weapons, to use the rifles as bludgeons, and strode forward, to bar Benjamin's way.

The uncanny man was right that Benjamin didn't know how to use a sword. But he did know how to wield a cutlass. Years and years of daily cutlass drill as a cadet, added to several encounters with pirates in the Southern Arc, meant his muscles well remembered how to use a blade. Add incandescent anger, and massive strength little diminished by his years, and he was a far more formidable opponent than anyone might expect.

The sword was special too, imbued with Charter marks that had flared into brilliant light when parrying the magic attack, and now limned the blade with gold. Benjamin parried an attempted butt stroke that saw the sword carve straight through the rifle and into its wielder, and pivoted on his heel; to drive the point over the other man's rifle and into his head.

Both of the grooms down, he advanced on the scrawny man, who backed away, those deep-set eyes suddenly wide in fright. Benjamin lunged, but his knees weren't up to it. He slipped on bloody mud and staggered forward, going down on all fours, losing his grip on the sword. He stared up, expecting yet another electric, white-bright flash, a sudden pain and nothing—

But the thin man was running away, until an arrow wreathed in golden fire struck him in the back of the neck, punching through so its barbed head stuck out the front. Astonishingly this did not slow him, but the first arrow was followed by another to the man's left leg, and another to his right. The golden fire from all three arrows spread up and down and across his spindly limbs and body, winding about him like unearthly rope. He tried to run on, but his steps became slower and closer until at last he fell. The ropes of golden fire tightened and tightened, until he no longer moved at all.

Benjamin slowly stood up. It took all his strength to do so, and his knees were in agony. He had never felt so weary. He looked behind him.

A very young man, a boy really, only fourteen or fifteen, stood near. He had a bow in his hand, with an arrow nocked but not drawn. To Benjamin he seemed like something out of a history book or a story, in a blue surcoat dusted with silver keys over an armored coat of small, interlocking plates, with a sword and dagger at his hip. He was very pale, and his black hair was tied in a queue.

Farther back, an older, gray-haired woman was on one knee next to Allison's body. She wore the same armor as the boy, and also bore a sword. But Benjamin's eye was drawn most to the bandolier across her chest. He saw the shape of the pouches, the handles protruding down, counted seven of them.

"Bells," he muttered, and reached for the fallen sword. "No, no necromancer!"

"Stay!" cried the boy. "We are not common necromancers. She is the Abhorsen. I am the Abhorsen-in-Waiting. Look, my Charter mark!"

He let got the arrow with his right hand, though he cunningly held it in place with his left against the bow, and brushed his hair back. Benjamin saw the mark there, glowing and shifting just as Allison's had in the kitchen. It seemed an age ago now. A thousand years and yesterday, when his sister was alive.

"The Abhorsen," he said heavily, letting his arm fall. "Allison said the Abhorsen would set things to rights. But I don't know where that donkey has gone. The bells are in the chest on its back."

The old woman left Allison and approached. She moved easily, though up closer Benjamin thought she was at least as old as he was, maybe older still.

"We met your donkey first, and quieted it with a spell," she said, flicking her eyes at her companion. "Terciel will fetch it now. Who are you?"

The boy nodded curtly and loped away. Benjamin tried to answer her question, but could not. He let out a sob, took a breath and coughed, coughed until he could cough no more. He found he was kneeling, but he could not stand up again. He wiped his mouth, heedless of the spots of his blood on his hand, and spoke.

"Benjamin Minoy. Allison's brother."

"Where did the bells come from?" asked the woman.

Benjamin told her. The millstream, the buried chest, Allison's desire to get it away from the village, their attempt to reach the fort. The Abhorsen listened, but he had the feeling she was listening to something else as well, something he couldn't hear or sense.

The boy, Terciel, brought the donkey back while Benjamin was telling his tale. The animal was unusually docile, its big brown eyes were strangely sleepy. Even without being hobbled, it did not wander when Terciel dropped its leading rope. It stood there patiently, not even lowering its head to snatch at tufts of grass.

"What now?" asked Benjamin. He needed to sit down. His knees hurt too much to keep kneeling. He lowered himself on to his side, and then rear, stretching his legs out in front. They were covered in blood. None of it was Allison's, it came from the two men he had killed. He wondered that he felt nothing for them, or cared what he had done. "Who, or what, was that thin man?"

"A man, once, in part," confirmed the Abhorsen. "Someone from this side, I think, who found some small source of Free Magic. A remnant entity of little worth, that entered into his body and whispered to him of greater power to be had, if he could find it. The bells in the chest would draw it like a moth to a raging fire, with a similar result. Even if he'd got them, he would not have wielded them long."

"He had a staff of bone," said Benjamin. He shuddered. "Made from human thighs, I'd say."

"Yes, we will take that away," said the Abhorsen. "And these bodies must be burned, including, I am sorry, your sister's. But there is something else to be done first."

"Burned? No, I will take her body—"

"You will not," said the Abhorsen quietly, but with absolute finality. "Other things may have been drawn to the bells, and still lurk about. An empty body is not a gift to be given to such creatures."

Benjamin wiped his eyes but did not object. Something about the way the Abhorsen spoke reminded him of Allison herself, of true knowledge, not to be gainsaid.

"Your sister is dead," continued the Abhorsen. She tilted her head, as if listening again to something Benjamin couldn't hear. "But she has not gone on."

He could only stare at her, incomprehension on his face.

"Her spirit waits for something, on the very border of Life and Death. Very few have the strength to do so, to stand against the river, and it can be the beginning of great evil. But I think that is not what is happening here. I have known Allison a little, over the years, and heard far more. The healer and midwife of Shrifby, greatly loved, greatly revered, a true servant of the Charter. Her power to remain comes from her calling, all those she brought into Life, they anchor her here. Not arrogance of will, a desire for power, nor fear of the final death."

"She always waited for me, to make sure I was all right," said Benjamin. Tears trailed down his cheeks, to be caught in his beard. He coughed again, and could not stop, until the Abhorsen drew marks in the air, and they fell like soft, shining rain upon his chest. Though the pain eased, he could not catch his breath.

"She waits for you still," said the Abhorsen gravely.

Benjamin smiled, and lay back. He could hardly breathe at all, but it did not trouble him. With the last of what little air remained to him, he spoke.

"I will not keep her waiting," he whispered, and was gone.

"Terciel. Stand guard," said the Abhorsen.

She drew her sword, and undid the flap on one of the pouches of her bandolier. Reaching in she drew a bell out by its clapper, with just two fingers, for it was the smallest of all seven bells. It was silver, like those in the chest, but there was none of the awful hot metal reek, and bright Charter marks played and danced upon the metal. The handle was not ebony, but warm, deeply polished mahogany.

Ice began to form upon the Abhorsen, a thin layer that came from nowhere, emerging on her face and hands to spread across her body, and she became completely still.

Tizanael, fifty-first of the long line of Abhorsens, braced herself against both the swift current and the leeching chill of the river of Death. It was a familiar action, honed over many decades, but she took no chances. The river would gladly drag her down and race her through the veiled mist of the First Gate that lay not far ahead, and thence through the other gates, to the Ninth and final portal from which there was no possible return.

She waded forward a few steps, listening and looking. The river of Death stretched as far as her aged, but still sharp, eyes could see to left and right, though the light was gray and dim and came from no visible source. A wall of dense fog cloaked the way ahead, only a few hundred paces away. She could hear the roar of the waterfall that was the First Gate, and the faint rippling of the current around her legs.

Something bright in the corner of her vision made her turn sideways, and raise both bell and sword. But she did not ring or the bell, nor lunge with the sword. A brief expression of surprise washed over her face, then she started to wade across the river, close to the border of Life, which she could feel a mere few steps to her left.

Tizanael was surprised because the river took the departed swiftly, dragged them down and carried them away, and though she knew Allison was very much imbued with Charter magic, and might delay a little, she had not imagined her spirit could stand against the current so close to Life.

But there she was. Washed out of all color, the same gray as everything about her, save for the Charter mark on her forehead, which glowed with the warm light of a well-banked fire, though one of golden flame. She was slightly bent over, reaching down to lift someone out of the water.

Tizanael watched as she drew her brother up. At first he was as he died, a huge bear of a man, already losing some definition of shape and visage. But Allison drew him close, and Tizanael let out a tiny gasp of surprise as the man's spirit shrank and changed, and golden light ran from Allison's Charter mark, limning her face, running down her arms and hands, spilling over on to the spirit of Benjamin Minoy.

"Allie!" he cried, and his voice and form were those of an eight-year-old boy. "I caught up!"

"Yes," said Allison.

The Abhorsen carefully replaced the bell Ranna. Sleep would be of no use here, but her well-practiced fingers unlooped the cover of Kibeth, the Walker, and her fingers reached in to grasp the clapper. But before she drew the bell, Allison turned toward the Abhorsen, and moved the boy to her side, still holding his hand. The river surged up around their legs, but it did not move them.

"You will not need to urge us onward, Abhorsen," said Allison. She looked down at Benjamin, her smile matching the one on his upturned face. "We're going for a lovely float, Ben. Like in your swimming lessons. Come, let us lie back and relax. You know."

"You won't let go, Allie?" asked Benjamin. His voice began high and squeaky as a child's, but it changed to gravelly bass as he spoke, and his spirit also transformed. He grew large, towering over his sister, once more in the shape of a massive old man. But he did not let go Allison's hand.

"Of course you won't," he said, shaking his head. "I thought myself a child again, for a moment, always asking you that. But you never did let go. You never did. And neither will I."

They knelt together, and lay back, still holding hands, and the river took them.

"Travel without regret," said the Abhorsen. "Do not look back."

She watched them float away, saw their eyes closing into dreamless sleep. Then she listened for the sound of the waterfall to increase, indicating the pair had gone through the First Gate. The roar came, and the current around her knees briefly increased. Still Tizanael remained, though she had no fear the two might return, or that they would fall prey to any of the entities that lurked beyond. Allison was so bright with Charter magic they would all recoil and hide, even the fell creatures who roamed the precincts beyond the farther gates.

But the Abhorsen stood, and wondered, for despite her long experience of Death, she had never seen the spirit of a grown man become a child, and the child back to the man. The river transformed and corrupted the spirits of those who lingered and delayed, but never so quickly, and never to her knowledge in such a fashion. She supposed in some way the child was the true essence of the man, and that, as ever, there were more mysteries in Death than could be known, even by an Abhorsen.

Terciel looked down at the dead man, and wondered what it must be like to have grown so large, and so old. Then he looked at Allison. The Charter mark on her forehead had the faintest light within it, but even as he watched it faded, and the mark was no more than a faint discoloration on her skin.

Ice cracked nearby. The Abhorsen had returned to Life. She shook droplets of chill water off her head, and met Terciel's gaze. He could tell something had got through her usual stern reserve, but not what had done so. Tizanael very rarely showed emotion of any kind. She would tell him in time, if he needed to know. If it wasn't part of his education, he would never find out what troubled her now.

"We must burn the bodies, and then talk to the Scouts at the Fort," she said abruptly. "They will want to know what has occurred. We will keep the donkey to transport the chest back to the House."

Terciel nodded gravely, and bent over Benjamin's body, calling up the marks for fire, cleansing, sleep, and peace, whispering their use-names under his breath. Tizanael was doing the same nearby, over Allison's body. In a moment, the corpses would burn, flesh and bone reduced to ash in seconds. Then there would be the Free magic sorcerer's body and his minions to be burned as well.

The Abhorsens' never-ending work, as Allison had described it.

Settings things to rights.

THE SENTENCE

Paul Tremblay

I think I'll start in middle of the summer of 2020 when me and my then partner Bracken rented a two-million-dollar home (according to Zillow) on Cape Cod for a week, which, crazy expensive house aside for a moment, was a big deal in our fledgling relationship, one that had been intensified by the crucible of the pandemic's early months as we'd only been dating since December, not quite a May-December romance thing as Bracken was six years younger, as sweet as a puppy and as manic as a seventies game show host, a former mixed-martial-arts bro until he tore up a knee, and in our early days I joked I wouldn't hold his youthful, or more youthful, violenting (my word) against him, and I didn't, mostly, anyway, neither of us could believe the dirt cheap rate for the Cape house when I happened to be online desperately searching for rentals, anything to briefly flee our cramped apartment quarantines, and the Cape house's owner had a last-minute cancellation, and well, if you remember, everything was on fire then, and yeah, that fire continues to burn, obviously, but you should've seen the place, how big it was with three levels, windows everywhere and every window had a view of a sheltered interior bay that gouged a hole in the elbow of Cape Cod, though, that bay wasn't very swimmable, or at least, I didn't think it was very swimmable because there was nothing but the thin strip of Nauset Beach separating us from a growing fleet of seals and great white sharks that in the last five years had started prowling those warming waters, but Bracken thought my shark fears were silly, which I didn't exactly appreciate, and he didn't go in the water above his scarred knee because he was more freaked out by all the horseshoe crabs, all of which was fine because swimming never mattered as our being there was about escape, escape to this make-believe house where we cooked on the outdoor grill and watched movies and played cribbage and rummy and fucked, which wasn't all that different than what we'd being doing at our apartments, except for the grill part, but it was different because we were at this gorgeous beach house that we would never be able to afford, not in a million years, and my favorite part was the east-facing main bedroom on the third floor that had French doors open to a small balcony, and my favorite part of the favorite part was that we left the curtains open and the blinds up so that as soon as the sun rose all the sunlight poured in, and I would just lie there, my eyes closed, bathed in the warm light, wishing those mornings would last forever, and the point of me telling you about those mornings in that house is that I spent the following years imagining myself still sleeping in that sun-washed bedroom whenever I could, and it started with our depressing return to my apartment after the rental week was up and the very next morning, in my cave-like, by comparison, bedroom, I kept my eyes shut and willed myself to transport to that Cape house bedroom with the French doors and calm bay waters and the ever-rising sun, and with repetition and practice, I got good at imagining and rebuilding that time and place to the point where I could fool myself into almost believing I wasn't in my shitty bedroom in my shitty apartment and that I was, in fact, lying in the third-floor bedroom of that house, and granted, in a way, I'd been practicing a similar kind of, let's call it visualization, my whole life because as a child I used to actively construct and then roam the halls of my memory palace after a teacher told me that designing a personalized memory palace would help my memory recall, as all I had to do was place objects and things I really wanted to remember in a room of my palace and then retrieval simply became a matter of finding the room in which I stored the memory, and of course, being a child of average intelligence (I can he honest)—though maybe I'm being a bit too self-flagellatory to ascribe intelligence or lack thereof to my not flourishing within the standard schooling hothouse—my memory palace was the suburban, no-frills three-bedroom one-and-half-bath house I grew up in, and no matter how many poems, equations, Greek myths, historical dates, I tried storing within the mental copy of my house, my memory was no better or no worse than anyone else's, as far as I could tell, but after the summer of 2020, I got good, really good at lying in my apartment bedroom in the morning and imagining I was instead at the beach house, which, I guess, became a one-room memory palace, and I know it sounds like I still remember that bedroom in great detail, but the worst part of this whole thing is that the details are now more like a story I once heard, some else's story, but I'm getting ahead of myself, so yeah, let me back up, but also fast-forward, maybe eighteen months—the longer I'm here the harder it is to remember time—and Bracken and I were sharing my apartment, but nearing the end of us, or more accurately, the end had already come but we didn't acknowledge it, and it was a rainy Sunday morning, Bracken was already up and out of bed, but I stayed behind to revisit the Cape house bedroom again, and I adjusted my position, screwed my eyes shut, took deep breaths, but I was failing to conjure up that room, but it really wasn't about conjuring the room itself, it was more about the feeling of the ocean breeze and warm sunlight, more about how I felt when I'd been there, but I was coming up with nothing, a blank, and when I was about to roll over and try again, I opened my eyes, and I was in another room—not the Cape house bedroom and not our bedroom—with walls that were wood paneled, darkly stained, and on the wall across from the foot of my bed and offset to my right was one lonely, shaded sconce, lit in a diminished, sad amber glow, below that was a full-length mirror, reflected in the mirror was a darkened bathroom, which I could not make out any details of, and I didn't want to because I was really afraid to look in the mirror, like so afraid I might die kind of fear, and the only blessing was that the image of this other room was gone as soon as I sat up, so I chalked it up to a bad dream even though I was awake, and yeah, maybe it was one of those waking/almost asleep kind of dreams, but as the next two weeks bled away, I saw that strange room again whenever tried to transport myself to the Cape house, and that goddamned image of the strange room lasted for only a blink, but with each reappearance it lasted for a longer blink, almost imperceptibly longer, sort of like the idea of halving a second, then halving a half second, and on and on forever but in reverse, and no matter how long or how frequent the image of that room hung around it didn't become familiar to me, I mean, I knew it's layout, or at least the part of the room that I was seeing, but what I mean is the weird room was not a place I recognized having ever been in and it wasn't warmly familiar or the least bit welcoming, and when I finally worked up the courage, or desperation, to tell Bracken about my seeing—no, my *being in*—the weird room, he told me he had recurring dreams too, and I said it wasn't a recurring dream, not exactly, and that I was seeing a real place, not that it was real in the apartment, but that it was real somewhere else, at least, that's what it felt like when I saw it, and he nodded and made I'm-here-for-you-and-I'm-listening sounds but couldn't wait to tell me he had recurring dreams about birds with large, oversized heads and tiny beaks and they always freaked him out, and I don't know why, but it was then that I knew he and I were through, and the split was amicable enough that we kept in touch for a while until we didn't have to be amicable anymore, and that's okay because every relationship isn't forever, you know, and I wish more people could be honest about that, well, on the third morning after Bracken moved out and I tried one more time to conjure the Cape room, there were the dark paneled walls, the sconce, the mirror, and the dark bathroom in the mirror and it was all the same, but this time, there was a pair of eyes hovering within the darkness of the bathroom contained within a darkened mirror, and in my memory now, though I don't think I can trust it much anymore, there was more than one pair, maybe even three pairs, and after blinking and shaking my head the strange room disappeared, and this time I blamed stress and my seismic personal life upheaval, and so I decided to stop the conjuring the Cape house bedroom thing (not daring to admit to myself that maybe I'd lost the ability to do so) since it was tied to Bracken and his big bird head, which is kind of mean of me, I know, but regardless of head size, I needed to move on, and I did, and the weird other room stopped appearing, for a time, a time that went fast, too fast, and well, life continued to happened, whether we (or me) wanted it to or not, and I won't bore with too many details but my dad died while mowing the lawn, not death by lawnmower, mind you, that wouldn't have been a boring detail, though Mom did find him sprawled in the yard with two blue jays perched on his back, no comment was made about the sizes of their heads in relation to their beaks, and if I make any light about Dad dying it's because his death brought a lot of dark that I don't want to talk about, but my mom was resilient, more resilient than I was, maybe too resilient, but who am I to judge given I've only dated a few (fine, three) people since Bracken and none of them for more than five months, not that I ever needed to be in a serious relationship to be happy, or content, and I do prefer content over "happy," which is an impossible, destructive ideal, well, Mom couldn't stand being alone, and to her credit she's self-aware enough to admit

that, again I'm not judging, but before the one year anniversary of Dad's death she moved to Vancouver, of all places, with a new partner who had made a mint off LCD light bulbs—that phrase being the extent of his career description I was given, and I didn't care enough to ask for more—and I only mention my personal stuff for some context, time context, as in the passage of time, as a way to measure it, because it's impossible to measure it now, seemingly, though maybe that's a balm because if I were to know how much time is passing in my present it might break my already broken head, but I'm getting ahead of myself again, which is understandable given the circumstances, and frankly, I think I'm holding up pretty well, all things considered, and I will regroup for one more verbal push here, and return to a post-ish pandemic world that returned to a new normal, which isn't accurate, so let's say that the world established a new normal, which is always the state of things if you think about it, so while life was happening, as described, my film news and review TikTok channel blew up and I began writing for movie content aggregator sites, which turned into a hybrid journalism gig, though writing was never my strength—come on, that's a joke—and instead of doing everything in my apartment or posting videos from local movie theaters, I was invited to travel to LA and to film sets in other cities and festivals in the US and Canada, and well, I must say, professionally, things were fucking great, going way better than I could've imagined, like, I couldn't believe that *Variety* (yeah, fucking *Variety*!) sent little old me on assignment to the Telluride Film Festival, which is one of the most prestigious and famous fests and Telluride itself is a small, chichi ski resort nestled within the middle, or the top of, really, the Rocky Mountains, and it was one of the most beautiful places I've ever been to, the downtown full of bougie shops and restaurants and surrounded by stunning views of steep, craggy mountains, and goddamn, the town was already at eight-thousand feet of elevation, which was no joke, asthma sufferer that I am, and I was not prepared for it, not in the least because as soon as the van stopped terrifying me on the ninety-minute, steeply pitched ride from the tiny airport in Montrose and dropped me in town, it was like I was breathing wet paste and I instantly had a headache and a fist-sized stitch in my chest, but I sucked it up because I was in fucking Telluride, press credentialed and everything, and on that first day, after my twelve hours of travel and no time to nap or freshen up, I was on a roof deck interviewing a young nepo star who stole the show playing Kristen Pfaff, the bassist of Courtney Love's nineties band Hole who died of a drug overdose, in the grunge-sploitation (her words) flick *Hole in Your Head*, and she insisted in the spirit of rock and roll that we make our first interview into a drinking game, and yeah, I should have drank more water than I did because by the time I made it to my chalet-style hotel and checked in, my headache was feral and once, finally, in my room I dumped my stuff at a small desk and ran into the bathroom, didn't even bother shutting the bathroom door behind me, and guzzled water directly from the sink tap, then took puffs from an inhaler and swallowed a handful of Tylenol and a melatonin gummy and a sleep gummy, and while sitting on the toilet I googled altitude sickness but reading the type on my phone made my head feel worse so I alternated holding my head in my hands and staring at my miserable self in the room's full-length mirror that was weirdly opposite the open bathroom door, and because I didn't need to see that anymore I dragged myself to bed and pooled under the covers without getting undressed, and, mercifully sleep came quickly, and when I woke up in the middle of the night it was the kind of waking that felt like I'd been asleep for days but in actuality I'd only been asleep for hours, and I was on my right side, which was unusual because I wasn't really a side-sleeper—normally I'm flat on my back or on my stomach—and it was kind of bright in the room because I'd left a single-bulb wall sconce on, one next to a mirror across from the bathroom, and holy shit, this was the room, this was THE room, not simply the vision I'd previously thought of as the weird room, but I was fucking there in the real one, sleeping in it, or not sleeping in it, and I sat up, and I blinked, and nothing changed, and the sum of all those half seconds I was yammering about before became full ones, and then stacked into minutes, and yeah, I was in that room, the one that I had preimagined or intuited or psychic-ed or whatever, and I giggled, and it was an awful sound, and I stared at the wooden walls and the sconce, and took it all in and then slowly came to a kind of conclusion, not that I concluded anything, which implies an answer, and I am not implying that, but there was something off about the lighting in the room, and it was an animal kind of feeling where the body knows before the mind and I scanned the rest of the room—something I'd never done before with the vision of the imagined room, yeah?—and darkness pooled in the corners unnaturally, like it wasn't supposed to be there, or, I mean, act like how it was acting, not that darkness can act, so let me say instead it was like someone had overshaded a painting, blurred out details, but it wasn't that purposeful, and by purposeful you could tell there wasn't an active hand, or an active mind that had willed that darkness into being, or nonbeing, and I know I'm not explaining it well, just know that the worst part, or the first worst part was that I could barely see the frames of the windows that were on the wall above the opposite side of the bed, I mean, they were there, and when I squinted I could make them out, but the frames didn't frame anything other than blackness, and I turned away so violently I spilled out of bed and hit the floor hard, which didn't change anything in the room and that was when I knew I was really in trouble, or the fact that I didn't have a headache anymore and I was breathing clear and easy as I stood up slowly and looked into that mirror, which didn't reflect me because of my vantage angle but reflected the inside of that dark bathroom, and also, reflected a hovering pair of eyes that were not mine, and there was only one pair and not three pairs of eyes like in one of my visions, though I couldn't be sure if there were two other sets of eyes there in the bathroom but they were closed eyes so I didn't see them in the reflection, and while I pondered that mystery and all the others I stood there for a long while, a length of time that was as unnatural as everything else, though maybe I should stop saying that it was and continues to be an unnatural experience, regardless, I stood there long enough to let my fear run out like grains of sand through my fingers and I decided to walk to the bathroom to see who or what was there, and the funny thing about a notion like letting fear run out is that it never actually does because as soon as I took one step toward the mirror/bathroom area of the room, the fear came roaring back, but I was brave and maybe stupid and maybe stupid brave and I walked toward the mirror until I saw my stalking image reflected along with the bathroom and the eyes, and I curled to my right and groped for a light switch that I never did find (not for a lack of groping) and before I knew it, I stood in the doorway of the dark bathroom and no one and no eyes were there, so I kept creeping forward, creeping inside, and no one was in the shower stall, and to my left no one but me in the bathroom mirror, and I watched myself slump back into a sitting position on the stupid fucking toilet, lid down, and I looked outside the bathroom to that mirror on the hotel wall and there were my eyes but the rest of me was as indistinct as the outline of the windows and the other parts of the room where the darkness pooled or gathered, and the thing is an indistinct outline of a body can't turn it's indistinct head or stand on indistinct legs or even wave a help-me indistinct hand, and you get the idea, and so, finally, the deal is that I've been in this place for a long time, longer than I dare to imagine, and I can't say for sure what it is that happened, is happening, but I have a notion, or a theory, and it's all because I dared to imagine, which maybe again I'm not being kind to myself, but as I figure it, I had an embolism or a stroke or an aneurism while at Telluride's punishing altitude, and honestly I couldn't care less how I died, but I'm pretty sure I did, and let's go forward with that assumption so that you and I can be on the same page, so to speak, so, I died and I didn't see a bright light or loved ones or whatever other cultural afterlife images that so many of you believe will happen because other folks have already implanted and hardwired those ideas and concepts and images into your brain, and because I'd so trained my odd little brain to conjure first a memory palace when I was a kid/teen, and then I was even better at the conjuring when it came to reliving or reclaiming the Cape house bedroom experience, and then, of course, the weird room, well, the weird room is what my dying brain, with its final electrical twitches and chemical dumps, cobbled together, this quote "afterlife," and I continue to experience it this way because some part of me must've subconsciously imagined that this weird room is what would be here for me when I died, and even though I'm dead, I continue to experience time differently because my final moments, my final seconds of life are stuck in the mode of halving-a-second-halving-a-half-second ad infinitum again, so yeah, I'm saying my brain and me are dead and gone and at the same time, my brain left me here, in Schrödinger's room, or some shit like that, and I know what I've described isn't exactly a bull's-eye because I can't explain why I saw a vision of the weird room before I was actually in it, though the easiest explanation is that the hotel room I checked into only looked sort of like the vision and my brain ran with it, so, there ya go and ain't life a mystery blah blah blah, and well, there's a part of me that wishes and wants to believe that I'm in a coma or that this infinite halving of time, the infinite halving of my final seconds on earth will end somehow or even that there is some sort of supernatural being doing this to me, no matter if it's the monotheistic assholes or, I don't know, maybe even the Greek gods, I mean, why the fuck not, though, I have to confess I don't know those stories all that well anymore, but I think about how I'd thought I'd seen three pairs of eyes in the mirror that one time and I vaguely remember some bullshit about the three-headed dog Cerberus, that three-headed fuck guarded the underworld or some shit, until someone took its place and set it free, but maybe that last bit is wrong, and like I said earlier (earlier in spoken words and not in time, though I think you're getting the gist of that now) I wasn't great at memorizing poems and facts and apparently Greek myths in school, so I think I'm confusing myths now, maybe even myths from other cultures, but hell, it doesn't matter because that's what is in my head, or was in my head, so the result is that even though I cannot close my eyes anymore and do the conjuring thing—believe me I've tried and continue to try—the hope I'm clutching too is that I can still somehow train my dying/dead brain and make it believe, truly believe there will be a someone else, there will be you—yes, you—and you'll be swimming along in your own life until you don't—and when I try real hard like now, I can see you, and I can give you a name and I think I'm so close into making you real—and when you die and you enter your own eternal room, not exactly the one I described, of course, but the one your mind made for yourself, and you'll see my eyes reflected in a mirror or a window or a brass frame and because you're a dumbass like me, you'll investigate, you won't be able to help yourself, that's the insidious part, and when you do, there will be a swap, you'll take my place, my sentence will be over, and, then, yours will be just beginning.

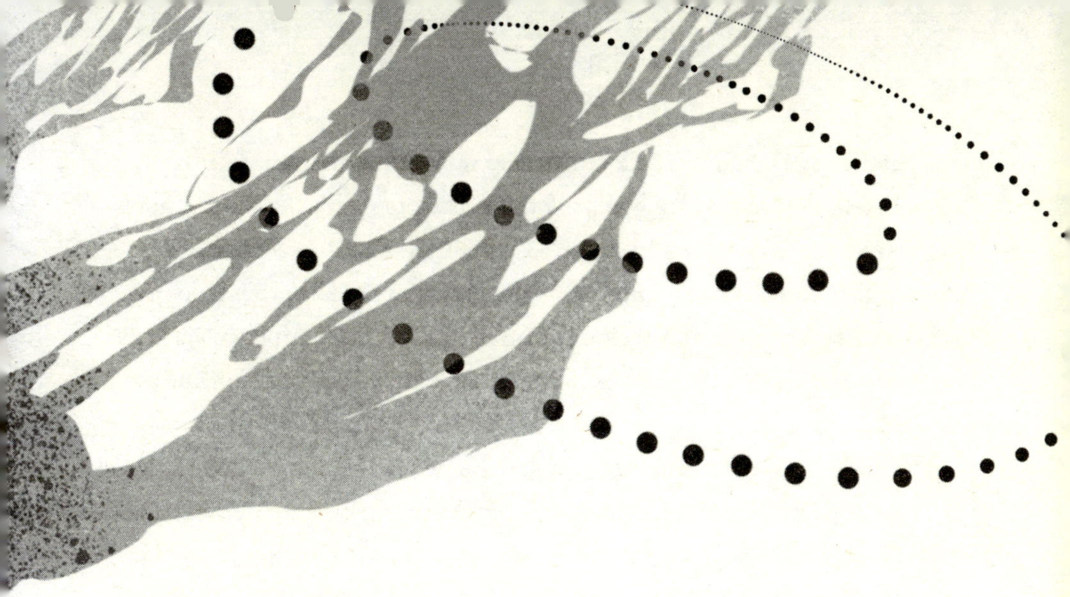

PERPETUAL GOD MACHINES OF THE ANCESTRAL KIND

Wole Talabi

1. THE LAW OF CONSERVATION OF SPIRITS

The consultation shrine was located on the seventy-sixth floor of the Akínmóyèró Institute of Spiritual Cosmology. It was well past midday. Sharp rays of sunlight cut their way through the windows, spilling onto the earthen floor like geometric paint. I was sitting on the floor facing my first and only client for the day, Bisi Shóńẹ́yìn.

I hardly ever took ìdáwò requests anymore, I preferred to spend my time in research. But the institute had a policy requiring that at least 20 percent of staff time be spent on client-facing practical divination, lest our skills ossify, and we lose ourselves in theories and incantations and equations about the fundamental nature of the universe that had no application or connection to our community. To be honest, I think they just thought it kept us humble. Immunization against the development of a god complex. Besides, Bisi Shóńẹ́yìn was a high-ranking member of the Ooni's cabinet, and she'd requested me.

Bisi was a quietly intimidating figure even though she was still young enough to be my daughter. Tall, with broad shoulders and keen, focused eyes. She was wearing a loose-fitting white blouse decorated with an intricate, appliquéd purple motif depicting a leopard atop a rocket. Commemorative material from the first Lunar war, of which she was a veteran. There was a wrapper tied tightly around her waist made from the same fabric. The purple gele around her head completely covered her hair but I could still see tiny tufts of tight gray curls peeking out from underneath. A matching purple shawl draped over her left shoulder so that its tip just touched the ground. She was kneeling with her legs folded underneath her, buttocks resting on the soles of her feet, back straight and hands on her thighs. The position did not look comfortable, but I didn't comment. She looked exactly like what her file said she was; a woman whose mind had accepted that she was now a politician but whose body would never forget that she used to be a soldier.

"You have the message for your ancestors prepared?" I asked, sitting with my own legs stretched out to the side and crossed over each other, bare feet facing the windows, the direct rays of sunlight warming my stiff soles.

She nodded. "Yes, Baba. I do."

Her lips barely moved, and she did not gesture with her hands. She radiated composure and control with every motion and movement. Fitting, for someone who held the position of Balogun in the Ooni's cabinet. And yet, I thought I saw something like anxiety or desperation in the wetness of her eyes, and in the constant clenching of her jaw.

"Excellent. Then let us begin."

Between us sat my quantum divination board. A perfect octagonal prism. White and smooth, with no visible seams or joints. Like a gemstone that had been hewn out of sacred rock. But it was nothing more than a complicated computer console with a hardline connection to the Higgs-Akínmóyèró field modulator at the base of the institute five hundred meters underground. A blinking red light ran around its border and there was a thin slit at its center from which a lightscreen was projected into the space above. An array of bright numbers, symbols, and characters suspended in the air between us like a galaxy of private stars. I gestured with my right hand and the lightscreen projection zoomed closer to me.

I swiped quickly, arranging the symbols into a digital Ọ̀pẹ̀lẹ̀ divination configuration. Age and lack of practice conspired to make me slow, but soon it was done. I began to recite the incantation that activated a localized multidimensional vibration of captive boson strings held in a stasis bubble within the Higgs-Akínmóyèró modulator. The chant was both song and code, an appeal to the fundamental nature of the universe itself to let Bisi Shónẹ́yìn communicate with her ancestors. After a few seconds, the bordering ring of red light turned blue, indicating that the multidimensional vibration was stabilized, and the channel was open.

"Speak now," I said to her. "They listen."

Bisi leaned forward, coming closer to the divination board even though she didn't have to. There was no recording device within. Every message had to be heard and translated into code by a Babaláwo who would transmit it using the specific multidimensional string vibration that had been accessed. Everyone leaned forward anyway.

I expected her to ask some question related to ongoing political matters at the Ooni's palace that had been on the holostreams recently, or perhaps something related to a personal familial issue. But to my surprise, she said, "Egun mi. Why have you been silent? Please say something, anything to show that you are still at my back."

That caught me off guard. In all my years I had heard people ask for all kinds of things from the ancestors—advice on romance, business, migration, politics, family disputes, even scientific queries, but I had never heard someone simply plead with their ancestors to speak to them because of course the ancestors always spoke to us. That was a given. Sometimes indirectly, as they often did in the past but directly too, especially now that we had mastered interdimensional communication with the spirit realm by manipulation of the Higgs-Akínmóyèró field. I was unsettled, but I think I hid it well enough. I quickly resumed my chant and swiped at the projected light symbols to encode the message and transmit it to the higher-dimensional compactified space-time coordinates where the spirits of all who have gone before, and those who are to come, dwell.

When I was done, I flicked my finger to send the lightscreen projection back to its place just above the divination board. The numbers and symbols of the Ọpẹ̀lẹ̀ flickered for a few moments and then collapsed into each other forming a single bright, blinking circle of light.

"For every call, there is a response," I said, speaking the ancient words that we have been using for almost a century, since Kọlá Akínmóyèró discovered how to temporarily unfold the compactified dimensions of the universe and shared his methodology. "You have spoken. Now, listen."

We sat there, silent, the circle steadily blinking at us as seconds, and then minutes, drifted by. My lower back began to ache, and I shifted my weight to relieve it. Bisi didn't move, she simply stared at the circle between us as though she could bring the message from compactified space-time to us by force of will. But as the time slowly ticked away, I could see the concern in Bisi's eyes increase even as my certainty of a response decayed rapidly. Could one calculate the half-life of hope?

Typically, for an ìdáwò, we received a response within a few seconds. Minutes, in some cases, if the field modulation was inefficient, which could happen with older hardware or with remote connections to the institute. Or if the multidimensional vibration was not fully stable when the message was transmitted—at the Planck scale such instabilities were always possible. However, the longest wait time ever recorded in the academic literature for a response was twenty-six minutes and eight seconds.

"For every call, there is a response," I repeated, when we hit the twenty-minute mark, trying to encourage Bisi and, if I am completely honest, myself. "We have spoken. We continue to listen."

She simply nodded and kept her eye trained on the circle like it was a target.

After half an hour, the circle of light stopped blinking, turned red and then flattened into a thin line before morphing into a string of text with the message:

> No response received. Process timed-out due to excess energy expenditure to maintain interdimensional string stability in Higgs-Akínmóyèró field bubble 00457801.

Bisi closed her eyes, shook her head, and sighed.

"I'm sorry," I said, pulling the lightscreen back toward me and swiping away the error message to pull up a detailed diagnostic log of the transmission. "That's very strange."

"Don't be." Bisi looked up at me, her eyes suddenly red in the bright light. There was a quiver in her lower lip and for a moment, she looked like she was about to cry. "That is what happened with the other Babaláwos too."

"This happened before? This exact same message?"

"Yes," she confirmed. "Twice."

"Why didn't you tell me when you arrived?"

"I was hoping you would have different results," she replied. "My colleague, the minister of science and technology recommended you. She said you were the best." Bisi glanced over my shoulder to all my plaques and awards hanging in the spaces between the old bones and empty gourds and leather charms that were displayed prominently along the shrine walls. Relics from my early career. They all seemed so useless in the face of what just happened.

"Besides, would it have made any difference to your approach?" she asked.

"Hmm. No," I admitted. "But you should have told me."

The diagnostic log showed nothing. The multidimensional vibration had been stable. The message had been encoded and transmitted without error. There was simply no response. Which was impossible.

"I have always felt their presence with me before now," she said, adjusting the shawl on her shoulder. "How do you Babaláwos always say it? That spirits exist in a part of the universe that we cannot perceive but which is always around us, always in contact with us?"

I nodded. She was mostly right, although described more accurately, spirits existed in compactified dimensions of our universe that were about 10^{-33}m across and could only influence tiny quantum fluctuations in space-time at the Planck scale, unless enough of them were doing it to become statistically significant. But that didn't matter. She knew enough.

"Even before the first ìdáwò when they didn't respond to me, I already felt their absence. In fact, that is why I first sought out a Babaláwo. I've never needed technology to communicate with my ancestors before."

She turned away from me and focused on the view from my shrine window—of clear blue sky and slowly drifting clouds and in the distance, the towering outline of one of the many orbital elevators that connected Earth to the space transit stations in the thermosphere. I was supposed to take one to go see my adopted daughter on the Ọ̀ṣùpá Lunar station in two weeks. She was about to turn sixty. A flock of white pigeons flew by in a *V* formation. I already knew I would have to cancel my plans.

"This is a curious problem you've brought to my attention," I told Bisi. "I will take a detailed look at the log over the next few days and discuss with my colleagues. The field of quantum divination is strange and complex, but I've dedicated my life to understanding and advancing it. I'm confident we can figure this out. I will send you a message once we have."

A cloud drifted in front of the sun, blocking its rays, and darkening the room. It felt like an omen.

"And what if you can't?" she asked, turning back to me, her eyes clear and focused again.

"Can't what?"

"Figure it out. Find any explanation." She rose to her feet keeping her back straight, like a tower unfurling.

"I doubt that will happen," I said, and then added, "when it comes to the ancestors, all questions have answers, it may just take time to find them. But we are dedicated to knowledge and the understanding of all things." I tried for an encouraging smile, but she was already moving toward the door.

"I have always felt the presence of my ancestors. Even during the Lunar war, I heard them whisper in my ear during difficult moments. I felt them guide my hand and calm me when I was most afraid. When the compression bombs were going off and lasers were tearing everyone around me to shreds, I could sense them collectively manipulate probability in my favor, giving me the luck I needed to survive. A millimeter here, a fragment of loose regolith there. My Egun have been faithful. I know they have not simply chosen to be quiet. It's like they have just disappeared," Bisi said, her voice low and hoarse like she was afraid of her own words.

"That is impossible. It would violate the law of conservation of spirits," I said, rising to my feet to follow her out. Spirits are never destroyed; they only change form. Death is nothing more than a transformation of spirit information into higher order dimensions where they exist until they achieve sufficient activation energy to cross the entropy barrier and return, reincarnated in some form. Even if one or several of them had reincarnated, that would not silence an entire ancestral line going back to the very first of us. But I admit, her question triggered a deep unease in my mind.

We walked to the elevators in silence. My bare feet were cold on the soft earthen floor, and I could feel my old hip pain returning. One of the semicircular elevator doors opened just as we reached it, our approach already detected by the sensors. Bisi entered the transparent pod and turned to face me, reflected sunlight haloing her.

"What if the law is wrong?" she asked.

I shook my head. "My dear, we've been doing ancestral research for decades and we have found no evidence that it is."

"Maybe what is happening to me is the evidence."

The elevator doors closed, taking Bisi away but leaving her problem churning in my mind.

2. THE SECOND LAW OF SPIRITUAL THERMODYNAMICS

I spent several hours the following week looking into the diagnostic log of Bisi Shóṇ́ẹyìn's ìdáwò, trying to figure out why her ancestors had gone silent, but I found nothing.

No response received.

The bright red letters of the error message haunted me, like graffiti sprayed onto my mind.

Frustratingly, I discovered that Bisi, like me, was the last of her bloodline. Her parents were both single children. As was she. That vaporized my most direct path of inquiry.

I asked my apprentice, Yinka Osuniyi, a quiet and brilliantly persistent young woman whom I know will make a great Iyaláwo one day, to check with the technicians at the Higgs-Akínmóyèró modulator.

"They processed one hundred and sixteen ìdáwò requests the same day as Bisi's," Yinka reported, her plump cheeks shiny in the light of my shrine as though they'd been rubbed with palm oil. She flicked her wrist to send me the summary data. "All of which proceeded without any problems. They reported no equipment glitches either."

A dead end.

Next, I requested the diagnostic logs of Bisi's previous ìdáwòs from the other Babaláwos and cross-referenced them against mine—checking everything from the connection strength to the Ọ̀pẹ̀lẹ̀ configuration and the probability position coordinates of the vibrating boson used to anchor the multidimensional data transmission. There were differences, of course, but nothing anomalous, no promising thread I could begin to pull at in hope for an unraveling.

When the frustration grew to a barely bearable level, I sent messages to my old friends and colleagues at the Bahia central shrine, the Lakota spiritual cosmology facility, the Noongar ancestral research center, the Chengdu spirit institute, and at the quantum research laboratory in Geneva, laying out the problem. They all sent messages back, expressing concern and sharing hypotheses but none of them had any concrete suggestions, or any confidence in their assertions and none of them even broached violation of the law of conservation of spirits as a possible explanation.

The question of Bisi's ancestral silence had fully set its claws into my mind. The push-pull between frustration at not knowing and anticipation of the joy of finally figuring out a solution did not allow my mind a moment's rest. I craved the satisfaction of calling Bisi back to my shrine and explaining to her what had happened. I yearned to see the look of relief in her eyes when I finally connected her to the ancestors that meant so much to her. It was a need I hadn't felt since my halcyon days at the institute.

And then, the following week, two things happened.

The first was that the problem of ancestral silence began to spread, like an infection.

Word arrived from a local Iyaláwo in Ìjẹ̀bú-Òde that multiple ìdáwòs with members of a family with deep roots to the land had failed. Her holographic message was a jumbled rant, hard to follow because she was so rattled by what had happened that she'd tried to reach out to her own ancestors for advice and had also been confronted with a deep and abiding silence. At least she'd had sufficient composure to send us her diagnostic logs. Yinka analyzed them for me and much like in Bisi Shónẹ́yìn's case, the logs showed no anomalies. But we now had evidence that it was not an isolated incident. The new case made it clear that some strange, previously unknown mechanism was at work. And then I began to receive follow-up messages from my colleagues in Dakota, Bahia, Chengdu, Whadjuk, Geneva, and cosmological research institutes around the world. They too were beginning to see failures in their attempts to contact their ancestors. Even the more traditional, less-direct means of contact that didn't involve multidimensional string vibrations and quantum tunneling, were going unanswered.

The second was that Bisi Shónẹ́yìn killed herself.

I was in my shrine when I saw the headline flash across my lightscreen, in the evening news bulletin. I froze and for a moment all I could hear was the thunder of my own heartbeat and my blood pounding in my head. My hands shook so much that I dropped my mug of tea. It shattered on the earthen floor, the noise bringing all the sounds of the world back in a rush.

I enlarged the lightscreen image and turned up the sound. A government spokesperson with narrow eyes and a face full of hard lines was explaining that Bisi had taken leave from her official duties and returned to her ancestral home in Òde-Ìdèpé. Her android home assistant had found her lying in her bedroom with her arms crossed over her chest, pale and still, with a bottle of poisonous aworoso seeds beside her.

I felt sick and off-balance, the weight of her death an unexpectedly heavy burden on my chest. I was surprised when the tears began to fall.

It was only later I would come to understand that I was crying not only for her per se, but for what her death represented. An unresolved mystery. The loss of an opportunity to explain to her what had happened.

At the institute, we are dedicated to the search for knowledge and the understanding of all things.

The ghost of my own words returned to me.

I stood up, wiped away the tears, and walked to my window just as the autocleaning nanobots embedded in the floor absorbed the last of my spilled tea and began to recycle the fired clay fragments of my mug, breaking it down to smaller, more digestible chunks.

The pink, yellow, and burnt-sienna light of sunset hit the edges of scattered clouds, giving them a scarlet glow and the orbital elevator in the distance was now just a towering silhouette. Below, the light sloshed over the Ilé-Ifẹ̀ metropolis which was buzzing with activity as though one of its most important denizens had not just been lost. The bioluminescent plants that covered many of the residential buildings were beginning to come alive.

Life and death. Always in equilibrium. Until now. The disappearance of ancestors meant loss of spirits, which would be a violation of a truth we had confirmed by calculating the increase of entropy associated with death. The energy loss associated with the unfolding of the spirit into its full dimensionality.

Death is nothing more than a transfer of information.

I needed a direct way of understanding what was happening in the dimension of the dead. I could try to contact Bisi, but it was folly to try to contact the recent dead when they had not yet had time to adjust to their new state of existence. Their messages tended to be garbled and incoherent. In that moment, with the sienna sunset afterglow from the high windows filtering in, the last of the sun's warmth on my skin, a thought settled in my belly. What about my own ancestors?

It had been so long since I had communed with them in any form. Ever since I'd been diagnosed with acute azoospermia and pronounced infertile. I hadn't even been sure I wanted children at the time, yet it had come as a blow to know that even if I did, the option was not available to me. The possibility collapsed like a bridge to a place I didn't know I wanted to go. I blamed my ancestors for allowing such a thing to happen during a heated ìdáwò, after which I had cut off direct communications with them, ignoring even their minor small acts of manifestation in my day-to-day life. Their whispers in the wind, their faces in dreams, their improbable coincidences.

Suddenly, I found myself wondering about them and if they were afflicted by this new, spreading silence.

It was against the rules to use institute facilities without an official request, and it was even more against the rules to perform an ìdáwò for oneself, but I didn't care. A nervous shiver slinked down my spine.

I walked gingerly to the center of my shrine where my quantum divination board sat and activated it. The ring of red light around its edges blinked three times before stabilizing and the bright white light projected out from the slit at its center. Fingers trembling, I quickly configured the symbols into a digital Ọ̀pẹ̀lẹ̀ and recited the incantation until the red light was blue.

I didn't even bother with words. I knew exactly what I wanted to ask.

<<Egun mi, if you are there, can you tell me what is happening to the other ancestors?>> I wrote directly in code and swiped to transmit.

A tyranny of silence pressed into me as I sat there, waiting to hear something, anything.

I listened and listened and listened until the fading orange light of sunset gave way to a purple-hued darkness and the automatic lights of the shrine came on. Still nothing. Ten minutes passed. I was about to send another message when I heard a sound transmitted back through the speakers on the side of the divination board. It was low and hard to hear, the pitch and intensity dopplering like its source was moving rapidly. It sounded like a scream, but I couldn't be sure.

<<Egun mi? Mama? Papa?>>

The sound continued for a few minutes and then . . . it stopped.

There was an extended silence until the blinking light circle collapsed into that dreaded red time-out message.

I sat there, trembling. My hands shaking and sweat beading my brow. My eyes were wet with tears. Tears of frustration, yes, but tears of anger too. I understood Bisi then, fully, and truly. My ancestors had abandoned me and left me no choice; I would have to follow them.

I went back to my desk and began work on a modified method of inquiry, one that would pierce the veil of dimensional silence.

The next morning, after swearing her to secrecy, I told Yinka what I had done and what I planned to do next. She gasped and put her hands to her mouth. "What?"

"I am going to unfold my spirit to higher order dimensionality," I repeated, and swiped my hand to transfer the entire night's worth of calculations and notes directly to her mobile lightscreen. The light of reflected numbers and symbols crawled across her skin like living tribal marks.

She pored over them for a few minutes, her eyes slowly widening as understanding began to crystallize in her mind.

"You mean you're going to die?"

"Yes." I forced a thin smile.

"But why?" she asked, swallowing, and cocking her head, her eyes glazed with tears.

"Isn't it obvious? I am going to find out what is happening to our ancestors. I will follow the trail of lost spirits."

The interdimensional transfer of spirit information that occurred at death was driven by a million variables and probabilities that fluctuated wildly at the string level. But those fluctuating probabilities eventually would pass through a specified nonzero value, which meant that, theoretically, if one could preselect a set of quantum conditions and simply wait for them to occur, then one could track the spirit as it crossed from life to death.

"But how will you come back?" she asked. I knew as well as she did, that she already knew the answer to that question.

"I won't," I told her, shaking my head.

Death is an irreversible process. There isn't enough energy in the universe to reduce the associated entropy. The unfolding and transfer of a spirit into higher dimensionality only proceeds in one direction, in accordance with the second law of Spiritual Thermodynamics. That was why whenever the ancestors came back, reincarnated, it was without any true memory of who they had once been—only fragments, like a half-remembered dream. The entropy cost of compressing a spirit into a less complex, embodied existence.

"I see," Yinka said, her voice dropping with the weight of the realization. "I hoped you would have figured out something . . . some way . . ." she whispered, looking back to my notes.

I stood and went to her, placing my hands on her shoulders. "No. There is no coming back. But my death will not be in vain. That's where you come in. I need you to conduct a tethered ìdáwò so that at the point of my death you can lock on to the information signature of my spirit and track my probability position coordinates as it unfolds to higher dimensionality. Once that link is established, quantum tunneling effects should ensure that we can continue to exchange messages in real time across the dimensionality barrier."

She stared at me with her mouth open as though shock was a weight.

The coordinates of information in higher order dimensions were an abstraction that could only be described in terms of pure mathematics. There was no correct analogy for it in our observable four-dimensional existence. It was difficult to explain that the people whom we'd once seen, touched, fought, kissed, hugged, made love to, sang songs with, and loved with a solid tangibility now existed only as streams of data encoded onto the floating surf of probabilities governed by the vibration of strings a hundred trillion-trillion times smaller than a proton.

"I have already sent a message to the Higgs-Akínmóyèró field modulation station chief, letting her know that I need unconstrained access for up to six hours for an important experiment," I continued. "That should give us enough time. I will observe what is happening on the other side and report back to you in real time. You must record everything meticulously. If what is happening to the ancestors should happen to me, I will try to describe it in as much detail as I can before I too am gone. And then you can carry on my work, finish the investigation." I forced a thin smile. "Perhaps they will even name the mechanism behind whatever we find after you."

"This is too much to sacrifice," Yinka protested, shaking her head.

"No, it is not," I insisted, raising my voice. "I am a drop in the ocean of humanity. A small part of the entire human community that is now under threat, a threat to our eternal spirits. There is no price too high." I paused and took a deep breath. "Besides, I am almost already an ancestor now, even though I have no direct descendants. And you know what our people say, 'Bí ọ̀mọdé bá ṣubú á wo iwájú; ágbà bá ṣubú á wẹ̀hìn.' *After a fall, a youngster looks ahead for help while an elder looks back for the cause.* I must go to the place where my ancestors dwell, even though I have cut myself off from them for a long time."

"But we need you here, Baba," Yinka whispered. Her voice was trembling and threatening to break my resolve.

"Child. I have lived long and achieved much. My generation has benefited from the guidance of those who came before. If I should die without resolving this, then the guilt of knowing that your generation will be adrift without guidance will torment me further. I have already failed Bisi Shónẹ́yìn. I cannot fail those who are to come. Do you understand?"

She nodded but she was fighting back tears.

"Thank you," I said. "Now, let us begin."

I stretched out my hand and let her help me to the center of my shrine where the quantum divination board sat ensconced in its black programmable nanomaterial cradle. The dark surface reflected light like a moonlit lake. I sat on the ground beside it, and it unfurled like a flower, revealing the seamless white and smooth quantum divination board within.

When my head and back were rested on the cool floor, Yinka retrieved the Oríokùnwaya—a helmetlike device with electrodes long enough to extend to the navel, which was used for taking recordings of the mind for upload to a quantum computer. It was transparent, with its internal assortment of tiny processors, wires, and circuitry visible, like a brain exposed. A single twisted run of cables extended from the crown of the helmet like a spinal cord.

"There." I pointed, turning my head slightly to the board. "Connect it."

I had reconfigured the Oríokùnwaya to connect to the quantum divination board and lock on to a spirit's information matrix, establishing a direct link between the dimensionality of the living and the dead. Yinka took the cable and plugged it into the divination board. And then she placed the Oríokùnwaya over my head. It felt tight and uncomfortable, and my neck was cranked up at an awkward angle, but I knew the pain and discomforts of the body wouldn't matter in a few moments, so I ignored them.

"Yinka, can you please take a memrionic recording of my mind for the institute's archives?"

She nodded, her eyes red and heavy with tears. Her oily cheeks were puffed up. I was more afraid than I was allowing myself to admit. Not fear of this death, but fear of a more permanent one, the one that may have befallen the ancestors. But this first death was the only way. To know, I needed to shed the cage of my body.

The memrionic recording took only a few minutes but it was enough time for my mind to wander. To think back to my own parents, whom I never knew. They died three days after I was born. They were nothing more than pictures and holograms to me until my first ìdáwò, when I heard them speak to me from higher dimensionality. It was a magical moment, and one of the reasons I had chosen to become a Babaláwo. I wondered briefly if I would see them when I crossed over. If I'd recognize them somehow as pure information—disembodied and floating atop the quantum sea.

"Recording complete," Yinka said, breaking the flow of my thoughts. "We can commence the err . . . transmission."

I forced a smile and nodded gently, as much as the helmet and the floor allowed. Yinka gave me an injection full of aworoso seed distillate. I pressed it and a shock of electricity ran through my body as it flowed into my system. I shivered, but only briefly. And then I relaxed as the poison began to shut down my vital organs.

"I'm sorry," I heard Yinka whisper. And I felt the touch of her trembling hand on my shoulder.

I felt no pain, the poison was so efficient. The traditional choice of kings and generals whose people had lost faith in them and were thus condemned to suicide, by community law. I found some comfort in that. I too was doing it for my community, the community of all humanity.

I stared up at the ceiling, the light from the windows still a warm memory on my face. My vision began to fade like a picture going out of focus and then the blurriness rapidly turned to darkness. Sounds developed a loud echo. I could almost feel my consciousness untethering from my body, drifting up and away from me but I knew it was nothing more than a trick of my mind. The afterlife has never been above or below, it has always been everywhere around us.

The last signal my body received before my spirit completely unfolded was Yinka's trembling voice reciting the ancient, ritual words, but they sounded different, because she'd modified them into a prayer. "For every call, there is a response," she said. "Baba Ireti, you go to seek the ancestors. I wait, and I listen. Go well."

And then, I was no more, swallowed whole by a nothing so potent I can only think of it in terms of mathematics—a collapsing of all probabilities to zero.

A perfect nil.

3. PERPETUAL GOD MACHINES

I emerged from nothingness into the dimensionality of the dead. Not a void, but a more complete rendition of our universe with its bubbling stew of quantum effects always at play—the microscale turmoil of a strange and wonderful universe.

I was without a body, but I felt something pressing upon my consciousness from all directions, like a wind of pure information. A potential difference of probabilities.

"Yinka?" I tried to call out, but there was no sound.

I tried to focus, to see around me, but there was no light. I tried to reach out and grab on to something, anything, but I couldn't. I couldn't control any aspect of my existence. I was a disembodied consciousness adrift in a subatomic spirit-sea. Fear overcame me, saturating my mind. It was a terror unlike any I had ever experienced. A raw and potent fear, undampened by the neurocircuitry of a body.

Then suddenly, something like a light appeared. At first a small dot in the darkness, it began to expand rapidly, becoming an iridescent fractal pattern that appeared to be advancing toward me. The silence was replaced by something like a low whistling and a chorus of voices, all speaking at once. The fear filling my mind spiked, but I could do nothing except observe. The iridescent fractal overran me, sweeping past in a blur of beautiful reds, yellows, pinks, blues, and a riot of colors I have never perceived before, an endless kaleidoscope moving in impossible patterns, folding in and out of each other constantly like I was endlessly falling into the boundary of a Mandelbrot set.

The press of the information wind against my consciousness grew more insistent. Gone was the darkness. Replaced by a fractal rendition of the universe. And then I saw them, the other ancestors, as glowing clumps of light embedded into the fractal background, like glowing galaxies sewn into the fabric of space-time. The chorus of voices was theirs.

Welcome. Run. You are one of us now. The fear. Something is not right. Allow yourself to understand. Be afraid. You are home. Relax. Don't let it take you. Let go of the fear. Flee, child.

There were so many voices. Contradicting each other. I couldn't make any sense of what they were saying but I began to grasp the nature of what was happening to me.

It was not real light. It was not real sound.

I was a spirit, nothing more than a persistent matrix of information, my expanded consciousness encoded in the surf of a subatomic sea of strings that made up the universe, so of course I couldn't truly "see" or "hear" anything. But my mind had constructed a framework for understanding this new environment—a model for this expanded realm of existence—using what was familiar. I was observing the oscillations of the universe at its most fundamental level, but my altered spirit-mind was processing that information with the only context it had. Sight. Sound. Sensation. The echoes of corporeality. But none of it was real.

"Yinka?" I tried again. Projecting my thoughts out, imagining them being transferred to four-dimensional space. And this time, after what seemed like a few seconds, I heard her reply.

"Baba Ireti! Ah, Baba, I can hear you!"

A sense of relief washed over me. The tethered ìdáwò process was working and my mind had reoriented itself enough to be coherent.

"Good," I said, trying project calm. "Are you recording this?"

"Yes," she confirmed. "Please tell me what you see?"

"Nothing I can describe accurately. Everything is strange—fractal here. And there is something like a wind, pushing me. Where am I?"

"You have arrived close to the last recorded probability position coordinates of Bisi Shónẹ́yìn's ancestors."

Good. The first recorded case of ancestral silence was a good place to begin my investigation.

The press of the consciousness wind grew stronger, and I focused on it. Willing my mind to understand what the wind physically represented. Eventually, I started to feel something like a pull in one direction, even though I could not tell what, with the constantly shifting fractality of the world. It was something vaguely magnetic pulling my raw, exposed consciousness toward it, drawing my spirit toward itself. That was when I realized I was moving.

"Are my coordinates changing?" I asked Yinka.

A moment. And then, "Yes. You're drifting closer to their last known coordinates."

"All right. I'll let it take me and see if it leads me to them." Not that I had much choice in the matter. I didn't know how to move in this higher-dimensional existence. Was this how all of us arrived in the afterlife? As patterns of superposed wave functions inscribed on the currents of probability—disembodied, disoriented, and disconnected, without as much as a psychopomp to soften the blow to our minds?

My consciousness continued to drift with the strange wind, caught in the pull of some unknown potential difference.

I wondered if everyone in the afterlife domain perceived things the same way, the fractal world, the clusters of light, the voices. Or if we all had our own models for understanding, which varied based on our most recent life experience in the four dimensions of embodied reality?

I tried to count the number of light clusters I could see but there were too many of them, all flickering translucent at a variety of distances from me like clouds of bioluminescent insects. We were all moving in the same direction at different speeds relative to each other.

"Yinka. There is something like a force here, attracting us. I can sense it all around. Like a bizarre gravitational field."

"Oh. Any idea what it would be?"

I thought about it, but no easy answers came to me.

The whistling sound I had been hearing since I first arrived suddenly resolved itself. The faraway information-voices of the other ancestors pressing against my disembodied mind was a cacophony of screams and cries of confusion.

What is happening? Help us. Run. You are one of us now. The fear. What is going on? Something is not right. Run. Why? The pull is too great. Be afraid. Run. Save us. It is eating us.

An intense surge of fear saturated my consciousness.

"I hear screaming," I told Yinka.

"Screaming?"

"Yes. Or something like it."

Our people have always said there was no heaven or hell. Only Orun. The place of the spirits. But the force, the screaming, perhaps hell had come to Orun. And I had willingly come to it.

A wave of terror flooded my mouthless mind. But curiosity too. I wanted to know what this strange new force was that could attract and obscure ancestral spirits, preventing them from communicating with the four-dimensional world of the living. And then a thought occurred to me that was so shocking, I went quiet. For how long, I don't know.

"Baba Ireti?"

"I have a theory," I said. "At the institute, Bisi asked me if it was possible for the law of conservation of spirits to be wrong. And I said it was impossible based on all we knew. But perhaps I was thinking too small. Perhaps it can be wrong in any given universe while holding true at a higher scale."

"What do you mean?" Yinka asked.

"For a long time, we could not prove that the spirit persisted beyond death because it was compactified into subatomic space all around us and was only observable at the quantum level. Not until the Higgs-Akínmóyèró grand unified resolution gave us the mathematical models to understand the physical nature of compactification. But in theory, the compactification of dimensions can be done in trillions of ways. We found one way that matched our observations and gave actionable predictions and so we assumed that theory of the universe was correct. But what if there is no one right compactification? What if they are all correct? And what if each viable compactification scheme produces a different space-time, a different reality with its own unique shape and order and physical constants."

"A multiverse?" Yinka said.

"Yes. A multiverse."

"And since we have observed that spirits can be temporarily conserved across dimensions as in our own universe up to this point, then perhaps such supersymmetry could apply to the multiverse at large. Perhaps there are random events at this scale that can transfer spirits from one universe to another."

"Like a higher order death that occurs sporadically?" Yinka asked.

"Yes. It must sound like baseless madness, I know. But I suspect that this singularity, and all the others popping up like it, could be the process by which spirits cross from one universe to another."

Excitement floated to the top of my consciousness, overtaking the fear. If true, this would be a major discovery.

"But if you're right, how could we have never observed this process before?" Yinka asked.

It was a good question. "I don't know. Perhaps it happened a long time ago when we couldn't understand it, before we understood and accessed hidden dimensions. Or perhaps our universe was not old enough and this is the first time it's happening to us."

There was only one way to know for sure. I would have to approach the singularity.

I focused all my spirit-mind in the direction of the force, trying to observe what I could of it. Suddenly I experienced an even deeper sense of dissociation, like all that I was had disappeared. Not unlike what had happened when I died and expanded into higher dimensionality. I felt the press of the wind against my consciousness increase in intensity. There was a sudden warp in the fractal universe's fabric, a giant wave in the quantum ocean.

"What happened?" Yinka asked, concern lacing her words. "Your probability position coordinates are changing fast. Too fast. The ìdáwò tether is weakening. I can't hold a lock on to you!"

Her voice was breaking. The sound was chopped up and missing bits in the middle even though I could still make out their meaning.

"I think the singularity has noticed me," I said, thinking of the observer effect. "It is pulling me faster."

"What was . . . Can you . . . Baba . . ."

"Yinka?"

"Baba—"

"Yinka?"

Nothing.

I was disconnected.

All I heard were the cries of the other ancestors caught in the current of this river of spirits, flowing toward the unknown force. The clusters of light blurred into each other as they zoomed faster toward the wellspring of the force. A subatomic spiritual singularity.

Run. The fear will trap you. Be afraid.

We were all caught in its pull and would all eventually be consumed by it, sooner or later. Some resisted more than others, slowing their consumption. But I had the mind of a scientist, and my curiosity had slipped on the viscous surface of whatever spirit-field this entity was manipulating to pull all of us into itself. I had crossed some point of no return, a Schwarzschild radius of reality. Now I was falling into it, accelerating, all I could do was continue to observe.

Hundreds of streams of brilliant ancestral light, like godwires heated to blinding white, all arced in infinite curves tending toward the singularity. Fractal whorls and patterns swept by.

I focused on the point we were tending toward and saw something like a hole in the universe, a perfect black circle into which all the light clusters of ancestral spirits were flowing, like someone had stabbed the belly of reality itself and left it to bleed out.

The screaming grew louder. The rippling of fractal patterns turned into warping, like a sheet being blown by a gale. The singularity grew as I accelerated toward it. I wondered what confused thoughts the other ancestors were receiving from me in this stream of the condemned. Was I projecting screaming too?

Up close, I could begin to see the outline of the singularity itself more clearly. Perfectly spherical, like an inverse sun. A lurid white glow licked at the fractal space around it, the color of dove wings, of Ọbatala the creator, of perfection. The arcs of ancestral light seemed to terminate where they contacted the singularity giving off the border glow, and as they did, the wailing voices of the ancestors began to merge into a single endless scream. A second, more permanent death? Or a transition to another universe?

Horrified as I was, I was also fascinated by something so inconceivable, so beyond our standard interpretation of spiritual cosmology. The incomprehensibly of it overwhelmed me.

At the center of the perfect darkness that ate the light of spirits, I saw a large red eye flutter open.

It fixed its gaze upon me and all at once, it knew me; completely and fully. I felt it latch onto my raw, awe-flavored curiosity like a hungry child and begin to feed. I could sense it analyzing the workings of my exposed pure mind, like an Oríokùnwaya. And I saw into it too. Saw deep into its fundamental nature. I began to know it as well as it knew me. And with that came absolute knowledge that I was right. The singularity was a subatomic connection between universes, a portal between realities. Spirits, like strings, are the fundamental building blocks of the mind of all universes and they are conserved across all possible realities. But I was also wrong. The singularity was not mindless, not some accidental result of physical constants crashing into each other. It was alive. It was conscious. It was growing. Which was why the ancestral voices were disappearing. It was consuming them. The singularity was a creature that blossomed at the borders of universes like moss growing in the hairline cracks along the wall of possibilities. Inhaling spirits and exhaling them into the vacuum wombs of other universes.

My mind was merging with it, the leading edge of my spirit bleeding into its very nature, becoming one with it, vibrating at the same frequency in all dimensions.

This then was the nature of existence. Multiple realities existing side by side, exchanging spirit information. And these creatures were living, breathing, perpetual god machines, transferring all the spirits that had and would ever exist from one universe to another, like neurons in the mind of the god that had first existed at the beginning of all things. Not a mind like our minds. But a unity of all minds. A wellspring of infinite cognitive potential. The sum of all spirits. The first and original ancestor. Egún Akọkọ.

My own fragment-mind reeled at the knowledge, even as I was subsumed by it, incorporated into the sweep of this strange and wonderful singularity.

It was beyond anything I could have imagined. My mind was filled with pure awe.

I tried to project a thought out, desperately wishing the tethered ìdáwò connection was not completely broken. Hoping that Yinka could somehow hear me and know what I knew. Tell the others. But it was too late. I had come too close to the eye of the abyss.

The lurid glare of the singularity's glow pulsed as spirits flowed into it like eviternal comets, long tails of light stretching back into a single curve beyond my perception. The fractal universe became blurry, and everything was swallowed by a fitful nightmare glow ringing the singularity.

I felt the pull of it grow exponentially and even the idea of resisting was gone from me. I could no longer maintain my mental integrity. I flowed into it, like all the other consumed ancestors before me. The rim of the singularity flared to a bright, blinding corona.

I entered the mind-mouth between universes.

The fear and curiosity and wonder vanished. Everything seemed to stop.

Whatever was left of my mind observed it as a field of white light, pure and purifying. My thoughts lost structure and drifted away from each other. I could no longer tell who or what or when I was. All my memories were superimposed over each other. And there were new memories too. Ones I did not recognize. I could see an infinity of selves in sharp relief, viewing all the possibilities of me. I could not distinguish between present and future; four dimensions from eleven. My spirit had become a field of possibilities, unfolded. What would happen, what had happened, what was happening, and what could have happened became indistinguishable from one another. A temporary flush of infinite rearrangement, the opposite of a nothing—an everything; my mind took on every configuration possible, an infinite number.

A slurry of moments unconstrained by probability. An explosion of possibility. Everywhere, every here, every when, every then.

I saw a million versions of my myself in my parents' arms, my father with his thick afro, broad smile, and overgrown stubble. My mother with her braided hair and her bright eyes and tribal marks. I changed but they stayed the same. Always the same. Always there, the way they had never been.

I saw my children too, the biological children I never had and my adopted daughters' children. So many children. Bright and tall and short and chubby and skinny, their skin glowing like polished leather. Looking up to an infinity of me like I was a star in their sky. A constantly morphing future ancestor they could hold on to.

I saw my ancestors reaching out for me, shapes and forms and shadows, hands out in an infinitude of welcoming gestures.

I would have wept if I could.

I was in a place of all possibility, all potential.

And then the infinite stream of my existence flowed into an ocean of even more possibility.

I merged. With the singularity. With the ancestors. With all the other spirits that had come before me.

Love and hate and wonder and envy and curiosity and fear and anger and disgust and joy and sadness and confusion and anxiety and surprise and everything, everything, became one. Lovers, sisters, friends, brothers, uncles, enemies, grandfathers, aunts, children, an infinity of spirits who had once been reassuringly enclosed within individual spirit-matrices that persisted beyond death, were now truly dead, and without their multidimensional ghosts. Liberated by union. I was all of them in that eternal moment. We were one. Naked minds exposed to each other; the skin of individuality stripped away.

Remade. Unfolded. Refolded. Integrated.

The stream flowing. An infinity of one. A singularity of spirits. A reconstituted aspect of the super-universal spirit that animated all things. Egún Akọkọ. The only way to cross the membranes between universes.

As one.

THE KEEPER OF THE DEAD

Tobi Ogundiran

There was someone in his study.

Having spent the better part of his day fishing at the pond behind the Tower, managing after several failed attempts to snare a large silver trout, the Keeper of the Dead had labored in his kitchen; salting and seasoning and frying until the trout developed just the right juicy crispy consistency. Then he had skipped up the stairs (almost whistling, Fates spare him) at the thought of digging into the trout, doubly giddy at the prospect of spending the rest of the evening reading one of his freshly acquired tomes.

His evening, to put it succinctly, had been carefully planned.

You can imagine, then, his shock at the sight of the intruder—a little girl, curled up in his study, in his favorite reading chair, flipping through his rare first edition of Wole Soyinka's *The Man Died*.

The Keeper came to an abrupt halt, heart in his mouth. (And if you insist you wouldn't have screamed from fright were you in his position, then you are a liar.)

The girl looked up. "Oh, hello!" she called brightly as though they were old acquaintances. "Are these your books? You have sooo many books!"

A waif of a child, skin stretched over fragile bones, she couldn't be more than seven or eight. The tome spread on her lap was more than half her size and her legs dangled a good three feet from the floor.

"Where are all the pictures?" she asked. "There are no pictures in this book."

"I . . ." The Keeper realized he was quite thoroughly discombobulated.

Sometimes the dead ended up in the wrong place; those who had met a particularly violent end, those who did not quite understand that they were dead. Or, he reasoned, it could be that one of his own spells, now several millennia old, would wear thin so that the dead did not go through to the Shores of Midnight. (The Keeper had long ceased to deal directly with the dead. He couldn't stand their sad eyes, nor stomach the stench of ripe desperation that oozed from them, and so he had automated the process—setting up wards to keep them on the path, spelling the canoes to ferry them across the Lake of Midnight—such that he never had to interact with them. But now and again, some slipped off the path, not making it to the Shores of Midnight, forcing the grumpy Keeper to hunt them down across his vast domain, find them, and march them to the Lake through which all dead souls must sail. They did not always go quietly, the dead, but he was Keeper and lord of this domain, and in the end they bowed to him.) So yes, stray souls appeared all over his domain.

But never, in all this time, had one gotten into his home.

Never, in all this time, had one made it into his *study*.

"From whence did you come?" he managed, finding his voice at last. "And *how* did you get in here?"

"I came through the door," she said. "It was open."

"Impossible!" spat the Keeper, for he would have known the very moment she crossed his threshold. He would have felt her dead aura and hastened to remedy the situation. Now came the slightly worrying notion that she had been here all this time, prancing about his home, flipping through his *books* (he shuddered at the thought) and he had failed to notice it. He wondered, now, how long she had been here, if it had been while he fished for trout, or while he cooked in the kitchen. He supposed it didn't matter. He would simply do away with her, and attend to his wardings.

The Keeper shut his eyes and began to mutter an incantation under his breath.

"What are you doing?"

The Keeper let loose a small scream he was not very proud of, even as he danced backward and nearly dropped his trout. In the few moments he had shut his eyes, the girl had silently walked up to him and was now looking up at him with large brown eyes, inspecting him as though *he* were the anomaly, as though *he* didn't belong.

"It is not very wise to creep up on me." Had he a heart—a real heart—it would have been thundering in his chest. "I am old and powerful and dangerous things befall those who startle—*attempt* to startle—me."

"Sorry," said the girl. "Your eyes were closed and you were muttering and I thought maybe you were having a seizure."

"A seizure." The Keeper's eye twitched. "A seizure? I was *banishing* you."

"Banishing me? Why?"

"You are dead, you shouldn't be here."

"Oh," said the child. Then, "Are you going to eat that fish? I'm hungry."

The Keeper watched the child attack his trout with alacrity. She **was** ***hungry, and*** he was very sorry to see the last of the fish vanish down her tiny throat. Dead souls exuded an aura. Something that explained the manner of their death. But this child . . . there was something about her. It was as though she were . . . he did not know what she was.

"The trout," said the child, smacking her lips. "It was really good. I was so very hungry."

Yes, you ate all my trout, you little rat. His stomach gave a loud growl and she paused, smiling up at him sheepishly. "Sorry."

"How did you die?" the Keeper asked, but she merely blinked at him.

Dead souls did not always remember how they died. Not initially. And . . . he sniffed. She was definitely fresh. Hadn't been here longer than a few hours. But she *was* dead. He knew she was. He just couldn't understand why his spells had no effect on her, why he couldn't simply vanish her to the Lake like he had done countless others before her. And therein lay his conundrum. He could not banish her until he worked out that one problem, so it wouldn't happen again. He would have to go through the library, peruse the ancient tomes to understand her provenance, how she died, and why he couldn't read her. The Keeper sighed. This was all starting to sound like work. All he wanted was some peace and quiet, and now, he would actually have to *work*.

"What is your name?"

"Enitan."

A Yoruba name. Good. He had a starting point.

"You will remain here until I am ready to banish you. You will touch nothing, most especially my books. You will look at nothing. You will not get in my way. Understood?"

On the Shores of Midnight broods a lone tower, which is the only structure to be seen for miles. Within its walls broods an even lonelier soul. He has kept his duty for a while, which is a short time, or a long time, depending on how one considers it. Look to the east. Do you see that long, sinuous mass? They are the souls of the dead, come from every walk of life, come from that place full of laughter and hope and passion and desire. Here they are now, assembled; slowly wending their way to the end. Perhaps your soul is one of them. No, you say? You are not yet dead, you say?

That is irrelevant.

The Keeper started awake, blinking blearily. He surmised by the sun rays stream-ing through the stained glass windows of his study it was morning. Dust motes swirled in the beam, and he had a moment to wrest his mind from the murky depths of sleep, before it all came flooding back.

The girl. The strange child.

He sat up abruptly, and there came a loud ripping sound. He had fallen asleep, his face pressed into *The Book of Lost Things*. He peeled the page from his cheek and settled it carefully in the book. Ruined. Everything was ruined. Ever since the appearance, nay, *intrusion*, of that girl. His cursed his bad luck. Eons of routine and peace disrupted because of her. And he did not like it one bit, no thank you.

"Good morning!"

"Gah!" he squealed, leaped back in his chair so violently that it tilted backward. There came a precious moment in which the Keeper windmilled, arms flapping desperately for balance, in which he teetered precariously on the hind legs of his chair. And then he fell, crashing violently to the floor in a chaos of robes and books.

As he lay there groaning, struggling to disentangle himself from the ruin of his chair, he glimpsed the child, perched high on one of his bookshelves, legs swinging as she bit into a tangerine.

He closed his eyes. "Why have the Fates cursed me so?" All he wanted was some peace and quiet. Was that so much to ask?

"Come down here," he growled. "Come down here right this second."

The girl plopped a last bit of tangerine in her mouth and scrabbled down the shelf, swinging from level to level. Several times it appeared she would fall, but her feet were sure, and within moments she was before him, looking up at him with those huge brown eyes. The Keeper had left her to her own devices the previous night while he pored through every book he could get his hands on, trying to understand her provenance and why his magic refused to work on her. He remembered the words blurring before his eyes until the warm nothingness of sleep overtook him. Which was odd, for he did not sleep. He hadn't slept in . . . well, he couldn't remember the last time he slept.

Curiouser and curiouser.

"Now," he said, panting. "Get out of my study."

Enitan pointed at the bowl on the table, bursting with mangoes and tangerine and papaya, all freshly washed and inviting. He hadn't even noticed it at first. "You didn't have dinner last night," said Enitan. "Because I ate your fish. So I went about the kitchen looking for what to cook but it was dreadfully empty! There were cobwebs and rat droppings in some of your cooking pots!"

The Keeper looked sharply at her. He had no need for food; centuries went by where he neither ate nor drank; but he could appreciate the taste of food and sometimes he did develop cravings; like yesterday, when he'd developed a Fates-awful craving for trout. Still, he was not about to be lectured by some child—and not a living one at that—about the state of his kitchen, or his pots for that matter. "Now listen here—"

"So I went out in the woods. Back home, I would forage—"

"You remember where you came from?"

She kept mum.

"Little girl. You *must* tell me if you remember something."

But the girl was adept at parrying. "I don't see anyone else here. Do you live alone?"

"Yes, but I don't see what that has to do with—"

"Don't you have any friends?"

"Friends? What are those?"

"You must be lonely." She looked at him slantwise, considering. "Is that why you're so grumpy all the time?"

"Grumpy?" He gaped at her. "*Grumpy?* Child, I am only grumpy because you have disrupted my peace and quiet! There is nothing I desire more this moment than for you to be gone! Lonely? Ha ha! What is loneliness to one like me? I have my books! Look around you, every day a new book appears in this library, great works of unfathomable literary esteem. Worth ten times a king's ransom and then some. My vast halls contain the lost library of Alexandria and countless others from civilizations humans have forgotten even existed! Civilizations that never even existed! Great works of literature *you* couldn't even begin to dream of. If I read a book a day for all eternity I still wouldn't be halfway through—" He broke off, wondering why he spoke so vehemently, why he felt the need to go on such long a tirade. Almost as though he were trying to convince her.

She offered him a sweet, knowing grin.

"You—" he choked, pointing a trembling finger at her. "You were . . ." The devil child had been trying to rile him up. And Fates be damned he had fallen for it. The Keeper felt heat crawl up his face as she burst into tinkling giggles.

The Keeper spun about on his heels and stumbled from the hall, Enitan's laughter trailing after him.

The Keeper spent the next few days avoiding Enitan. He locked himself in his study and spelled shut the doors and windows. He also spelled close the crawl spaces (after seeing her scrabble down the bookshelf he had no doubt she could slip through one of the crawl spaces that led into his library).

On the fifth day he looked up to realize he had generally been a prisoner in his own home, and what a ridiculous thing indeed it was to hide from a little girl. A little dead girl. Enough.

He threw open the doors and marched out . . . stopping dead in his tracks. He had expected to find her camped out in the hallway like some puppy craving his attention. But the hallway was empty.

"Girl!" he called. "Come to me!"

Nothing.

"I command you! Show yourself this very moment!"

There was nothing. Just his voice thrown back at him by the stone walls. The Keeper stood there a moment, a slow grin breaking across his face. She was gone. Unable to torment him any further she had left this place, perhaps left the same way she came and gone to the Lake of Midnight. Followed the other dead souls to where they belonged. He twirled around, letting loose a hoot of joy. Granted he had been unable to get to the root of how she came to be here in the first place, or how she was resistant to his spells, but that didn't matter. She was gone, and he would need not do any work!

The Keeper stalked from room to room, noting with increasing distress the absence of dereliction. The cushions were fluffed up, the floors swept, the cobwebs that lurked in the corners long gone. Torches guttered in their sconces, flames dancing merrily as they banished the perpetual gloom and wetness of his halls, leaving in its place a . . . a general warmth, a homey warmth—not that he *cared* for any of that. Books he had left strewn about with abandon were neatly stacked, and for the first time in a long time he caught his reflection in the mirrors. Everything glistened with a newness as when he first made them.

"What in all the realms . . . ?" He breathed.

First came shame. An unpleasant emotion he was not accustomed to. It wormed around his heart. But on the heels of that: anger. How dare she presume to clean his place, impose her will on his home? How dare she confuse his tolerance . . . for hospitality? With a wave of his hand everything returned to its original state. Cobwebs stretched across the high ceiling, and grime caked the stained windows and gloom and filth and dankness reigned supreme once more.

The Keeper had dealt with wily spirits. There were those who did not want to go, and employed all manner of cunning their feeble minds could conjure to remain here. He had been offered kingdoms, jewels, and artifacts—even sex by lascivious spirits. But he was not a man. Had never been a man. And did not share their weaknesses. He had dealt with all manner of cunning, yes. But this . . . this was a different flavor.

He marched out into the garden, where he found Enitan seated on a low boulder, book in her hand as she read aloud to her attentive audience, which was a group of cats.

There were large tabbies and barn cats and black cats and spotted cats, cats big and small, all of them arranged about Enitan, who might as well have been the cat queen herself, given how rapturously they listened to her.

The Keeper stood there for a moment, gaping in silent wonderment. He had never seen so many cats gathered. Not because he never paid them any mind (he did) but because they were wild and temperamental creatures. They slipped in and out of realms at will, and not even he, who was lord of this domain, had managed to master them. Sometimes he glimpsed one or two when he ventured into the forest. But they kept their distance, and he kept his distance, and he was quite happy with the arrangement. That is, until now.

Fury clouded his mind. "You brought vermin here?"

Enitan looked up at him. "They're not vermin. They're my friends—"

"NO!" he thundered. "THEY DO NOT BELONG HERE. *YOU* DO NOT BELONG HERE. FOR YOU ARE DEAD, DO YOU UNDERSTAND? DEAD!"

As he spoke the skies darkened and the moon turned blood red, bathing the garden in an eerie crimson light. Birds scattered from the trees. Enitan shrank back from his terrible regard, for now he appeared before her in his true form, formidable and a terror to behold. Her eyes widened with fear and her lips trembled and she burst into tears. The Keeper could almost taste the despair that wafted from her, and he found that . . . he did not revel in it. In the past he had taken great pleasure in visiting terror on recalcitrant spirits, in bringing them to heel. But now . . . he searched his mind and found he could not enjoy her fear. Perhaps it was the way she shied away from him, hugging her knees to her chest; perhaps it was the way the cats swarmed toward her in protection, hackles raised, a chorus of disapproving hisses directed at him; perhaps it was because in that instant he could see that she was no stranger to fear. That fear had been a constant and unwelcome companion in her life.

The Keeper's fury melted away as he regarded her with fresh eyes. His conjurations dissipated and the sky was the blue of morning once more, and sun shone golden and bright.

"Stop it," he said softly. "Stop crying. I'm—" He could not *say* he was sorry. He flapped his hands rather uselessly, at a loss for what to do. "Carry on . . ."

The Keeper spun about on his heels and practically flew from the garden.

They settled into a truce of sorts. The Keeper allowed Enitan to do as she pleased, which did not irk him. Well, except for the cats. They were everywhere. He could not walk without tripping on one of the blasted creatures, who would give him a baleful stare from underfoot before slinking away.

"Where did you find these vermi—cats?" he said to Enitan once at lunch.

"They found me," she said. "I was reading in the garden when Muna came—"

"Muna?"

Enitan pointed to the large tabby in her lap, who was purring so loudly he could almost feel the table vibrate.

"You . . . you *named* them?"

"No, silly. They told me their names." She cocked her head at him. "What is *your* name?"

"I don't have one."

She frowned. "Everyone has a name."

"Well, I have no need for one. There is only me."

"Then how do you know you're you?"

"Whatever . . . do you mean?"

Enitan lifted Muna (to the cat's great discontentment) and presented her to the Keeper. "This is Muna!" she declared. "She is a cat, yes. But she has a name, so she knows *who* she is. How do you know who you are, if you don't have a name?"

"I know who I am. I am the Keeper of the Dead." He had felt no need to define himself beyond his function. "I am neither human nor animal. Surely you know that, little girl. I do not abide by your rules."

She thought about that a moment. "If you only have a title, then you are replaceable. And I don't think you want to be replaced."

"I am one of a kind. I cannot be replaced."

She considered him. "I will call you Grumpy."

"You will not."

"Okay, Grumpy."

Later that evening the Keeper tried to instruct her in fishing.

"You must lure the trout with bait," he said, impaling wriggling worms on his hook. "And wait. Much of fishing is waiting. You might ask why I simply do not command them to my hook, but some things must be done the proper way, and I do not mind the time—*what are you doing?*"

Enitan was splashing noisily in the shallows. She dived into the water and after a moment came up sopping wet and laughing, a large trout flapping in her small hands.

"I caught one!" she cried. "I caught one! Bring the basket—!"

But the fish was so big it wobbled her frail form and slipped from her grasp, flashing silver in the late noon sun before splashing into the water and away.

"I had it! I *had* it!"

And then she was laughing, bent over with mirth. And never had the Keeper seen such expression of delight on anyone's face. And how could he, when all he ever saw were the desperate and morose faces of the dead? And it wasn't until he felt a tug at the corners of his lips, and realized that he too was smiling that it dawned on him that he had let this go too far.

The Keeper shook Enitan gently awake. "Child . . . Child . . ."

But she would not wake. She merely turned in her sleep and resumed her soft snores. The Keeper cursed softly. He had half a mind to leave her, but after a few moments of deliberation, he wrapped her up in the blanket and carried her out of the room. She settled snugly into the crook of his neck as he descended the stairs, her breath warm on his cheek.

The night was dark and chill. But it wasn't really night. Where the Keeper might manipulate the rest of his domain into a semblance of day and night and even seasons; here, on the Shores of Midnight, it was forever dark. The Keeper approached the lone canoe bobbing in the black water, gently settling Enitan into the bow seat. Then he stepped in, seized the oars and began to row.

(Look closely. Do you see those other canoes in the water, as numerous as the stars? Do you see the countless souls crammed into the vessels? They are the souls of the dead, sailing into the burgeoning dark.)

The Keeper watched Enitan stir awake. She blinked first at him, then around, but not before the Keeper made it so she could not see the others, so that all she saw was the endless blackness of the Lake.

Enitan frowned. "Where are we going?"

"On an adventure," said the Keeper. "I want to show you something."

Her eyes lit up at that.

Once they were close the Keeper stepped out of the canoe and onto the water. He began to push. He did not need to push. He could have simply willed it across, but he needed to be there until the end. He would do this one thing for her.

"Look!" Enitan cried, pointing ahead. "Look!"

The Lake sloped into a vast and turbulent whirlpool, which spun like water rushing down a drain. Indeed the boat increased in speed once it was caught in the currents. Where the rest of the Lake was inky blackness; the whirlpool shone bright, blindingly bright, as though lit from below by the light of a sun. And the boats, in their hundreds, in their thousands, in their hundreds of thousands, rushed toward that point of light. At once a chorus of voices filled the night: the dead screaming in fear of what lay beyond the light. They begged the Keeper to save them, but he shut out their cries.

"We're going to drown!" cried Enitan. "We have to turn back!"

"No. That is where we must go."

"Why?"

"I told you. It is an adventure."

"But . . ." The girl looked from the whirlpool to him, her eyes searching. "What is in there?"

Damned if he knew. Perhaps there was nothing. Perhaps there was something more.

"I'm scared," she whispered.

"It's all right. I am right behind you." The words were ash on his tongue.

Enitan nodded, flashed a brief smile and turned to watch their fast approach. It was then the Keeper realized she trusted him. Trusted that he would keep her safe, that his words were true.

Never had he loathed anything as he loathed himself in that moment.

When the girl turned back to look at him, he had stopped pushing the canoe but stood still on the water, the vessel fast careening away from him. Ten feet. Twenty feet. Thirty—

"Father!" she cried, her face taut with alarm. "Fa—!"

The canoe plunged into the whirlpool and then she was gone.

By the time the Keeper returned to his hallowed halls he had convinced himself that he did the right thing.

"It is my duty," he announced to his books. "She was dead. She did not belong here."

She had called him "Father." Why did she have to call him Father?

Guilt wrapped around his neck like a noose, slowly tightening. He ignored it and returned to business as usual.

Or tried to.

The Keeper searched for solace in his books, and spent long days reading of things yet to be, of things which shall never be, of things that once had been. But the joy was leached from reading, and he found his eyes tracing the same lines over and over again. He went trout fishing only to be confronted with the memory of Enitan's tinkling laughter, of her splashing in the shallows, of the pure and unfettered delight that illumined her childish face.

Worse were the human traits he'd picked up. He still sat at the table for regular meals which he didn't need; he found himself snoozing to the twitter of birds in the garden (his dreams haunted by Enitan's cries of "Father!"). Once he started awake in his study to find the cats, more of them than he cared to count, perched in the shelves, on his table, on the sills—on every surface they could find—watching him. They knew what he had done and he could see the judgment in their eyes.

"Away!" he said weakly. "Away with you." And when they didn't leave, added: "I did what I had to do."

Every day the Keeper wandered the vast halls of his home. And every day the Keeper realized just how strangely empty and . . . lonely it was. These halls that he had known since the Fates first formed him from nothing; these halls, his home, whose silent walls had comforted him in his long existence, now felt strangely lonely. The girl had been here such a short while and had left an indelible mark on him. To be so thoroughly changed by a child, him, the Keeper of the Dead! He who was immovable and constant and never-changing!

"This won't do," he said into the silence. "This won't do at all."

In response Muna the cat plopped onto the chair, the one Enitan often sat in, and proceeded to silently judge him. The Keeper glowered at her. He was sick of those yellow eyes, sick of the judgment and contempt he saw in them. Growling, he grabbed a heavy bronze candelabra and chucked it at the feline: Muna hissed, dodging the projectile before darting out of the room in indignation, tail raised high.

The chair had toppled backward as Muna flew out of it. It crashed to the floor and something came flying out of its cushions, skidding toward the Keeper.

It was a book. One bound in emerald crocodile leather. He traced a finger over the gold clasp before cracking it open.

Writing splashed across the pages. Not the meticulous hand of monks that filled some of his other books, but a scrawl, barely legible.

Slowly, the Keeper began to read.

Once there lived a girl. She was the light of her mother's heart, who was a very rich and prosperous railway magnate. And for a long while they lived happily ever after. But bliss soon curdled when her mother died, shredded to ribbons under one of her own trains. Unbeknownst to the girl her mother had left her all her fortune, but had also left her in the care of her father who coveted the riches, and conspired with his new wife to claim it for himself.

"We cannot steal the fortune. The will is airtight; I am merely custodian until she comes into her own."

"And if she never comes into her own?"

The man looked into his new wife's eyes and took her meaning. "I cannot . . . I cannot kill my own child."

And so they lured the little girl into the cellar and held her prisoner. For years the girl endured in the deep and dark, surviving on rats and voles. They could not kill her. They would not kill her. And when people asked about her they would say, "Oh she's away at school, our brilliant Enitan." Or, "She just went out to visit with friends. You only just missed her!"

It didn't take long for the little girl to realize this was to be her life. Alone in the dark and the cold she began to dream up a different reality (and which of us, when confronted with a terrible life, have not escaped into the bliss of dreams?). She dreamed a different father. One who loved her and cared for her and did not keep her in the dark so she might wither away. All this she scribbled in her book.

The girl's father and stepmother lived above in splendor and bliss, and fattened themselves on her inheritance, while the world forgot about her. But she did not perish, nor did she wither. And after many years the wicked stepmother unlocked the rusted chains that bound the cellar door to find the frail form of the snoozing girl, clutching her book to her breast. And she pried the book from the sleeping child and read it and flew into a rage at all she had written, for daring to dream a better world, a better life, than the one foisted upon her. The wicked stepmother burned the book. But the girl had written all of her wishes into the book, and the burning of wishes is as old as time, and there is magic in that act, and the world must listen. In her folly the wicked stepmother granted the girl what she wanted.

And so, the girl vanished from that world, from that cruel, cruel existence, into a better one.

The book dropped from the Keeper's hands as he staggered backward.

"No!" he breathed, collapsing in his chair. He grabbed a fistful of his hair, nearly tearing them out by the roots. "Dear Fates, *what have I done?*"

This was Enitan's story. She had come here in search of something better and he had treated her badly. He had . . . good gods, he sent her to the lake!

Hadn't he felt the aura around her? The fear and despair. If only he had paid more attention he would have seen it. But he had been too preoccupied ridding himself of her, with fulfilling his duty.

He was no different from her father.

She had called him "Father" when in truth he was no different from her real father.

"No," he gasped wagging his head like a flea-ridden mutt. "No, no, no, no, *no*."

And then the Keeper was flying from his study and stumbling down the stairs, his world spinning, his ears ringing. Into the canoe and across the Lake of Midnight he went until he was staring into the whirlpool, into that vast and swirling whorl of light. He couldn't go in there, not even if he willed it so. What happened to souls who went in there? Was Enitan in there? Was she still . . . alive?

He could not answer that question. But he knew who could.

Back in his study the Keeper removed the cloth covering the mirror. It was an ancient piece wrought of pure silver, a heavy old-fashioned frame carved around it. The Keeper contemplated his haggard reflection, the rows and rows of dusty books, his red-rimmed eyes. He recited:

Spindle spinner, dest'ny weaver.
F'rever mothers o' this world and nether.
By wool and yarn and thimble and needle
Shew thy face in the black of the crack!

Nothing.

The Fates were coy and did not always answer summons.

"Come on!" he begged. "Please!" Wiping the snot from his nose, he tried again.

Spindle spinner, dest'ny weaver
F'rever mother o' world and nether
By wool and yarn and thimble and needle
Shew thy face in the black of the crack!

The mirror fractured.

"Well say your piece since you've called us here," said a voice.

The Keeper wheeled about to find the Crone perched in his chair, crocheting.

"I made a mistake, I—" He gulped. "I sent a child—a *living* child into the Lake. Please bring her back."

"Ha!" barked the Crone. "Why don't you ask for the moon while you're at it?"

"What the Lake has taken cannot be given," said the Mother, studying her reflection in the mirror.

"Can't it?" It was the Maiden who said this, and it was to her the Keeper turned, hopeful as a puppy who's heard his master's voice.

"If the girl was not dead, then she did not belong in the Lake."

"The Lake will not give her back. Unless . . ."

"Unless?" he croaked, eyes darting between the Fates who regarded him, identical smiles on their faces.

"You must give yourself in exchange," they chorused.

"Yes!" he gasped, without thought.

"I don't think he understands what it means," mused the Maiden.

"Whatever it means," said the Keeper. "I'll do it. If it means she can . . . she can live."

A man stands outside a lopsided bookshop. Around him yuletide is in full bloom: garlands dangle over doors and lampposts and fairy lights twine through roofs and trees to light up the street in the colors of Christmas. And riding the wind is that most infectious spirit of the season. Folk call out cheery salutations as they make their way down the street; even the mutts wag their tails as they prance about, sniffing hopefully at passersby who oblige them. Here, a man scatters crumbs to cooing pigeons; there a woman twirls to a busker's jaunty tune. And just down at the street corner two lovers share a kiss, entwined in an embrace.

But let us consider the man who stands outside the bookshop. You might take in his countenance, the rough corners of his lips, and call him grumpy. But he is not grumpy, not really; it is merely his resting expression.

A girl darts out of the bookshop. Her cheeks are plump and her eyes are full of delight. "Look what I got!" she cries, waving an emerald crocodile leather-bound book in his face.

"A book?" he says, amused.

"A diary," she counters, rolling her eyes, just as a large black cat comes bounding out of the shop to twine about her leg.

"What do you plan to write in there?" he asks. "How I am the best father in the whole world? How much you love love *love* me?"

"Eeew!" She scrunches up her nose, but her eyes twinkle with delight and she bursts into tinkering giggles as he tickles her.

"I will write . . ."

And whatever you think it is that she writes, that is the truth.

NOW WATCH ME AS YOU HOLD YOUR BREATH

Silvia Park

In our third year of university, my best friend Rinko became obsessed with indie bands. For as long as I had known her, she had never not been in a relationship, except that fall semester. It was her longest dry spell and she was determined to snag a wannabe rockstar boyfriend. She'd submit fan surveys to indie bands with sticker pictures of the three of us in virtual cat ears, which made even Aya look cute and harmless. One of the bands eventually called Rinko's number and we met in a karaoke room. The bassist was a better singer than the vocalist, and they all sang other people's songs better than they sang their own.

Rinko liked vocalists. Aya preferred drummers, and I got whoever was left over. I didn't mind last pick. But that night, I got the drummer and he was unusually handsome. I understood soon enough why Rinko had paired me with him. He was a Korean exchange student, not completely fluent. His phone wallpaper was a blue-haired Lolita. I was small and cute enough, I guess, to fit that aesthetic. If handsome, outgoing drummers could also be otakus, then maybe I was his type.

"I drew this myself when I was ten," he said.

Not bad for a ten-year-old, I thought. I praised him generously and admitted that despite having once been a Western painting major, I couldn't draw people at all.

"She's obsessed with drawing insects," Rinko chimed in.

I was known as "Insect Girl" around campus after my last work, which had won a prize. I re-created the memorial for a dead praying mantis I had found on the ground. It had laid sanctified in a tiny circle of pebbles and prayer beads. I made a human-sized statue of it from copper wire and glued a mix of fake and real succulents to give it a fungal sort of rot. It was supposed to be interactive: you could step into the circle of prayer beads and lie down beside the dead praying mantis and be the little spoon. Or big spoon, depending on your size.

The drummer wanted to see pictures of the installation, but my Cloud loaded too slowly so we moved on to livelier conversation, like visual kei and anime—his favorite being *Fullmetal Alchemist*—and eventually dead mothers. His mother had passed away last year of cancer. She had loved his drawings; his Lolita drawing used to be *her* phone wallpaper. His voice trembled when he recounted this. I thought sharing my own story might come across as attention-seeking, but I told him that my mother too—my father also, actually—had died when I was in high school. From an accident.

"Both your parents?" he exclaimed. "Wow, that's really, yeah."

People really didn't know how to deal with death, especially if they started weighing who had it worse.

"But you know what? It might be better that way. I get that it's super painful for the people left behind. But you know, for the person who dies, it's better if it's quick."

"I can see that," I said.

The others seemed to be having a good time. By the end of the night we'd made plans with the indie band to meet again at the end of the month for Halloween. Rinko declared, "My costume is going to be no makeup," and everyone laughed because she was beautiful—so beautiful, a band member of Arashi had once complimented her at a jazz bar.

The drummer tapped my shoulder. "Do you want to exchange LINE?"

I had been told often that I had a sweet, childlike face, which seemed to suggest only pedophiles would find me attractive. Proof that the face does not reflect the soul. After my parents died, I'd met plenty of vile, horrible people with the most pristine faces.

The vocalist was one of those. At the start of the mixer, he said we could order anything. He summoned a constant stream of melon sodas and strawberry parfaits and honey toast, wholesome-sounding food. He had the kind of long platinum-blond hair that only a rocker could pull off. Rinko asked if she could put her finger through his earring and I knew she was too drunk to hear herself.

That night I got shit-faced. We were probably drugged. All signs pointed to the scummy vocalist, who had at one point walked into the room generously carrying a tray full of electric-blue drinks. The air felt sticky and the room sloshed blue, like a slow, sleepy tidal wave. Everything seemed out of reach. Feeling sick, I got up without saying anything. The drummer followed me. I crouched in the hall and threw up. He panicked and left, saying he would grab some paper towels.

I wiped my mouth with the back of my hand and got to my feet. I couldn't find Rinko, so I went to look for Aya.

I passed by the karaoke rooms. Most were dim. Some with a glow from deep within, the lyrics unfolding across the big TV screen. Disco lights flittered while shadows swayed and danced, clapping slowly to a beat. One room was completely dark. But the music was on. Sweet and low. ABBA's "Dancing Queen."

I couldn't really remember what had happened that night, but I did find Aya.

A few weeks later, I met Aya at a department store in Namba. We were going to use the handicap-accessible bathroom to change into our costumes together before we joined the boys for the Halloween parade.

Rinko was late, which we had planned for. We waited at a popular European café and ordered their seasonal parfait. When my parfait arrived, I clapped in excitement and took a picture. I'd learned to feign delight ever since I started therapy so I could feel the trim of it. Fake it until you feel it, no?

"You don't really have to do that," Aya said, picking up the long thin parfait spoon.

"Take pictures?"

Aya just shook her head and smiled down at her parfait. "This is exquisite, isn't it?"

The parfait was an ecosystem unto itself, with carefully segregated layers of treasure, like an RPG dungeon. The top was studded with purple and orange jack-o'-lantern macarons, grinning in adorable malice. Underneath scoops of runny cinnamon ice cream was the crunchy soil of granola with candied pumpkin. Cubes of fluffy cake soaked in the milky cinnamon. Aya ate slowly, excavating each layer. When the stickiness dripped over her fingers, she licked around the knuckle and locked eyes with me.

"Do you like watching me eat?" Aya said.

"You're so thin, but you enjoy it so much."

"I'm always hungry," she sighed.

Rinko finally showed up, blue pigtails flouncing, armed with a reasonable excuse. Her train had stalled at a station. An office lady was found partially eaten on the tracks. All the passengers had filed out in an orderly fashion. She followed the crowd out of the train station and walked for a good ten minutes through the neighborhood, eventually cutting through a small dingy mall to catch the train at the next station.

Rinko had also seen the body—covered up by a blue sheet, weighed down with a brick, but the wind had flipped it over for just a bit, and she saw a flash of black hair.

We soothed her and each held her hands. Poor Rinko, Aya said, stroking Rinko's blue bangs. So horrible, I said.

Rinko let go of my hand to put her palm over her chest and took a breath. "It must have happened for a reason."

Aya and I exchanged glances but wisely we said nothing. These accidents did happen all the time. You could download an app to keep track, although the numbers were probably unreliable. The bodies didn't always show up, and when they did, it was usually a man, shredded like a lost kite. Also, it was considered bad luck when the body reappeared. It felt unclean.

We got up and paid for our parfaits and coffee. Now that Rinko was here, we went upstairs to change into our Halloween costumes, but the accessible bathroom was unexpectedly occupied. A man lined up behind us, standing close enough to taste Rinko's perfume.

"What time are we meeting the indie band?" I asked.

"I can call them," Rinko said. "But don't you have the drummer's number?"

She knocked her shoulder against mine. Her teasing tone loosened in my chest a small knot, tightly clogged like a ball of hair inside a drain.

"Did you hear their vocalist disappeared?" I said.

"Oh my God, yes!" Rinko's cheeks turned pink and she glanced up at Aya. "They had to cancel their last gig."

I heard a click. The man behind us held his phone low and steady, as if he'd been angling for a glimpse. Only Rinko was wearing a skirt.

I stared at his phone like I wanted to crush it with my mind, but Aya was watching the man with wide opaque eyes. A thrill, like an ice pick, pierced me. I imagined Aya stalking this creep. I imagined her leading him into one of the alleys outside and they'd find a dark corner and I'd get to watch.

A woman stepped out of the accessible bathroom and looked startled to see a line. Aya backed out at the last second, saying she'd use a separate stall. Rinko cooed at Aya's gap moe, how cute for our cool and calm Aya to be so shy. Aya had also changed in private when we went on that trip to Arima Onsen. I had wondered then if she was hiding something on her body, like a scar.

As soon as the door sealed shut, Rinko split open her duffel bag. Wings spilled out, attached to Anna Sui-style corsets, lacy and violent. They were held upright by old bra wiring and the lace was a seamless chiffon blend. Rinko was a good designer but a brilliant patterner. She could close her eyes and tell the type of fabric from touch, whether it was rayon or polyester or cotton-on-polyester to mimic the slide of silk.

Rinko turned her back to me as she changed, spine curling to show off the knobs. When she peeled off her tight scallop-edged cardigan, the bandage on her neck came away. The bruise was now a pale jade green, but you could still make out the shapes of fingers. I pretended not to notice. The last time I had called attention to the bruise, it hadn't gone over so well.

Rinko patted the bandage flat then asked me to help her put on her wings. "Can you pull it tight?"

"Your waist is already so small."

"It's okay, I don't need to breathe!"

I twined the shoestrings twice around each finger and pulled. "How are you feeling?"

I was talking about the train incident, but Rinko exhaled, a fluttery sigh. "I'm in love."

Who is it this time? I thought. I said, "Oh?"

"I think I love Aya."

"*Love*-love?"

"Love-love."

"Are you going to tell her?"

After a second, Rinko said, "Tighter."

Ah. I had made a mistake. I was supposed to act surprised, instead I hid it. In not giving Rinko the reaction she craved, I had put her on the defensive. But I was too shocked to react properly. And a little annoyed. Rinko had never shown interest in women, so why now? Why Aya?

Rinko put her hand on her ribs and took a deep breath. "Okay, I'll do yours."

"I can't believe you like Aya," I said, coaxing now.

"She's so mature and untouchable, like she knows her way in the world and everyone will move aside for her."

She rambled on like this. I found the reasons to be vague and pretty typical, but I kept nodding. I was reminded of our high school days when she used to call me late at night and talk about the soccer team captain, our art teacher, that gallery owner who had slipped her a business card, instead of what was really bothering her. Rinko was raised by her grandmother, after her mother had walked out on her father when she was eleven, and sometime around high school, her grandmother began to leave the house and wander the streets in a fluttering nightgown. Until one day, it happened. Her grandmother disappeared.

Clean, was how Rinko called it. For her end-year project at Kyogei, she designed a series of white funeral kimono for her grandmother and posed them using upcycled hangers in the various movements of her grandmother as she went about her day, cooking, vacuuming, gardening, darning Rinko's socks. A professor called it "sentimental" during crit, leaving it up to us to decipher his tone.

"Would you have sex with me?" Rinko said.

"What?" I snapped out of my daze and looked down at my fingers. Striped red from how hard I'd yanked as I'd tied up her corset.

"How would you feel if I sprang this on you? Would you have sex with me?"

"I like you and I would have sex with you," I said. "But I also value our friendship very much."

She'd asked this question before when we were in high school. It was like a test.

"You're so cute," Rinko said, and patted my head. I smiled but I knew to be wary. Rinko could just as easily withdraw the forgiveness she'd extended.

"Are you going to tell Aya?"

Instead of answering, Rinko peeled the bandage from her neck and threw it in the trash.

Outside, she twirled for Aya, who was also wearing the butterfly wings. Somehow Aya had done up her corset by herself.

The man with the phone was no longer there. Aya was smiling. Her skin glowed, her eyes now glossy as a green-black beetle shell. Rinko had told me Aya had all the right ingredients—tall and skinny with a small face, big eyes, red rosebud mouth—but they didn't add up quite right.

At the time, I had thought Rinko was being cruel, subtly putting down other girls, but now I could see what she'd meant. Aya looked unnerving when she was satiated.

From Namba Station, we followed a crowd toward Dotonbori and met up with the indie band on the other side of the bridge. I recognized the drummer from the other end of the bridge. He was jumping around like a monkey, taking pictures of the Glico Man, a big neon sign of a runner with his arms thrown in the air.

"Hey!" The drummer sounded relieved to see me, as if we'd been separated by the crowd. He asked if I could take a picture of him and the Glico Man. He threw his arms in the same victory pose. "Do you want a picture too?"

"Not really," I said.

"What are you dressed as?"

"I don't know, a dark fairy? And you're supposed to be . . . ?"

"Sailor . . . Venus!"

He made a pose that was unlikely to be correct. He urged his bandmates to join. The squad of *Sailor Moon*s lined up in front of us and lifted their skirts, flashing their boxers. Rinko cackled, called the cross-dressing "clichéd, but hot." Aya snapped a picture of all of us together. When I went up to look at our picture, Aya wasn't holding her usual iPhone.

It was a bigger phone, with a big thumbprint smudged on the screen. She smiled at the expression on my face and tucked away the phone before I could say a word.

"Is that your new vocalist? He's so pretty," Aya murmured.

The newcomer stood to the side, clutching his pointy elbows. He was small-boned enough to pass for Sailor Mercury, if Sailor Mercury had a septum nose ring and a scowl on her face.

"No touch!" The drummer stepped in front of Aya, blocking her off with his arms. "This is my little brother. He's sixteen."

Aya and Rinko laughed. "Is your vocalist still missing?" I said.

"Yeah, it's been two weeks."

The drummer didn't sound too cut up about it. Apparently, no one had any idea what had happened to the vocalist. Not the vocalist's friends or his parents who had funded his fifteen-mat LDK apartment and monthly allowance of 200,000 yen.

"So, do you think he was eaten?" I said.

"You can't just ask that!" Rinko cried.

I was 100 percent sure that the vocalist had spiked our drinks that night. The truth was, I had a black hole in my stomach for alcohol. I almost never got drunk. But I kept blacking out. I couldn't remember if I had taken Rinko home. It had always been my job to worry about her since middle school, and aside from the year after my parents' accident, I'd fretted after her in college too. She had so much friction with other girls, who were jealous and judgmental, Rinko said, of how she dated older men who covered her rent and her allowance and art materials.

Rinko had gotten in trouble before, but not like this. After our karaoke night with the indie band, she'd skipped uni for a whole week and showed up on Tuesday for the afternoon crit, swallowed up in a thick hoodie. Without her blue eye shadow and thick mascara, she looked simultaneously very young and very old.

I'd asked about the bruise on her neck. She'd waved it off. The vocalist got carried away. Boys watched too much porn. Then, she admitted that she had a panic attack and she'd locked herself in the toilet stall, the way she used to hide from her father whenever he got drunk. I listened to her and soothed her, so she could soften and crumble and I would become the shoulder she needed. She said why do men do this to me? I said it was okay to not date. She said she wasn't like me. She needed someone to be fully happy. I said I get that, I just wished she'd be a little more careful. She abruptly lifted her head and glared at me. Are you saying it was my fault? Are you victim-blaming me?

For about a week, Rinko ignored my texts. Tonight was the first time we'd spoken about something that wasn't cordial, like school. And now she had latched on to Aya like this. They were whispering together, arm in arm. Watching Aya put her herringbone scarf around Rinko and Rinko burrow her face into Aya's shoulder, I felt like I'd eaten a hive of wasps.

Rinko looked so frothily happy. She bubbled over with a vitality that was beyond me, while I was standing on a lower plane, watching everyone else above live in a lush, nubile 3D world where they could see things and hear things and taste things and smell things I would never be able to grasp. Love put stars in their grapefruit-sized eyes.

Whenever I nursed these heavy thoughts about love, I thought of sex to comfort myself. I'd always found sex alien and horrific, like those deep-sea creatures that evolved into tantalizing shapes for reasons only knowable to nature. Rinko used to reassure me that I hadn't found the right person yet. My parents had taken it for granted too that I would marry one day and have children, their grandchildren.

Occasionally I would realize I hadn't thought about sex in weeks, maybe months. So I'd look up porn during class or I'd stare kind of gormlessly at our professor. It amazed me to think that he had a sex organ hidden in his pants. That everyone did. It felt uncomfortable shaping these thoughts and once I gained some lucidity, they usually turned violent. I'd imagine man-eating birds attacking the classroom. I'd imagine an earthquake and demons crawling out of the cracks. My classmates screaming while the birds and demons descended on us.

What brought me pleasure was how I could dissipate these thoughts, have them vanish with the rake of my fingers. The world felt safe and malleable in my hands. I could end it at any time.

"You look really cute," the drummer said.

I mimicked Rinko and twirled for him. Whenever I channeled Rinko, I could be playful and confident. I thought about asking the drummer if he'd want to have sex with me, but even as a joke, the question felt unsafe now. Joking about sex used to make me feel normal. Another thing karaoke night had ruined.

The parade kept growing, and I was feeling hot and stuffy. The strap of my Vivienne Westwood purse cut into my shoulder. One of my wings was dragging close to the ground; they were too big for me. Rinko must have cut corners by designing just one size that fitted Aya and her.

"I hate being a butterfly," I whispered to the drummer. "My wings are falling apart."

"Did you know butterfly wings are waterproof? You put one in water and it can still fly away."

"I guess that's like me. I'm alcohol-proof," I said. "I don't get drunk."

He took off his blond wig and held it, studying it like a piece of tapestry, looking anywhere but at me. I hadn't been sure about the rest of the band, but watching him now, I knew.

"What do you think happened to your vocalist?"

The drummer shrugged. "What do you wish happened to him?"

"I think he was eaten."

His eyes finally met mine. "What makes you so sure?"

I shrugged back, but mysteriously. "Maybe sixty percent sure," I said.

"That's not very high," the drummer said, almost sadly.

We dipped out of the parade and found an empty spot in front of a closed pharmacy. I sat down on the stoop. I was sweating even though my shoulders were bare and cold, from the wind, the unforgiving cinch of my corset. The others joined us a second later, Rinko breathless with laughter, yet she cried out, "This crowd is going to kill us!"

"Last year, there was the Halloween crowd crush in Itaewon," the drummer said.

I asked him if he was there. He wasn't, but his little brother was. "It was crazy, right?" The drummer raised his voice for his brother to hear. "Crazy! Itaewon crowd crush."

His brother rolled his eyes. "*Luckily*," the drummer said, as he turned back to me, "no one we knew died. But most of the victims were girls." He held up his hands as if he was holding an invisible waist. "Their rib cages are smaller."

Beside us, away from the stoop, Rinko was arguing with the bassist, as they compared maps, trying to locate the closest and cheapest izakaya.

Aya, as if taking her chance, pulled away from Rinko and sidled up to the drummer's little brother, who was sitting alone at few steps below me, close to my feet, and offered him a cigarette, which he eagerly accepted.

"No smoking!" the drummer said, but in English for some reason. He karate-chopped his brother's wrist.

The brother sniped back something that sounded like Korean for "You're a loser" or "Asshole," before stomping off into the crowd.

"You're a loving older brother," Aya said.

She handed the drummer a different cigarette, a peace offering, which he only grudgingly accepted. Aya often intimidated men. I used to think it was her height, maybe her wide smile which could turn small and hungry when you looked askance; I thought these men were being losers, too fragile of heart. But Aya eventually got along with everyone. Once she started to speak, her voice had this lulling effect. She knew how to lean into people without invading their space, as she did right now—reaching out to light the drummer's cigarette, and then hers.

"What were you two talking about?" she said.

"The crowd crush in Korea," I said, but the drummer spoke over me, "I was asking her why she thinks our vocalist was eaten."

"It's not uncommon, no?" Aya said. Her collarbones stood out stark as knives when she took a drag of her cigarette. "One or two people vanish per week."

"Rinko thinks a person disappears for a reason," I said. "Like it was fate. They were chosen."

"I don't know about that," Aya said, exhaling. "I think it's luck."

I thought her tone was a bit too casual, as if it had nothing to do with her.

"Bad luck," the drummer said. "Very bad luck."

"Some people deserve it," I said.

Aya laughed, choking a little on the cigarette smoke. As she wiped at her mouth, we got to share our secret look. The curve of her rosebud mouth. I felt a warm stirring inside me. I had always felt protective toward people who didn't really need nor want my help.

But so did Aya, who would feed me from time to time, bringing me bars of dark chocolate when I would work alone in the studio past closing time and the whole school was pitch-black and no one was around. Once, she asked if I walked home alone every night. She asked if I wanted to disappear.

She might be the only one in the world who cared about me.

Rinko and the bassist had finally settled on an izakaya. Now acting all chummy, the bassist tried to loop his arm around Rinko, but she shoved him away. We were all surprised, Rinko most of all. The bassist, making a face, apologized with a smarting sullenness and Rinko tried to gloss it over, but the mood had definitely sunk. So when the others started heading toward the izakaya, the drummer said he would join them later after he'd finished his cigarette; I said I'd stay with him.

"Do you smoke?" he asked.

I shook my head. My father had quit around the time I was born, so I was trying to . . . I mean of course I no longer had to support him. But I couldn't stop.

"I know they're killing us," the drummer said, staring at the burning end of his cigarette. "But we have to accept it, right? Living with the risk. We pick and choose our battles."

He tapped out another cigarette onto his palm. "Excuse me, I'm going to call my brother."

After a minute, it was clear the little brother wasn't picking up. The drummer hung up and complained about the cold as he tugged down at the hem of his skirt. "I thought lighting up would warm me up, but this skirt is too much."

"The skirt is supposed to be even shorter, so points off for lack of realism."

He laughed. "You know, you have a cute voice, but you say kind of scary things."

"Do you like it?"

"I guess I do." He gave a small cough. "I'm sorry I didn't come back for you. The truth is you barfed on me. My favorite T-shirt. Supreme Akira collaboration."

"Oh, I'm sorry."

"See? You're mocking me! But it's okay, it was a black T-shirt. And now it's a cool memory." He scratched his head under his yellow-haired Sailor Venus wig. "The rest of my memories still feel hazy. I feel like I was hallucinating."

"I know what you mean. I think we were drugged."

"Yeah!"

After a shaky laugh, he tried to calm his nerves with his cigarette. Now that it was just the two of us, I realized he was acting very different from that night. He no longer tried to fill up silence with awkward chatter.

A while later, he said, "Did you see anything?"

I thought of the phone Aya had stolen. The look of wipeout bliss on her face. Sixty percent was a bit low. It was closer to seventy-five. "Ahh . . . I don't know. I was dizzy too."

He nodded, but I could tell he wasn't all that convinced. "Have you ever had someone disappear?"

"Someone I know?"

"Yeah."

"I don't think so. But we can't be sure, right?"

"What about your parents?"

"That was a car accident. My final year in high school."

"Oh, that sucks."

"Yeah. The timing. You know what prep school's like. I was producing a hundred drawings a week."

I had hardly talked to my parents during that period. If I failed the college exam, I'd have to do it over again for a whole year, and plenty of students failed once or twice before they got into Kyogei. So, every time my mother slipped into my room to bring me a plate of sliced fruit, I would snap at her to leave me alone. I later found the voice message my father had left me. He said our dog might have eaten a fallen grape so they were driving her to the vet.

It was February. Highway. Sharp curve. Black ice.

Sometimes, randomly, like when I would be walking across campus, I would forget where I was going and I'd just stand there for a moment. I would wonder, Why couldn't I have been in the car? My mother and my father and our dog, Momo. We could have been together. Instead they had left me behind.

"But I passed my exam." I made a victory sign. "I got into Kyogei."

"Hell yeah," said the drummer. We high-fived.

I texted Rinko for the address of the izakaya but hesitated before I hit send, be- cause now I had been conditioned not to expect an answer. The drummer and I joined the crowd. We held hands to stick together. I searched for the flap of butterfly wings, and he was craning his head too, probably looking for his brother, who was dressed as Sailor Mercury. I bet it felt weird to worry for a boy who could be mistaken for a girl.

A pair of men stood wearing angel and devil wings, cupping each other's hip. Cat girls held their tails like a hangman's rope. Pikachu kissed cigarettes with a wet turtle-beaked kappa. Women swaggered in sumo costumes, bumping into whoever they wanted. Crowding the udon stall was the entire *One Piece* crew and a lush white wicked fox, fur on the chin spiked with udon juice. Three girls posed in kiddie overalls streaked in red blood, one wielding a ludicrous kitchen knife. She giggled, dangerous and high-pitched.

I felt dangerous too. The drummer followed as I led him through the crowd. My wings flapped weakly. Rinko and Aya were gone, but blending among these monsters, I felt calm, like a hunter. Who was I hunting for? A woman's head on a long, winding rubbery-looking neck peered over the crowd.

I thought about the drummer's question. If my parents had vanished, would that have made their deaths feel different, instead of completely senseless? Rinko was convinced her grandmother's disappearance gave her death meaning. Could I have deluded myself the same way if I hadn't been brought in to see their bodies?

Rinko and I had a fight related to this, after the karaoke night. We said terrible things to each other. The worst part was, when I tried to smooth it over through text, it led to more misunderstandings. We fought entirely over text even though we'd see each other on campus. I'd tried to collect my thoughts and sent her messages to apologize despite the risk; I knew Rinko would screenshot and dissect my texts with other people, but I needed her to know I wasn't blaming her for what had happened. I needed her to understand my position.

My view of the world was quite simple. Your parents are supposed to die before you. If you live a natural life, that is. It is unnatural for the child to die first. That means all of this—*sexlovemarriage*—is supposed to be a buffer for the loss you will eventually face. All the more if you love your parents like I did. So, I understood where Rinko was coming from. She wants to love and be loved and make up for all the ways her parents hadn't loved her. And one day, Rinko will find the right person. She will fall in love and marry and have sex and babies. But what happens to someone like me if all of that feels unnatural? How am I supposed to make up for my loss?

Rinko bought me an edible flower bouquet, of all things. She brought it to the gallery opening for my prize-winning praying mantis. It was a luxurious bouquet of fruit arranged into flowers, apple roses and banana lilies and tangerine daisies, and it must have cost more than 10,000 yen, which I knew took a huge chunk out of Rinko's budget.

At the end of the street, a small crowd was dancing to ABBA's "Dancing Queen." I saw Rinko's blue braids whipping around before I heard her call my name. Rinko, snug in Aya's scarf, jumped up and down, waving at us. One of her wings was torn, but she didn't seem to care. I waved back but the drummer wouldn't let go of my hand so our hands went up in the air together, like we'd won a three-legged race.

Rinko gasped. "Are you two together now?"

I tried to drop the drummer's hand, but he wouldn't let go. It was like all his talk about cigarettes and risk and acceptance had gone out the window the moment we saw Aya.

"Where are the rest of the *Sailor Moon* boys?" I asked.

Aya placed her chin on Rinko's shoulder. She pressed a kiss against the old bruise, then nibbled on it. "Stooop, don't eat me," Rinko laughed, then she looked at me, something triumphant in her eyes, as they swayed together to the dancing beat.

The drummer's grip on my hand tightened.

He saw it too, didn't he?

After I had vomited on his favorite T-shirt, I'd gone to look for my friends. I checked every karaoke room. I wanted to lie down. As I teetered past a dark room, I heard the song. ABBA's "Dancing Queen." Snuffling sex noises. Someone on the floor and someone on top. I saw the vocalist's blinding slash of platinum hair. The person on top was too tall to be Rinko. I was immediately embarrassed and ashamed for Aya. My instinct was to leave, but the vocalist made a choked noise, a soft, cloying whine. I'd never heard a man make that kind of noise, not even in porn. He was flat on his back, hair bright as a crescent moon. Aya was straddling him. She had him pinned with just her hands but her arms looked strange, smooth and curved like a pair of flesh-colored scythes. Nuzzling her heart-shaped face into his neck, she nibbled his jugular. Her teeth were little red fingers caressing and tearing into his skin.

Her eyes, liquid-black, locked on mine. She dislodged her mandibles from his throat and bent over him. Neither of us breathed. The vocalist was still rutting against her, legs twitching. His hand touched her face helplessly. When I blinked, she bit into his finger. Like she was waiting for my reaction. I gave her the tiniest nod and then she swooped down, latching her jaws on his face. He was still thrusting and twitching. She watched me watch her eat.

It wasn't quick at all. It didn't seem painless. It was a slow, devouring excavation.

"Where's my brother?" the drummer said.

"Didn't he leave earlier?" Aya said, eyes unblinking.

With that, the drummer finally released my hand. He asked Rinko about the rest of his bandmates.

"I can call them," Rinko said, turning around. "I'll tell them we're going someplace else."

She moved away from the dancing crowd and the drummer followed her, and it was just me and Aya. I noticed one of her boots was untied. I was staring at her feet, unable to look her in the eye. She asked me, from somewhere above, if I wanted a softcream.

"We were so worried," Aya whispered. "Did you see the emergency alert? Someone was found partially eaten in a Don Quixote."

"Another woman?"

She shook her head. "A *Sailor Moon*."

"Oh," I said. "Which one?"

"Don't worry. No one we know." Aya held out an ice cream cone. Matcha and strawberry swirl. "Want a bite?"

I mouthed at the ice cream, watching her. Too milky. I couldn't tell the matcha and strawberry apart. "Parfait and now softcream. You must be super full."

Aya shook her head, regretful. "I'm always hungry."

"Are you going to eat Rinko?"

"Maybe," Aya said. "Or maybe she'll eat me first." She licked her ice cream, little red darts of her tongue. "I like it when you watch."

I did too.

Until that night, sex had made no sense to me. Why do we have sex when men eat and women are eaten? Of course, there's gay sex and pan sex and poly sex but then society calls all that stuff unnatural, even though barely anyone has sex for procreation these days. Sex is still imprinted into our genes. So, why didn't I want it? Why didn't I want to love? Was I just broken, like Rinko said? Because of my parents' accident? She said I needed therapy, which was a fair suggestion, but she said it like she didn't think it would help. And I was so sure I had always been like this. All throughout middle school and most of high school.

So it didn't matter. I was going to be like this forever.

Then I saw Aya that night. Aya who made sex seem so miraculous and natural. Of course she has sex. She's hungry. She could have any partner. She chose the vocalist and he deserved it. Yet, when Aya has sex, she loves her partner. She loves them so much she wants to become one with them.

We finished the ice cream together. Aya wiped the stickiness from my mouth with her handkerchief. She could act so motherly sometimes.

"Would you let me draw you?" I asked.

"Of course. I love your art. I think you're a genius."

Pleasure, like no other. I flushed everywhere. My nose felt slightly stuffed as if I was going to cry.

"Rinko said my art is cold. That I have this dark, broken view of the world and that's why my art is full of such bitterness."

"I don't think it's cold or bitter at all. I find it so comforting."

"Comforting?"

"Mm-hmm. You're not fooled by beauty. Beauty is usually a trap by design. Yet you see the ugly as beautiful and the beautiful as ugly. It's comforting. One day you'll be famous and others will see it too."

I remembered how touched I was when Aya and Rinko had come to the gallery for my prize-winning installation. Rinko took a picture of Aya and shared it on our group chat. It was Aya lying as if dead beside the praying mantis, her lanky frame curled tight as a shrimp. She had buried her face into the sunken chest, which was covered in fake and dying succulents.

Did Aya love Rinko? Could Aya love someone like me? I didn't have an answer for either, but I knew this. Aya wanted me to live.

Rinko returned to us, without the drummer. "No one's picking up. Let's just go to a bar. I bet we can score free drinks."

My phone quivered. Maybe it was another emergency alert, or a text from the drummer. I silenced my phone and tucked it away deep into my purse. "Let's go to an owl café!" I said. "I want an owl parfait!"

"Yes!" Rinko said.

She linked her arms around each of us. I really had no right to be mad at her. Deep down, I thought of her as broken too. Needing someone to be fully happy, what are you but incomplete?

Together, we cleaved our way through the crowded street. When Aya bent down to fix her bootlace, Rinko tugged me ahead and said breathlessly into my ear, "Thank you."

"For what?"

"For being so brave. You make me feel brave. It's not weird, right?"

My throat closed. I was false in almost everything I say, but in this instance, I wanted to be true for her. "No," I said. "It's not weird. There's nothing unnatural about love."

Rinko tightened her arm around mine. Her laughter frothed, her face was flushed and pale, bright red spots on her cheeks.

"I love you," I said. "I love Aya. I love you both."

"Oh wow, you're drunk!"

I wished I could get drunk.

I wished Rinko and Aya fell in love. I wished they had sex. I wished they didn't. I wished sex didn't exist. What a divine 2D world it would be. Violence would become pure. Violence for the sake of violence. Love for the sake of love. I was bursting with love. I loved Halloween. I loved the parade, the freedom, the secrets. I loved parfaits and their sacred layers. I loved my Kyogei professor who said I surprised her. I loved the notes my mother used to tuck into my father's lunchbox. My dog and her wheezy breath. Rinko who loosened my corset and urged, *Breathe*. The way my father would briskly massage my mother's shoulders when she was upset, like she was a boxer about to enter the ring. I loved being a girl even though I felt so small and weak. I loved girls who were anything but. Aya who made more sense than anyone else in the world. The voice message my father had left me. Don't worry, we'll be back soon. Focus on your art. What do you want for dinner?

We'll get it on the way home.

THE INVOCATION OF THE GHOST, THE EXORCISM OF THE MUSE

Isabel J. Kim

The eastern tradition draws the corpus in ink. The western tradition paints the corpus in oil. Studies done in immigrant communities claim a 15 percent higher success rate in dispelling "ethnic" hauntings when using "ethnic" painting techniques. The irony is that sheaths of rice paper and a crematory ash inkstick are infinitely more portable than a canvas and decomp-paints, turpentine, linseed oil.

Maybe using oil paints makes sense out in the country, where everyone owns a car and there's room to set up an easel, where there are old churches and battlegrounds and rows of unrelenting corn. Or in the suburbs with the dead malls and hushed-up violence. Maybe the oils make sense for old-money ghosts, ghosts with histories beyond the sighing whisper of *I used to be alive, and now I'm not*. Maybe those ghosts won't animate anything less than a portrait in the style of John Singer Sargent.

"Sorry, ghost," Woojin said as he stood in the living room of 321 West Seventy-Sixth Street, while doing his warm-up sketches—stark outlines of faces, eyes, delicate threads of ink creating strands of hair. "It's just me."

The ghost didn't respond. No one else did, either. Woojin was alone in the honey-colored living room. The late afternoon sun illuminated the rice paper on the plastic-covered Noguchi table. His clients were somewhere upstairs. Woojin thought about the unimaginable luxury of having two floors in Manhattan.

Woojin lived in a one-bedroom in LIC that he had exorcised the week he got off the plane, right before classes started. The ghost that had lived there had been born before the apartment building had been built. He had been a good conversationalist with a thick, unplaceable accent. Woojin had offered to let the ghost stay, but the ghost had declined, citing that he was tired of haunting a place he could no longer recognize.

So, Woojin lived alone and commuted to Manhattan, carrying a beat-up old Jansport filled with brushes, inksticks, rice paper, and empty Tupperware for water, slinging it on his back when he took the F train to do his exorcisms. Just another way immigrants are taking all the jobs.

There are a lot of Asian exorcists, just the same way there are a lot of Asian laundromat owners, or a lot of Asian violin players. Americans like their immigrants in boxes, and exorcism fits neatly in the intersectional between "spiritual" (martial arts masters) and "technical" (scientists, engineers, computer science majors), the same slot that "graphic design" fills in the art department, which is why a full two-thirds of the international students in the graduate art program at the New School are tacitly concentrating in product/graphic/industrial design. That and the money. Always, the money.

"You know that I do conceptual installation art, like sculpture and stuff," Woojin had said when Yichen had explained his theory. They had been drinking. "Sculpture and stuff" was the best description Woojin could manage for the jet-black spears and ashy ink that created his installations. The way paranatural ink spilled through his dreams.

"You're an outlier and should not have been counted," Yichen had said, patting Woojin on the cheek tenderly. "You're part of the problem. I've seen your website, you're all about *updating the classics*, you've packaged orientalism for them in a nice neat space-age package."

"Well, you're a sellout," Woojin had said. Yichen was going to work at his brother's company after he graduated. Yichen's family had money.

"And you're a creepy little ghostbuster, but I love you anyway," Yichen had said, and flagged the waiter for another round of drinks. The rest of the night was a blank space in Woojin's memory, which restarted the next morning, which turned into a hungover blur of grabbing his supplies and getting on the train, which turned into the here and now, the supposedly haunted apartment and his supplies spread all across a two-thousand-dollar table.

Woojin would have killed a man for a cup of coffee. He was sweating under his collar. He felt queasy and out of place in the jewel-box apartment. But he had a job to do. He closed his eyes and tried to untangle any psychic influence from his own thoughts. He was going to call his mother tonight and talk about what nonsense his dad had been up to. He was going to ask his brother about his severely lacking love life and get yelled at in response. He would be going home for summer break soon, and in the meantime there were his friends here, his business, and he was happy most of the time, really, he was—but, ah, his family. Why was he so nostalgic about his family? There it was.

He opened his eyes, feeling immensely more cheerful.

"Stop that," he said, and felt a cold wind blow across his face. He grinned. He had the specter pinned now. It was some sort of ghost of nostalgia, maybe. A ghost of familial regret. It felt like a woman. Sometimes ghosts felt gendered, sometimes they didn't. A lot of people had strong feelings about their gender before they died, but there's a shockingly large proportion of the population that never really *thought* about it, and then they died, and then it turned out that that gender was never really part of their internal compass.

But this ghost feels *maternal*, in a way that some ghosts feel. Ghosts that are leaving people behind who still need them. Ghosts who had children or particularly favored younger siblings. It had dredged up memories of his family and home, rather than memories of his friends, or his work.

Woojin wiped his ink basin and poured water back into the shallow black stone rectangle, before grinding his crematory ash stick against it. Black ink dissolved into the water. He unrolled his mat and took his favorite brush out. The head was made of hair from his last haircut. The remains of his last, bad dye job were visible at the ends. The body was made from bamboo grown in a cemetery.

Woojin visualized the ghost in his head. Not its appearance. Its appearance was secondary. Appearance was the vessel for the ghost, the same way the body was the vessel for the living, and the important thing was making sure that the drawing was a more attractive target for the ghost than his body. If the ghost possessed his body—well, they made movies about that sort of thing. It would end badly. But only very powerful ghosts could overpower an already ensouled sack of meat. Woojin wasn't particularly worried.

He dipped the brush in the ink. He closed his eyes. He painted.

The paint sank into the paper, the drag of the brush against the grain a familiar vibration through his fingers and up his arm. He let the ghost move his hand in the shape it wanted. She wasn't fighting him, which was good.

Woojin opened his eyes. He'd drawn a woman. She was elegant, with big eyes and long dark hair that had been braided in a heavy rope that rested on her shoulder. She looked young to have died, but she also had dark ink wash under her eyes, so maybe it was sickness that killed her.

She smiled prettily at him. "Hello, witch." She had the slightest hint of an accent, similar to Woojin's.

He smiled back. "Hello, madam. I'm here to ask you to please stop scaring the new tenants, and to ask whether you would like my assistance in passing on."

She shook her head. "No, thank you."

Woojin frowned. "Why not?"

She had sunken into his drawing so readily. Usually the ghosts that cooperated were the ones ready to move on, the ones who were tired of haunting the same set of rooms and were causing trouble so that an exorcist would be called.

"I called you here for a reason. I have a request for you. I would like for you to find my son. I will pay."

Woojin blinked. "What?"

The drawing smiled again. "I'll pay. If you find my son, I will tell you my name, and I will give you the names and passwords to investment accounts my husband never learned of, and you may send me onwards."

Woojin had never had a ghost as a client before.

"What do you want with him?"

"I just want to see how he's doing," the ghost said.

That was too simple. It sounded like a lie. Ghosts were notorious liars. They would say anything to get what they wanted—just like living people. But she was very together, and very calm. Maybe she did just want to see her son once more before passing on.

"There's a quarter of a million dollars in my accounts," the ghost continued.

Woojin choked on his own spit.

"It's yours, if you take me to him."

"I can't be *bribed*," Woojin lied. He didn't know what he would do with a quarter-million dollars, that was a ridiculous sum of money.

"Then can you be begged? I died when my son was very young, witch. He and his father moved soon after my death. I remember watching them leave. He cried as his father carried him over the threshold. He was barely three. He would be twenty-three, now. I would like to see him before I rest."

The woman in the portrait looked around Woojin's age. Early to mid-twenties. But she had been a mother by then. Woojin couldn't imagine having children.

Her kid would be Woojin's age.

A quarter-million dollars.

"I can't promise anything," Woojin said. "This is a big city. And he might not even be here anymore. And I can't keep you forever, if I can't find them. But what is his name?"

The ghost portrait beamed at him, wider than the pretty little smile that she had given him before. "Young Yejun. Or, Yejun Young."

Woojin nodded. "Okay, Ms. Young. I'll go find your boy. But first, I'm going to go tell the Johnsons that I've exorcised you. So please be quiet while I tell them that you're gone."

Ms. Young dipped her head and put an ink finger to her mouth. Woojin put the stone inkwell on the corner of the paper to keep her from blowing away and went to tell the Johnsons that he had definitely exorcised the ghost that had been plaguing their home, and that he was requesting his payment now, please. Cash preferred.

Woojin carefully rolled Ms. Young's portrait in a reed mat so that it wouldn't be squished in his bag before packing it up along with his other supplies. He exited the apartment with many thanks from the Johnsons and a white envelope with two hundred dollars inside. He didn't feel bad about the lie—he was fulfilling the spirit of their request, if not the technical details. He ambled over to the subway and descended down into the tunnel.

"Oh, they renovated the station," Ms. Young said. Ghosts captured in portraits weren't bound by their drawn eyes. The portrait was more of a mobile location for them to haunt.

"It's been a long time," Woojin said, popping an AirPod in his ear. He would look just look like he was having a phone conversation. "Do you have any ideas on where your son might be? I can do my own research, but I'd like to hear your perspective."

"My son was so young when I died," Ms. Young said. "His father worked—works, perhaps?—in finance. You know, the big banks around Fiftieth Street. I don't think they left the city after I died, though I might be wrong. My son would be done with college, now, unless he took a gap year, or maybe he finished on time and is working. Or maybe he moved? I don't *know* where he could be, it's been so long . . ."

Ms. Young's voice began reverberating into the jagged harmonics that characterized a de-coalescing ghost. The sort of ghost that wasn't a person anymore, only a lingering emotion that had claws and teeth.

"Tell me about your son," Woojin said hastily. "What he was like. Take your time, Ms. Young. I'm not going anywhere."

The F train arrived, and he got in. Ms. Young was quiet as he walked into the train car and leaned against a pole. Ms. Young was a thrum of simmering emotion that slowly subsided into a pool of calm. Woojin was surprised by how strong she was, after all these years.

They rattled together through the dark subway tunnels and emerged onto the elevated line across the river, sunshine streaming through the windows. Woojin liked people watching in the city. When he had moved to the States, he had been surprised by the sheer variety of people and what they wore. The colors, the textures, the way that no matter what you looked like, you were never going to be the strangest person sitting in the subway seat. The ghosts were the same. It was fantastic.

"He was a good boy. Sweet," Ms. Young says, almost too softly to be heard over the sound of the train. "You can tell, even when they're that young. Yejun was always so gentle with the cat. And he was so cheerful. A little ray of sunshine. I don't know where he got it from, not me or his father, but it was so nice."

She trailed off.

"I know this doesn't help you," she said, almost a whisper.

"It helps," Woojin lied. It didn't help. But he could imagine the little boy and his mother, and the apartment he had just left, filled with toys for the kid and the cat.

"You're a nice boy, too," she said, and then she was quiet for the rest of the journey back to Woojin's apartment.

He felt almost a little ashamed, pulling the soul-portrait out in his little one-bedroom. His place was a mess, especially compared to the apartment they had just left.

"Oh, your prints!" Ms. Young said with audible delight.

Woojin used his wall as studio storage space. He had a habit of ripping pages out of his sketchbooks and spreading them out haphazardly. Detailed, lovingly rendered drawings of joints and muscles. Sharp, abstract shapes. Sketches of three-dimensional monuments. Diagrams of spiraling currents, appended with notes on the flow of air through space. Together, they created a mosaic of his thoughts, like his head had been unspooled and pinned onto the plaster.

"You like them?" Woojin asked, setting his bag on the desk and turning on his computer.

"They're wonderful," she said, and Woojin had to wonder about her, this dead upper-class lady bribing him from beyond the grave, who thought that the heavy strokes of his art were wonderful. He thinks they could have been friends, in a world where they had lived at the same time. She could have been his patron, or something.

He opened a search engine and typed in *Young Yejun*. The page populated immediately, line after line of Facebook profiles, LinkedIn profiles, Twitter profiles, Instagram profiles, Woojin's dismay growing with each new profile that showed up. There were so many people in the world. All he knew about Young Yejun is that he had been a cute toddler. He didn't even know if he was in New York.

He had to start somewhere. He typed in *Young Yejun New York* and watched a slightly narrower set of results appear. Still far too many. Rows and rows and rows.

He sighed. "Okay, Ms. Young, let's get started."

Ms. Young's son was another type of ghost. He had no digital profile. Woojin's scrolled through a lot of Young boys, but none of them were hers, or at least she was unable to see them on the computer. Something about the digital screen creating a blind spot for her, where Woojin has to describe the images rather than her viewing them. She shook her painted head after each guy, though sometimes she hesitated at the descriptions. It was all so uncertain. After a few hours, her paint started to unspool across the paper, and they stopped for the night.

Woojin hung her portrait on the wall, next to his sketches of his artwork. She watched as he worked.

"What are you making?"

"It's just homework," he said, holding the sketchbook up so that Ms. Young could see more easily. There were little drawings of different installations, each a hypothetical rendering of the gallery space. "Well, just working on ideas for my thesis, more like. More sketches for the wall."

"What are you imagining, when you draw these things?"

Woojin had been thinking about loci. And ghost portraits. And what called people home. He didn't want to tell Ms. Young about that. He thought it might make her sad.

"It's about longing," he said finally. "How a place never leaves you. About how you end up stuck somewhere."

"Oh, I know about being stuck somewhere," she sighed. He didn't know if she meant being trapped as a ghost in the apartment, or in his drawing. Or if she meant something from her life—being an immigrant, or her marriage, or having her child. He didn't ask. It would feel cheap, and it might destabilize her. Most of Woojin's knowledge of being trapped came from the ghosts he talked to. He himself felt very free, too free, in fact, overwhelmed by the choices for his future. Would he stay in the States? Would he work in industry? Would he go back to Korea? Would he try teaching? The future to him, felt like a great big sky, and sometimes he wondered if he was falling into it from a plane without a parachute.

"I have to figure out what the final version will be," he said. "But I'm just working through iterations, now."

"I like the black drapery in the last one," Ms. Young said.

"That's going to be made of rice paper. The ink is going to pool down and drip all over the floor, if I make it," Woojin said. He had been dreaming of big black pools of charcoal dripping from cloth, drying slowly and leaving the ash in organic shapes. Maybe into the outline of a body.

The next morning, Woojin took the sketches to critique and was bloodlessly eviscerated, his drawings pinned on the white gallery wall and dissected by the other students. The word *derivative* was used, along with the words *seeming sort of tonally vacant* and *ungrounded in any meaningful tradition, which is kind of a shame because I know you're classically trained in Chinese calligraphy, right?* The professor eventually drew the execution to a close by asking Woojin whether he had any response to the critique.

Woojin wanted to defend himself. He wanted to say that it was his heritage and he wasn't building on air, here, he was building on his own work. That every week he went out into the city and drew the dead from their hiding places, that this sketch was a representation of how it felt, inside, to ink ghosts and commune with them. Therein lay the issue, though. He knew he was drawing from emotions that he only understood secondhand—he talked to the ghosts, he felt the barest wisp of their feelings, but they were ink and he was meat. He could only guess at how they felt. If his sketch felt hollow, it was because his own emotions underpinning the work were hollow.

"Thanks for the feedback," he said. "I don't have any responses."

Afterward, he headed to his studio space to sulk in peace. Yichen came and found him.

"They really ripped you up," he said. "My God. Bloodbath."

Yichen's sketches and mock-ups—sculptures made from broken porcelain, reconstructed to look like weapons—had gotten a similar dressing down. But it didn't matter for Yichen, who was going to work in industry.

"Yeah, well," Woojin said. "It sometimes feels like if the first person to speak gets a little negative, we get into a sort of negative spiral."

"Unlucky," Yichen said, and handed Woojin a little Yakult drink. Woojin examined it and then ripped the top open.

"I haven't drunk one of these without soju in years," Woojin said. He drank. Cool, sweet, vaguely yogurty. He had drunk these all the time as a kid. He wondered if they sold them in China, too, whether these featured in Yichen's memories as well.

"There's three packs of them in the communal fridge, if you want more."

"Thanks."

Yichen drank his own drink. "I liked your mock-up, for what it's worth."

"It was a little half-baked. I've been too busy to really put my statement together," Woojin admitted.

"Oh yeah? Work, or something?"

Yichen knew about the part-time exorcisms. It wasn't like Woojin tried to hide the ghosts, it was just that for most people, exorcist was a job in the same way psychic or palm reader was a job. His job helped people sleep at night, if they believed, and otherwise, they dismissed it. But Yichen was from somewhere else, the same way that Woojin was from somewhere else, somewhere where the Christianity only papered over the old superstitions, where Confucianism held hands with old myths and shamans, and it was actually a little refreshing, that he would believe Woojin when Woojin said that he was being hired by a ghost.

So Woojin started with the house on the Upper West Side and the request from the ghost to find her son, and ended with how there was a ghost in his apartment now, who was growing more frustrated by the day. He described Mrs. Young, and listed all the ways he had tried to find Yejun Young. Yichen listened while drinking three more Yakults. When Woojin was finished with his story, Yichen tossed the last Yakult into the trash, and frowning, pulled his phone out.

"I think I might know the guy," Yichen said, and showed Woojin an Instagram profile of a man, about their age, who looked like the half-white, gender-bent version of Ms. Young.

*Woojin used the big department Epson printer to print a few high-resolution pho-*tographs of "Jonathan Yejun Young" on the good photography paper. He thought that maybe Ms. Young would be better able to see if the object he was showing to her was closer to "art" and not "a screen." Woojin wondered what would happen if he poured a little crematory ash into the ink cartridge. He shivered to think about how realistic the resulting ghosts would be. That would be some real horror movie shit. Ghosts grew stronger with verisimilitude, and it was a fine line between making a ghost too weak to speak and making the ghost so strong that it could climb out of the drawing and start wreaking physical havoc. Woojin had heard horror stories about exorcists who had lost control of their trapped spirits, and he had no intention of being one of them. Some of them had taken over their summoner's bodies, it had been rumored. There was a psychic in the East Village who was rumored to be a dead lady who had taken over a teenage girl who had gotten in over her head. Woojin hadn't verified whether that was true or not.

But this and other stories were why, outside of his exorcist work, Woojin's art was abstract. No representation for ghosts to cling to.

The photographs finished printing, and Woojin cut them to size. Jonathan-Yejun looked like an okay guy, if a little bit boring. His Instagram profile indicated that he was an MBA student at Stern—which immediately prejudiced Woojin against him—and that he was very fond of his cat—which made Woojin soften, just a little.

The name was wrong, but the rest of it was right. And it wasn't uncommon for kids to take a western name, if they were in the west, and this kid was half-white, anyway. So Jonathan-Yejun was probably the right kid. He looked exactly right.

Woojin shoved the photos in his bag, next to his work equipment, and was careful not to smudge them with ink when he took out his supplies to do his two scheduled exorcisms. One was in a deli that had suffered a lot of broken cups and plates, and another in an old lady's rent-stabilized apartment in the Lower East Side. There wasn't any ghost in her apartment, but he did the drawing and all the associated pageantry, and it was worth it for the look of relief on her face. He only charged her half price.

Then Woojin went home, and pinned the photos across from Ms. Young on the opposite wall.

"Can you see these? Is this your Yejun?"

He watched as her eyes darted from drawn edge to edge.

"That's him," she said. "That's my son. That's my boy. Take me to him."

Ms. Young's voice began going strange with the harmonics at the end, and the lights began to flicker. Woojin was a little afraid that he had used too much detail when drawing her, that she was spiraling out of his control. He wondered if he should just exorcise her here and now, while he had her pinned.

But the money. And her son. Woojin wasn't immune to sob stories. It was a bad trait in an exorcist—that was how ghosts took advantage of you. The man who had taught Woojin to paint, when he was much younger, had drilled that into Woojin's head. You could not help ghosts. They were dead and beyond helping. But this pretty young woman, who spoke his language with an old-fashioned accent and who had died in this international city where he was still a little lonely, she tugged at his heartstrings.

"Okay, Ms. Young. We'll go find him. But please, let me handle the approach. Please? He goes to my school, and I don't want to cause any fuss. *Please.*"

The lights stuttered back to normal.

"All right," she said. "But please, be quick."

Woojin settled for staking out the business school lobby, with Ms. Young carefully sequestered in his backpack and a sketchbook in hand. It was remarkable, the places that would let you loiter, as long as you looked like a harmless artist and had a student ID. He picked a comfortable seat with a good view of passersby and settled in for the long haul.

Day after day, Woojin sat there and sketched badly, surreptitiously watching and waiting for Jonathan-Yejun to walk through the doors.

Ms. Young was getting impatient. She never spoke in public, but was growing increasingly demanding in private. Woojin was afraid that if he didn't find her son soon, she would completely unravel. He felt like a character in an old folktale, or a creepypasta. Coming home to his angry ghost. He resolved to exorcise her at the end of the week, regardless of what happened. She was getting dangerous. There was a reason that the ink-and-paper was meant to be a temporary solution, not a permanent one.

But on the fourth day, Jonathan-Yejun walked in.

Asian American haircut—short, styled like white hair, grown-up frat-boy business fit, talking on his phone with someone as he walked across the hall. Woojin nearly swallowed his tongue. He forced himself to remain calm. He got up and followed Jonathan-Yejun in. Woojin pretended to be texting while he followed Jonathan-Yejun through the hallways, up the second set of stairs and to the bookable study rooms, which were all in a row on the third-floor balconies. Jonathan-Yejun typed in the code for one of the rooms, and Woojin watched and memorized the sequence of numbers.

He waited a few minutes before walking over and sliding the portrait of Ms. Young out.

"I found him," he told her. "Please be quiet until we get inside, though."

Ms. Young nodded, and Woojin slid the portrait back into the bag before punching the door code in and opening it. Jonathan looked up, mid-sentence, breaking off his conversation. He looked confused. His cell phone was on the table, and there was a call visible on the screen. Speakerphone.

"Hello, my name is Woojin Joo. Your mom asked me to find you."

It was too subtle, but Woojin had never been in this position before and he figured that it made more sense to couch the truth, in case they had gotten the wrong man, in case the person on the other side of the phone call would cause problems. Jonathan-Yejun looked confused.

"What are you talking about? I'm on the phone with her right now."

"Um," Woojin said. He wasn't sure how to respond to that. He wondered if he had found the wrong guy. Maybe this man just had an uncanny resemblance to Ms. Young.

"Honey, who are you talking to?" someone said over the speakerphone. The voice didn't sound like a girlfriend. It sounded distinctly maternal. It sounded American.

And then Ms. Young screamed from inside his bag.

The scream threw a physical shock wave through the room, throwing the phone and Jonathan-Yejun's laptop and his papers into the air, followed by the table cracking in half, Jonathan-Yejun himself thrown against the wall. Woojin fell to the floor, and the drawing of Ms. Young flew out of his bag and hung in the air like it was suspended from invisible wires, rotating in the air.

The lines of Ms. Young's drawing stuttered like sound waves. Paint began to drip off the rice paper, pooling on the floor, and the rest of Ms. Young's body began to fill out the sheet, her hands straining at the edges of the drawing. An icelike fear crystalized in Woojin's stomach.

He had left her too long. She had grown too powerful. She thought this was her son and saw that he had a new mother, and now she was trying to crawl out of the ink he had captured her in. Her hope had turned to resentment. She was radiating malice. She was going to become the sort of ghost that couldn't be reasoned with, the sort of ghost that could only be sent to their second death, the death that was complete destruction.

He didn't want to do that to Ms. Young, and moreover, he didn't know how. He was just a cut-rate back-alley part-time exorcist. He had never summoned such a powerful ghost. He hadn't known she had this force of will—but he should have known, he shouldn't have negotiated with her, he should have expelled her when he saw her.

SHE STOLE MY SON, Ms. Young's voice reverberated from all around them, as the painting rotated to face him. The paint on the walls began to peel.

"Holy fuck," Jonathan shouted. "What the fuck did you do!"

"It's a ghost," Woojin shouted back. "Are you sure this is your son?"

BLOOD OF MY BLOOD, Ms. Young's voice echoed, as if she was quoting something ancient and terrible. Her portrait rotated to face Jonathan.

His face went slack, the confusion melting from his face, condensing into a sort of terrified wonder.

"Umma," Jonathan said. "Umma, is that—"

But it was too late. Ms. Young was already crawling out of the painting, now, the ink dripping out as she gained flesh and form and she was pulling herself out and once she turned from a 2D to a 3D object, it would become impossible for Woojin to contain her. He couldn't run and get a better exorcist. There was no time. Woojin had no good ideas.

But if he didn't act, she might destroy the building and all of the people in it.

Woojin ripped his bag open and pulled out his human-hair brush from the bamboo mat it had been wrapped in, dropping down to his knees and dragging the brush through the ink pool collecting on the floor before closing his eyes. He painted across his face by memory. The arc of an eye, the dramatic swish for the nose, the slash for the mouth and the paint around the edge of his face, from his chin to his hairline. Let it be what it needs to be. It would be ugly, but it was a face.

This was a bad idea. This was a bad idea beyond bad ideas. But it would contain her, desperately, hopefully. He sent a prayer to any gods or benevolent spirits who might be watching. Then he took a deep breath and ran forward, face-first into the paper hoping, that as he had been taught, that a living body would be a more instinctively attractive host for a ghost than any dead and pulped wood.

His wet face hit the paper. She fell into him, like cold rain, and he was—

—dancing with her husband on her wedding night and she's so nervous but she smiles and—

—five years old and he has new yellow boots and he's kicking his feet and—

—she's eating ice cream and it's the first time she's had gelato and it's pure delight and—

—sitting in exams and he's wondering why he has to study so much and he's—

—getting her driver's license and feeling relief in her stomach and—

—he's on a plane and he's nervous and excited about moving somewhere new and—

—she's holding her son and she's nervous and excited about him entering her life, and—

The wind had stopped. Woojin was crying. The room was in disarray around them. There was no ink bleeding from anything. The page with Ms. Young's portrait was a deep black, lying on the floor like a scrap of burned paper.

"You're dead, Ms. Young," Woojin said, his voice hoarse, as if he had been screaming. "It's over. I'm sorry. It was beautiful, but it's over."

"But I don't want it to be over," Ms. Young said, using his mouth and sounding so plaintive and sad and lost that he almost forgave her for all the trouble and mess she had caused.

"But it is," he said, and the tears were dripping from his chin, now. He couldn't tell if they were hers or his. He wiped his tears and his nose. He was so sad that she was dead. She was so sad that she was dead. He looked back at Jonathan, who was staring at them as if he was seeing something beyond Woojin's face, covered in ink. As if it was his dead mother staring back. Woojin wondered what he would see if he looked in the mirror.

"I've let your dead mom possess me," Woojin said, which was followed by Ms. Young using his mouth to say, "I'm sorry I scared you. Who were you talking to?"

"That was my stepmom," Jonathan said hoarsely. "She married my dad when I was seven. She raised me after you died. I have a picture of you on my nightstand."

"Did you miss me? Do you love me?" Ms. Young said. The fervor in her voice strained Woojin's vocal cords.

"I did," Jonathan said, his voice cracking in the middle of his two-word sentence.

"Did you grow up well? Are you having a good life?" At least she was staying within a normal human register.

"I did. I am."

"You have to go now," Woojin said, stretching his mouth and pulling control back away from Ms. Young. "You're dead, Ms. Young, and you've seen your son, and you need to move on."

"I'm almost done," she said, wresting his mouth from his control. To his horror, Woojin found he was unable to pull control of his mouth back. He tried to look away from Jonathan, and found that he couldn't. His heart hammered in his chest.

Ms. Young stepped Woojin's body toward Jonathan. Woojin wanted to warn him, but his mouth wouldn't move. Woojin had miscalculated, again. He should have known that what Ms. Young's original request had been a ruse. He shouldn't have tried to contain her with his body. He shouldn't have been so softhearted.

"St-st-step back," Woojin finally managed to mangle out of his lips. "G-get-"

He took control back for the briefest moment, and then Ms. Young snapped his mouth shut and kept advancing. She took step after step. Woojin wanted to call out, to tell Jonathan to run, to get out of the room, that all his good intentions didn't mean anything anymore. But he was unable to. Ms. Young was in control. Jonathan finally stepped back, but it was too late. Ms. Young grabbed him with supernatural speed.

And she hugged Jonathan, using Woojin's body. Clasped him in Woojin's arms and tucked Jonathan's head against his shoulder, used her hand to hold the back of his neck like Jonathan was a small child. She took a long, shuddering breath using Woojin's lungs.

"You're both good boys," she said through Woojin's mouth. "Thank you."

And Ms. Young let go.

The psychic presence that had locked Woojin's muscles and bones evaporated. He was left with a string of numbers, a username, and a password floating in his mind's eye as he embraced Jonathan, who was essentially a stranger.

He hastily pulled back.

"Sorry. I didn't expect . . ." Woojin trailed off. He didn't know how to explain everything that had just happened.

"You're crying," Jonathan said.

"She was crying," Woojin said, and kindly did not mention the tears streaming silently down Jonathan's face.

They cleaned up the room the best they could. They wiped ink from the broken table and the floor. They stacked broken chair legs against the wall.

"I think the rest of it we can call facilities for, I'll make something up for them. But I don't know what to do with this," Jonathan said, holding up the black drawing.

"We need to burn it," Woojin said. "I'll do that."

"Can I come?"

"Sure," Woojin said, surprised. He took the paper from Jonathan. It felt inert. No ghost. Ms. Young was truly gone. He felt sorry about that, again. He still felt the memory of her holding her son for the first time. He hadn't known a person could feel that way about another person.

After Woojin washed the ink from his face in the business school's men's bathroom, he guided Jonathan through the warren of studios, out to Woojin's little drywall cubicle. They talked a little, on the way. Woojin learned more about Jonathan's stepmom, who Jonathan had been figuring out summer family vacation plans with. That he had a little half sister. That both of them had been at the rooftop grad school mixer last month arranged by the Asian grad students organization, though they hadn't talked.

"These are really cool," Jonathan said, gesturing at the sketches lining the wall.

"Thanks," Woojin said, and knew that he would be redoing all of them. He was imagining black ash and ink in a box and that box being something you could step inside. He was imagining digging a hole in the gallery floor and covering everything but a pinprick opening. He was imagining someone else getting the story you had always wanted to live within. He was imagining being alive, so briefly, after having been dead.

It had felt so strange to have had Ms. Young inside him. To feel what she felt. He wondered if it was wrong, to use a dead woman's grief. It had felt like his own grief, in the moment. They had been his tears and his body. But he felt weirder about it than he did about taking the money.

Woojin and Jonathan built a small fire on a glass palette, perched a little precariously on the fire escape outside of Woojin's studio. They used cardboard and scrap wood from one of Woojin's classmate's projects. The clear yellow fire crackled merrily, against the background of the Manhattan skyline.

"Can you paint me a portrait of her? One that isn't like. Haunted," Jonathan said. He showed Woojin a photo of her, on his phone. In it, Ms. Young was alive and in color and smiling and holding a little kid who must have been Jonathan. She looked like her ghost except for all the ways she didn't.

"Yeah, I can do that," Woojin said. "I'm sorry for your loss. I'm sort of sorry I brought her to you at all."

"No, it was good," Jonathan said, staring at the flames. "I guess this must be like, every weekend for you, though, huh?"

"This was the first time a ghost has possessed me," Woojin admitted, staring at the little pyre. He bit his lip. He thought about Ms. Young, how she had been so sad and so alive. How he had never asked her why she had wanted to find her son. How she had left so quickly and lightly, after hugging him, even when he had imagined such ill intent from her. He would call his mom when he got home, Woojin decided. He would call his mom and talk about normal things. Regular life things. She would complain about whatever his father was doing and ask if he was eating well, and he would say yes.

He pulled the black page out and held it out to Jonathan. "Ready?"

Jonathan took the paper, and took a deep breath. "Okay. Let's do this."

Jonathan fed his mother's portrait to the fire. It felt oddly solemn. Like something private. Like a funeral pyre. Woojin stepped back inside. He went to the fridge, and got out two of the little Yakult drinks. He thought about doing a portrait of Ms. Young. How he would draw her. How he wanted to paint her in color and not only in ink. Like she had looked when she had been alive.

Woojin brought the Yakult where Jonathan was sitting cross-legged by the smoldering embers. He held it out.

"Here," Woojin said.

"I haven't had one of these since I was a kid," Jonathan said, and drank.

DEATH LETTERS

Vajra Chandrasekera

Younger brother Naryman,

I have terrible news. Our beloved eldest brother Amoghi has been killed in the war and his blood has been lost to us. More soon.

Your elder sister Ferride

All the letters are handwritten; the handwriting will grow progressively worse, which is counterintuitive since this first letter is the one most obviously written in haste. But it is written in the clearest hand, the cursive almost flowing, the diacritic vowel strokes so crisp you can still see the anger of the pen, the depth of feeling embossed into the yellowing foolscap. The first letter is also unique in that it is the only one written on a sheet of unused paper; being also the shortest letter, the paper is mostly blank, the entire body of the letter compressed into a single tight line. Even after all this time, the letter seems to vibrate in the hand, to buzz like a wasp, a long pent-up sting.

The mentions of familial relationships specifying "younger brother" and "elder sister" may seem insistent and passive-aggressive, but in the cultural context of the source chronotope, they were near-automatic prefixes that in practice were generally applicable to virtually anyone, not just immediate family, functioning as honorific, endearment, or assertion of kinship, fellowship, political affiliation, or implied social obligation. In this case, however, the letters imply a close family relationship: they are generally believed to have been siblings or first cousins.

Younger brother Naryman,

It has taken me an additional week to write this letter with what scant details I know so far. I apologize for the delay, but I knew there would be a cost in time. This is why I sent you that brief first letter, so that you would know as soon as possible, and have opportunity to pray for eldest brother Amoghi while you awaited further details, and to understand the depth of the loss of his blood to our fields. I hope you received the news in that spirit. I have not heard from you, but no doubt this letter shall cross your initial reply in the post.

I anticipate that your first question would be "What war?" as I remembered, only a day after sending my first letter, that you and Amoghi have not been on speaking terms for a while, and moreover, you have not lived on the island in over a decade and do not know the state of our wars. For all you know, a new war could have kindled itself since the troubles ended. I may reassure you that it has not. We remain at peace, though the peace grows ever more impoverished. Inflation has been dire. We have found it ever more difficult to make do with our lands unworked. It has now been sixteen harvests since our parental revenants disintegrated and the fields first became untended. We are a salaried house now, to our shame. Our three paltry incomes combined have made this survivable, but it remains as unpleasant as ever to trade our own labor instead of being supported by our dead, as is our historical and familial right. Modernity brings many humiliations.

I do not say this to arouse your pity or elicit offers of assistance from abroad. We have managed this long with the fields fallow, and with Amoghi gone, there is one less mouth to feed. His was the hungriest, as I'm sure you remember, and his army salary and bonuses combined amounted to the smallest income, only forty-six escudo a month. So if anything his death relieves our burden somewhat. I mention this solely to explain why he took the offer to go fight in the Wild Fields, despite the great risk and the gamble of his initial investments, which Duygul and I sponsored upon his sincere and urgent request.

The offer first reached us through an agency I will not name in writing since what they asked was not legal. The offer required Amoghi to desert his nation's military and travel far abroad to join that of another. He was being sought, as were many of his peers, as cheap soldiers experienced in war. They were cheap from the perspective of the armies fighting in the Wild Fields, of course, the Anteans and the Roxolani. But the offer was staggering to us: 1,500 escudos a month and eligibility for Antean citizenship for Amoghi and his dependents if he served one year. He offered to list Duygul and myself as his dependents, since none of us have spouses nor children. The agency fee was 250 escudos, and Duygul and I paid it for him. But then the agency stopped responding to messages, and we could not reestablish contact with them. It seemed as if we had been swindled. There was a time of some recrimination among us. You, too, were implicated in our arguments then. Having left us behind doesn't free you from the angers of family. It only means you don't have to listen to it.

Amoghi was undeterred, however. He reached out cautiously to his peers in the army, and eventually heard back about such offers from many agencies. The most reputable one, the one that seemed to have actually placed some fellow soldiers in gainful employment in the Wild Fields, on both Antean and Roxolani sides depending on the availability of work, was much more expensive than the agency that has first approached us, but after some rigorous discussion, we decided together, the three of us, that perhaps one had to pay more for the thing to be done right.

The fee for the second agency was 2,000 escudos up front and half the salary for the first three months. The advance payment came out of our savings, Duygul and mine, and effectively emptied them. But this time, it was not in vain. In a matter of weeks, Amoghi had received a commission and left for the Wild Fields. We got few letters from him, but he confirmed his safe arrival, without mentioning anything about where he was or what he was doing so as to not anger the censors. He had promised to send money home once the first three months were done and he had settled with the agency.

He did manage to send money home once, before his death. Seven hundred and fifty escudos, arriving some six months after his departure, in the form of a check drawn on an Antean bank, delivered slowly by the old neighborhood postman—old Mukhul, you must remember him, even more bowed and gray than he was when you still lived here. That was how we knew for sure Amoghi was fighting on the Antean side. The next information we received, almost two months later, was the notice of his death.

This letter grows overlong. I shall send this and wait for your responses before I say more. I reiterate that I ask nothing of you. I am simply keeping you informed.

Your elder sister Ferride

The second letter is written on the backs of pages torn from a calendar, the cheap kind that hangs on a wall, each month to be torn away as it passes. This is fortuitous, as it provides much of the reasoning for dating the letters, though there remain extent debates about how out-of-date the calendar might have been at the time the letters were written. Some of the dates on the calendar side are circled in what appears to be the same ink as the letter. The significance is unknown. There are no notes on the calendar side to match handwriting. Neither the paper nor the ink can be dated by conventional forensics, of course, as they are from a different regime of poetics. We are forced to rely on the text itself. The nations or polities here called Roxol and Antea (?) have not been identified. There are many extant debates about possible transcription and translation errors. Unfortunately, scholarly and public interest continue to focus on the more sensational and urgent aspects of the last three letters, leaving these details under-investigated.

Brother Naryman,

I have received both your responses to my letters. I must say I do not care for your tone or your insinuations. It was uncouth of you to suggest that I am demanding money from you when I have clearly indicated that I am not doing so. It was childish of you to bleed onto the page, and gauche to do so in such volumes. You have not outgrown your penchant for the dramatic. However, since you have provided me with your blood, I have done exactly as you suggested—without whatever irony or sarcasm you may have intended. I refuse to be shamed or to apologize, which was clearly your intention. I have instead chosen to read your offer as quite literal and sincere.

Therefore, after having extricated a tincture of your blood from the paper, I have used it to grow revenants in your name. I suppose they are technically not revenants, as you are still alive. I find the dissymmetry pleasing, as you were always the one who objected most strongly to the raising of our ancestral revenants upon their deathbeds. Even when you were so little, when our parents raised our grandmothers to join their husbands in the fields. You always said you would rather leave than live off their dead labor. And now here you are, not only part of that tradition but doing so while still alive—in contravention of ancient practice, ritual, and your own ideology and principles. How delicious it all is.

I am further delighted to inform you that the magistrate accepted my petition with your letter as evidence. The successful raising of the revenants indicates, to the letter of the law, your legal death. You have now formally been declared dead in absentia. I am sure this is of no concern to you since you have long since renounced your citizenship and declared your intention to never return to the island, but the main reason I write once more after all these months is to inform you that you may not return to the island even if you change your mind, as you have now been placed on a watch list. It seems our solution is not that uncommon. Other left-behind families of the diaspora too have turned the absent into dead labor to sustain themselves and support the economy. The formal, if somewhat secretive government policy, as I have learned, is to declare you not only legally dead but to avoid at all costs the coincidence of life and death on our soil. If you attempt to return, even as a tourist, you will be disappeared. Naturally I wish only the best for you, so consider yourself warned.

You will also be pleased to learn that your revenants—we extricated enough blood for quite the flock of them—are working well. The fields have been cleared and replanted, and we await a successful harvest. Duygul should be able to stop working by next year, and me too within a few more seasons. We so look forward to the leisure. It's too bad that you are not able to reap the benefits of your own revenants' labor, and must toil away at whatever incomprehensible precarities you use to survive the heart of the metropole.

Ferride

The third letter is written on the backs of five small photographs. The photographs themselves are black-and-white, much faded. They seem to depict five small children in either costume or period clothing—the bobbin lace details are a giveaway from an age of much finer revenant motor control. It is natural to posit that these are family photographs, and that four of the children are the named siblings or cousins, but it is impossible to tell for certain.

Naryman,

I write with great hesitation now, as I did not intend to contact you again or to respond to your most recent and incoherent letter. Your grammar is atrocious as always, but I can barely read your hand now. It is evident that you forget more of your mother tongue with every passing year, but it seems that after your bleeding, your hand shakes more. I wonder now if this is a consequence of drawing so many revenants from living marrowmeal. Perhaps there are good reasons this is forbidden by ritual and tradition. Still, a consequence of adapting to the times, don't you think?

You write with seeming concern not for yourself but for us, and for your former homeland. I assure you we are quite fine, and thriving. I don't know what you read of us in the foreign newspapers, but as always they lie and exaggerate. There have been no outbreaks, no great calamity. There were a few incidents that get played up for drama. Some people like attention. I will clarify the truth to set your mind at ease, out of nothing more than affection as your elder sister.

First, the farm is doing very well. We are thriving. Both Duygul and I have been able to quit our salaried jobs, which is a great relief, and return to the slower, more elegant life we were accustomed to as children. Your revenants are doing a wonderful job standing in as field-workers and house staff alike. We have bought a little more land and intend to cultivate it further, as we have managed to raise a few more revenants from what's left of the bloodied letter. Duygul has been doing wonderful work experimenting with homeopathic dilution techniques. Our production ratios are well on the way to setting an all-time provincial record, perhaps even an all-island record if we keep it up. The houses that initiated this practice, including ours, are now seen as pioneers, and we are widely imitated, with heavy citation of the legal precedent of my petition that allowed us to change our fortunes. Many of your diaspora-kin have been willing to send back blood to support their houses. I hear in most cases they do so in a more dignified manner than you chose to.

As I said, there have been some isolated incidents, both on our farm and elsewhere. Old Mukhul was put to some trouble when he cycled up one day with the post. He has since retired, or perhaps been reassigned to some other area. The new postman is a revenant. This is an excellent move by the postal service and a signal that our government has at least some forward-thinking persons in it. It avoids trouble neatly.

Similarly, I have heard a few reports from other farms. Revenants are the perfect workers—they are completely obedient to their callers, hardly speak, never tire, and require no pay—but there is only so much work for them to do, and idle revenants have a tendency to wander and get into trouble. This is one reason we are acquiring new land, to keep them busy. But not everyone is so conscientious, and flocks of idle revenants wandering around without work to keep them busy is the proximate cause of all the troubles you speak of. It is an easily solved problem. Their callers simply need to give them more work.

The path to prosperity is never without setbacks, little brother. But prosperity is where we are headed. There is nothing to worry yourself about. Your concerns about your own condition are clearly only paranoia. You were always a hypochondriac. My advice would be to eat more red meat and stop bothering your foreign doctors. They have very little understanding of our techniques, and you do not want to end up as one of their scientific curiosities.

The fourth, and penultimate letter, is written in the margins of pages torn from a book. The words are written at an angle, to be read diagonally one at a time as the reader rotates the page. There is a sense of practice to this, as if Ferride had a great deal of experience in using such pages for correspondence. The book itself has been tentatively identified as *That Sweet Belling*, a then-contemporary collection of short stories by a writer whose name is unknown but published under the epithet Undying Eminence. The short story whose pages have been used to write this letter is incomplete, but it appears to be a satirical drama about a middle-class couple, both well-intentioned academics, concerned about the difficulty of replacing their single revenant servant, who is slowly decaying into senescence, and whose malfunction takes the form of lengthy delusional conversations with an absent son, who may or may not be a younger version of the husband of the couple. As is common in the fiction of the period, the revenant is depicted as far more self-aware and articulate than was the reality.

The letter lacks a sign-off from Ferride, and it is possible there was more to it.

The fifth and final letter has no text, and cannot be reproduced here. It is simply a single small scrap of rough paper, roughly rectangular but jagged all around as if it had been ripped from a larger sheet. It is unknown whether this letter was written by Ferride or someone else: The only reason to consider it part of this sequence is that this was how and where it was found.

The scrap has been soaked overlong in blood until the fibers of the paper were swollen with it, and then dried to a hardened, flaking crisp. It has already partially disintegrated from careless handling and is now kept in airtight containment. There are only faint traces of writing on the page. The ink has long been suborned by blood and is no longer legible. It has been suggested that the markings indicate diagrams or perhaps invocatory poetics rather than the ordinary prose of a letter. This, too, is one of the reasons for the letter to have been kept in containment for a very long time. There are concerns about what might happen if some further minuscule flake of blood-rotted paper were to make contact with the naked air when our societies still struggle so deeply with the problem of ever-growing surplus labor. Global productivity is the highest it has ever been. We pray at night to till our own fields again.

VARANASI

Priya Sharma

Death is easy, but dying is the hardest thing in the world.

I knew you were ill as soon as I opened the door, just like I knew it was you, even though I'd not seen you in forty years. I just hoped that you'd spent some of that time living.

Your birth is a family legend. Mum kept repeating it at her end. She never stopped asking when you were coming home.

We always want the ones who aren't there. And you should've been there. Only we had no idea how to find you. Mum's final thoughts were of you, her beautiful boy, who came out blue and limp. The panicked midwife wrestled with the umbilical cord that garroted you while she shouted for her colleague to fast bleep the pediatrician.

Our burly father was unflappable. He drained corpses of their blood and pumped in embalming fluid, massaging the body to distribute it throughout the tissues. He packed their orifices with wadding to prevent leakage. He was implacable in his quiet consolation of even the most extreme displays of grief. Yet he slid down the wall into a heap when he saw you like that. Everyone who knew him laughed at that, safe in the knowledge that you survived.

Nobody except me gets the real point of that story.

Even your birth was a preparation for death.

You come in, without explanation, and go upstairs to your childhood room as if it was only yesterday that you walked out. It's a guest room now. I can hear you moving about. A door closing. The shower running.

I go to the foot of the stairs several times and stand there. Time hasn't blunted my anger. It's a good six hours before I stop shaking and I finish playing out the dressing down I'm going to give you, but I'll retain some composure. I make you a cup of coffee and then put it on a tray with the sugar bowl and milk jug as an afterthought. I've no idea how you take it.

You're still in bed. You're gaunt, skin leathery from the sun. Your hair is now clean and tied back, which highlights how far it's receded. That causes a pang, as to me you're still a snub-nosed boy with brown hair verging on red, cut short to reveal the circular whorl at your crown. Your eyes flutter and open, as if aware of the scrutiny.

"Hello, Lucy." You pull yourself up. "Milk and two sugars, please."

"This is easy for you, isn't it?"

"Not as easy as you think." You take a slurp from the mug. "How are you?"

"That's it. That's all I get? It's hard to paraphrase the last four decades, so you'll forgive me for not trying."

You don't rise to it.

"Where's Michelle?"

Our older sister.

"She works for the Inland Revenue."

"Jesus, that's a bit extreme of her, isn't it?"

I refuse to laugh, even though it's funny.

"You're here because you want something."

"I don't want anything. I'm tired, Lucy. I just wanted to see you again. Spend some time with you."

I don't care what you want. What *I* want is to take a strip off you, but something in your face stops me. You *do* look tired. Bone weary and gray. That T-shirt hangs off you. Your silver rings are loose on your hands.

"Uncle Pete?"

"Multiple myeloma. It was nasty."

Dad's younger brother was a cheerful man. We loved him. I never understood why he was alone.

"How were Mum and Dad at the end?"

"Bloody awful. Mum went first with lung fibrosis. Do you know what that's like? Dad with prostate cancer." The need to hurt him is a poison that floods my mouth. "You've no idea what it's like to lay out your own parents."

"I didn't think you'd do that yourself."

"Why wouldn't I?"

I insisted on it, but I was unprepared, despite my profession. Every step was painful. The interminable paperwork that dogs us, even after we've gone. I bathed Mum's body for the final time. I washed her hair. I fitted spiked caps under her eyelids to keep them closed and make her repose look restful. I dressed her: underwear, tights, her favorite blouse and skirt, her nicest shoes. I applied a little makeup and then cut and painted her nails. Then last of all I put on her best gold earrings, her engagement ring and wedding band. Only then did I let Dad come in on his walking frame to say goodbye.

Covid robbed my father of those last dignities. All I was allowed to do was put his bagged body straight into a coffin.

"I looked after them." I thump my chest. "*I did that.* You should have been there. They loved you. They were sick with worry from all those years of not knowing where you were. Whether you were dead or not."

And I needed you.

"They were scared of me. Were they relieved when I left?"

Dad bellowed at you for not going to school. For not helping at home. For going out at all hours. Mum questioned you endlessly. *Is it drugs? Is it a girl? Is it a boy? Just talk to us.*

"They were scared *for* you. They just didn't know what to do to help you."

You don't hear me.

"Do you remember what Dad used to say? *Death is just like getting out of one car and into another.*"

"Dad didn't say that. He was quoting John Lennon."

Dad, the Beatles fan. Michelle was "Michelle-My-Belle," I was his "Diamond in the Sky," and you were always "Hey Jude." You'd run to him and leap into his arms. Where did that love go?

"Where the hell have you been all this time?"

"Everywhere."

You're infuriating. Nothing I say seems to touch you.

"Do you mind if I look around?"

I don't believe in premonitions. No omens predicted your arrival. Still, an odd thing has been happening recently.

My body is starting to remember what my mind hides. It happens randomly. I'll have locked my car away in the garage and be walking in from the yard to the mortuary. Or I'll be bringing in a doctor from the office to view a body, so that they can complete the cremation forms. All unremarkable events, but my heart starts to hammer and my mouth goes dry.

The old woman's lips were moving. She was talking to you.

I grasp my chest. A deep pain, within my breast. The image is a wound, as fresh and painful as the day it was made.

Our family have been undertakers for generations. Seventy years of Kirkland and Sons. A vocation that dominated everything. Death keeps unsociable hours. Christmas, birthdays, bank holidays. Dad always answered the call.

Only I remain. Kirkland's daughter. I changed everything when I took over. Out with the dark Axminster carpets and bronze-yellow curtains and matching lampshades. I renamed the Viewing Room as the "Room of Remembrance" and put in patio doors so that families can sit with their loved one but still see the trees and sky. I encourage them to open the doors and step outside if they wish.

The office where I talk to the bereaved is light and airy. The heavy brown furniture has gone, replaced with light oak. The only nod to my family is the framed portrait of our grandmother, in her mayoral robes and chain.

"You've done a great job. This must have cost a lot."

Here we go. At least you've got to the point quickly.

"There aren't any pockets in shrouds." I'll make you work for whatever it is you're after.

"You've done all this for the business, but I don't think you've spent anything on yourself. What else have you done besides work?"

Am I so easy to read? I wish you *had* asked me for money now.

We've reached the corridor that runs behind the office to the mortuary. I can't read your expression, but I see you properly now, without the shadow of the little boy I still love. Your tiredness is absolute. You look like you've seen everything and are exhausted.

"Are you sure you want to go in there?"

It's a stupid question. We're here now. There's no choice. The present is always intercut with the past.

Dr. Brace used to be a regular when we were kids. She'd come to view one of her deceased patients and then come upstairs to our kitchen. She'd fill in the cremation forms while Mum made her a cup of tea. She even had her own mug. I always knew she was around because I heard them laughing together.

I last saw Dr. Brace about eighteen months before she died.

"I've come to see you in a professional capacity." She pulled a folder from her bag. For a crazy moment I thought I was about to have some kind of medical examination, even though she'd been retired for years. "I want to get this all sorted and pay for it so that my children don't have to worry about it."

She looked me in the eye until the last moment when her gaze swerved. "Only if you feel comfortable doing it."

It must have been difficult for her to keep walking back in here to do her job after what happened.

"Of course." My answer was smooth and professional, leaving room for all kinds of uncertainties in her mind.

She nodded as if she'd expected this and opened the folder.

"Are you planning this for a specific reason?"

"No, just thinking ahead."

We talked about what music she wanted, her clothes, and the order of service. I showed her catalogs of coffins, and we talked about cars. Then costs.

"Is that everything?"

"Pretty much."

She didn't get up. She clutched the folder on her lap. It was clear that she had other business to resolve.

"I used to worry about you children. You were in and out of here all the time. Far too young to be around this business. It's all totally different now, of course. A child wouldn't be allowed anywhere near."

Not worried enough to bring it up with Mum during one of your cozy chats.

"And then, what happened to Jude . . . I can't imagine what he went through."

I don't need to imagine. I saw it.

"I've never made a mistake like that. Not before and not since. I offered to talk to Jude but your Mum wouldn't hear of it."

It was the only time that Maria Brace talked with me directly about what happened. She was earnest, not defensive. No wonder she was so well loved.

"Has he ever been in touch?"

"I got a postcard from him about five years after he left. From Varanasi, in India. We all looked for him over the years." I don't mention that I even went out there and hired people to help me. "He either doesn't want to be found or he's dead."

She grasped the edge of the desk as if to steady herself.

"I'm sorry, Lucy. I'm so sorry."

I leaned over and put my hand on hers. Not because I felt anything but because it was the right thing to do.

I still have your postcard in my desk drawer. Mum and Dad were hurt that it was addressed only to me. You'd written "Lucy, you are the Koh-i-Noor Diamond" in your scrawling hand and signed your name with an *X* underneath.

I had to look up what that was. You'd dubbed me the largest cut diamond in the world.

The card had the word *Varanasi* in a tiny blue font on it. An old Indian man in a loincloth stood at the bottom of huge stone steps that led down to a river. He held up a lotus flower in his cupped hands. There was a temple in the background.

I had to look up Varanasi too. The Indian city of pilgrimage. To die there, on the banks of Mother Ganges is to break the endless cycles of birth and death. To be free of the Karmic Wheel.

My abiding memories of it are the press of bodies, the rising sun, temples, flower sellers, and the smell of sandalwood and smoke.

The Manikarnika Ghat is the most auspicious site for cremation in all of India. There were huge stacks of wood. A swaddled body was brought down on a bamboo stretcher. A woman cried as it was doused in water from the Ganges and then set alight. She used the loose end of her sari to cover her face, which contorted in pain. Loss has a universal language. Watching her I was stricken by the idea that you had come here to die.

There's no spare time when you run an all-consuming family business and have three children. As soon as we could answer the phone politely and take a message, we did. We made cups of tea. Michelle learned about invoicing. She was a terror for numbers. She chewed them up and spat them out. Michelle looked after me when I was little, and I looked after you in turn. It's a shame I don't see much of her.

The first moment I recall being conscious of the family business was a stinking hot day in June. I walked in through the gates into the backyard. I normally went to the back door of the main house, to go up the back stairs to the upper floors where we lived. On the far side of the ground floor was the entrance to the mortuary. I could hear voices from deep inside. Uncle Peter was singing along to the radio.

The outer annex contained the washing machine and dryer. Dark suits and ties were hung on a rail. Then there was the door into the mortuary proper. Dad's voice joined Peter's in a sweeping falsetto. I stepped inside. The first thing that I noticed was that it was wonderfully cool.

The human landscape was unmistakable under its white sheet, but a hand had escaped and hung from the trolley. It was a man's, with long fingers and with a smattering of dark hair on the back. I stared.

Uncle Peter saw me first, the song dying in his throat. Dad was drying his hands.

"What's that?" I pointed.

"You know what it is. It's a hand." Mum walked over slowly. She didn't do fuss. She wouldn't tolerate hysterics. "This man has died. Do you remember how we talked about dying? We're getting him ready for his family to come and say goodbye."

I didn't move.

"Are you hungry? Michelle's home. Go and ask her to get you a drink and biscuit."

She stepped in front of him. Even now, I don't know which one of us she was trying to protect.

Death, not sex, is the last taboo. We've lost our skills for grieving in Britain. We should feel free to wail and tear our hair. Bathe our dead and anoint them with oils. Fall to our knees at the magnitude of our loss. Have a proper wake where we can commune with the deceased, toast them, and tell stories of them late into the night. Have a parade of mourners walking beside the hearse through their hometown.

We should have shrines to them in our lounges and surround them with incense, chrysanthemums, oranges, and Ferrero Rocher. We should build them coffins in the shape of a favorite musical instrument or animal, painted in bright colors. Or hold a sky burial. A tower of silence. Let vultures consume their flesh so that their soul can fly free. Instead we worry about death certificates, informing their electricity provider, and canceling direct debits.

I see it as my job to make the nuts and bolts of the funeral as easy to deal with as possible to give those left behind room to grieve. To get the dead and the living where they need to go.

Thinking about that lifeless hand kept me awake. It was dark outside. I picked up my alarm clock. It was eleven p.m. I'd heard the phone go earlier in the evening, then Dad's voice. He hung up and called Uncle Peter. *We've got a pickup at St. Anslem's. I'll swing by and get you. It's on the way.*

I crept into your room to wait for him. It overlooked the yard, with the garages at the far end. I climbed onto your bed to look out.

"Lucy, get off." Your face was crumpled from the sleep.

"Shh."

Headlights swung into the yard, then died. Dad was home.

You stood on the bed next to me and peered out. Dad got out and went inside, while Pete opened the rear doors of the van. The yard light went on. Dad wheeled out the trolley and together they eased out the body in its bag. They took it inside.

Your breath quickened. You pushed yourself under my arm.

A moment later Dad came back outside. He'd turned off the yard light and all we could see was his outline and his sneaky cigarette that was a pinch of orange in the night. It flared with each puff. Then he let out a cry and fell to the ground.

*You won't recognize the mortuary. I've remodeled it and updated all the equip*ment, sinks, slabs, the lot. All the storage is fitted, so it looks sleek and minimalist. The crematorium sends back ashes in plastic urns. My parents stored them on an old pine bookcase in an alcove that I hated. Now they're in a large glossy unit with sliding doors. Sometimes I find tiny bone fragments in ashes as I decant them into proper urns. The embalming equipment is gone. I didn't want to learn. Most funeral directors get someone in to do it when it's needed. We're a closed-casket country, on the whole. The same with the funeral cars. I only keep the hearses and hire whatever else is needed.

"Hello."

It's Richard. He's balling up his plastic apron and washing his hands. He looks like a surgeon.

He's startled that I've brought someone back here, but he holds out a hand in welcome. You take it.

"Richard, this is Jude."

"I'm Lucy's brother."

Richard glances at me. I never talk to him about you. I'm sure he's heard.

"Richard's worked with me for years. He's going to take over when I retire." Chew on that.

I want the business to go to someone that I trust. That this community trusts. He has the right temperament for the job.

"I'll leave you two alone."

And Richard is good at reading the room.

*You're waiting for something. I don't want to oblige but if I don't, I'm only pro*longing this.

"Are you afraid to be in here?" I ask.

"No. It was a long time ago. Aren't you?"

"I was at first." Getting over it was an act of pure will. "Like you said, it was a long time ago. Maria Brace made a mistake when she pronounced that woman dead. She was dying, certainly, but still alive when Dad brought her in."

"She was dead."

"Don't be ridiculous."

"You know it's true."

"No."

I back away. You follow. I'm suddenly afraid of the hidden strength in those emaciated arms.

"You've seen thousands of corpses. Stop lying to yourself."

I'm backed against a worktop, your face so close to mine that I can smell the stale coffee on your breath. It's so bright in here. All the gleaming steel and white tile hurts my eyes.

"Our purpose is similar. We get the dead where they need to go."

You're taller than me. I lean back to get farther away from you. You gather me up in your arms. I can't remember the last time anyone held me.

"I know you remember," you whisper in my ear.

I start to cry. The abscess is lanced.

When I say, "Yes, she was dead," you hold me tighter. There's that pain again, flaring bright inside me.

Uncle Peter was at Dad's side as soon as he heard him shout, then he rushed back in, screaming for Mum. Dad was on the floor. Feet thundered on the stairs. Mum and Michelle. We followed. Mum was at the bottom of the stairs, calling an ambulance, her back to us. She turned at the last moment as Jude and I passed her. She made a fierce face at me and pointed to both Jude and me, then back up the stairs.

It was the only time that I ever disobeyed her. We never spoke of it, even after what happened. I went out to Dad, with Jude following.

When someone has a cardiac arrest it means their heart has stopped. They are dead. Resuscitation isn't guaranteed. CPR only restarts the heart for one in a hundred. Of those, only one in a hundred are as they were before the critical event. Lack of oxygen damages the liver, kidneys, the heart muscle, and the brain.

Uncle Peter saved Dad's life. He got straight to work, fingers locked, arms straight, and the heels of his hands on Dad's sternum. Mum flinched as she heard Dad's ribs crack. Then Peter blew into his mouth, before starting the whole cycle again. He kept Dad going long enough for the paramedics to restart his heart with a defibrillator.

I didn't see any of that because I realized you weren't next to me. I hadn't noticed your hand slip from mine. I looked over my shoulder. The mortuary door was open.

I went inside, looking for you. I didn't want you to see the dead man's hand. I needn't have worried. Not about him, anyway. He was stored in the fridge.

The fluorescent strip lights were unremitting.

Dad and Peter had brought in an old woman's body. The upper part of the bag was unzipped. White wisps were all that remained of her hair. Waxy, yellow skin was stretched over her skull. Her eyes were sunken. She wore a baby-blue nightgown with white lace at the neck.

She was sat up.

Her torso was twisted so that she could clasp your head in her hands. She'd lifted you off the ground, your head tipped back, your feet dangling. You were clawing her, gasping.

She leaned down, her lips moving close to your ear.

What did she say to you?

She moved her mouth to yours and for an awful moment I thought she was going to kiss you, but when her lips parted a thin gray plume of smoke poured from her and into you. It was dense, not ethereal and hazy. I thought you'd choke on it. Her thumbs marked the plumpness of your cheeks.

Urine ran down your leg and pooled at your feet.

Then the old woman went limp, her lifeless body pitching from the trolley. Her legs remained tangled in the black body bag. She'd dropped you and you lay beside her on the floor.

That's when I started to scream, fit to raise the dead.

My head and chest throb from crying. My face feels so tight that the skin could split open like wet tissue paper. We're side by side, sat on the floor with our backs to the cupboards.

"What do the dead tell you?"

"I imagine it's the same sort of conversations that you have with their family. Sometimes they're angry. Sometimes they're relieved. But they're as lost as we are and miss us as much as we miss them. Grief is all the love that remains which we don't know what to do with. They feel it too."

"Grief feels like fear."

"That it does."

"I saw her—she went . . ." I lack the language. "Where did she go?"

You inch closer, your upper arm against mine.

"I don't know. It can't be bad though, Lucy? I'd know if it was, wouldn't I?"

I put my arm around your shoulder. There's that pain in my chest again. "Of course you'd know. It can't be wrong. It's *you*."

We sit in silence for a while.

"I'm sorry that I didn't come back for Mum and Dad. I was a coward. You've been lonely, haven't you?"

"I have my work. What about you?"

"The same. I have my vocation."

A thought occurs to me. "Are there others like you?"

"Yes. There's always some of us in Varanasi. We're drawn there."

"The Holy City."

"It feels good to be among people who do what I do. The dying flock to us."

All those souls breaking free of the wheel. It sounds peaceful.

"Why have you come back, Jude? Are you sick?"

"No, I've looked like this for years. What I do, it takes it out of me. We all look terrible." You put your forefinger right on the painful point in my chest. You're crying. "You were always there for me. You're the Koh-i-Noor diamond, so I've brought Varanasi to you."

THE LEAVING SEASON

Angela Slatter

The first thing Burt knows about it is when he wakes to find Hilda gone.

Her side of the bed is empty, and when he puts his hand against the hollow where she'd lain the sheets were cold. No trace of warmth. His wife of fifty years had been absent for some time.

She might be in the kitchen, but that seemed unlikely; he'd always been the early riser, heading out before her. He'd grab the breakfast/lunch she'd packed for him the night before. Burt didn't hold with large cooked breakfasts, not because he didn't want Hilda going to trouble, no. Just his digestion was a bit tricky, so a few sandwiches sat better in his stomach. He'd put on the kettle though, just before he left, rejoiced in the click-click-click-whoosh of the gas the second before he walked through the back door, so she'd have to wake up when it began to scream, and get out of bed to shift the damned thing off the stove.

On bad days, she'd called it his cold war. On worse ones, she said he was a shit and she should never have married him.

Now, he rises and wanders through the rooms, looking for her, a bit bewildered, with decreasing hope and increasing rage.

No sign of her.

It's only when he sets foot on the long narrow verandah, scans the dawn horizon—dry earth, scrubby grass, stunted trees, rolling dust golden red with the fresh sun—does he realize what day it is.

The day he's ignored forever, though he's known other men wakened to empty beds and homes, saw it happen to his own father, his brother, best friend, worst enemy, and any number of dickheads down at the Royal.

The start of the season.

When Burt goes back inside, still with a tiny bit of hope, he notices the deer's head over the fireplace that only gets lit on the coldest of nights, the frostiest of Outback mornings because he's firmly of the mindset that everyone can just put on an extra jumper. The buck, twelve-point, shot in Scotland and its head mounted, shipped out here by his great-grandfather at great expense to adorn the farmhouse, is old and dusty. Above eye height, easy to ignore—which Hilda's always done, has hated the thing since first she moved in, tried to talk him into getting rid of it and finally settled for passive neglect of it.

Well, that deer's head is lying on the polished hardwood floor. Both its antlers have snapped off, and if he's not very much mistaken, at least two branches are missing. Along with his wife. The hope flickers and dies.

Hilda had been feeling it for weeks, though she didn't identify it at first.

Just that sense of being off—*bit crook*, she'd have said, if Burt had bothered to ask, which he never did—which was neither here nor there. No point complaining, her mother had always said, nobody listens, which was precisely how Hilda had found her existence to be. Margery had warned her, Hilda would admit that now; now that Margery was long dead and still in the ground of the station next over to the one Hilda had spent her married life in. Hearing all these stories about how hardy the men of the bush were, how hardy and tough and unmoved. How many head of cattle or sheep they ran on their land, how they survived fires and droughts and flooding rains, how they were the backbone of the nation. But no one ever mentioned the women who fed them and bedded them, birthed their children, kept their houses clean, saw the tears no one else was privy to and took the blows that came quickly because Christ forbid a man show any feelings without that shot of shame afterward to make him swing his fist this way and that like he might be able to wipe away the memory. Make her forget too. Wash it away with all the filthy work clothes, bake it away in a great wave of pumpkin scones and sponge cakes, fold it up tight with the sun-dried sheets and the chenille bedspreads and shove it into the back of the cupboard.

Where was she?

Oh, out in the garden, what was left of it.

She's taken the hoe to it, meant to tidy things up, harvest the last of the lettuces before the rabbits got to them. But there was only carnage, everything hacked and disgorged from the earth, the symmetry of the rows destroyed, and the wooden handle of the tool held so tight in her arthritic hands she could feel splinters trying to worm their way through her calloused palms.

Or she assumed it has been her.

Couldn't be anyone else, could it? No one else had come and put the tool in her hands after they'd made a hash of everything. She *must* have done it. One of those fugue states her daughters had discussed once, when they talked to her about menopause, or tried to, asked how it had been for her.

"Didn't notice it," she'd said. Because what was the point of talking about it. No point complaining, nobody listens. Deep down, however, though she wouldn't admit it, was that little core of bitterness. Jealousy. That these girls *did* talk about it. *Could* talk about it. Might find answers that she never had a chance to look for—didn't know she was *allowed*. Her mother and grandmother and all the women around her had pursed their lips, gritted their teeth, and just got on with it. Ignored the screams of their own bodies. Aches and pains in joints and muscles. Wombs contracting as if to extract themselves, tearing loose from moorings. Blinding headaches, thoughts that drifted away as soon as they were thought, ideas forgotten, slippery as eels and gone; *Why did I go into this bloody room?*

And all the women in a long line before her, some whispering *Just suffer like we did—do you think you're better than us?* And then others, strident, louder, women men wouldn't *like*, yelling: *Shout! Scream! Who cares if they don't like you? Don't swallow this pain, it's poison! Don't feed it to your daughters!* Part of her cheers them, those women, thinks she could have been one, given the right circumstances—but the weight of training, of grooming bears down too heavy, crushing rebellion and resistance. Somewhere inside her, she knows it's not a default setting, this passivity; it's habit.

Boys are so easy to raise! Girls are so much trouble!

She'd repeated that adage to her daughters when both were pregnant, discussing their worries about the sex of their respective fetuses. Grace had looked her dead in the eye and said "Boys are easy if you let them run wild, don't teach them anything or insist on better behavior or make them suffer consequences. If you spent less time trying to crush girls into a pleasing shape, and using some of that time on boys? Maybe things would get better."

Hilda remembers stammering and stuttering in reply, leaving the room in a huff, telling herself Grace and Evelyn were ingrates. *Little bitches.* But deep inside she knew it was jealousy of their confidence. Anger because she knew they were right; that she'd not done her best by them. Taught them the wrong things.

She doesn't know where her daughters got it, that audacity, that voice, the fearlessness. *Wasn't me,* she thinks with shame.

Ouch!

One of the splinters has broken through as she's squeezed the handle more tightly without thinking. Blood blossoms, looks like a flower as it wells almost elegantly until there's suddenly too much of it, she's there without a tissue or a hankie, and small red drops fall, spherical and slow, to the dirt.

If he put his mind to it, Burt could recall when his mother went missing.

He and Charlie were ten and eleven, just at the age when mums seemed less necessary and more annoying. That was the lesson their father taught them. *Don't be bloody sissies. Get out of the kitchen, your mother doesn't need any help in there, that's her job. Get outside and play sport. That's woman's work and no son of mine will be a bloody—*

Words Burt would have repeated to his sons, if he'd had any. But no, Hilda was only good for daughters.

Some days he'd dream, still, of his mum. Of the time before he wasn't allowed to love her or listen to her. When he could curl up on the armchair in the lounge room right next to her, feel the warmth of her, the crisp cotton of her housedress and apron over the top to keep it clean, smell her lilac perfume, her clean skin, and whatever she'd baked that day. When she'd read him and Charlie bedtime stories to send them off to sleep.

And while he didn't forget tenderness—Christ knew he'd used it to lure Hilda in—he simply couldn't be bothered making it part of his everyday habits. Nor kindness, nor gentleness, nor anything that cost him nothing or pleased his wife. Because he'd married her, he didn't have to do anything more. Wasn't that what she wanted? He'd got what he wanted. It never occurred to him to wonder why they were so miserable.

Burt shakes his head. He hasn't left the house; sheep and cattle remain untended. Outside the kelpies have mostly given up barking their upset at this change in routine, just the occasional howl to register a continuing protest.

He's sitting in the kitchen, drinking from an enamel cup of too-strong tea that went cold ages ago.

His mum.

Standing between his dad and him and Charlie, taking blows so they didn't have to. Growing thin and silent and pale, though his father called her "fat bitch." Always there like sword and shield, until the night the lights came. Until she walked into them. Until she left her boys behind, maybe because she could see that no matter how much she loved them, they'd still turn out like their father. Maybe that was why it was so easy for her to go. Yet he'd never thought, ever, that behaving differently toward Hilda might stave off the same event in his own life.

The lump in her breast comes as a surprise, she doesn't know why; Aunt Ead, Great-Grandma Tib, Cousin Ozanne, all went that way.

Somehow, Hilda thought she was too old for that sort of thing.

The doctor gave her a pitying look when that had tumbled from her lips. Started to tell her about the operation and treatment and survival rates and hair loss and the tattoos they'd put on her boob to make sure they got the radiation in the right place.

But Hilda knew she wouldn't have the treatment. That the thing growing in her chest was, if not meant to be there, then at least a means to an end. An exit.

She's wasted her life, getting all the things she was told she should want, all the things she was told were all she needed. She shouldn't have married Burt, shouldn't have married at all. Shouldn't have had her girls—should have let them be someone else's daughters. In a way, she thinks, they are; they came out of her, but their personalities, their independence, their refusal to let someone put a boot on their necks? That came from somewhere else. They're someone else's daughters. She wonders, idly, if every mother suspects her child is an alien, a foreign object. Unrecognizable.

And that thing growing inside her was a child of another stripe, a dark one, perhaps her only true child, borne of bitterness and disappointment and bad choices. Letting others tell her what she wanted and needed, listening to them though the voice in her head—the one that was gradually drowned out—said *no.* She should have left town, left the stations, gone to the city, found a job, studied, done anything but what she had. Didn't have to be a forever job or a forever home—just needed to be an experience of something new.

Because she didn't need a career, but Jesus H. Christ she'd needed an identity that was her own. An idea of who she was. What she wanted to be, could have been. Was never given a chance to discover. Because all she became was a something to someone else: wife to a husband, mother to children, feeder of chickens and lambs and jackaroos, baker of cakes for church sales, tender of vegetable gardens, cleaner of toilets, maker of beds, darner of socks.

And now she's the cultivator of something else.

Something just for herself.

Burt thinks, a couple of times, of calling the girls.

But he's not sure where their numbers are to be found because Hilda took care of that. There'll be a little address book, he supposes, that she keeps somewhere, all the names and numbers of people, the details of and connections to the network she built up throughout their marriage to make things easier. Things he didn't have to think about: doctor, dentist, daughters, bank, gas, electricity, accounts at the IGA in town, the chemist, even the feedstore. All the mail she opened, all the bills she paid, the letters she read and answered, the Christmas and birthday cards she wrote and signed for both of them.

Besides, the girls hadn't been out here for years.

Not since that last fight.

Not since he'd spat the last bit of spite at them, saw a final thread snipped and the way their bodies sort of sagged as they fell away from the house and their parents, almost drooped before they went to the red Mitsubishi Triton and took off in a cloud of dust and disappointment.

He hadn't really expected them not to return.

Hadn't ever expected them to say *Enough* and mean it.

But he'd seen the look in Hilda's eyes then and knew the habitual animosity that spouses have for each other, that routine contempt, had turned into something else. An alchemical reaction morphing ordinary dislike into pure golden hatred.

How was he to know there'd be consequences to his actions?

That daughters are never as forgiving as their mothers.

And even if he could find that little address book—Did it have a pink cover? Did he remember a small pink book in her hands?—even if he could find those numbers, make his thick fingers dial, what would he say?

She's gone.

Season's come.

What do I do?

He had, he knew, no remaining credit in his daughters' affections, and for all he'd spent years growling to be left alone, driving his family away, for the first time Burt was actually alone.

And it wasn't anything like he'd hoped it would be.

Finally, Hilda wakes in the middle of the night—morning, really, two a.m.— pins and needles in her body moving in a wave. She imagines it, visually, like those of banks of lights you see on TV, this row then the next. A radiating wheel of pain in her left breast. And the heat—she hasn't felt this sort of fever since the last kick of menopause—is burning through her bushfire fast. But the sheets beneath her are dry, not a trace of sweat, not at all damp.

Burt's snoring the way he always has, the way she learned to block out a hundred years ago when they first got married, when they first had kids and she was the only one to get up to them in the dark hours. Had to learn how to not hear him or she knew, just *knew*, she'd find herself putting a pillow over his face and holding it there hard for three and a half minutes, maybe four just to be safe.

Hilda sits up, swings her legs over the side of the mattress, feet touch the floor, cold wood, the shellac a little sticky in the weather. Can't work out what woke her until she sees the flare of warm light through the curtains, a slow and gentle strobing. Welcoming. She hisses "Burt? Burt!" but he doesn't wake, even when she half turns, feels the catch in her side at the odd angle, and shakes him. He snores louder, farts. She doesn't bother with her slippers.

In the lounge room, the light is brighter, stronger, a little more urgent. Still gentle though, somehow no faster. Hilda's seized, however, with the sense that she's underdressed, that she needs something special to make herself stand out—and Christ knows, Hilda's never stood out a day in her life, at least not after she met Burt, because look where standing out had got her, attracting his attention. But now, right now, she needed *something*.

She scans the room, spies the hated deer head, the sad thing whose eyes plucked at her every time she looked at it by accident. Those antlers.

It's surprisingly easy to get off the wall, a little push and it dislodges; she steps out of the way so as not to be impaled. Doesn't worry about the noise, Burt won't wake. When it hits the floor—gouging furrows in the polished wood—the antlers break off, and branches snap individually, neatly, into jigsaw puzzle pieces. Just the right size and weight she needs.

They don't hurt, not really, when she puts them to her own skull, presses the sharp broken ends into her coarse silver-gray hair, into the scalp that shows pinky-white beneath it. Not much blood, not too much warm on her temples, cheeks, neck. Quickly done, quickly fused, suddenly solid.

Her crown of horns; crown of thorns.

Queenly, she thinks, nods. Feels the antlers bow and sway with the motion of her head.

Hilda opens the front door, floats onto the verandah.

The lights are out past the yard fence now, or maybe that's where they always were. They're moving, getting farther away. Determinedly, she paces forward, down the creaking wooden steps and into the dirt and dead grass of the post-summer lawn. Doesn't feel the bindis or sharp cutting little stones beneath her bare feet. Seems to see, in the weak glow, other footprints ahead of her. A pathway walked by other women, when their time comes, when they turn their backs on what no longer (or never did) serves them, and stride into the night with its gently strobing lights, the quiet promising hush of the darkness.

In the evening, Burt has a shower, puts on the newest of his blue cotton shirts and jeans, the leather belt that still has a shine to it and the smell of dubbin wax. Not much point polishing the boots, given the ubiquitous dust, but he gives them a brush nonetheless—he once heard one of his daughters (can't remember which one, generally found them indistinguishable), say that a woman judges a man by the state of his shoes and watch. He doesn't have a watch, hasn't worn one in years because the hours tick through his bones and he can tell you the time down to the minute without the aid of a timepiece; feels the sun in its rising and falling. Yet didn't know his wife's leaving season was on its way.

He climbs in the old ute, takes the long driveway toward the highway that leads into town. Almost a straight shot to the Royal. The publican is ten, fifteen, twenty years younger than he is. Barb, a widow. Frequently courted but never caught. It doesn't occur to Burt there's a reason for her to remain single, that it's her choice—she already had one husband and found that to be more than enough, his death a happy relief—but Burt simply thinks that if he makes an offer she's obliged to accept out of politeness. Don't all women owe men politeness? Just to hear him out. That's how you get them, after all.

He a widowman, with something to offer.

In the twin glare of the ute's lights, there's a flash of white.

Thin legs, a faded pink nightgown, silvery hair, and a crown of antlers growing from her head. She turns toward the sound of the engine. Burt thinks from the hostility spreading across her face—otherwise rendered smooth and blank by the brightness of the headlights—that she recognizes him. And he's so taken aback, so pinned and fascinated by this unexpected sight that he doesn't brake or swerve or even just slow.

But Hilda's suddenly growing, looming large large large, impossibly so.

His wife squares her shoulders, settles her feet into the dirt for purchase, drops her head, antlers pointed in the direction of the oncoming vehicle, and begins her charge . . .

THE GRAND OPENING

Stephen Graham Jones

Townhomes, town-homes, town *homes*, "townomes."

Redding has said that word so many times that it's lost its meaning, has melted into . . . not a sound exactly, though if it were a sound that sound would be hammers hammering, but a feeling: a nail, being driven into his hand, his head, this job he's coming to realize is his life.

"How many units, again?" he asks Chuckles, who's trying to get a baseboard level on a floor that most definitely isn't.

"Don't think about it," Chuckles says around the lollipop in his mouth.

But Redding already is thinking about it: ninety-six. Ninety-six units in an impossible eight months, after a seventy-odd complex last fall, and probably a hundred-top coming soon.

Not *top*, though, Redding reminds himself. *Top* is restaurant talk: "You've got that five-top by the door?" a server might say to someone passing through the kitchen.

Redding can hardly remember working in that seafood place, though. He does know he'll never eat shrimp again—finding that package that had gone bad isn't a thing his mind can let go of. And, anyway, didn't that restaurant burn down or something? No: Gilbert, who was Chuckles before Chuckles was, had shown him the newspaper article on a lunch, two or three complexes ago: it had exploded. And then, Redding guesses, burned.

Who cares.

"Like this," he says to Chuckles, and drops down to his knees to help with the baseboard.

As long as none of the ramrods are looking over your shoulder, doing their quality-control thing, you can, if you know what you're doing, sort of shave the bottom of the baseboards to roll with the uneven flooring, so the tops, at least, read level.

"Watch for Floyd," Redding says, posting Chuckles at the door, and inside of twenty minutes, once again, this next baseboard is passable. It's not the floor crew's fault, either, Redding knows. It's the clowns who pour the foundations. Well, really, it's the clay that goes down for nearly twenty feet this close to the creek. Yeah, if longevity is a concern, you can drop pylons down to the bedrock, get all these townhomes stable and level, but . . . how long will people even live in these?

Judging by all the shortcuts each crew's been taking, not long. There's supposed to be fiberboard behind the showers, the pipes in the exterior walls are supposed to be insulated, the registers are supposed to anchor into studs, not just Sheetrock, and on and on. If the supervisor doesn't see it, though? If the incoming residents don't have to know for five or six years?

In the company's books, that's a success.

And even if there's blowback, well, all the swarms of Reddings and Chuckles and Gilberts are just punching a clock, hammering nails for pennies on the hour, so they don't catch any of that, are already on the other side of town, leaning another cardboard complex up against the sky.

It's a living, if not much of a life.

For lunch, Redding sits halfway up the carpeted stairs, Chuckles down at the bottom, each of them contemplatively gnawing on their ham and mustard sandwiches and drinking from their thermoses.

"How can there be this many people?" Redding finally says around a bite.

"Be glad there are," Chuckles says.

It's the difference between the two of them, Redding thinks: Chuckles doesn't want to have to think about the bigger picture.

More and more, though, Redding can't help it.

This is better money than the restaurant, sure. But the work, it's so unchanging, so constant. At least in the restaurant there were new customers every night, and when corporate sent down a new menu, and new packages off the reefer trucks, that was some variation.

Unlike here. Unlike this.

Looking ahead, Redding can see himself hammering finishing nails into baseboards until one day, when he runs his hair out of his eyes with his arm, that hair will be thin and crackly. And then, a few years after that, the hair will be gone altogether, and then some other Chuckles will find him collapsed over his ten thousandth ham and mustard sandwich.

Do they even clock you out when that happens?

Do they just bury you in the townhome's lawn, so long as the landscapers haven't rolled the sod down yet?

"Would you want to be buried here?" Redding says down to Chuckles.

"Why do I always get paired with you?" Chuckles asks back. "Why can't I work with someone who had forty on the game last night?"

Redding, up where Chuckles can't see, sort of shrugs in understanding. He knows he shouldn't always be trying to interrogate the world, shakes answers and meaning and whatever from it. Gilbert, before he went wherever, called Redding "the Philosopher with a Hammer," and Redding had never liked that, could hear the insult in it. But it wasn't exactly wrong, either.

"I mean, how many of these can we build before townhomes are all there is?" Redding asks.

"You want to build something else, that it?" Chuckles asks back, balling up the foil his sandwich had been in and arcing it grandly out the back door, for some other crew to pick up.

"Just, where does it end?" Redding asks.

"Let's hope it doesn't," Floyd says suddenly, from beside the staircase. He's not looking at Redding and Chuckles, is doing what he always does: staring down into his clipboard. And scowling.

Redding flinches, caught, and Chuckles stands too fast, knocking his thermos over, gurgling water onto the new, plastic-smelling carpet.

Chuckles collects it, whips the bandanna from around his neck to dab at the spill.

"But speaking of ending," Floyd repeats. "This unit was supposed to have been completed . . ." He raises his clipboard, studies it through his reading glasses, peels his lips back from his teeth. He looks up to Redding and Chuckles to deliver what comes next: "This unit was supposed to have been finished four *days* ago? Cleaning crew's supposed to be in here right now, cleaning up all you two's *messes*. New resident's scheduled—" He looks up, around, at all the unfinishedness, his hands on his hips, his reading glasses hanging on their lanyard at his chest. "What have you two been doing in here?"

"Had to wait for electrical," Chuckles says, making zero eye contact.

"Had to be up to code," Redding adds, which he hopes is the silver bullet for the schedule being fried.

Floyd hisses, that silver bullet sizzling into his frustration.

"But how can . . ." Redding adds, more hesitant. "You mean residents are going to be moving in before the whole complex is even finished?"

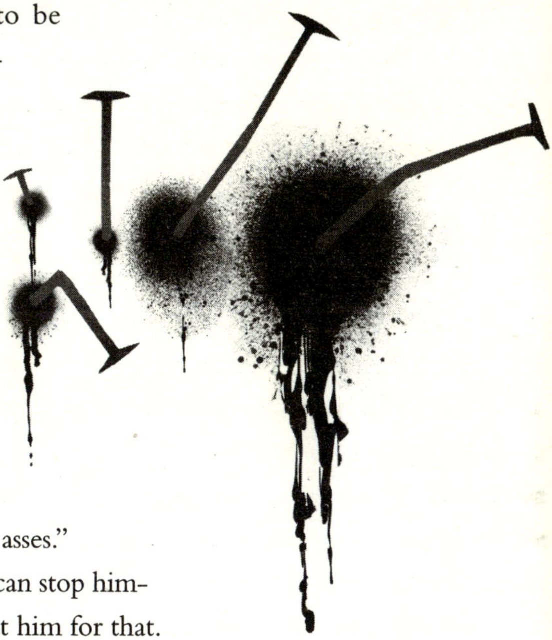

"It's a rolling system," Floyd says. "Stupid, yeah. Parking lot's not even painted yet. What, are they going to wear hard hats when they go check their mail? I don't know. Above my pay grade. All I know is that there's more and more of them coming, and we have to keep up, be ready, or it's our asses."

"*Our*," Redding says before he can stop himself, and Chuckles flashes *No* eyes at him for that.

But it's true.

Sure, Floyd might get chewed out if a new resident shows up to find none of the switch plates screwed in yet, but that's nothing to the chewing-out Floyd will give Redding and Chuckles.

"I'll bury you here myself," Floyd says, meaning he had been listening longer than he let on.

He glares each of them down for a solid five seconds each, which is probably in the supervisor manual under "How to Get More Productivity with Nonverbal Threats," and then spins away, is on to the next unit over, to do the same thing there.

Because the residents are coming.

Because we're behind, we're behind.

Faster, faster.

Never mind that that kind of urgency, mixed with power tools, can only lead to accidents, which *really* fry the schedule.

But that's above Redding's pay grade.

"Welp, lunch is over, I guess," he says, coming down the stairs, avoiding the wet spot in the carpet.

"What did you mean, about that?" Chuckles says, not working yet, just drinking the last of his water down, or whatever he keeps in his thermos.

"That if we don't—"

"No, about the burying," Chuckles says, leaning over to see into the unfinished living room, it looks like. For if Floyd's playing possum in there, ready to pounce, flatten some heads with his clipboard.

"Nothing," Redding says, not wanting to lead Chuckles back through the circuitous way he got there.

He should learn to just punch the clock, turn his thinking off and not turn it back on until that five o'clock whistle. *If* then, right? Why not just tamp all his questions about life and meaning and the world flat, into a steady dial tone, right? Wouldn't that be happier? Easier? Not to think, just to do.

Like Chuckles.

Except now Chuckles looks to be maybe thinking, oops.

Redding should have just kept his trap shut, he knows.

"It made me remember something, though," Chuckles says. "About my big brother. I ever tell you about him?"

"Big brother?" Redding says, leading the two of them into the kitchen.

The boxes of pull handles are in a neat pyramid stacked precariously on the thin ribbon of counter in front of the sink, which Redding has decided must be the night crew's version of fun: If you accidentally knock that pyramid over, all those small boxes tumbles into the sink.

The things that are hilarious at three in the morning, man.

Or, the things that are hilarious when nobody with a clipboard is around, to clock what illegal substances you might be floating on, to get through this dark shift.

Who cares.

And, the pyramid is sort of fun. Like a mysterious structure left by a lost people, for the day crew to make sense of.

"Yeah, Timothy," Chuckles says. "He used to hold me upside down by the feet over the toilet, and flush it over and over, me screaming the whole time."

"I made you think of that?" Redding asks, carefully removing the topmost box of pull handles and tossing it back to Chuckles.

They can talk, but only so long as they're working. Well, so long as they look busy. But, after a while, looking busy might as well be working.

Things you eventually learn, working by the hour.

"No, that's just who he was," Chuckles says, clunking down to his knees the way he does, that always unnerves Redding. They're both wearing kneepads, but still, it jars your whole body, to just drop like that, like a puppet whose strings just got cut.

"I'll start on the top," Redding says, opening the next box.

"He was nine years older," Chuckles says, finger-tightening his first pull handle. It's their system: They get them all finger-tight, then come through as a team, one holding the handle steady on the pull-side while the other uses the electric screwdriver to tighten. Over and over, into eternity.

"So you're a mistake, then," Redding says with a halfway grin.

"Like you're not?" Chuckles says back with one of his signature chuckles, spinning another handle down to its door.

It's a joke, is nothing, but it manages to send Redding back to the seafood restaurant for some reason.

It's one of those days, isn't it?

One of those ones that are so much longer, because you get caught up in your own head, can't find your way out.

"And this has something to do with burying, what?" Redding says, holding the screw post of two handles in his mouth at once, which is a thing the new resident will never have to know about. They'll move in assuming their saliva will be the first spit to coat this place.

Wrong, always.

"I had forgotten it until before," Chuckles says, knee-walking over to the cabinets under the sink. "We had gone to my grandma's funeral. This was before the wreck."

"What wreck?"

Chuckles stops spinning his next pull handle on, kind of zones out like dredging something up. Then, "Just . . . this was before that. After the reception or whatever the part after the funeral's called."

"Wake?"

"Isn't that before?"

"The opposite of that, then?" Redding says.

"It's really hard to tell you something when you stop me every six words," Chuckles says, *not* chuckling this time.

"What did your brother tell you about burying?" Redding says then, enunciating over-clearly like speaking to a kid.

"I asked him what was going to happen to her now, Granny Lu," Chuckles says.

Granny Lu, Redding repeats in his head. *Grannylu, Grannilu, Granlu.*

You can do it with any word.

"He asked me back didn't I know why she was all dressed up," Chuckles goes on. "I didn't know. I guess I was, like, six, here? Maybe five. It was a long time ago."

"Back when you were gullible," Redding completes for him.

Chuckles shrugs, spins a pull handle into its hole fast enough that it pinches the skin of his finger. He jerks that finger up to his mouth fast, to hide it in his mouth.

Not only saliva, then, Redding tells himself. Some blood too.

"Why was she dressed up?" he asks, trying to play along, not slow things down.

Chuckles looks up to him, his eyes somehow scared, which Redding doesn't much care for. In remembering this, though, he can see that Chuckles has dialed back to his six-year-old self, sort of. That innocent sort of thinking, where you believe everything your amazing big brother tells you. It's gospel, every word.

"He told me it was for her big entrance," Chuckles says, rocking back and forth on his knee pads. "Timothy, he hated being called Tim, he—he said that the way coffins are built, the bottom opens too, right? Like an upside-down hatch or something. I guess there's hinges on one side."

Redding strongly suspects Chuckles is saying this about hinges because that's what they were installing two days ago, but he doesn't say anything.

"It opens?" he asks instead.

"Yeah," Chuckles says. "But only after it's covered with dirt on top. And—and the hole, the grave, it's not only six feet deep. That's the thing. The hatch opens down into that, into a staircase Granny Lu was going to walk down, into her new life."

"Hunh," Redding says, not working now either—but ready to, if they hear boots in the living room. "So, Tim, Timothy, he was mean like a brother has to be, but he was nice too, wasn't he?"

"What do you mean?" Chuckles asks.

"What he was making up for you," Redding says with a shrug, because this is so obvious. "He was telling you a story that let your grandmother still be alive. Just, somewhere else. Somewhere she needed nice clothes for."

Chuckles considers this, considers it some more.

"Sometimes he would let my hair touch the water in the toilet," he finally says.

"I'm not saying he was *nice*," Redding says, spinning another pull handle in. "I'm saying it was cool of him to do that for you."

"Maybe," Chuckles says. "But, I got in trouble at my uncle's funeral when I was twelve, for reaching into the coffin beside him and pushing down to see if the door under him opened. It made the whole thing fall over."

Redding chuckles now, likes that image, that scene.

"So it was all a big, long joke he was pulling," he says, shifting gears. "Your brother. He was setting you up for that, wasn't he?"

"I was a stupid kid," Chuckles says.

"Who grew into a—" Redding can't help but start to say, but the lollipop stick zinging at him stops it short, and then, for about thirty seconds, it's another battle, each of them throwing whatever they can find at each other.

Until Floyd's standing in the doorway.

Redding gulps, studies the floor like inspecting it for irregularities he's going to need to address.

"Um, um," Chuckles tries, probably feeling around for an excuse, but there's no excuse.

"And I wonder why we're behind schedule," Floyd finally says, clapping his clipboard against the doorjamb just like a dad might double his belt over and slap it together to show what it can do. He looks like he's trying, and barely succeeding, to control his fury.

"You're each on until *nine* tonight," he finally decrees. "But I'll be clocking you out now."

Redding winces to lose those hours.

But there's nothing to do about it.

"What about dinner?" Chuckles asks.

It's a good question. Each of them only packed lunch, and the burrito truck is always gone by two.

"What about it?" Floyd says back, staring each of them down in turn again.

"We'll eat after," Redding says for both of them, filling in the blank Floyd's left, and, apparently, passing this single-question pop quiz: Floyd nods gravely, shrugs, and turns, is gone again.

Or not.

With him, you never can tell.

For the next eight and half hours, Redding and Chuckles work for free, finishing the kitchen, the switch plates, the two bathroom thresholds, and then tightening all the knobs on and adjusting the hinges so the doors swing and seat right. It's tedious, all this stuff at the end, but, like Floyd says, it's the first thing the new residents have to complain about, so it has to be up to snuff.

On the way out, their tool belts over their shoulders even though it's more awkward to carry them like that, since you have to always be hitching them back in place, Redding says sorry to Chuckles.

"I started it," Chuckles says back with a shrug. "It's me who should apologize."

"No, for—your uncle's funeral," Redding says. "That was a cruel trick your brother pulled."

"But it was nice too, like you said, right?" Chuckles asks.

Redding claps Chuckles on his non–tool belt shoulder in reply, and they slope off for the bus stop like they've done every day for who knows how long. Like they'll *do* every day for however long the future goes—for forever, it feels like. Because there's always new residents coming in.

Luckily, the bus is late—Redding only remembers his thermos when he clocks Chuckles picking at a faded sticker on the side of his.

"What?" Chuckles asks, when Redding stands all at once.

"Here," Redding says, handing his tool belt down to Chuckles. "Don't—don't let the bus leave without me?"

"I can't—" Chuckles says, standing now as well, and Redding knows that you can't hold a bus, especially one already behind schedule, but screw it, he's already running back to the town house they just finished out. Safety-toe boots aren't made for speed, but Redding tries to use them that way anyway.

He climbs the tall chain-link fence instead of going the long way around through the gate, falls onto the new shrubs landscaping should have known better than to already plant, and crashes into the now-finished unit, just stands there on the tile entrance, squinting to try to remember where he might have left his thermos.

The half bath under the stairs, yes! He knows it's there because, to fill it in that sink, he had to lay it over and run the water slow. It would only ever get two-thirds full, so he and Chuckles had been back there all day, but the kitchen faucet was all sputtery and messed up, which they didn't want to have to report, so: the half bath, where he was laying that ornery threshold down.

Redding walks quietly through the living room, can't help but imagining the couch there, the television against that wall, a family photo hung up right here, one of those tall thin tables right here, to balance an urn on—

An *urn*?

Redding stops, doesn't know why he would kick an *urn* up.

Then he grins: Do they have trapdoors in their bases too?

Ha.

Chuckles. Such an idiot.

On the way past where that urn might someday be, Redding caresses that space in the air, and almost feels the lid sliding off, and a smell coming up from there.

Rotten shrimp.

Redding has to gag a bit, and step back.

Just like he did when he found that bag of stink and crawling wrongness.

Step back into . . . into what?

And why does the seafood job keep rising for him today?

Doesn't matter. Probably because he hasn't had dinner.

Who cares.

The thermos.

It's right where Redding knew it would be. He doesn't even have to turn the light on to find it.

He grabs it, nodding success to himself, then stills, listening hard for the air brakes on the bus.

What he hears instead are footsteps creaking the first couple of stairs, up at the top.

A spike of fear jabs into Redding's chest, and he feels caught, exposed, guilty.

But—but it's not Floyd, Floyd has to be gone, he can't be here with his clipboard all day.

Can he?

No.

It's the whacked-out night crew. That's who it has to be. They're up there balancing a gift-stack of soaps or something in a pyramid upstairs, who knows what they do. But now they heard a sound downstairs where it's supposed to be empty, so are halfway down the stairs, listening just like Redding is.

He steps out of the half bath, wants to beeline the front door, hop the fence, race for Chuckles and the bus stop.

But . . . he's never seen the night crew, either. What if it's some shadow version of him and Chuckles, right? Not stacking the soaps, but zinging them at each other?

Ha.

"Hey," Redding calls ahead, not wanting to scare whoever's there, and, instead of retracing his path back through the living room, he steps around to the bottom of the stairs.

"Where am I?" whoever's on the stairs says back, though.

Redding looks up to them, to him.

It's a guy, a man, maybe late thirties.

He's holding the handrail tight-tight like he's never seen one before, is only halfway down the stairs.

Behind him, the lights off, is just endless blackness, going up and up, to . . .

A dim rectangle in the ceiling? An opening of some kind, now shut? Do these townhomes have grand attics up there, what? They don't, Redding knows. He would have had to put pull handles on the attic hatch, had there been one.

And, *hatch* isn't the right word, quite.

Trapdoor?

One tapered at the foot end.

Redding brings his eyes back to this man. This man who doesn't know where he is, who's standing there so gingerly, parentheses of uncertainty around his eyes.

He's wearing a nice suit, nice shoes.

And . . . and his cheeks are pink with makeup? And—and there's dirt crumbling off his shoulder, sifting down from his hair.

Redding steps back fast, feeling for the wall, and what his groping hand finds is the handle of an industrial stove, the gas hissing on fast, filling the huge stainless-steel kitchen Redding's about to crash through, dislodging a hanging pan such that, when it falls, it's going to spark.

And—and blow the whole restaurant up.

Along with Redding.

He swallows, watching this dead man come down the stairs. He swallows, shaking his head no faster and faster.

The new resident is here, right on schedule.

And, in Redding's closet back at *his* townhome, there's a nice suit too, isn't there? In its long plastic sleeve? Its tapes from another time, another era.

Redding's breathing fast now, and too deep, and then, and then—

He's running out the front door, he's crashing over the fence, and Chuckles is getting on the bus, is halfway on the bus, trying to keep it there longer, because his friend is coming, his friend is almost here, and Redding is running, he's reaching with the thermos he knows now he should have left behind, he's almost there, and then the distance between them stretches out into forever.

Just like this job.

This life.

This death.

THIS IS WHAT HAPPENS WHEN YOU DIE

Catherynne M. Valente

The universe, long declared to be axiomatically infinite, is not entirely without bound or limit.

It is only *nearly* so.

The great unfeeling void, sparsely punctuated by spheres of fire, spheres of dust, spheres of wind, and spheres of stone, does, of course, expand on and on, out and out, past any capability of measure. In every direction all at once, further than the mind can grasp on any given Tuesday during which the mind is also expected to perform rational functions or operate heavy machinery like coffee machines or forklifts or marriage.

And stops, just short of forever.

Only to contract, and cool, and regret, understand its many faults, and promise to change. To learn. To grow. To make better choices next time. To finally get it right. It is the limit that triggers contraction and expansion. A tide booming against a cliff, and rolling back out to sea.

No language on any world on which life has risen, flourished or stagnated, withered or ascended, has evolved a word sufficient to communicate both the sprawling grandeur and peculiar disappointment of *infinite minus one decimal point.* Let alone infinity minus 37.149 (repeating) kilometers, which is much closer to the truth.

Nor does any technological means, owned or operated by any currently active civilization, exist with which to detect, locate, or observe this boundary, nor what lies beyond/beneath/beside/below/between it, way down deep below the bottom of the black. By any currently active definition of *currently.*

Or *active.*

Or *technology.*

And yet, there it lies.

The barren distance between the last lonely floating silver spangle of galactic filament and the terminus of all matter is unfathomably greater than the distances between those comparatively overcrowded, wild and slatternly reaches where all other galaxies, elements, dust, disaster, sorrow, elation, fusion, loneliness, and light move and weep.

It is a long way to fall on the day you die.

On the day I died.

But fall you will; fall did I. Past that last glittering safety net of time, consequence, and experience. Past home and worry; past mantle and core, pole and orbit. Past any region of space ever graced by the miracle of a single star or mote of hopeful dust. Past the final, intellect-sundering crevasse of *nothing* whose depth and breadth approaches endlessness in and of itself.

And then a little further still.

There was always so much more space in you than matter. So much more emptiness than its opposite. And this is not only your nature, but the nature of everything.

The matter in you must die. The space cannot.

The hollow between your atoms, that lightless un-organ that once fused all that is unrepeatable, unquellable, unannihilatable in you to your faltering flesh, may survive these countless light-eons of descent. It may not. It is so easy to get lost. To forget. To want to forget. A little void can so easily melt away into the great one. Into peace, into silence, into the relief of unthought and unbeing, black butter releasing in a black pan.

But if the depths of you, painless, thoughtless, dreamless, helped only by gravity and momentum produced by other stellar bodies, resist these vast temptations, one day (though days are meaningless), one lucky hour (though hours are meaningless), your feet (though by then you will barely remember that you ever had feet) will find, against all logic or faith, solid ground.

It is nothing like you, or anyone you know, wanted. It is nothing like any enfleshed being has the capacity to even so much as hallucinate. It is not heaven. It is not hell. It is no bardo, no sheol, nor any purgatory. There was never enough order or purpose in the universe for such things.

It simply is.

Nothing that follows this paragraph is true. At least, not exactly. Not in the way the facts of gravity or heat exchange or nuclear fission are true. Each word that attempts to perform its usual duties dissolves on the surface of what it describes like a child's stickers placed on the surface of the sea. Each sign that approaches the actual nature of its signifier immediately begins to lose cohesion around the edges; shudders, bursts, floats away on an aimless eddy.

It's not their fault. They're good words. They tried. They always try.

What lies there, lies on a circlet of earth (though its chemical composition would not recognize our earth, even as a passing acquaintance) possessing a diameter of roughly five hundred kilometers and a variable thickness averaging out to eleven kilometers.

Most of the time.

Beyond that, above it, beside it: only absence. The universe stretches upward from this disc of black hardscrabble in its yawning semi-conical geometry; the saucer in which the teacup of all things rests.

There is sometimes a tree in this place (which is not a tree). There is sometimes a still pond (which is not water). There are sometimes lights (which are more than light). Though muffled by the blanketing cosmos, there is sometimes sound (which obeys no laws of sound).

But there is always a house, even if it both is, and never was, or will be, only a house.

The house at the end of us has no architecture of its own. The tree has no specific species. The pond is open to constructive criticism. No two beings would agree on their most basic details. This place exists in the fusion of perception and longing the way the sun exists in the fusion of helium and hydrogen. And trace elements: memory, attachment, aesthetic resonance, desire. Regret. Guilt. Exhaustion. Magnesium. Iron.

It is simply The House. The Last House.

You will find the house walled and doored, glassed and gabled, paneled, lit, and jointed out of everything the word *home* has ever meant to say in any language. Out of dim, lovely memories of sun through kitchen windows, or great icicles toothing all the way down from eaves to new snowbanks. Or out of dreams of finery you once yearned for in great detail, grand spaces, clean lines, carefully chosen colors. Or cobbled together out of both, neither, all. A hallway racing through every hallway you ever knew or imagined, your heels clicking then clodding then hushed down polished pine into stone tile into packed dirt into rugs of a thousand intricate patterns. This bedroom, that dining table, your mother's study, your best friend's treehouse, your father's porch swing, the parlor of a Victorian writer you saw recreated in a museum when you were young, the parlor where you imagined you'd read cozy detective novels during rainstorms when you grew old.

The bones of the house are your bones. It builds itself out of you. Out of all that comes most effortlessly to mind when you remember, poorly and dimly: safety, warmth, welcome, ease. It has no consistent nature or essence or even purpose, except to be *comprehensible*. Immediately, instinctively, comfortably. The house exists to be understood. To be known.

So did you. So did I.

In the star system we call Auriga, there is a planet covered in oceans of liquid xenon through which vast, slow, rainbow serpents move like glaciers through valleys. The aquatic intelligence of these serpents is gentle, uninsistent, but as beyond ours as we are beyond dandelions. The name of this species is an exhalation of a precise number of pale, hard, blue-violet bubbles that takes a year to release. Their individual names are longer still.

The bubbles of their language collect on the seabed, hundreds of trillions of them, buffeted by heavy, frigid currents, floating and rolling and tumbling into and against one another for millions of years past and billions more to come, until the seas grow too full and the surface too near.

This is the Poem-of-All.

Every single idea, startled exclamation, accidental (or on purpose) profanity, profession of love, declaration of enmity, geometric proof ever exhaled by a kilometer-long serpent the color of a pearl on fire. Nothing lost. Nothing forgotten. Every utterance preserved. Yet the bubbles are never wasted or wasteful. Every cry of pain or pleasure or discovery or warning creates a new home for mollusks, for coral, for the sweet, soft, frilled, intellectless echinoderms on which the serpents feast.

The scions of Auriga conceive of almost nothing as we do. They experience mathematics emotionally, each number and operation felt individually and profoundly, combining and recombining; an angle of grief, a proof of ardor. They understand gender as a series of musical tones. A tune stuck in their heads. They perceive cold as pleasure and time as jewelry. These leviathans conquered their stars long ago, found conquest too sad to bear, returned to teach their world, and the seas upon it, to travel as a ship unto itself and so outlive their sun when it, inevitably, one day, can no longer hold herself together for the sake of her children. Ever since, their appetite for peace has rivaled ours for sugar and fat.

A human house has less than no meaning to a kilometer-long diamond-toothed ice-eel. A tree is nothing. A pond; less than a drop of rain.

One of these dragon-whales, whose personal name still houses glass crabs (which are not crabs) and neon oarfish (which are not oarfish) somewhere in the depths of that distant sea, came to rest here a century or nine ago. In the place where you will stand, she (ascending subdominant B#) found a cozy cathedral of compressed water-slabs and gelatinous filter-walls, shimmering invitingly in the night. Living coral gardens full of the choicest urchins and starfish, lamps of quiet green-white bioluminescence, balconies of clustered bubble-syllables, not one of which uttered by a stranger. The tree rose up as a tower of albino kelp, the pond a hillock of dry desert.

If one of those hapless echinoderms whose flavor Auriga's living kaleidoscopes so relish, as they all ricochet back and forth together on their ship-of-seas between the arms of the galaxy, were to waft and flutter through the lightless nul-eons to the house, it would find an open seafloor strewn with millions of those bubbles, each one singing: *They are gone now, you are safe. Gone, gone, gone.*

When I came to this place, I saw my best friend's old house waiting in the cellar of the void. From when we were little. When we were new. The dark walnut slippery floors, the tall dusty windows, the banister we swung wide round as we fell laughing up the stairs, the hush (mummy's working) and the noise (daddy's home). The secret half-closet in the attic where we disappeared to tell our secrets, kept our treasures, hid from pain. The shadow of the chestnut tree in her front garden flinging gray-black leaves along the cream-colored walls, though there were no chestnuts to cast them.

Yet when I glanced into the guest room, I saw the dark velvets and orchids, perfectly organized closets and brocade-curtained bed I always meant to have when I grew up.

Yet when I peeked out beyond the kitchen archway, I saw my grandparents' enormous living room where we always went for holidays, watercolors and silver plates on the wall, ancient electric organ still stuck on bossa nova, stuck now until the heat-death of love.

The house will be different for you. But it is never different. It does not change. It was not built. It cannot crumble. It only exists, all the ways it can. All the ways home, all in the same place at the same time.

I do not know these things because I am dead. There was no flash of blinding revelation, no lifting of the veil. I know these things because of the lunarium. That is where I learned about the house, the tree, the pond, the frozen sea-snakes of Auriga who wear decades as diadems. Where I sunk my questions, to catch hungry answers. That is where you will sink yours, too.

The lunarium is the constant heart of the house. No matter whether or not any home you've known or heard of had one, the house at the bottom of the black does. A room from which to contemplate the lattice of experiential phenomena and contextual associations which your mind is capable of interpreting as the moon. Night, secrecy, romance, quiet. Tides, illumination, solitude, dreams, inspiration. Things hidden, things mad, things ancient, things studied and wondered at. Light reflected, and therefore gentle. Hours stolen, and therefore kind.

Because you are human, these impressions all together are understood as deep moonlight pouring through tall windows that form the better part of every wall of a grand and elegant conservatory.

But the lunarium needn't be a room at all.

Not long before you, only an eon or nine, a zinzolin arrived at the house. The zinzolin could never imagine any connection between moonlight and night, nor secrecy, nor romance, nor dreams nor quiet nor loneliness. Their home lies near the crux of the Southern Cross. A precious single pink-black world orbiting a green star, caged in a lattice of innumerable moons. We can see this star easily from Earth, but not as it truly is. Our eyes cannot process its light as green, any more than you could come to the house and find a zinzol's cozy home.

But that does not make the star white, nor death simple, nor the house a physical structure in a tangible place.

The moons whizzing around that black-ruby world are not even cousins to our enormous lifeless satellite, not the first of the or the seventh or the seven hundredth of them. Tiny incandescent fists of unceasingly fusing and unfusing helium, hydrogen, selenium, tungsten, phosphorus, and gaseous gold. Even the largest only as far across as a diamond in a wedding ring. Suns, except that they orbit a planet. Moons, except that they borrow light from no one.

On the surface below, little can thrive: quilted hectares of veined rose-and-jet vegetation, free of the chains of chlorophyll. Magmic fistulas boring endlessly through quiet stone like earthworms. Onyx mountains. Glucose rivers. It is the moons themselves that live, and think, and yearn, and call themselves the zinzolin.

To a zinzol, moonlight is life. It is energy. It is sex and adrenaline and food. It is noon in high summer. It is the circus come to town, the first morning of the spring fair, the orchestra warming up a million cellos and tubas in all their finest clothes. Moonlight is noise, activity, ambition, dancing on the village green! Friendship, feasting, family all in one place at last. Hugs at the door; kisses by the sea.

Having no useful limbs or physical needs, the zinzolin have never developed one cell of technology. Nothing you or I would recognize as the least component of sentient civilization. No drive to conquer, defend, or overcome—what does a moon fear? What could they hoard; what could be taken from them? Orreries of constantly-detonating fireflies are subject neither to the necessities of the elements nor the pressure of privation. And all around, in every direction, a voidland empty of habitable systems millions of light-years wide separates them from both the danger and temptation of outsiders.

They simply live.

Zinzolin culture exists in pure thought; in their connection, communication, kinkeeping. Memory. Fabulation. The patterns of their fusion, moonspots and moonflares, magnetic pulses and storms, coronal mass ejections, plasma downflows and spicules and lunar prominences, arcing through the vacuum, back and forth over the poles, meridians, continents like flying buttresses—these comprise the whole of their language, their arts, sport, mathematics, war. Their orbits demarcate the seasons of their lives. Gravity clusters them into companions, mentors, comrades, clans, or collides them into estrangement, enmity, shame, trauma.

And when one of these infinitesimally tiny stars bursts into the tiny shimmering hiccup of a micronova, or loses its fuel to the whipping exospheric currents, or even hurls itself down the gravity well in answerless despair, that is their death. That is their end.

Had a tiny wisp of liquid electricity that once lived as a zinzolin found your hushed conservatory and your soft blue moonlight falling silently as snow through the window glass, it would have called that beguiling place hell through the last shreds of its sanity. One moon only? Its light mute, stupid, without information, identity, without selfhood? Such horrors lie beyond the most ornate of zinzolin imaginations.

Few zinzolin make it this far. Something inseparable from their deepest being can only rarely resist the oceanic calm of the long void between existence and the house. Stars they are; the boiling-cold nothing is their mother. But the last time a zinzol stubborned its way down here, to the very dregs of the darkening bottle, it found the lunarium dressed as bright as pink-black days of wonder. Bright as the circus. Bright as the spring fair. Bright as dancers on the village green. It marveled not at a tree, but at a spume of joyful plasma. It became fascinated staring, not into a pond, but into the clouds of a tiny planet slowly rotating a few feet above the flat black grit.

But I am not a living moon. When I walk through moonlight (which is not moonlight) as I understand it, I feel what you feel in the night. My imagination prickles like skin. I run my fingertips (which are not really fingertips) along the wall (which is not a wall) and when I speak, if I speak, I whisper, though I am alone.

For me, the lunarium is all glass. I can look out and see across the disc, toward a familiar chestnut tree and an unremarkable pond, then up toward everything that ever mattered. I find some panes of glass missing. Some splintered. And a few, a precious, beautiful few, full of green grapes covered in melting frost.

Just so exactly like the ruined old greenhouse suckerfished to the cheek of the crumbling Cape Cod my parents rented one autumn long wintered and gone. I used to hide in that greenhouse, to pretend I was someone else and draw pictures of what I imagined the wide world beyond childhood to be. The real owners kept rusting tools in there. Outgrown bikes and roller skates and toys. An old hot tub. I met a girl my age on the cold, gray beach that week, and for a week she was my cold, gray sister. We collected shattered shells along the shoreline. We told each other different names than our old boring well-worn ones, more splendid names, more promising. We'd sit in the steaming water after and make up stories about witches and lighthouses and wild black horses only we could tame. Who we, being little, would become, when we got big. Reached up our hands toward the panes of frosted glass, toward the green net of wild grapevines slowly devouring it all from the outside. Crushing the iron crossbars, worming its way in, toward the wet heat, toward my new sister and me, punching hopeful clusters of half-frozen fruit so desperately against the glass it burst. Even when the nights made us shiver, we could reach up and pick the baffled grapes, suck innocent juice from innocent fingers. Pretend we were queens. Pretend we were grown.

You don't have to use the lunarium. The house has many rooms, many halls, many stairs. You can board it up, paint over the boards, hang the painting of the jester in the black hat your mother took from house to house to stare malevolently at yet another living room on them, and pretend you don't care. It makes no difference. Nothing does. There is no compulsion in this place. It simply is. You simply are. What remains of you will find nothing left of *must* now.

But you'll choose to. Eventually.

Everyone chooses to. Eventually.

Time means even less than physics in the house. It was only ever a way to organize reality into something useful. But it is difficult for a mind to lose the habit of linearity. When you lived, you *swam* in air. So much air you rarely lent the concept of the thing the smallest thought until and unless you hadn't any left. You never worried about using it all up or managing it wisely, and only a few ever did. Time exists here, but only as air exists in a storm. Too much of it, moving too fast, or too slow, changing too often, to take note of every individual molecule, every sudden gust, every hour, every terasecond.

But time still matters just enough that sooner or later, even if you tell yourself you won't, you will go looking for the moonlight, and it will find you. Clean and still, shafting down from some far-off vanished night, refracted by glass, carved into shapes by the suggestions of arches at the crown of my windowed lunarium walls, sashes, muntins, cladding, curtains thin as cat's breath. Columns of broken silver on a rug-blanketed floor. Never quite enough to read by; enough to make the shadows dance.

Yet you will see everything so clearly, so clearly.

Cast-iron staircases spiral up like beanstalks. Blue shadows ladder up great henges of overstuffed bookshelves rising from the baseboards, so far and so high their upper stories are hidden in cloud-banks. Few volumes bear any likeness to another, except in clusters of related works, here and there, there and here. Folios, chapbooks, hymnals, scrolls. Pulp paperbacks, quartos, bestiaries, psalters, encyclopedias. Grimoires, dictionaries, comics, monographs, wax tablets, slabs of stone. Vellum, papyrus, A4 white, parchment, cloth. Leather, wood, cardstock, vinyl.

Even if, by the time you die, humans read only luminous text that unspools itself at twice the speed of thought across the concave surfaces of hydrocolloidal lenses surgically fused to the iris, you will still find your lunarium dusty with books (which are not really books) you must hold in what you still believe are your hands. We cannot help ourselves. As we perceive night, silence, mystery as moonlight, so we understand wisdom, knowledge, profundity as ancient books on a shadowy shelf. And so the lunarium's bookshelves (which are not really bookshelves) stretch on and on, skyscrapers in an abandoned city. Between them, long burnished floorboards wind like alleys and closes. Like grand boulevards, too, avenued by lamps and candlesticks taller than cypresses.

Every once in a while, walking the miles between monolith-bookshelves,

I find another in a series of rain-oranged tricycles and bicycles from that old rented greenhouse by the lake, each left behind in its turn like a snail outgrowing shells. Every once in a while, I hear the pop of a glass pane shatter under the pressure of cold green grapes.

You and I are lucky. The evolutionary equations of our five fingers on each hand, our two cooperating eyes, our heavy single head and soft, bendable midsection produced such cozy methods for the transfer of information. Others might envy us, if for little else.

At the head of the stellar serpent called Draco pulses a binary star called Thuban. Thuban is almost done with this vale of trials. Ancient, hoary, exhausted. Everything Thuban shines on is quick, hot, loud, young, multitudinous. Two hundred worlds and ten thousand moons. The local system whirls like a grand wheel of dancers around a midnight meadow. In and out, over and under, stamping and clapping. Each bristling with cities. Each humming with technology.

Which planet first birthed the hell-faced fey of Thuban none now know. But these worlds belong to the Elytra.

And the Elytra belong to no one.

Small, volatile, clever: glass-frilled, six-armed dragonfly-crabs the length of a longbow's arrow. Their thoraxes have no physical connection to their abdomens, yet the two halves function as one, bifurcated by a free-floating tetrahedral organ that thumps a hundred thousand rhythms like a contrabass string furiously struck, again and again and over again besides.

Oh, sacral ponask, color of wine, luster of pearl! Heart, brain, soul, weapon, instrument of love! Those oilglass wings, that opal-onyx exoskeleton, these arms, skull, tail, eyes like upturned goblets—all of it little more than a support system for one pulsating, oleaginous pyramid.

When the needle-jawed mouth of an Elyt speaks, the ponask bongs out a wild, complexifying underbeat. Elytrial language requires both. The buzz, click, clattle, chirr of malachitinous mandibles communicate information. The ponask communicates intent in syncopation. Nouns, articles, participles, vocatives issue from the mouth; verbs thrum an accompaniment from the grease-garnet of their gullet. Facts from the larynx, feeling from the ponask, always the ponask.

Not one among them can lie, though they long to. Their words may say: *I (love) you, darling mine,* but the truthful ponask throbs *I would rather (have suckled) the meat from each of your vertebra individually than (ever have known) any syllable of your name.*

The Elytra are agitators, battlers, inventors and conquerors to the least of their kind. So reckless, these mayflies, with the brief firework of their existence! Thuban's worlds spin fast and orbit faster. By our calendar, each Elyt nymph lives less than ten years. By theirs, a thousand and more. They believe their lifespans long and luxurious. They believe they have time enough for foolishness. In truth they die often and in great numbers, suffering the wounds of works unfinished. Many have walked these grounds.

All Elytrial doctrines teach variations on a theme: to live in peace is a waste of industry, imagination, and the vigor of all life. Family and elite squad are one unit: the sworn Ennead, the nine-as-one. To *contend* is the whole of joy. To *take* is better than to *have.* To grapple, more noble than to embrace. To measure yourself against the measure of another—how else to know your worth? Come, kindred! To harvest only! Never to till! Never to wait! Never to stop! Never to yield!

The Elytrial week sets aside one holy day for rest, for lovemaking, and most especially for declarations of new wars. Whether with neighbor or parent or prospective mate or distant species matters nothing: all wars are as equally loved and valued as children.

No Elyt could accept information derived from a mute, passive book that cannot so much as grip a phratrile blade. There's no *juice* in it. Nor could any Elyt tolerate the essential confinement of any version of the house, let alone the lunarium. When the thump-chittering sworn Enneads, inseparable even by death, the universe and time entire, scream though the end of everything, they immediately divide themselves into factions. The factions divide the black disc, the tree, the pond, the house into territories. I would tell you how they perceive these things, but they barely notice them except as mission objectives, enemy territory and homefront, high ground and low, treasure and blood.

The Elytra then, blessed in bliss, clash joyfully one against the other for supremacy.

But they no longer own any true flesh to take injury, any more than you or I do, only the memory of it. The habit. When a warrior's swollen ponask suffers a scratch, a blow, a vivisection, a catastrophic deventriculation, a portion of understanding opens inside her faceted skull like origami unfolding. The more dire the wound, the more significant and interesting the knowledge gained.

For the trillion teeming young of Thuban Draconis, this endless mutilation toward wisdom feels as cozy as a library.

But you are like me. You attended a school I would recognize. I spent rain-prisoned days turning pages your fingers would know well, on sofas you would not find strange. The lunarium's archipelago of books and cabinets and ferns and fireplaces and shadows (which are not really books or cabinets or ferns or fireplaces or shadows) make the same unconsidered sense to me that they will to you. Delicate little escritoires and broad, solid draftsman's tables, beside tables and banquet tables as long as riverbanks, each with their own stools, cushions, mats, deep, heavy chairs to hold a body like the hand of a giant.

And somewhere deep in the geography of the lunarium, somewhere different every time you want it and go looking, there will be a tray of tea or coffee or whiskey or wine laid out just as you remember once liking it, light-millennia ago. Somewhere in this forest of moonlight; hot, hidden, waiting.

All these many things together produce particular, specific feelings, the way a clutch of gardenias and heliotrope and lime branches in a copper vase would produce their particular, specific scents, separate and together. The emotion of gardenias permeate everything. The feeling of lime blossoms in the walls. The velvets. The leather. The vanilla pang of heliotrope in the curtains and the dust.

In this room lives the peculiar thickness of nighttime when you alone are awake in a full house all asleep.

In this room lives the held breaths of parents rocking clutch-fisted babies whose eyes have finally, *finally* closed.

In this room lives the thrilled stretching of those star-bought hours where what is possible has no limit.

On the bookshelves lives everything.

And it is yours.

It is mine, too.

Everything that ever was. Everything that could have been. Everything imagined. Everything known. Everything that ever might or will be or could have been. It is all here. You have only to wander, to explore, to summit, to excavate, to find.

How the story ends. How it proceeded, while you were falling. How it began. No matter how great or small the question itself, the answers haunt the lunar shadows and dog your footsteps.

What made a slop of algae and mushrooms stand up and think itself capable of painting horses on a cave wall, of burning old bones to fly, of forgiveness and of its opposite.

Where you lost your keys, every time you lost your keys.

Who the child you miscarried at nineteen would have grown up to be.

Whether there ever was any such place as Atlantis.

Who really wrote Shakespeare's plays.

Every single second in the life of the butter churn you didn't buy at that farm stand because your friend said it was stupid, you can buy all the butter you want at the shop, but oh, how the stains of a century's fat-lashings shimmered like Jupiter's stripes!

How to travel faster than light.

Why your mother felt such bile when she looked at you that you fled over and over to another child's beautiful home, to a broken greenhouse, anywhere, everywhere but here.

The true nature and purpose of black holes.

Why your father didn't stop it.

The solutions to the Navier-Stokes equations.

What happened to every craft lost in the Bermuda Triangle.

If there were ever mermaids or unicorns, anywhere, on any world, by even the loosest definitions.

The names of everyone you never knew loved you to distraction and back.

The meaning of every mysterious hieroglyph, rune, henge, temple mound.

The life and times of every individual mason, prostitute, astronomer, brewer, weaver, child who laughed and warmed the stones of every ancient ruin, found and unfound.

What you could have done to save your marriage. If saving your marriage would have made everything worse, or better.

The text of every lost poem, play, book, treatise, volume, song.

Every broken sculpture, every burned painting, every work discarded unfinished by masters and fools alike. And you will not experience these things as illustrations or flat type, but as it would have felt to see, hear, read, know them when they were new as dawn, in their time, in their context, performed by great talents born and withered before recording devices and after, anyone and everyone who loved them.

Every time you nearly died and didn't know it.

Every time you nearly had it all and didn't know that, either.

Why zebras could never be domesticated.

Who you might have been if you had been born other than you were.

Each perfect work that existed in the minds of its maker before it fell from grace, through mortal error, to become the finished work known to all.

Indexes of the house's appearance as others experienced it.

Herbariums of all the trees the tree has been.

All the waters and unwaters of the pond.

The most intimate, dawn-snapped thoughts of everyone who will live in the house where you died after you've gone, and before you came. The house where you were born. Your college dormitory.

What lilies and what ferns your grandchildren planted in your garden, knowing you'd never see it now, digging in the good dark earth all the same.

But you did see it. You can. You will.

Alongside the fate of every shipwreck, vanished treasure, missing plane.

Every galumphing thought your dogs ever had. The sleek internal monologues of all your cats.

What happened to your babies, and theirs, and theirs thereafter.

If humanity will survive, if we will thrive and stretch our hands up toward the stars like children reaching through steam and snow to pluck a green grape out of a glass sky.

Whether you yourself are remembered, for a year after you were gone. For as long as your grandchildren knew your name. For a century. Or forgotten in a day.

Who you should have married instead.

How the regime ended.

Whether there ever was or could be any such thing as real magic.

Every possible outcome of every war as it occurred in a timeline where that was the only difference. Every laugh that did or did not echo out into a sunny happy afternoon in a timeline where nothing was hard.

What you could have done differently. What anyone could have. What you did so profoundly right. What a rainbow ice-worm dreams under an ocean of ice. What a moon fears. Why a dragonfly fights. It's all there.

It is a reward. It is a punishment.

It is not a reward. It is not a punishment.

The despot may pleasure himself for a geological age, chasing his own importance from volume to volume, but he will also watch time devour him like krill, and his name, too, will soon enough become nothing and no one, not even remembered as a shadow among shadows.

The saint may delight in the deeds and near-deeds, almosts and nevers and might haves of others without an iota of self-interest, but she will also inevitably discover all the lives she might have lived, the ecstasy of meaning she might have known, if only, for one moment, she had loved herself and the fallen world just as it was.

Even in a place time cannot cower, it might take a millennium and four just to study the face of every child you might have had, with every person you met, or might have, or never did, whose probability of loving you was other than zero. Every child that might have resulted from a kiss leaned toward moments later, a night without commuter traffic that began sooner, the specific genes that did or did not combine in the millisecond of conception, all those millions that might have been yours, just as yours as the ones that were or were not. You will experience them in the same way as all those lost plays and symphonies, exactly as it would have felt to love them and be aggravated by them and keep them and lose them. The exact weight of a child's body as they once and never sat beside you, so small and new, drawn gravitationally to your lap, your shoulder, the sweat of your July skin, the heat of their origin, while you wrote a story about death you hoped was true.

It might take more than that to understand the rapture and the agony of Aurigan math, or learn to belt out a single nursery song in zinzol, or experience every lifetime your lost loves might have, did, or never could live without you.

And much, much longer to love them again, through all that could ever and never be.

I cannot say how long it takes to love every version of yourself that way. With that expansive grace. With that beggaring acceptance.

I cannot say.

In the End was the Word, and the Word will be with you, and the Word is you.

It was always you.

It was me, too.

It was all of us.

No one is alone in this place, though we cannot see each other, quite. The land underneath the light is five hundred kilometers in diameter. And there are so many of us. But what is left of us is the space between the atoms we once were, and that has no objective dimension. We move against and around and through each other like electrons rising and falling within a single object, like hydrogen brushing the cheek of oxygen inside a wave. Like onionskin pages stuck together, each typeset letter so important, so bold, yet so thin they all fade, echoing down and back and forward again, into every other, without end.

I feel them sometimes. I will feel you, when you walk up your grandfather's staircase while I walk down my own, from my third house, where life was soft for a moment. You will feel me, when you stand in the kitchen you earned in your best year, while I place my palm against the window through which I watched my father leave.

We will not be together, exactly. We will rest our hands in the same place. Yours on top of mine. We will see and hear nothing. But we will feel a weight that is not our own. Catch a scent that is not a memory. Cigarettes smoked to the nub before the invention of gaslight, seal blubber, the war-musk of the ponask, chlorine-soaked grapes at midnight.

And sometimes, oh, sometimes, we will leave the house. We will leave the house and walk across the black regolith to the pond. Without knowing why, only that something in us was ragged, rent, broken open, a wound in the shape of a pond.

Hello, we will say to the obsidian surface of the pond, in which reflects the whole of the universe as it expands above. In which reflects our own dear, familiar face, not as it was, but as we imagined, as we saw our faces in our thoughts, when we were free of mirrors.

Hello, the pond will say back, and most of the time it will speak in our own voice, as the house does. But every so often, eon on eon, one of the others will also have felt the same pull of the pond, in the same moment, and in that synchronicity, we will see someone else in the deep, rush-fringed water. Hear another voice from out the glimmering, translated between bodies, of water, of memory.

I'm sorry, your mother will say back.

I forgive you, your lovers will whisper.

Let's go for a drive, kiddo, just you and me, your father will beckon.

Who did you turn into when you grew up? Your childhood friend will ask. *Why didn't you ever want to play at your house?*

The sum of the squares of a triangle's short sides equals the square of the unbearable pressure on my pectoral fins as I watched my first young hatch and flow out laughing into the cold-thickened sea to live and yearn and become wiser than I, the Aurigan rainbow serpent will opine. *But there are no positive integers greater than two that can satisfy the equation of having lost you.*

If it would take millennia to know all the children you might have had, art you might have made, nations you could and could not have conquered; moments, mere moments, that could have changed everything, for you, for someone: a touch of a finger, a gentle smile, a breath and a stop in the midst of rage at some poor shift-worker to say: *we are both more space than matter, so a refund on this button-down shirt doesn't matter at all, I just forgot that it was only a broken piece of the void and so am I. Come home with me and let me make you dinner,* then there is no numbering of galactic ages that can encompass the time you will spend walking back and forth to the pond, just in case your baby is there this time. Walking for the surprises waiting in the little ripples of cause and effect that still, somehow, occur here. No accounting of what those waters will give. Or what they will take.

But in the end, even amongst the lunarium and the many rooms of the comprehensible house, and the pond, it's too much to spend eternity like that. You would go mad. You would forget you were ever other than mad. You would forget you *were*, long past the chance for the hot cold dark of you to melt into the hot cold dark of all. Time may be an exploitable system, but it is not an illusion.

For a sea-serpent, or a moon, or a dragonfly, it is harder. It usually takes longer, when it already takes forever. But we are lucky. We are human. We know what to do with a tree.

You climb it.

When we were little.

When I get big.

We have told the truth, all along, in every language. From Alpha Draconis to Sol Tertius. When we are alive we are little.

But oh, one day we will get big. How big we will get. From where you lie now, from where you cough and wince and call for someone, anyone, to hold you, you cannot imagine.

When the lunarium holds no more mysteries, when the pond has borne its gifts and its tortures up through the silt, you will, without knowing why, keep walking. Beyond the marsh. Across the black earth. Five hundred kilometers.

And you will, in your exhaustion, an exhaustion only the space between atoms can possibly know, you will lean against the tree. Any tree, every tree, every tree you loved and told your secrets to in the summer and carved someone's name in, the tree of trees whose branches kept you in shade, whose emptiness let the snow in, who bore witness over the land that knew you before you came and after you were gone, the tree of which you ate the fruit without hesitation until wine juice flowed down your chin. You will lean against it, and somehow, beyond all probability, its rough, kind bark will be warm.

And you will begin to climb.

This is the process. The same process everything suffers, moves through, around, under, above, in every cell, in every space.

You lived. And you died. You contracted, cooled, regretted. Understood your many faults. Promised to change. To learn. To grow. To make better choices next time. To finally get it right. And you will slowly climb the best tree you can imagine, out of all the trees you've known or dreamed, and gently, ever so gently, come up against your limit.

You will stop. You will look back.

And you will expand.

You will spill out, in every direction at the same time. Like entropy. Like everything. And as you grow, as you stretch, you will feel physics as you feel fear, as you feel hope. A weight in your chest that is no longer a chest. A lump in your throat that is no longer a throat. A pain behind your eyelids that are no longer eyelids. Just the habit of eyelids. Of a chest. Of a throat. You will feel it all.

Gravity will become all the sensations of passion and love. You will know, as physically as you have ever known a broken bone or a bashed skull, the pain and guilt of black holes helplessly pulling all matter in toward them to drown. The sensations of gelatinous proto-planets coalescing will land on your long-dusted sensorium just as packing hopeful boxes into a moving truck once did, the colors of nebulae exploding in you like inspiration and new beginnings; asteroid collisions as work well completed. You'll feel the storms of Jupiter like butterflies in your stomach (which hasn't been a stomach in forty thousand years). You'll physically endure the shearing, obliterating force of the galactic core—and it will be the feeling of homesickness. Boundless love in the unfurling leaves of a trillion strange forests, a child's excitement at the click, click, click of their first roller coaster in the winds of a billion worlds. You'll undergo the fission and fusion of every star and it will all come bubbling out of you like repressed laughter you can't keep inside no matter how much you know you should.

It will not stay inside.

This is how you live. For the rest of the rest. Whether you were bad or good or nothing particularly. You will feel, as cleanly as a stubbed toe, the life of constellations, and know that as the feeling of families you've made. The stars whose heat you feel like a sunburn on a beach vacation with your mother long ago, your daughter long ago, your son, your teacher who never understood you—*is* your mother long ago, your siblings, your daughter, your son, your bosses, your students, your friends, your enemies, your teacher who just wanted everyone to be okay.

All these things, you will feel, not as a void melting into a void, but as yourself. The self you have lived within for so long now. Your inescapable self. Those wrists, that gut, stratospheric clouds along your hairline, those kind wrinkles at the corners of your pulsars, those creaking joints of your magnetic poles, those aching orbits, bearing up through the miles. And miles. And miles. Your shattered shell, collected on a cold shore, feeling the cosmos as it feels itself. As it always did. As the stars you see tonight, the light you run from to cool shade tomorrow, the firm ground beneath your feet always was, even if it could not possibly be known: all the loving, knowing dead still so close by. Not one grain of pollen you can touch, not one swelling borealis you can see, not one speck of darkness in the night that does not already live and dream and love the space between your atoms it will one day know as a friend.

And so will I. I am not ready to climb yet. But so will I.

So will a kilometer-long iridescent ocean-wyrm who wears the span of their lives as a collar of jewels. So will a moon the size of a thumbnail who only knows how to live in flashes of light. So will a dragonfly whose heart is a wine-colored pyramid that (feels) so loudly it cannot (lie). All of us. Together. In the dark. In the light. In the beauty of it, beyond what any thought was meant to bear.

And you will know us all. The least of us, and the greatest. You will look us in the eye of our galactic core. We will see you as you are; you will see us. Knowing is the end of unknowing, which is the end of pain. We'll be waiting for you on the underside of forever. And we will stand one beside the other, in every way *together* can be understood, in a house at the end of the world. Whatever world we loved. Whatever world loved us, or hated us, or never noticed our foot upon its sphere. For always. For all ways. Bright as the circus. Bright as the spring fair. Bright as dancers on the village green.

Take my hand (which is not a hand).

Take your time (which is nothing).

And I will meet you in the sky when we are both big.

THE WELL OF THE MARTIAN QUEENS

Tamsyn Muir

The **Queenswell** or **Well of the Martian Queens** is the common name for what is properly designated **Martian Royal Shaft Grave 7**, located in Margaritifer Terra a little to the northeast of Aram Chaos on Mars. It is the largest and most complex single burial site yet discovered on the surface of Mars and has been a major focus of Martian archaeology since it was discovered in MY 131 by a team from Heidelberg University.

HISTORICAL CONTEXT

Shaft burial was common from the earliest stages of Martian civilization. In the oldest and simplest shaft graves, dating back to the time of the Second Empire, a circular shaft was dug down to a depth of one or two meters in the rock. Coffin-sized horizontal niches were then cut sideways, extending away from the central shaft like spokes from a wheel: the largest of this early type, Martian Royal Shaft Grave 12, has space for a total of twenty-six bodies arranged in two layers of thirteen niches. The shaft was left clear (although presumably covered by some sort of lid or capstone to prevent unwanted access) for as long as the grave remained in use and was then filled in with a mixture of sand and rubble once all the available niches had been occupied.

In its earliest form, shaft burial seems to have been reserved as a privilege of royalty. During the late Third Empire, and most strikingly during the

Fourth Empire, it became the normal style of burial for wealthy individuals: a high-status Martian family of the Fourth Empire would normally possess an ancestral shaft mausoleum in which generations of family members would be interred side by side. These graves increasingly became opportunities to showcase the family's wealth and power: Many Fourth Empire shaft graves are constructed almost like an apartment building in reverse, with a descending central stairwell (often elaborately decorated with wall carvings) allowing access to individual tombs. A representative example of this high style, Martian Shaft Grave 39, consists of a 5-meter square shaft that descends into the rock to a depth of 113.7 meters; a total of eighteen "landings," stone ledges that extend into the shaft and were originally connected by flights of metal steps, give access to multiroom tomb structures (often referred to by archaeologists as "apartments"). Each of these separate tombs includes a burial room and a couple of subsidiary rooms for religious rituals and the storage of grave goods. Generally, even the later and more complex tombs continue the old model of allotting a single "entrance" for each interred individual; toward the end of the Fourth Empire a trend emerged for "family apartments" where a given generation of family members would all be buried in the same tomb, albeit usually still in different chambers.

Perhaps in response to the proliferation of the style among private families, royal shaft graves during the same period became even larger and more monumental—vast subsurface structures which would have required years of difficult excavation and construction. Even against this backdrop, however, Royal Shaft Grave 7 stands out.

DISCOVERY

MRSG 7 was discovered by drone flyover during a mineralogical survey of Margaritifer Terra undertaken in MY 131 by Heidelberg University's Department of Areological Science. The university immediately assembled an areoarchaeological expedition led by Professor Anna Neumann, which set out four months later from Sinai Base. Neumann vividly describes the experience in her autobiography, *In the Footsteps of the Queens*:

We drew near the edge of the pit... Multiple drone sweeps had established that the rim was structurally sound, with no evidence of crumbling or collapse, and yet it was hard to suppress a sense of foreboding. Given the limitations on telemetry range, it had been judged too risky to send a drone into the shaft itself—any loss of control might have caused accidental damage to whatever was inside. We had very little idea of what might be waiting for us below...

Sophie [Becker, Neumann's research assistant] did not want us to get too close. "We ought to wait for the heavy team," I remember her saying [a reference to the second team of the expedition, who were following in a truck that carried the bulk of the surveying equipment]. But I could not wait. I do not consider myself a romantic, and I have read too many history books to be tempted by the chance to appear in one; and yet the appeal—of being the first human to set her living eyes upon what I already suspected was the grandest structure anywhere on the Martian surface—seemed all at once too great to resist...

[After some discussion, Neumann's team members secure her with a safety harness and a line, and she approaches the edge of the shaft alone.]

When I was still perhaps a couple of meters from the edge, I found I could no longer remain on my feet. The wide Martian sky overhead, and the knowledge of the great emptiness yawning ahead of me, seemed to render me impossibly small. I lowered myself to my hands and knees and continued in this manner until I could peer over the edge . . . I have never experienced anything like that moment. I stared down into the vertiginous darkness of the past, and it was as if a soft hand came to rest between my shoulder blades; then, gently but firmly, it began to push, urging my head and upper body forward and over the lip of the pit. Simian reflex asserted itself and I flattened myself into the red dust, my gloved hands scrabbling for purchase, hoping for a friendly tree branch or a vine I could use to arrest the fall I knew had already begun—but the smooth alien stone offered me nothing so earthly or familiar...

I was, of course, altogether safe—lying prone on horizontal rock, with only the upper part of my head extended past the pit's edge, there was physically no way I could fall. And yet to this day I still feel that, if I had not been on the line, I would have fallen.

The expedition was marred by tragedy only a few days later, when Becker actually did fall from an upper section of the stairs. A subsequent inquiry found that she had tried to explore the shaft by herself, without safety equipment or support from her team members and with only a flashlight for visibility—in fact, the rest of the team was asleep in their pods when the incident occurred, and did not discover that Becker was missing until the following morning.

LAYOUT

At the center of MRSG 7 is a single circular shaft which descends to a current depth of 417.8 meters (1370.7 feet). The floor at the bottom of the shaft is a tightly packed mixture of sand and rubble that clearly postdates the original construction, but ground-penetrating radar has established that the actual lowest point—that is, the level at which the original builders stopped digging downward—is only another couple of meters farther down. The lowest tomb entrance, QW85, is nearly 50 meters above the shaft floor, and below that point there are no further signs of tomb excavation; presumably more tombs would have been dug out over time if the overall shaft grave had not been abandoned.

Many of the larger royal graves use carved stone steps rather than the metal gantry-type arrangement that seems to have predominated in nonroyal versions, and MRSG 7 is no exception. A single spiral staircase, carved from the rock at the same time the shaft was originally dug, runs all the way from the surface to the bottom. The staircase is a little over a meter in width (see "Spiral effect" below) and is broken by flat sections ("landings") after every twenty-fifth step; these landings, which are no wider than the steps and curve slightly to follow the wall of the shaft, permit access to the doors of the tombs themselves. In other words, although the individual tombs were not excavated until they were required (see "History and Usage" below), the shaft was dug with a prearranged layout in mind: the original builders mapped out the future position of each entrance, offsetting each one some way around the shaft from the one above it so that no two tombs would be built directly on top of each other, and then left the landings "blank" for future construction.

(Some scholars, such as Roberto Manza of the University of Padua, have argued that the shaft was repeatedly extended downward as the need arose—that the original excavation went no deeper than twenty or thirty meters, and that at various future points the current ruler ordered another few "layers" to be added on. The primary evidence against this is the lack of any discontinuity, however tiny, in the construction of the staircase; close inspection has revealed no trace of stone carving being halted and then resumed at a later date, or of textural differences in the stone which would suggest multiple discrete stages of excavation over hundreds or thousands of years. Other scholars have pointed out that, as impractical as it might seem to dig a shaft with space for nearly a hundred future tombs, this very impracticality would serve as a striking display of dynastic confidence—a way of making clear that the current line of queens would extend almost incomprehensibly far into the future.)

While it was in use, the shaft would almost certainly have been decorated and protected by some sort of canopy superstructure, to reduce weathering and atmospheric erosion. Stone and metal fixtures have been found around the edge of the pit which were probably used to anchor such a system, although no actual remains of it have survived.

THE "SPIRAL EFFECT"

One peculiarity of MRSG 7's construction not found in any other known shaft grave, royal or private, is that its diameter narrows at a slight but consistent rate. The diameter at surface level is 60.4 meters (198.2 feet), but by the current lowest level of the shaft this has narrowed to 52.2 meters (171.3 feet). In combination with this, the width of the spiral staircase running around the wall of the shaft actually widens as it descends, from very slightly less than 1 meter (3.3 feet) at the top to 1.6 meters (5.2 feet) at the point where the stairs currently terminate.

There is no obvious structural reason for either of these features, and yet the absolutely consistent rate of change—which would have required careful prior engineering and pinpoint accuracy in excavation—dispels any reasonable possibility of their being accidental. The aesthetic effect is slight but perceptible if viewed from above, and to most human viewers it tends to accentuate the impact of height vertigo, as alluded to in Professor Neumann's firsthand account. Some scholars have suggested that the Martian builders had such an effect in mind (see "Ritual Aspects" below); others, however, have cautioned that given our very limited knowledge of Martian sense organs or neurochemistry, it is dangerous to assume that the Martians even experienced vertigo, let alone that they would have designed a structure specifically to evoke it. Opponents of this theory have also pointed to the lack of evidence for any kind of safety rail or banister ever having existed on the stairs' inner edge (the metal safety railing seen in modern images of the staircase was installed by archaeological teams working at the site). If the Martians suffered from vertigo in the way humans do, it is argued, having such a narrow staircase at such a height would simply have been too dangerous to be practical.

HISTORY AND USAGE

Although the precise dating of the Fifth Empire—believed to be the longest period of rule by a single Martian dynasty, and widely regarded as a high-water mark for Martian civilization in general—remains a topic of debate, nearly all scholars agree that MRSG 7 spans its whole length. Its earliest burial, QW1, is the tomb of Queen Iron (so called because, in the still mostly undeciphered Martian writing system, her royal name is written with the glyph for "iron" as its most prominent element). Queen Iron's accession to the imperial throne is treated by historians as the foundation date of the Fifth Empire. At the other end matters are more uncertain but given that the burials in MRSG 7 terminate some way before the shaft itself does (see "Layout" above), and that no other shaft grave with the iconography of Fifth Empire rulers has yet been found, it is likely that the lowest tomb—QW85—was constructed for the dynasty's final queen.

The tombs in MRSG vary widely in size and complexity, with a general trend for the lower (i.e., later) tombs to be more extensive and elaborate than those above. QW1, despite the historical importance of its occupant, is very simple and plain in construction: the entrance doorway leads into a ritual antechamber, which is connected by a short corridor to a "treasure room" of grave goods, which in turn gives access through a pair of iron double doors into the burial room itself. Some of the later tombs, on the other hand, are extraordinarily complex: QW66, believed to be the largest, contains a total of twenty-seven individual rooms ranging in size from small storage chambers to a grandly decorated hypostyle hall, and has its burial chamber concealed behind an elaborate system of hidden doors. Some architectural trends appear and then disappear during a particular sequence of tombs, such as the prevalence of stepped floors in QW19–QW30, or the distinctive curved "gutter" around the edge of the burial chamber that is found only in QW68, QW69, and QW70 (and the purpose of which remains unknown).

Each tomb was presumably constructed during the reign of its eventual occupant. Some tombs show signs of alteration during their construction—most obviously QW71, in which an original plan for an extensive and elaborate tomb seems to have been hastily abandoned in favor of something much smaller: not only is the layout much simpler than that of either QW70 or QW72, but one passageway cut into the rock leads nowhere, while another sizable room was carved out but never furnished or decorated, simply sealed off behind a fake wall. Given that the royal mummy in QW71 appears to have died at a young age, it is likely that the tomb had to be made ready at very short notice before its builders had carried out most of their plans.

Every tomb except the lowest, QW85, is occupied by a single royal mummy. Most of these were embalmed according to late Martian funerary practice and laid to rest in the conventional posture of queenship—supine, knees slightly raised, wrist-spurs locked together over the lower abdomen. The quality of embalming, and hence the current state of preservation, varies widely: the mummy in QW49 is the single best-preserved Martian corpse known to modern science, with even the skin markings surviving to an extraordinary degree of detail, whereas the mummy in the only slightly later QW52 seems to have been very ineptly prepared—no attempt has been made to open the coffin, since CAT scans suggest that little more than an undifferentiated mass of decayed matter remains inside.

Most of the later tombs also contain at least one additional mummified body, but anatomy makes clear that these are never of the royal caste and therefore are presumably not blood relations of the tomb's inhabitant. In some cases they are most likely to be slaves or servants who were mummified as part of the queen's funerary rites: the famous "Hall of the Dead" in QW21, a long corridor leading to the burial chamber, is lined by a total of sixteen niches, each containing a single mummy in a standing position. In other cases they may be branch family members or even royal consorts (although if so, none is ever interred in the queen's own chamber, or with anything approaching the honor accorded to the queen herself).

RITUAL ASPECTS

Scholarly knowledge of Martian ritual, including funerary ritual, remains very partial, and no claim made about the ritual functions of MRSG 7 has been wholly free from controversy. The most widely accepted theory, known as "filial interment," is that burial in the shaft grave marked a crucial public moment of transition between the reigns of consecutive queens. According to this theory, a Fifth Empire queen would have started construction on her own tomb as soon as she came to the throne—possibly even before. When she died, her daughter and successor would have supervised the ceremony of interment—perhaps only being crowned as the true queen once her mother was installed in the tomb.

The best-known account of this ceremony, and one which is often erroneously taken as fact, is the one offered by Jeremiah Powell in his bestselling book *Secrets of the Queenswell*. Powell writes:

> Like all the most powerful symbols, this one was anything but subtle. The young princess, clad in a ceremonial garment, leads her mother's funeral procession to the edge of the colossal pit. She begins to walk down the narrow, winding stair into the darkness . . . The crowds watch as she disappears from their sight—and, following her in single file, the whole train of mourners and attendants carrying aloft the glittering coffin of the late queen, its jewels and ornaments

flashing in the Martian sun. All vanish into the abyss. A breathless hush descends.

What they do down there in the depths—what rituals they perform in the claustrophobic, torchlit chambers of the tomb, what prayers are spoken, what obsequies fulfilled—no one may know. This is the business of the queens, and the queens alone. There are tales, of course—rumors of blood offerings, of secret names, of death-gods unknown to ordinary folk. But rumors they remain.

The second before they see her, an expectant murmur rises anew. The onlookers know, somehow, that she has climbed almost all the way back up the stairs again, that a new star is about to rise. Then all of a sudden there she is: one small figure, emerging from the steps to stand on the edge of the pit looking out at the people—*her* people, now. The crown has been placed upon her head. Down in the dark the door has been sealed on her mother's corpse, never again to be opened. There has been no break—no awkward discontinuity while the throne lay empty. Before the very eyes of her subjects, the ruler went down into death and was reborn. The queen is dead. Long live the queen.

Much of this description is either conjectural or wholly fictional—there is no direct evidence that the new queen personally participated in the funeral rites in the way Powell describes, beyond a few sculptural friezes whose content may be symbolic rather than literal, and recent archaeological findings suggest that the tombs of early queens *were* sometimes reopened (either for ritual purposes or simply for maintenance). But Powell's account seized hold of the public imagination as soon as it was published and remains for many people the defining image of a Martian royal funeral.

(A variant theory of uncertain origin, though clearly one inspired by Powell's interpretation, claims that the old queen would have been taken down into the pit while still living; she would have lived out her final hours or days in the tomb itself, with her daughter only re-emerging once she was dead. This is obviously very unlikely, as it would require the entire process of mummification—a highly complex procedure which must have involved multiple specialist attendants working over several days—to take place inside the tomb.)

SCHOLARLY SIGNIFICANCE

The discovery of MRSG 7 is generally regarded as the single most significant event in areoarchaeology since the Argyre cache was found in MY 44. Following the preliminary investigations of Neumann's first expedition—which descended nearly halfway into the shaft but did not attempt to open any of the tombs—successive teams of archaeologists from both Terran and Martian universities have undertaken almost continuous study at the site.

MRSG 7 is a particularly important asset not only because of its scale and historical importance, but because of its unexpectedly good state of preservation. The widespread social collapse that brought about the end of the Sixth Empire, and the ensuing period known to historians as the Martian Anarchy, saw violent and indiscriminate looting and vandalism of ancient sites. Some royal graves, such as MRSG 3, were stripped completely bare; others seem to have been temporarily repurposed for shelter or storage, with little thought for the original occupants. There is almost no trace of such activity at the Queenswell. A total of three tombs (QW2, QW4, and QW5) show signs of having been broken into, but in each case the looting seems to have remained small-scale—the theft of light and easy-to-carry items like statuettes and discs, rather than any systematic attempt to empty the tomb of its contents, and with no sign of vandalism or damage for its own sake. Some scholars argue that the presence of royalist forces at Great Xanthe nearby acted as a deterrent to would-be robbers even after Martial social cohesion had largely collapsed, whereas others, including Powell, suggest that religious or superstitious awe of the site itself may have protected it from the treatment that befell many smaller and less impressive monuments.

Today, every tomb in the complex has been investigated to at least some extent, although a number of those farther down the shaft have not been entered by archaeologists; instead, miniature lidar drones have been deployed to survey and record images of the interior without the need for the door to be fully breached. In a recent report, the Martian Archaeology Institute in

Pavo estimated that only 25–30 percent of the total contents of MRSG 7 had received "detailed study," and that decades more work would be needed just to properly catalog the sheer number and variety of artifacts contained in the tombs.

As an active areoarchaeological excavation, the site remains off-limits to tourists; the MAI says it has begun a process of "informal consultation" about allowing limited access for supervised tour parties at least to the edge of the pit, pending the resolution of ongoing health and safety concerns.

QW85 AND THE "MISSING MUMMY"

The first serious expedition aimed at lidar-surveying the contents of each tomb, preliminary to actual excavation, was carried out in MY 132–133 by a larger team again under the supervision of Neumann. It was able to establish the presence of a royal coffin in every single tomb except the very lowest, QW85.

The last few tombs in MRSG 7 are very formulaic in their layout: by the declining years of the Fifth Empire, rulers had apparently lost their taste for architectural innovation and preferred to replicate a conventional form with only minor adjustments. QW85 in particular is almost a carbon copy of its immediate predecessor QW84, although slightly smaller and lacking one or two decorative elements. The position of the burial chamber was therefore very obvious, even on a basic scan—but, unlike the burial chamber in every other tomb surveyed, it was completely empty. Nor did the scan detect any other large objects anywhere else in the tomb of the size and dimensions necessary for a coffin, royal or otherwise.

For the next nineteen years, the "missing mummy" became an object of both scholarly and public conjecture. A joint team from Victoria University of Wellington and the University of Cambridge entered the tomb in MY 140. Its findings suggested that the tomb was complete and had not been abandoned during its construction—every chamber in QW84 had an exact equivalent in QW85, and all had been finished and decorated with no trace of incomplete work—but that it had simply never been used for burial: not only was there no coffin, there were no grave goods, personal belongings, religious offerings, or anything of the kind. Yet the door had been closed and sealed in the customary way.

The "greatest unsolved mystery in Martian archaeology" received an unexpected and partial solution in MY 151 with the discovery of the Lost Queen's Tomb, nearly two thousand kilometers away in Terra Sabaea. This small and otherwise unremarkable semi-surface tomb, of the kind popular for private use in the late Fifth and early Sixth empires, showed signs of extensive looting: almost no trace of grave goods remained, and the coffin itself had apparently been flung over onto its side. The mummy, mostly buried in sand in one corner of the tomb—perhaps still lying where it had been discarded by grave robbers—was in very poor condition, with one arm missing, one leg detached below the knee, and extensive damage to the tissues; but the anatomical profile was unmistakably that of the royal caste, and the overall standard of mummification appeared to be very high, higher than would have been available to any but the wealthiest Martian families. Genetic sequencing established, to a 98.7 percent degree of certainty, that this mysterious mummy was in fact the direct descendant of the one in QW84—and therefore almost certainly the intended occupant of QW85.

No explanation of this unusual burial has yet found general acceptance, although many have been proposed. If the mummy had originally been buried in QW85 and then later moved elsewhere, it is hard to see why the original tomb would have been so completely cleared of its contents, or why the door would then have been resealed on an empty set of rooms. The sealed door of QW85 is thought by some scholars to represent a "symbolic burial"—a way to preserve the ritual of sealing a deceased queen in her tomb, even though the priests and courtiers who performed it had no actual body to bury. Powell suggests that the queen was "exiled"—that, following her death, she was for some religious or political reason forbidden burial in her ancestral monument; critics of this theory have asked why her body still seems to have received the highest possible level of care in its mummification, quite what would be expected for a queen of the Fifth Empire, and why it had to be moved such an enormously long distance from the customary site.

Neumann's autobiography was published a few years before the discovery of the Lost Queen. Shortly before her death, she published a revised second edition of the book which—along with some minor changes—added a short final chapter on QW85 and its displaced inhabitant. She concludes:

> The simplest explanation owes nothing to dynastic policy, nothing to religious disfavor or to social upheaval; it is a very human explanation, and perhaps therefore it has no place in a study of the Martians, who for all their closeness to us remain so alien in essence. Perhaps Queen 85, while she yet lived, came to the edge of that great pit as I once did. Perhaps, as I did, she looked down into that vast black spiral, that inverted tower of death plunging down farther than any human eye—any Martian eye?—could hope to reach . . . Perhaps she saw her own tomb waiting for her there, far below, beneath the layered treasures and the layered sins of her long and illustrious line. And perhaps, like me, she found she did not want to go in.

The QW85 mummy is now kept in climate-controlled storage at the Martian Planetary Museum in Olympus, pending discussion about its potential future reinterment.

SEE ALSO

THE HEART IN SERVICE TO HUNGER

Nghi Vo

I killed the cockerels in the morning and at eight o'clock they hit the table for Mr. Page's birthday, gleaming with butter, gizzards simmered and strained into gravy, and garnished with rosemary and thyme. I stood by the door, trying not to drowse because I had been up since before dawn, and as she went by, Mrs. Page pinched my arm hard.

"Where is Rose?" She had perfected the trick of hissing without moving her lips. She was even still smiling.

"Rose is in the kitchen, ma'am," I whispered, with my head ducked down to keep anyone from guessing I could talk. "The dessert course still needs tending."

Mrs. Page's smile widened to show her teeth, and the sound she made was small but sharp, a reminder that her displeasure had consequences. She turned back to her guests, the Marburys, doctor and missus, who did not seem to care in the least that there was not a matched set of Oriental girls at the door to serve.

The apple compotes with mint of course needed no minding at all, and they came to the table in the blue-glazed bowls with a silver-plated spoon by each one. I watched to make sure that the first bites were a success, and then my eyes drifted closed again. I imagined myself floating free of my body, trickling through the cracked window in the kitchen like steam. The town of Hollycross diminished beneath me, and soon I flew over the fields scarred with dirt roads, over the broad brown river that cut the land in two, so high and so far that I laughed, turning to Xiulan to say, *Hey, look how far we've gone.*

Dinner ended, and the party moved into the parlor. The Pages weren't wealthy enough for separate parlors, one for the men, one for the women, but they pretended, the men by the window overlooking the field, the women making do by the hearth. They did the nothing they were so very fond of, and it wasn't until the clock chimed eleven that they left and I was allowed to start cleaning.

"Where *is* Rose?" Mrs. Page asked, yawning as she followed Mr. Page up the stairs, but she didn't expect an answer, and gathering up the cigarette butts and dumping out the ashes, I didn't give her one.

Instead, I scraped the plates into the smaller cast-iron pot, and to that I added the cockerel heads I had stashed that morning. I covered it all with water and stoked up the fire in the stove again, setting it to boil as I cleaned. After twelve years in service, I prepared my excuses with the food, that the scraps were bound for the trash, I could pay for the wood, I was only so hungry after working all day, but tonight I didn't need them. By the time the clock in the hall struck one, I was pouring the broth into a tin bowl. This I carried silently up the back stairs, the separate ones that didn't stop on the second floor where the Pages slept, no matter how convenient it would be.

The door to the room we shared was tall and narrow, the top perpetually in shadow from whatever candle or lamp we carried to light our way. Xiulan had stolen a pencil from the Pages' nephew's schoolbag when he was visiting and written a series of characters across the top. She had a tidy hand, every character neatly spaced and none larger than the other. It looked like art to me.

"How pretty. What does it say?"

She rolled her eyes at my ignorance, but pointed to each one, sounding them out as if there was a chance I would see and remember them. When she spoke Cantonese, her words slithered like snakes in my head, the sounds familiar but without meaning.

"But what does it mean?"

"It's an ancient curse meant to keep us safe," she said gravely, and then her face broke apart like a plate, unable to contain the joke, and she laughed. She had such a loud, terrible laugh. "It means *Go the fuck away!*"

Our door was heavy, but it locked from the outside. I opened it with one hand, the tin bowl and my candle balanced in the other, and in the darkness, I saw the shape under the blankets shift.

"My?"

"Who else would it be bringing you good food, huh?"

I shut the door behind me and set the candle and the broth onto the little table by the bed. It held my tin of rice powder, her tiny mirror and tweezers, and a box of candle stubs too short to burn. When we had enough, we could melt them together and have a whole one, and nothing would be lost or wasted.

"Did you use the pot today?"

"I tried."

"Well, one less trip down the stairs for me," I said trying to sound cheerful. "Here, turn over."

She did as I said, and I helped her shift up on her pillow. By the unstable light of the candle, she looked like carved bone, like some unkind knife had hollowed out her cheeks, the flesh around her eyes. She held her lips pursed like an old woman whose teeth pained her, but she still had enough spirit to make a face at the bowl.

"Oh you little peasant! You left the heads in."

I laughed, because the stewed heads, beaks and all, floated to the top of the broth when she stirred, glaring up at her as if angry they were dead.

"What, take them out and waste the brains on the neighborhood cats when you need them so badly?"

I plucked one of the heads from the broth and cracked it open with my teeth, sucking off the slivers of meat and spitting the bones into my handkerchief. I pried out the cockerel's brain with my pinkie nail and pressed it to Xiulan's lips. She closed against me for a moment, but when she opened, she sucked the gritty scrap off my finger.

"There, isn't that good?"

"It's shit," she said, her chin on her breast. For a moment, I thought she was looking down at the still bowl in her lap, but with a flinch, I realized she was only resting from the effort of swearing at me.

"Xiulan—"

"I want fried milk."

"Well, I want a flying horse and a million dollars, but—"

"It's real," she insisted. "It's real, and you would know it if you weren't born in a barn."

"It wasn't a barn, it was just that the pig got to come into the house," I said, refusing to be baited. "All right, Miss Guangzhou, you can tell me all about how you fry milk if you at least try to drink some more of that peasant broth."

She drank down two gulps of broth with ill grace. We waited to see if she would keep it down, and then she pushed it toward me.

"No more bird brains. Look. Look. You curdle cow's milk with rice starch, ground finer than that stuff you smack on your face. All right? And then you mix it with eggs, and you cool it in a vat of water, cold as you can get, and when it's solid, you cut it up."

"Right. Right. You cut up milk."

She slapped my arm in irritation. I was pleased she had the strength to make it sting.

"You cut it up. You roll it in bread crumbs, and then you fry it in hot oil. There. That's fried milk. It's delicious. I don't want chicken brains, I want fried milk."

"I'll run to the kitchen immediately and wake up the chief cook and all his apprentices. I'll make them buy a cow from the Pearl River and source oil from India, and I'll lay in the fire with the perfumed wood from California, and—"

"Foolish!"

Still she laughed, just a shadow of the hyena she used to be. I finished off the soup and set the bowl aside before I stripped off my dress and hung it up.

It was a warm night, but when I slipped under the sheet, I found her cold to the touch. She rolled toward me, murmuring at how warm I was, but I didn't feel warm in the least.

I came to work for the Pages first. I followed my mother and father from the port of Saigon all the way to New Orleans, and when they were carried away by one of the annual city fevers, I went to work in the home of one of my father's employers as a maid. I was almost fifteen years old before I decided that I would like to be paid for my service, and seventeen before I could make my escape. I passed from employer to employer, working my way up the Mississippi River until I landed with the newly wealthy Pages in Hollycross.

I worked side by side with their old maid for six months before she went off to stay with family, and then it was just me, running up and down the stairs, scrubbing the steps, pretending to be three servants while the Pages learned to present themselves to polite society. It's a kind of living death, that kind of work, a blur of aching muscles and pressure-bruised fingers from the endless cleaning, smelling like sweat and vinegar while pretending you don't. I don't think I looked up from my work at all until Mrs. Page announced they were getting a new girl.

Xiulan came in with the cherrywood secretary and the new silver salver, neat as a penny in blue from the missionary school, and Mrs. Page admired us together, calling us matched when I was taller, heavier, and a good several shades darker besides.

"Oh, that's nice, very nice indeed," she said. "All right then. You can be Rose, and you can be Peony, and we shall all get on very well. Peony, show Rose up to the room. You can start showing her her duties tomorrow."

I looked at this other girl who was meant to be my mirror, who was anything but with her hard mouth and her square shoulders, missionary-raised with a godly bow to her head. Silently, I did as I was told, leading her up the dark stairs, feeling her disapproving gaze on my back.

I was almost at the top when she reached up and pinched my ass so hard I thought a goose had bitten me, stifling a yelp as she cackled.

"Oh, Peony, Peony, what are my duties?" she sang. "Peony, tell me if the sky is blue or purple, Peony, tell me if dogs bite or if white people eat garbage, Peony, I'm too stupid to know!"

I covered my mouth at her impudence, and from the lower step, she looked up at me, her eyes so wide and deep I imagined falling into them, drowning in that darkness as we laughed and laughed at a joke just for us.

I slept for a few hours before slipping out from under the covers and tucking them more securely around Xiulan. She barely stirred as I did, didn't make a sound as I put on my gray dress with the green pinstripes, my day-to-day uniform. I powdered my face like Xiulan never needed to, sprinkled orris root into my hair to absorb the grease, and I started for the door when she grabbed my hand.

"What's the matter?"

"I can hear the butcher," she hissed. "I can hear the cleaver hit the block, can't you hear it? He's cutting roast duck."

I listened, heard nothing but the singing of the too-early birds, a dog barking somewhere close by. From the house and from the kitchen, there was nothing.

"Sis . . ."

"I *hear* it. Bring it to me. Bring me the pieces he's cut thick and fat, bring me the skin. It's fine if there's bone in, I'll eat that too. Just not the heads, all right?"

I laughed, shaking my head and closing my free hand over hers before I pulled away.

"Okay. Okay, not the heads."

She blinked, and her mouth did something strange. A smile, perhaps, though illness had made her lips thin and her teeth prominent.

"You're laughing at me," she said sulkily, and I leaned down to kiss her mouth. Her breath had a metallic taste to it, and I drew back quickly.

"If there's duck, you can be sure I'll get it for you," I promised.

Mrs. Page was in a temper that day, the downstairs clouded with her angry disapproval. I had a good trick of being invisible even as I cooked and cleaned, but over and over again, she found me, shoving my head toward some stain or other, grabbing my arm to march me to some room that had been neglected.

The house was properly too large for only two girls inside and a man who came once a week to tend the gardens, but the Pages were new to their money. They hadn't figured that out yet, and until they did, it would be Xiulan and I sprinting up and down the stairs, burning ourselves in the kitchen, scrubbing the silver until our fingers were black with tarnish.

"And the linens came back from the laundry with grease stains. This doesn't happen when we do it at home. We still have the wringer and board, there's no reason to send the washing out if they're not going to do better than we can."

Than I *can,* I thought.

That night, in anticipation of hours up to my elbows in suds and the skin peeling back from my fingernails in the lye solution, I lifted the roast up from the plate, carving away a chunk of pork before setting it back down.

I wrapped the stolen portion in a kitchen towel and stuck it in unused pot when I went to serve dinner.

"Where is Rose?" Mrs. Page demanded when I appeared with the food, but I was saved from answering by Mr. Page, who squinted at me over the top of the evening paper.

"Isn't that Rose?" he asked, perplexed, and Mrs. Page glared at him, allowing me to beat a hasty retreat back to the kitchen.

I didn't mind, honestly. I could have been Rose as easily as I was Peony. We wore the same dresses, put our hair into the same tight braids that we pinned up like crowns over the top of our heads. The differences between us were for us to explore at night in the attic, the way Xiulan's back and chest were dappled with dark spots, the way my hair formed fluffy waves when it was loose and hers fell as straight as a knife. When we came, she held her breath and I yelped. Afterward, I might cry, and sometimes she laughed. Different, but not for anyone else to see.

I opened our door that night to a foul and familiar smell. I had worked a while at the hospital in St. Louis, and it was nothing to me to wash her and place her gently on a clean blanket on the floor while I stripped the bed. The whole time, she made a crying sound, her eyes pooled with sticky, scanty tears, and she kept saying she was sorry.

As Mrs. Page said, we had a wringer and a washboard. I cleaned our bedding and hung it up from the branches of the trees in the back. The sheets would be stained with sap and windfall berries by the time I went back for it, but it would smell like the outdoors, and the Pages wouldn't see it easily from the house. Her nightdress, I hung with care from the branches of the apple tree, and it floated in in the night breeze, the lace edge playfully skimming the tall grass.

When I got back, I climbed onto the bare mattress with Xiulan, resting my head on my arm and laying my hand on her sharp hipbone. My spare nightgown draped over her like a shroud, and I shook that unlucky, unlucky image out of my head.

"Sis. Sis, there you are."

"Don't say sorry again. You sound stupid when you do," I said, making my voice hard. If you were too tender with her, she would break into tears.

She said something too soft for me to hear, and my hand tightened on her hip.

"Hey—"

"I said *duck blood soup*," she snapped, and I laughed with relief. "Honestly, it's easy enough, you must know it."

"Yeah, yeah I do. Cut a duck's throat, bleed it into a bowl, add some fish sauce to keep it from going lumpy. Mix it up, throw in whatever greens—"

"Sweet basil and mint!"

"Sure, why not. Throw in whatever greens you have growing. Mix it all up, and drink it fresh. I wouldn't drink it if it wasn't. When I was a kid, Ma got a baby peccary, slit its throat to make soup."

"What's—" Xiulan stopped, gathered her strength. She had refused the pork I had stolen. "What's a peccary?"

"A kind of pig. She made it with beaver too, but that was pretty bad."

"Vietnamese, eating trash," she said contemptuously.

"Yeah, well, you know folks from Guangzhou. You eat everything with legs but the table."

It made her laugh. She'd told me that joke herself. Then she got quiet, and she didn't talk anymore.

I went to sleep dreaming about Xiulan bending over a big silver bowl, asking me if I wanted her to stand up. I said *No, no, don't,* because I knew if she did, I'd see the cut where the big knife had slid across her throat, and they'd bled her dry.

I woke up with her thin legs wrapped tight around my thigh and her hand clutched on my shoulder.

"What are you doing?" I mumbled before I realized, and then I held her until she got too tired and gave up, falling on my shoulder with an exhausted angry cry.

"It's okay, sis," I said. "You get better, and we'll sneak into Mr. Page's bed again, do it when they're visiting the relatives."

She turned her face from me and wouldn't say anything even when I kissed her shoulder. I remembered that they went to visit Mr. Page's relatives in October, months from now. I pushed the distance between now and October away, as well as the words *too long* and *won't last.*

I dressed quickly, already late, but I paused at the door. Xiulan's back was still turned to me, but if I listened, I could hear the rustle of her voice, dry grass in an exhausted summer wind.

They eat living fish in the islands to the west. They nail them to planks and peel back the skin. Do you think that would be good?

I was already late getting downstairs, and I ran from task to task, one ear out for the Pages stirring in their rooms. It was impossible to do it all, even before Xiulan had fallen ill, and now I was shaving every chore as thin as paper, sweeping the floors and throwing open the curtains only on the rooms I guessed would be used that day, lighting the stove and leaving it to heat on its own while I saw to the orders for the butcher and the greengrocer. If you were unlucky, you'd burn the house down, but I don't know a single maid who didn't occasionally bet on her luck if there was a chance it would keep her mistress off her back.

It was the grim kind of game that every maid played every day, how much work she needed to do to escape a scolding or a beating, how much work she could leave for another day so she had a moment to breathe or eat. You win your life back by stealing it. I was good at this game, better than Xiulan, but no matter how good you are, it's not a game you can win every day of your life. Eventually, you get too tired, and when you get tired, you get clumsy. The coal scuttle gets dumped on the rug, you miss the dead mouse in the dining room, you forget to turn your face when a guest is passing in the hall. You lose, and I nearly lost that morning, bringing breakfast to the table.

Mr. Page ate his buttered toast and bacon without complaint, but when Mrs. Page cracked open her soft-boiled egg, she gazed at it with a frown, as if her only indulgence for the year had been spoiled. My fingers twitched as she pointedly picked up one of the fingers of toast and dipped it in, drawing only a smear of yellow from the overcooked egg. We both examined it, and with a sigh, she laid it down on the plate beside her eggcup. I stared at her food just a beat too long before jerking my eyes away. My own breakfast of cornmeal porridge had been hours ago already.

"This is unacceptable. You know that, don't you?"

"Yes, ma'am. I'm sorry, ma'am."

Mrs. Page was a woman who prided herself on her control. Even when she stood, scooped up the broken egg and pitched it hard against my chest, she didn't shout. Mr. Page flinched but only lifted his paper to shield himself from her ire as I caught the egg to prevent it from striking the ground. Mrs. Page breathed hard as if she had shouted.

"Clean yourself before you run for the rest of the washing," she said, sitting back down and picking up a dry finger of toast. "And I want Rose serving at dinner."

"Ma'am, I'm sorry, but Rose is feeling poorly."

She didn't look up, but her lips tightened, and unexpected tears glittered in her eyes. She was hard, but brittle as well. Mr. Page ignored us both.

"Then I suppose you will have to do it. *Why* are you bothering me with this?"

"Yes, ma'am. I'm sorry, ma'am."

Back in the kitchen, I separated the egg from its shell, eating what I could and throwing the rest out before I sponged off my dress. They kept us so hungry, they all did. I didn't know a maid who wouldn't risk a hiding for some extra food, for one day where the hunger didn't ring in her ears. The egg tasted unfairly good, something I should have sneaked up to Xiulan, and later that night, when I half crawled up the stairs to our room, she could smell it or something like it.

"You smell good," she whispered. "You smell so good. What have you been eating?"

"Here. Look. I fried some cornmeal porridge for you. It's still fresh, here."

She mouthed a few crumbs, but they fell out again, wet and soggy down her chin. I set the fried porridge on our table, maybe she could try again later, and slid into bed next to her.

She pressed her face to my throat with momentary strength, her fingers digging into my shoulders. Her fingers tightened, and then, exhausted, she released me. I took her hands in mine, ignoring the chill to rub them gently loose again.

"I don't want fried porridge."

"All right. What do you want?"

For a long moment, I thought she wouldn't speak, but then she found her words.

"Sparrows," she said at last. "So many sparrows, caught in a weighted net. You have to pluck them, singe them over open flame to get all the down off, and then you fry them in hot oil. That's all. That's easy. You leave the heads and feet on. You ought to like that."

I imagined going to Hollycross's market square with a weighted net, casting it over and over to catch the hordes of little brown birds that gathered for the dropped food and spilled grain. I would look like a madwoman, stuffing sparrows into a basket, smiling apologetically at the people who stared.

Xiulan wants it, I'd tell them, and that would have to be enough for them because it had always been enough for me.

"Do you want sparrows to eat?" I asked, and there was another long pause. I thought she was gathering her strength for a response, or perhaps she had fallen asleep, but then she started to cry without water running down her face. Even if I had brought her a hundred sparrows, she wouldn't be able to eat them.

"I'm hungry, so hungry, sis." She whispered it over and over as I fell asleep, her breath rattling like dice in my ear.

Mrs. Page handed me a pamphlet the next day, folded open to a page of insectile text.

"There. For tomorrow," she said, and I squinted at the letters, sounding them out. She had forgotten that Xiulan was the better reader between the two of us, or maybe she didn't care.

It was a recipe for roast chicken in half-mourning. You peeled the skin back, applied butter and a scatter of aromatic mushrooms underneath and then roasted the whole thing. The end result was somewhat ghastly, meant to resemble a chicken gently laid over with a speckled mourning veil, but in fact, it looked more like some kind of parasite to me, dark and feasting greedily on the chicken before the server the Pages hired to carve ever touched it.

He was a game-looking older man who came with his own uniform, and taking his meal in the kitchen much later, he shook his head.

"What they won't eat," he said, and the phrase stuck with me as I washed the dishes, drying them and putting them away. What *wouldn't* they eat? The list seemed endless, especially to someone born in Vietnam and raised in New Orleans, especially compared to someone who had grown up in Guangzhou and tagged along with her grandmother to the live markets. They didn't have words for the birds and wild game that appeared in the cages there, ready to have their necks wrung.

"But we'd pluck them at home," Xiulan had said, wrinkling her nose. "That way, they came cleaner to the kitchen."

That night, I climbed the stairs to our room with a bowl of broth strained so carefully through a piece of white cloth that it was almost clear. No salt beyond what was in the roast, no cockerel heads this time.

"Sis, I don't want that," she said, but she allowed me to sit beside her, spooning the broth between her cracked lips. Her mouth was too dry and tight to allow the sharp edges of the spoon past it without hurting her, so I sneaked downstairs again to find the glass eyedropper that Mr. Page used to fill his pens with ink.

I washed it out as well as I could, and I used it to feed Xiulan her broth drop by drop until as much flowed down her throat as down her chin. She turned her face away, and I took her hand in mine.

"What do you want to eat, sis?" I whispered, but she wouldn't or couldn't say.

I woke up when it was still pitch-black outside, and at first, I didn't understand why. No one had called me, nothing had touched me, and I realized that was what had awakened me, the nothing.

When I held my breath, the room was completely silent. The hand I held was cold, and when I squeezed it desperately, the flesh didn't spring back.

In that moment, I could have done anything. I might have started screaming. I might have started crying. I might have opened the window and flown all the way back to New Orleans and from there out over the vast blue sea.

Instead.

Instead, I went back to sleep.

The things you know when you're asleep are different from what you know when you're awake. When I was asleep, Xiulan wouldn't be dead. She might chase me through a forest hung with corpses, or she might always be one room away in the boarding house I worked in Natchez, or she might sit silently in the pew at First Presbyterian, holding a bowl in her lap that slowly filled with blood from her mouth, but oh, she wouldn't be dead.

I slept, the last good sleep I would ever have, and when I woke up with dawn just lightly scratching the sky, I thought I was sleeping still, because there was a rattling sound beside me, a draft finding its way out of a dry and acrid house.

"Sis," she said. "I'm so hungry."

In the kitchen, staring at the eggs in the pan, I thought about bones. I thought about how people said they were down to skin and bones, as if they had nothing left, and how that just wasn't true. When the meat was gone, skin and bones remained, and you could fry the skin to crackling in its own fat, and of course the bones went into the pot. The marrow was the good part, but there were the knobs of cartilage at the ends, the shreds of meat that you missed.

You boiled the bones over and over again until they went soft and rubbery, until all the strength had gone out of them and gone into you instead. You kept on until you were drinking the ghost of the thing that had died to feed you, or maybe the memory of it, and you kept on because it was better than drinking nothing at all.

Mr. Page gave me the same distracted nod he always did when I served him. Mrs. Page, her back never touching the chair, tapped her way around her egg in the eggcup, removing the top suspiciously. She relaxed when she found it good, as if it was a relief she did not have to reprimand me. I watched her tap a single shake of salt into the egg and commence eating it in tiny bites, my own presence erased from her world now that I had served my purpose.

My own hunger hung low in my belly, a familiar and exhausting weight. I had waited too long to start my own breakfast before I had to tend to the eggs. When the cast-iron cooled, I would peel the dark brown scraps from the pan, eat them before I started the washing, maybe dab a tiny bit of butter on my tongue to keep me going. It was easier to think of my own hunger than it was of Xiulan's.

Before I fled that morning, she had cried from the other side of the bed. For all her boasts and bullying and bluster, Xiulan was always an enormous crybaby. She would cry for the girls she missed from the mission, for a beaten horse in the street. She would cry because someone was cruel to her or because she remembered someone being cruel to her, and I would take her into my arms and kiss her until she stopped.

I started to do just that this morning, but then on some instinct, I rolled back instead, out of the bed and onto the floor with a great thump. It left a bruise the size of a saucer on my hip, but I watched as Xiulan's hand struck the place where I had lain. It slid from under the covers like a spider—it was already terrifying to me how I had held it. It dug its nails momentarily into the bed, and then it softened with despair or disappointment.

"Get me something to eat, sis," she whispered, and I nodded hard, seizing up my clothes to dress on the landing. As I buttoned my shoes, I heard her turn over in the bed. I heard, clearer than I should have, the sound of her breath, forced out of her body by some exhausting, remorseless pressure, by some *hunger*, and with a shudder, I turned the lock on the door.

The Pages were still replete after the success of their dinner the night before. Mrs. Page directed me to make something simple and plain for them, and the barley in pork was certainly that. Mr. Page ate with the stolid indifference with which he ate everything else. Mrs. Page ate it liked a picky child, and afterward, she followed me to the kitchen, going through the pantry as if she were searching for something. It hadn't been that long ago, I reckoned, that she had done most of her own cooking. Now she was trapped in that strange space of being too rich to cook her own food, too poor to have it cooked the way she liked, and she slammed the canisters of cornmeal and flour around as if they had displeased her.

"You must keep on top of the pantry," she said angrily. "Look at this. And this. All of it stale and in need of a shift."

She opened a canister of rice from the back, making a disgusted noise before she shoved it in my face. The rice had taken on weevils, their brown bodies not much larger than the grains of rice themselves. When the light fell on them, they burrowed down into the white only to be revealed again when Mrs. Page gave the canister another hard shake. For a moment, I thought she would dump the whole thing over my head.

"I'm sorry, ma'am," I said, careful not to whine. "I can wash it, take them out."

The adults would at least float to the top in the milky rice water. The eggs and grubs wouldn't.

She thrust the open canister to my chest, so hard I cried out. I clutched it frantically to keep it from falling to the floor and dropping rice and vermin everywhere (*no time for more sweeping, no time, no time left at all*) and she swept by me angrily.

"No. Throw it out, throw it all out, and order fresh."

Of course I didn't. I cooked it after she and Mr. Page went to bed, while I was wavering on my feet and struggling to keep my eyes open.

If you fall asleep and pitch forward, your face will strike the stove and all the skin will peel off, just like that poor boy in Galena, I told myself, and it kept me upright and stirring gently until the water boiled away and the weevily rice puffed up. I took it off the heat before I would have if I were cooking it for myself—Xiulan liked rice a little tough, putting up some fight.

I packed the rice into a round bowl before upending it on one of the Sunday-best blue dishes, leaving a perfect mound behind. It was pretty like food never was unless we were making it for each other, and I carried it carefully up the back stairs to her, lifting my candle high so that I wouldn't stumble.

I set the candle in the niche in the wall and reached for the latch one-handed. Before I could lift it, however, something scrabbled at the toes of my right foot. I jerked back reflexively, imagining mice, and I saw Xiulan's small fingers, slid underneath the door, reaching, and for just a split second before she pulled them back, clenched in frustration with the nails dug into the floor as they would have been into my foot.

"Sis," I whispered, clutching the plate as if there was ever a chance it was going to save me, and from behind the door, Xiulan wailed.

"I'm hungry. I'm so hungry, please, I'm just so hungry."

My head echoed with her whimpers. I would never stop hearing them. I bumped down on the floor before I realized my knees had given way. Somehow the mound of rice stayed intact on top of the plate, and I held it on my lap as I sat on the top step next to the door, and Xiulan cried for how hungry she was.

I didn't sleep. Instead, I watched until the candle choked on its own melted wax as Xiulan reached under the door for me. In the darkness, I listened as she prowled on all fours from door to bed and back again. Her words dissolved into weeping by dawn; I thought in that kind of scrubbed-clear, too-long-awake way that she must run out of tears soon.

Eventually, the night gave way, and the door at the base of the stairs swung open, slamming against the wall with force.

"Rose! Peony!"

I tried to tell her not to come up, there was no need, we had only slept in, *Sorry, so sorry, Mrs. Page,* but then she was on the stairs, her voice rising as she lifted her lamp.

"I have had quite enough of this nonsense. I will dismiss both of you for this ridiculous—Peony, for God's sake, get up, what in the world are— Is that my mother's plate?"

I staggered up on legs that had gone numb and tingling from my long vigil on the stairs, and she jerked the plate away from me with fury, scattering rice down her skirts and mine. With an angry snarl, she thrust her lamp into the niche and put the plate under her arm, turning to the door.

"Rose, you come out of there at once. I have had enough of this malingering; do you hear me?"

I moved forward, so dazed with weariness and hunger that I am no longer sure what I meant to do. I hoped I meant to help her, but instead she struck me a resounding blow to the side of my head, and the two halves of the plate fell to the floor. I fell back with my ears ringing, nearly falling down the stairs before I grabbed hard for the banister with my head lowered against another blow. That was why I didn't see the moment when she lifted the latch.

She managed to say *Rose* one last time, and then Xiulan was on her, a desperate thing all flying arms and loose hair, her fingers clawing at Mrs. Page's body as if she could tear it open. She might have done it, split her belly open like an overripe gourd gone soft in the yard, but Mrs. Page's corset prevented it, better than armor with twenty-four lengths of whalebone sewn to her sides. Mrs. Page uttered a noise that sounded more offended than anything else, and Xiulan leaned down, her mouth opened so wide it seemed to take up half her face, and clamped her teeth on the right side of Mrs. Page's jaw, shearing through the skin of her face as if it were thin silk and crunching down on the bone with terrible strength.

Mrs. Page uttered only half a scream—it was cut off when Xiulan tossed her head and ripped away Mrs. Page's lower jaw. I saw the red meat of her face, the flash of her white teeth, and the way her tongue lolled out trying to shape the wheezing bellow of air escaping her lungs.

Then Xiulan seized Mrs. Page by the head, slamming her with stunning force against the floor, and when she leaned in moaning, I saw her draw our mistress's tongue into her mouth and bite down just before I stumbled down the stairs.

I was moving so fast that I was almost on my hands and knees when I burst into the kitchen, where Mr. Page was just entering.

"Where's breakfast?" he asked, and I shook my head, pointing behind me. "Mrs. Page. Oh, it's Mrs. Page."

Alarmed, he thrust me aside and ran up the stairs. I heard his thumping footsteps. I heard him swear, and then I heard him scream, and I closed the door to the stairs deliberately. I realized that there was a latch on this door as well, again from the outside.

How little they trust us, I thought numbly. *But then, imagine trusting someone as hungry as a maid. Who knows what she might do for a full belly and something good in her mouth?*

Two days later, I picked up a paper someone had discarded on a bench at Chi-cago's Union Station. As the trains roared out from their dens, I found the story about the couple dead in Hollycross, killed in a fire that had started in their kitchen. Their two Oriental maids were wanted for questioning, and below the text were rough ink drawings of two identical girls, their faces round and solemn with squinted eyes like raisins in raw dough. I threw the paper away hurriedly, and I returned to where Xiulan waited on the platform with our single suitcase.

"There you are. Did you find anything?" she asked.

In response, I tore the sausage roll I'd purchased in two. I gave her the larger half, and she ate it with a kind of scientific curiosity, her jaw moving up and down as if someone had once told her how to chew but never shown her. If I looked too closely, the motion of her chewing would bring on a kind of dizzying nausea, or perhaps it was only the memory, too strong, of that brief moment when I had seen two tongues protruding between her lips.

Instead, I focused on my half of the sausage roll. The white bread held a gray thumbprint where the vendor held it too hard, and there was a kind of rubbery quality to the meat that made me want to gag. The mustard helped some, and I finished it off. I started to wipe my fingers on the side of my skirt—it wasn't like it was getting any cleaner—when Xiulan made an impatient sound and took my hand, swabbing my fingers with her handkerchief.

When they were clean, she held my hand for a moment. We'd spent endless nights examining our hands, pressing them together to see the difference in size, kissing them, tasting them.

Now she turned my hand over to see my palm, running her fingers along the heart line and the life line, the mound at the base of my thumb, the shockingly sensitive skin between my fingers. She lifted her head to meet my eyes, and then she brought my hand up to her mouth.

I thought of Mrs. Page's tongue. I thought of Mr. Page, hollowed out so that he seemed like an empty basket, the liver, lungs, heart, and intestines all gone.

I held my breath, and she only kissed my fingertips before letting me go. Around us, the people stirred, gathering up their things as the train pulled up to the platform.

"Thank you for buying us food," she said softly. "But sis, I'm *hungry*."

Her eyes flickered to the other people on the platform with us, and then she turned her gaze back to me with a smile.

"Of course you'll find me something good to eat."

Linking her arm through mine, we got onto the train.

DOWN THE INTERSTATE

E. Lily Yu

Lee Evenson Brown watched the thick fog that lidded the interstate gather in a glitter on his windshield. It was the fog, he figured, that had slowed traffic to a crawl, red brake lights glowing everywhere in hellish repose. If he could have rolled down his window and punched the fog, he would have. He settled for flipping the bird at the fog and muttering a string of obscenities.

The fog had wiped away all sense of time. The car's clock showed *20*, whatever that meant. It had shown *20* for a while now. Lee wasn't sure if some dying circuit had erased the first two digits, which did not reappear when he hit the display, or if something else was at fault.

He had tried turning on the radio to relieve the blank monotony of the drive, but no matter what station he scanned to, the radio hissed. Now and again, dialing between stations, he picked up a faint and distant suggestion of voices and music, difficult to distinguish from the static. It never lasted for long.

Lee was used to certainty, to having or inventing the answers and shouting them if necessary. He did not like the formlessness of his situation any more than he liked the stuffing of a sofa escaping its corduroy bounds, or a potential customer's vague, hand-waved *maybe later*, or an errant interest payment.

The vehicles around him were packed too tightly at present for him to change lanes, and no one seemed inclined to yield. Although he could have sworn that no one was moving, that none of them were getting anywhere, in an appalling magic trick, cars on his left and right kept passing him, moving with infinitesimally greater speed.

In spite of the cosmic injustice occurring in the left and right lanes, Lee reserved his purest hatred for what was behind him: a lifted pickup with aftermarket LED headlights like a nuclear explosion. Whenever he glanced at his mirrors, his eyeballs stung, and the back of his head throbbed with a nasty headache. The white and greenish beams knifed straight through his skull.

Every so often the pickup driver leaned on his horn.

"Jackass," Lee said. A memory tugged at him. Hadn't he driven a Silverado once, king on his throne, riding the tail of anyone ahead of him? How had he wound up in this crappy early Kia with shit for tires? It must be a rental, but when—?

"A stupid decision like that? Must have been you," Lee said to Cindie, who was sitting mutely beside him, staring out the window into the fog. "Some lunk of a salesman at the rental counter pushing the paper over, sign here, baby, you'll love it. You never even read what you were signing. You never asked yourself, what will my husband—"

Ex-husband. They had divorced over a decade ago. He hadn't seen her in years.

Of course his passenger wasn't Cindie. Why had he thought it was Cindie? No one would ever mistake his mother's wispy white curls for Cindie's thick and sandy waves. His mother was shivering in her cross-hatched hospital gown, dark thumbprints under her eyes.

Lee inched the car forward.

"Who let you leave the hospital like this?" he grumbled. "Not even in your own clothes."

"It's all right," she said. "They were rushed, that's all. Nice people, for the most part. I had a call button. One of the nurses gave me ice chips whenever I asked."

"They should have treated you better."

"Oh, I didn't care. For the most part I was lying in bed wondering how you were doing, were you sleeping well, when would I see you—"

"Don't give me that. You know I had to work. Cindie was sucking me dry, the bitch."

Cindie had fled without asking for alimony, and all Lee paid was child support, but what his mother didn't know couldn't hurt her.

"Don't call my mom that."

Andrea glowered at him from the passenger seat, her eyes hot, wet, and sloppy with mascara, arms crossed over the seat belt. Her mouth was silvery with braces and crossed with hot pink bands. She had taken after him, which he and Cindie had quietly agreed was a tragedy: wiry brown hair, craters of acne, teeth that elbowed each other out of the way. Lee had paid for the braces without arguing.

She had also inherited his temper.

"Oh for chrissake," Lee said. "You weren't here a moment ago—"

A gap opened in the left lane like a miracle, like the Red Sea parting, and Lee swung into it. He braked hard as the car in front of him stopped. Around him rose a disapproving chorus of horns.

"You are a *terrible* driver," Andrea informed him. "You're rude and a chauvinist pig and you didn't come to *any* of my concerts even though Mom kept saying you would. She covered for you. Got me two bunches of tulips each time and said one was from you. But that was a *lie*."

"Quit yapping," Lee said.

"You're so stupid you don't even know where you're going."

"If you don't shut your mouth—"

"You'll what, crash the car?"

Without taking his eyes off the road, Lee backhanded his daughter across her face. Or he tried to. His hand hit a man's chest instead and bounced off buttons.

"I'd ask if I raised you to smack kids," his father said, "but—"

"You did," Lee said, gripping the top of the wheel. "You taught me that."

"Though I had better form. Don't think I missed."

Lee's knuckles whitened on the wheel. "Are you bragging?"

"About being a worse father? Wasn't much of a competition." His father leaned back and studied the car in front of them. "How long you been on this road?"

The clock read *27*, which meant nothing. Lee said, "Dunno."

"Decades? A century? Whose car is this?"

"Rental," Lee said. "Useless piece of shit."

"I used to call you that."

"When you wanted to sit on the sofa and I didn't get up fast enough. When girls turned me down. When I swung and missed."

"It was embarrassing, having a kid like you," his father said. "Not one you can show off around the guys. Runty thing, punches like a girl, trips and falls while walking. Now you know what it was like."

"Andrea's fine. Good grades. Takes care of her mom."

"Has an asshole father."

"She'll survive it. I did."

His father grunted. "You're quicker with the comebacks."

"Sure, now that I hit as hard as you."

"That tap? That was nothing."

"Oh yeah?"

His father's sigh was like the emptying of a bottle. "Think you coulda turned things around, with a few more years. Maybe not with Cindie, but with Andrea. Me, I couldn't have done anything. But I wish you got that time."

"You could have quit drinking."

"Didn't want to." His father squinted at Lee. "Both you and Mary Lou were heavy. Needing things. Crying. Six beers, and neither of you existed. I was the funniest guy in the room. It felt like being young again. Can you imagine it? Not having Andrea? Not having to write those checks?"

"Get out," Lee said. "Hitchhike or walk. I don't care."

The passenger door didn't open, but the car was empty again. Lee squeezed the wheel, took a breath, and bellowed at the enveloping fog, the traffic, the clock that now showed *32*. He banged a fist into the felted roof, then the top of the dash, roaring until he was out of air.

"Why?" he shouted. "*Why?* I didn't ask for a father like that! I didn't ask to be born!"

The only reply he received was the blatting of a sixteen-wheeler's horn. Its grille loomed in his rearview mirror.

Move.

How many times had he done the same thing?

His chest sore and sour, Lee eased up on the brake and edged forward.

Lights flickered in the distance, white and red. The fog softened and rounded them.

Emergency vehicles. Lee barely glanced in their direction. The interstate still approximated a parking lot. If there was an accident ahead, it was possible that traffic would clear up past the crash.

He felt no excitement at the thought.

Yellow left-turn signals began blinking through the fog. One by one, graceless as hippos, cars merged left. This slowed things further.

The interstate's five lanes of traffic funneled into a single lane. As he approached the tangle of emergency vehicles, Lee's headlights swept white sparks through a spray of shattered glass on the ground.

The line of cars in which he sat crept past parked police cars, two firetrucks, and three mangled vehicles.

The cars had rammed into each other, hoods buckling, bumpers crumpling, their black tangled innards spilling into view. A sheeted body on a stretcher was being carried off, arms flung sticklike to either side, the hands half curled, a crimson stain on the shroud above the torso. The vivid color in that endless gray shocked him.

Although it was impossible, Lee felt suddenly sure that the body under the sheet was his own. He could hear the brakes screeching as his foot pressed down, wheels sliding on the fog-slick road, the thump and crunch of metal, the sharp high tones of glass breaking.

"Get up," he mumbled, staring at the body.

The trucker behind him honked. A space of fifteen feet had opened between Lee and the car in front of him. He let his car roll past the accident.

The lights of the emergency vehicles glimmered in his rearview mirror before receding from view. Cars began smearing themselves again across all five lanes. This did not improve traffic in the slightest, even after the three-car pileup was miles behind him. Somehow, Lee was not surprised.

The clock showed *64*.

It occurred to him that the Kia should have run out of gas ages ago. But the fuel gauge never wavered. The needle pointed steadily at a quarter tank.

Lee slunk forward a foot or two when traffic allowed, as the numbers on the clock ticked up with exasperating slowness: *67*, *68*, *69*. He did not know if the clock was counting days or weeks or months. If there was a sun somewhere behind the fog, it neither rose nor set.

"It's my fault, Cindie, isn't it," he said dully. "It's always my fault. That's what you wanted me to say—"

"Actually, what I wanted was a 'thank you' now and then," Cindie said.

"For what?"

His passenger was silent.

"Fine," Lee said. "It was nice having someone to talk to," he said. "Someone to hold."

"Someone to nitpick," Cindie said, turning her face toward him. "Someone to blame."

"All right. You were someone I could blame."

"You did that plenty."

"Both of us did. But it was nice not being alone."

Cindie said, "I preferred to be alone."

"You had Andrea."

"She wasn't as difficult as you."

"Thank you for Andrea," Lee said. "For raising her, when I wasn't there."

"She got very good at drums," Cindie said. "Made it to regionals. You should have come to hear her. You should have called and said hello."

"I should have," Lee said. He was sick of cars and fog, sick of the interstate, sick of himself and his opinions. "I'm sorry."

"You *should* be," Andrea said, hugging herself. She wore an oversized hoodie and was taller now than she had been before. Her braces were gone. "Mom made me stand up and speak at the memorial service. I had to dig up nice things to say about you. Nice things! I had two."

"Two's better than zero," Lee said. "What were they?"

"You paid for my braces and you didn't shoot Mom. You only hit her."

"Ah," Lee said, staring at the dented bumper in front of him.

"Mom grabbed my elbow and yanked me away so your cousin could speak next. She yelled at me after. Said I'd regret it someday. 'You only get one Dad,' she said."

"If I could do it all over," Lee said, "I'd have gone to your concerts."

He was alone. The interstate stretched endlessly before him, red lights winding into the fog.

The clock showed *81.* The pickup with the magnesium-flash lights had wound up behind him again, blaring its horn, but he found himself unable to either wet his mouth to spit or fill his gorge with spite.

"I should have come to see you, Ma."

"You were working. You had your own life."

His long string of jobs—insurance agent, car salesman, regional manager, and so on—seemed as insubstantial and unimportant as fluff.

He felt her hand alight, delicate as a butterfly, on the back of his.

Lee said, "Never asked what you dreamed about, when you were a girl. Never knew who you were. You were just there."

"Most children are like that."

"I didn't know who anyone was. Not Cindie. Not Andrea. Not you."

"That might be true."

"Except for my father. I know he was a jerk."

His mother laughed. "He could be that, sometimes."

"Sometimes?"

"There were reasons I fell for him, back in Okaloosa. What do you think Cindie saw in you?"

"It didn't last."

"It doesn't always. Your father made his choices. So did you."

"I failed them."

She snorted. "Think you were the first? Did you really think you were original?" She gestured out the window. "This one cheated on his wife. That one sabotaged her friend. Millions of failures. Nothing special. Fail and get on with it."

The light pressure on his hand vanished. Lee knew without looking that no one sat beside him.

The vehicles around him remained. They were the only points of interest in that unwavering twilight. He no longer saw them as obstacles and objects of hostility, but as so many strangers on a sluggish river, floating together from nowhere to nothing. He drifted among them, as lost as the rest.

The fog thinned around him, revealing depth and detail.

From the scabby pickup in front of him came a large hand that in one smooth motion flicked a cigarette into the road. Before it was retracted, Lee saw that the hand was muscled, calloused, the nails trimmed and darkened with dirt—a working man's hand. The driver of the hatchback on his right wore sunglasses and a scarf, her face impassive. She drummed her perfect oval nails in a skittery rhythm on the top of the wheel. A line of rubber ducks sat along the bottom of her windshield.

In the red sedan on his left, a child in the back seat huffed onto the window and drew faces on the glass. Seeing that he had Lee's attention, he dragged the tip of his nose down the fogged window, turning his nostrils up. The woman driving the car, who Lee assumed was the boy's mother, grimaced and said something inaudible to the child.

The clock showed *97*.

"That's not right," Lee said to himself, as the child slouched, sulking. "This isn't a place for kids."

Andrea hadn't really been in his car. She wasn't on the interstate with him. Andrea had gone to college in a chaos of laundry baskets and bedding, leaving both him and Cindie behind. That was what children were supposed to do: grow up. Leave.

He rolled down his window and waved until he caught the eye of the other driver.

"Excuse me," Lee said. "Is that your son? Why is your son with you?"

Her eyes were dark and hopeless, the skin beneath them heavy. "I've been asking myself that. It was a rollover crash. Drunk young man. We were going home from my sister's."

"You can't get him to—he can't get out?"

"Can anyone?"

The car in front of her crawled forward. She did the same. Lee waited impatiently for her to come back into shouting distance.

"I haven't seen any exits," Lee said. "Have you?"

"No, but there'll be an exit onto a turnpike. We'll pass it sooner or later. I don't know how I know that. I just do."

"What's the toll?"

"No clue. Doesn't matter, though, because I don't have any money. I checked."

Lee dug through the heap of receipts and tissues in his car's center console. A borrowed car, then, and not a rental. Beneath the paper detritus, his fingers closed on a quarter, reassuringly solid. He wondered why he hadn't thought to look before.

"Can you show me where to go?" he called to the other car.

"Follow me," she said.

It took some time, since traffic was as clotted as it always was, but eventually Lee maneuvered his Kia behind her scuffed Toyota Camry.

He had a possibility, a future, to anticipate now. He began to notice the dents and dings on bumpers, cracked windshields, one battered passenger door. "Character-filled," Cindie would have called it. An elderly man drove a busload of seniors with furious concentration, eyebrows bristling.

Whenever the Camry he was tailing flicked on its turn signal, Lee did the same. Their merges proved impossible to coordinate, though, and Lee often ended up a car or two behind.

Like two pawns traversing a chessboard, they made their way into the rightmost lane. Then Lee found himself veering onto a long concrete interchange that hadn't been signposted anywhere. Without his guide, he would have missed it in the fog.

The interchange deposited them onto a broad toll plaza fortified with dark-glassed booths. CASH ONLY glowed in green letters over each lane. The sky above them was blue and clear. Behind them, thick fog crouched low over the interstate.

A sign said: ALL VEHICLES $2.75.

Lee had been scrabbling in the cupholders and glove compartment whenever his car was not in motion. He had accumulated eleven quarters, which sat warm and heavy in his left hand.

The Camry ahead of him swung to the side and parked. She beckoned for him to drive ahead.

Lee leaned out of his window. "Keep going!" he bawled.

The woman hesitated.

"Go!"

After a moment, she restarted her engine, and her car entered one of the toll lanes.

Lee swerved onto the striped median between booths, hopped out, and marched up to the toll collector's window. Her gray-green polo had KAREN H. stitched over the pocket.

She raised an eyebrow. "You can't park there."

Lee thrust his fistful of quarters at her. "This is for them," he said, indicating the Camry.

The boy in the back seat stared at him.

Lee said, "Let them through."

The toll collector shrugged, counted the quarters, and waved the red Camry through the rising gate. The mother said, "Sir—"

"Move it," Lee said. "You're blocking traffic. I'll be right behind you." He put on his most professional smile.

She nodded and pulled away.

Lee turned to admire the gleaming chrome and trim of vehicles approaching the tollbooths, the marine curves of gray concrete, the clouds like torn-out sofa stuffing. He could even appreciate the queasy smell of diesel and gasoline.

The tollbooth operator cleared her throat.

"Sorry," Lee said. "That was all the money I had. Which way back to the interstate? Or do you ticket me first?"

"You can go through," she said, covering a yawn.

"What?"

"Somebody paid for you. Now get off the median."

Lee climbed back into the Kia—lovely, loyal thing, he thought, patting the dash—and peeled into the toll lane. A thought occurred to him, and he rolled down the window.

"Was *she* paid for? I mean, before I got here."

Karen nodded.

"What are you going to do with the $2.75?"

"Cup of coffee," she said, stifling another yawn. "From the vending machine. Two obols a cup. Sludge, but what else can you find around here?"

She hit several switches. CASH ONLY went dark, replaced by a red X.

The gate rose. She flapped her hand at him.

Lee drove through.

The turnpike was straight, bright, and nearly empty. He arrowed down it, trees blurring to either side. At intervals, roofs and power lines jutted above the sound barriers, glimpsed and gone. The landscape was unfamiliar, and there was no map anywhere in the car, but Lee realized that he knew where he was going, where he had been going all this time.

Somewhere ahead of him, miles away, was the exit where he would turn off for home.

UNCLE HERMIT

Kaaron Warren

We were all at the table the day I went to the hermitage for the first time and discovered my true talent. Dad, tired after facilitating three funerals in a row but fired up with all of us around, pouring drinks, "get that into ya," not caring that two of his sons had given up the booze and one was allergic to the chemicals in the cheap red wine Dad favored. "Get that into ya." Mum and all of the brothers mocking him. Mum faking drunk, lolling about. I stopped her flashing her boobs. "Bridge too far, Mum," I told her. "Always the family protector, Sarah," she said.

My oldest brother and his wife and their two cute-as-button kids—six and eight, dressed like pall bearers—bringing out the plates of food left behind by mourners. There's a deep and long-abiding superstition that no funeral food should be wasted. So, we ate it or we gave it away. We didn't care it was dead people's food. We relished those little pies, those tiny dried-out sandwiches, those gelid, overly sweet tarts. Bowls of nuts, pretzels, chips, salt gathered on their bases thick and tasty when you licked it from your fingertips. Bite-sized quiches, pastry triangles, a pyramid of spring rolls, cold and transparent with grease. Or "grief" as we called it. When I was a child, playing around our funeral home in all the nooks and crannies, I heard the word *grief* so often, when someone said, "that fried chicken is full of grease" I thought it was the same thing. So in my family we have griefy chips and chicken, when we want to indulge.

Johnno, my weightlifting brother-in-law, joined the table with a slab of very rare steak he had brought with him and thrown on the grill for a minute or two. Blood running from it, him grinning over it. Nothing with it but his beloved hot sauce. His knuckles reddened and my sister's arm bruised and no one says a thing. Their son is thirteen, Johnno's from a previous relationship. The kid calls my sister Mumsy; she doesn't seem to realize he's being sarcastic. No one talks about what happened to his real mum. My dad, the world's neatest eater, even a bottle of wine in, watching Johnno wipe his mouth with the back of his hand. Watching him lift a finger for someone (and he didn't care who) to get him another beer. The collected aunts and uncles, the cousins, the nieces and nephews were all getting their own drinks, getting louder by the minute, having a good time. I hoped no client came knocking out of hours; it wasn't a good look for a funeral home.

And my grandmother there in all her finery, never one to miss a chance to dress up. She piled up her own plate and another one besides. "It's for Uncle Hermit," she said.

My dad passed her a good-sized brandy and gave her a pat. "He's been gone a long time, he doesn't need anything to eat," he said.

"It doesn't hurt to leave it for him," Grandma said. "He looked after me, I look after him." She stood up, holding Uncle Hermit's plate. My dad tried to take it from her. He always says he'll deliver it to Uncle Hermit but of course he doesn't, although he knows where to go.

She topped the plate with a thick slice of Spam. "He loves Spam," she said.

"That was our father. Don't you remember? How pissed off he got when there wasn't a spare tin?" my oldest uncle said.

Grandma drank off her brandy and Dad poured her another.

My mum: "She doesn't need any more, look at her," under her breath the same way she berated all of us when she wanted to.

"Tell us about Uncle Hermit," one of the grandkids said. I had to laugh; we used to do this. When we were kids, it was, *Tell us the scary story, Grandma.* We built a whole thing around him, filling in the gaps she never said.

"He lives up in the bushes," Johnno's kid, the oldest grandkid said, thirteen years old, prime "scare the shit out of your cousins" age. "And if you don't feed him enough, he's gonna come spit on your food." Later, I saw him do this, spit on food. Like father like son, already.

"He only eats funeral food," one of the younger cousins said. "And he only eats it once it's all gone bad and moldy."

My grandmother said, "He doesn't live in the bushes. He lives in a hermitage made from dead people's furniture."

"This place is full of ghosts," one of my cousins said. "How could it not be? They are every single where. They hang around anyone who hangs around dead bodies." He screwed up his face. He was one of those who found the funeral business disgusting. Who hated the fact my parents lived in this good big house next door to the funeral parlor where most of us worked.

"Done is done," my dad said. "Puritans believe the body without the soul is an abhorrent thing. A funeral director can't feel that way. Our family's motto: Done is done. All we deal with is the body, we are not here to think about the afterlife. Don't you worry about what comes next. This is all you need to worry about."

He slapped his chest.

"You mean your man boobs?" one of the uncles said. Hilarity.

I think Dad's wrong. There is a comfort in a belief in the afterlife. This is why we want to talk to loved ones' ghosts. To be sure they are okay. To give comfort that in the afterlife we'll be reunited. And so they can reassure us we did nothing wrong. That there are no ill feelings.

I said this out loud and half the family killed themselves laughing.

"Anyway," Dad said. "We're here to celebrate fifty years of De'ath business, with thanks to our great-grandparents all those years ago wanting to have a place where people could come for decent funerals without fake smiles and all the rest. And for our mother and father for keeping it all happening. And to all of us as well." He raised his glass to Grandma and she bowed her head.

He'd had plenty of brandy, too. "Here's to the joy and security it's brought us all," he said, with tears in his eyes.

Security, sure. And we were never hungry. There was always food left over after the wakes. Sometimes the bereaved family took it with them but mostly they didn't. Mostly they forgot about food. We catered for the wakes, by preference, a way to make money but also to take the worry from them. And to avoid food that stained, like beetroot dip. Other times, mourners would bring their own food in. As a kid I loved this, because the leftovers provided a good variety. I tasted food from all over.

"Here's to our mother and father," Dad said again. All his siblings shut their eyes when Grandfather was mentioned, blocking him out. He'd done a runner when my dad was about sixteen, left the family in the lurch. We all raised our glasses. Drank. And drank some more.

My oldest brother said, "Sarah, before you get too drunk could you please pop next door and take the belongings?" by which he meant he'd laid out a person for burial and he wanted me to take a photo of her things. Nobody would steal from a dead person, not even the worst of us. But the photo is perhaps proof, a record of what there is, to double-check and show the family. I *could* steal. I'm the one making the record. But I want none of their stuff.

I finished one last drink. "Business out the front," I said. "Party out the back. We should call this place the Mullet Funeral Home." It wasn't the first time I'd made this joke, but it still got a laugh. Seriously, the contrast between our family life at home, and our serious and dedicated work life in the funeral home, deserved the nickname.

I let myself into the funeral parlor. It was cold, and I quickly moved to the room where we held belongings, and where there were comfortable chairs, and tables with boxes of tissues. The dearly departed's belongings were in a plastic box. I dusted and polished the sideboard and laid the belongings out nicely, moving them around until they sung to me. Until they told a story. A pipe, a watch, a money clip. A creased photograph. A small smooth piece of glass. I added a bright green apple and took my photo.

By the time I got back to the table, they were getting stuck into dessert. Caramel slice, lemon slice, oat biscuits. The best of home cooking. All of it left over from funerals in the last couple of days. We thought ourselves lucky, but dealing with the dead was a shameful thing in a small town. Everyone knew what we knew. And we were the De'aths, a name my sisters married to get away from.

I embraced it, as a kid and now. I wouldn't change my name for anything. Certainly not to my boyfriend's. Sarah Grover? I don't think so. Behind his back, my brothers called him Groveler. He showed up just as someone pulled a selection of cakes out of the freezer. "Usual cast of thousands?" he said, looking around the room at all my relatives. He didn't kiss me, instead going around to the men to shake hands. Groveling. He didn't need to impress me, but the menfolk? "Gary, mate!" they all said, as if they hadn't called him Groveler minutes earlier.

Feeling huffy, I sat with a plate of stale sandwiches, peeling the bread off to get at the chicken loaf inside. I stuffed my face and no one noticed.

Then Gary came over and rubbed his face on my cheek. "Dusty!" I said.

He was our carpenter, making the coffins and the stands and bookshelves for anyone who asked. Johnno reckons he's after my money and the family business. We've all done well out of it.

He tried to kiss Grandma's cheek but she recoiled. "You've got the dust of someone on you. My husband used to come kiss me like that." She smiled. "He was a great woodcarver, that man." There were pieces of his work around our house. A wooden plate, a stirring spoon, a lion's head that sat on a bookcase.

"No, it's just wood dust. I made one out of her kitchen table. She was a much beloved." This was something we prided ourselves on; we provided coffins made from the furniture of the deceased. It was a no-waste kind of thing. Not all the mourners wanted it, but those that did loved it.

"The table she died at. The table she absorbed into," Grandma said.

In the awkward silence that followed, I moved things around, setting up a still life. I couldn't help it. Everything looked better that way. The saltshaker one of my nephews deliberately tipped over across the table. And someone's false teeth out on the table, no one will confess to them but there's Dad with his gums flapping.

"Shhh, everyone, Sarah's making art, shhhh, she needs quiet to be a genius. We're not dead, Sarah, leave it alone." One of my sisters. They all paused for a moment to laugh at me then moved on, as they always did.

My boyfriend took a photo of my setup, saying, "You can paint it later, it'll look great." Which was sweet, but I couldn't tell if he meant it or if he was just . . . groveling.

Johnno's kid, ready with a perfect sense on how to dig, how to hurt, said, "Auntie Sarah, look, I did one too. It's called the Fat Triangle." He'd piled up a pyramid of food and circled it with sugar cubes.

The family, as a group, paused before laughing. I swallowed the mouthful of chicken loaf I had.

It all stepped up a notch then, adults loud, kids loud, things being knocked over and no one caring. My grandmother shrugged her shoulders to her ears. She never did like loud noises. I was with her on that; I preferred the quiet.

"Come on, Grandma," I said. "I'll take you to see your uncle." I picked up the plate of food she'd set aside. We'd all seen this mythical plate forever. Grandma heading out the door, Dad sometimes going with her. I used to

think the hermitage was up the back of our place. All of the yard was overgrown, but once you got past the washing line, it was impenetrable. As a child I thought the hermitage was somewhere in that overgrown yard but was never brave enough to seek it out. I was terrified of the stories of Uncle Hermit, and of his hermitage. I never went back there. My two oldest brothers did, coming back with animal bones and booze bottles with a few centimeters of liquid in the bottom, and sometimes underwear. They brought stories of a small shelter made out of branches, and there were more empty bottles and a firepit just outside it. Anytime they tried to drag me there, telling me the ghosts were asking for me, I'd hide.

My boyfriend was watching football with the men. They were digging deep into the whiskey and would be messed up by the time the game was over.

"I'll see you later," I told him. "At home."

"Yes, you will," he said. He took his eyes off the TV to wink at me and right then I knew I'd dump him. I'm not like my sister, sticking with an awful boyfriend, marrying him, having kids. She came in with a bowl of chips and some beer. Put them down, kissed Johnno's hand.

"You've got her well trained," my boyfriend said.

I was leaving him, for damn sure.

Mum was cranky with Dad for being drunk and getting his mother drunk and so he said, "I'll come too," and whispered to me, "We'll just go to the pub," and off we went. Grandma in the passenger seat, humming away. I drove. Dad in the back seat. I asked Grandma to tell me the story again, of Uncle Hermit, and she and my dad, the two of them, and I filled in the gaps because I'd heard it a hundred times. The three of us told his story on the way to visit him with a plate full of dead people's food.

So: My great-great-great-grand-uncle was something called an ornamental hermit, contracted to live in the garden shed of Effingham House, by a wealthy family, long gone and forgotten. I only realized as an adult that there was no such thing as Effingham House. Fucking Ham House, was the family nickname, small revenge for his life spent small and pointless, to bring rich people more good fortune. The rich family paid for his meals, in return for him sitting in their garden hermitage, quietly. It was a thing they did in the UK, apparently.

And by all accounts this was the best place for him; he terrorized every one of his eleven siblings and could not be trusted around women. He never married. There is a strain of the family attributed to him, though, because his last act before entering the hermitage, never to emerge, was to take a young married woman by force. This is in the family's lore. It isn't official. That part of the family remains under another name and want nothing to do with any of us.

They never did.

That uncle lived to be at least a hundred. He never took a drop of alcohol and some say that's how he lived so long. No one is sure when he died. The wealthy family who had hired him forgot about him over time, sending up fewer and fewer meals until he stopped relying on them and foraged in the garden he had grown from vegetable scraps, instead. His hermitage grew over with weeds and birds' nests. It grew over with ivy and moss. A tree fell, and another, and the hermitage was lost to sight. No one remembered he was alive.

Some would say he received the imprisonment he deserved.

Grandma says he was a man possessed. That he was a conduit for passing souls, a throughfare, a throughway, and each left an impression upon him.

As a girl, my grandmother would sit outside the hermitage and sing to him. For comfort. Later she did it for others. Singing outside the jail for condemned men. Singing at births and stillbirths.

Singing loudly when her husband beat the children or her (by which I mean my own father among them, it's why he's a gentle man now and no violence), singing as that same man spoke with ineffable kindness to the bereaved and gave them hope and a belief in the afterlife.

She had a voice like an angel.

My grandmother was the only one who visited Uncle Hermit. She was lonely too, and almost voiceless then. She took him food from funerals. Letting him take on the sins.

He had a life of solitude and contemplation. An utter and complete lack of conversation. You couldn't say silence; even then without the noises of society, it would have been awash with birdcall, tree creak, limb fall, animal call, and other poetry of nature.

He didn't read or write. In the end, did he think in words? Or were they gone, too, leaving behind an impression, a *feeling*? That space filled with the ability to hear the dead in inanimate objects and to draw them out in his eventual, desperate need for company? I loved hearing Grandma speak, tell her story. I reached over to touch her leg, wanting contact, before returning my grip to the steering wheel.

"He always gave me comfort, no matter what went on. Even when my darling died." She shrank into herself, tears falling quietly.

"She's forgotten how awful your grandfather was," Dad said in my ear.

"We should go to the Hermitage, Dad," I said. "It'll make her feel better. She said it always gives her comfort. We'll go to the pub on the way back."

Grandma said, "She can cope. She's more sensible than the rest of them." I think it was the nicest thing she'd ever said to me.

We drove for maybe half an hour. Grandma told us about her young married life, painting a pretty picture that wasn't true. Dad said nothing unless he was directing me where to go, even when she spoke about his father, although he too needed to touch her, stretching out to hold her hand for a moment

I parked in the driveway of the old mansion, the one we'd always called Effingham House. It wasn't named at all, and was long since uninhabited, used now for weddings and other parties, rich people pretending to be even richer for a few hours. I didn't know the history of the place, beyond that once the family (who'd hired Uncle Hermit to sit in their yard, and forgotten him) suffered a scandal, they lost it all and everyone in the town said good riddance. Maybe if they hadn't forgotten Uncle Hermit they'd still be there.

We didn't care about the house itself, though. It was through the back, along a path that ended abruptly at hedges and brambles. It had been a while since she'd been here. Dad pulled aside the vines and cleared the path, enough for us to walk through at least.

And there was the hermitage. You could see its stonework through the branches and bushes surrounding it, through the piles of twigs, the leaves in mounds, the collected debris of snack food that seems to gather in even the most isolated of places. I stepped forward to clear it away.

My grandmother watched over as I worked, humming. She said, "He's still in there. You be careful."

"He's long dead, Grandma," I said. "We're just here for the memory of him. Where's he buried?" I asked. "Should we take the food here?" But neither of them answered me.

"He used to whisper to me through the crack in the door. Him bending down or squatting because I was sat there with my back against it. He's the one told me to marry your dad. He's the one told me a beating was good for me. He's the one told me boys will be boys."

"Why did you ever come back?" I said. I was angry that anyone had said these things to her, and that she'd listened.

"Because he had secrets to tell. Things to teach me."

I cleared away the last of the debris, enough to be able to open the door toward us. The smell that seeped out was milder than I'd expected, more like a bonfire made of moldy leaves than anything else. Dad cleared the small window, I pulled the door wider open, and poked my head in.

The smell got me first; I knew the smell of death, old and new. This was old death, bones only just connected by the last sinews, held together by mummified skin. His body sat on a chair, his mummified hand around a glass, tin plate at his feet. Bones of mice in that plate. Across his lap an ornate walking stick, dark rosewood, the handle a lion's head. A still life right there.

"He's here!" I called out. Grandmother shrieked and I added, "He's dead! Don't worry! He's dead!"

She was crying. "He wasn't so bad," she said.

"He bloody was, Mum."

Dad took another nip of brandy and handed the flask to his mother. She drank the rest of it.

"You guys!" I said. I was horrified at how little they cared. "We need to get him out of here."

Grandma said, "We're going to leave him where he is. There's no other place for him." I realized they both knew the skeleton was there. "They'd pull this hermitage down and then where would his soul go? Better it stays absorbed in these walls."

This is what Uncle Hermit had taught her and what she believed. What my dad believed too, it seemed. That when a person dies, their soul is absorbed into the walls around them. Or into an object, if there are no walls. Like a book, or a pottery mug. Something porous.

"You can see this if you look closely enough," Grandma said. "A stain that shifts, or a bump in the wall that sometimes moves. A blurring of the lines. It leaves a layer of grease."

The two of them swore me to secrecy. "It'd be bad for business," Dad said. "No one would trust us. That's why we've left him."

Grandma said, "I met him in the darkness. He had to do all the things he did, act nasty, to keep the evil spirits away. He didn't mean it." She shifted sideways and Dad propped her up. She had a bad leg, and a bad eye. And she was tired. "I saw it happen. Through the window. I called to him. He reached out. But he cut his own throat, he'd had enough, and I could see a fluttering lifting and breathing in the walls."

"Can't we just bury him?" I said, but I saw the wall move at the suggestion.

So we left the bones there.

Dad said, "We'll bring Johnno next time," and my grandmother nodded. Two bloody drunks talking rubbish.

I felt very proud though. They'd trusted me enough to show me this. I was ready. I'd find out some of the others knew, but none of them cared. We were all too used to the family business, to keeping secrets, keeping quiet. Whatever a bereaved family member sobbed, that stayed with us and never got any further.

We kept the secrets.

I didn't get back to the hermitage until the middle of summer. I thought about it often, though, and about Uncle Hermit, sitting there surrounded by his meager belongings. I began to scrawl sketches of the hermitage, with a glimpse through the window. I never drew him though, sitting there in his bones. Only his things. I dreamed of what else he might have around him, and these I gathered in a basket. It felt louche and artistic to do it this way, rather than cramming everything into a tote bag.

The hermitage walls were cold to the touch. In this summer heat, it was a pleasure. I rested first one cheek and then the other, letting my face chill. I felt nothing beyond that wall. No caress from Uncle Hermit. Then I unpacked the basket.

A packet of butter, unopened. The same of cheddar cheese. An old book, gold lettering indecipherable (the point being that no one read these old books, they were simply for show). There was a copper goblet; in this I rested a bunch of white grapes, then on reflection changed them for purple grapes. A bottle of wine (or beer, for the congruity) and a thick bronze arm-band. All of these placed on the table in front of the skeleton.

A candle, just snuffed out. A copper bowl with droplets of moisture. An open book. A jar of murky water.

I set my tripod up outside. Light inside dark, muted. Shadows enough. The light was better and the distance afforded a different look at the objects, rendering them unfamiliar, separating them from "self."

I would leave it here overnight and come back again, day after day, until I had it right. Dozens of versions of the same thing, and the grapes changing, and the butter too, melting and setting again. I loved all of this and could see life changing before my eyes.

As for the walls, they changed too. Bulging at times and then indenting. If I was tired enough, they seemed to pulsate. At times I saw crawling insects, feelers waving through apparent cracks and then disappearing.

I started to draw what I saw as well as photograph it, as if I could capture it better that way. I moved the objects he'd had with him. The dish. The empty tin of Spam. The whiskey bottle.

"These are very good," Mum said. She liked the drawings best. This was the first real praise I'd ever had from her so I kept at it. I painted, I drew, I worked with pastels. I was the happiest I'd been in a long time. I still used the camera to take a record of the dearly departed's belongings, but beyond that, I worked with paint, pencil, pastel.

I needed somewhere to lay out my hermitage artworks, so I turned on the lights in the gallery room, set up a heater, and got to work.

This was my favorite place in the funeral parlor. There were hooks from where the paintings of Jesus used to hang when we were more religious, and photos of my great-grandparents, and of the place when it was first built. This is where we lay out photos and flowers ready to present, but mostly it stays empty. I think I'm the only one who goes in there. It is dark and cold. There's a griefy film over everything, as there is in any unused room, once you know where to look. It settles when a room has been empty for a while. In a certain light, you can see these griefy droplets lifting off a body.

Once my grandmother pointed the grime out to me, I saw it everywhere. I saw it here, in the hermitage, and I tried to capture it as I painted my still life.

I hung my art there and the progression of it, the changes in the walls, gave me new faith in my own abilities. So when I heard a bereaved client say to my father, "I just want something to remember him by," I had an idea. I took her aside and showed her my work. I said, "Some say, death is absorption. You become a part of your surroundings. This might be an object, or a place. I can paint your husband's still life from objects and make that his memorial. It will be *him*."

I didn't know if this was true or not, but I believed it. I took the photos but I drew as well, and painted. I added life. I added ghosts, and a shimmering.

That client was so happy with what I did she spread the word, and people started to ask for me. No one minded me being in the room as they made arrangements with my parents or my brothers (my sisters not part of the business once they changed their names). Grieving people often want witnesses.

Each painting I did reflected not only the beloved, but different ideas of what happens after death. In the afterlife. I painted heaven, hell. I painted walls thick with absorbed ghosts. I painted ghosts. I painted griefy surfaces, shiny and awful to the touch.

I painted nothing.

At last, I found myself with a role in the family business beyond simply taking photographs of belongings. My paintings drew out the souls. My still life paintings summed up their lives. I made visual obituaries. What would be in mine? A melting bowl of chocolate mousse. A half-filled wine bottle. Crusty bread rolls. Carnations or rhododendrons, dropping petals, so that each iteration of the painting will change.

I worked in the rooms we stored the cadavers in, wanting the greasiness there, the last of the soul settling on the surfaces. Everything was griefy to the touch, like unwashed hair. Like the top of a kitchen cupboard. I ran a film over everything I painted. Even the frames were grimy to the touch.

People loved the insects I painted emerging and disappearing in the wall behind. And they loved to find his face, to say, "there he is" in the walls. They loved that I gave them proof of a soul, even though they should all be terrified of being absorbed. Terrified that that is all the afterlife had to offer. I took commissions, of course I did, and I spoke on podcasts where they sought answers I pretended to have. I said, "When we die people like to sum us up. 'She was a great singer,' or 'They slept with my wife.' The whole life summed up in a few sentences. The still life does the same. Freezes a person in place. Photography can do this, but in art there is freedom to fantasize, catastrophize, imagine." I said, "Every painting is a still life, really."

I called my pieces Still Life by Sarah De'ath.

I broke up with Gary and all he said was, "Can I still hang out with your brothers?" which made me so irritated we ended up not having sex that one last time. Which goes to explain to a small degree why I spent so much time with a man who came in to see us about burying his mother.

I really found this bereaved son attractive. He made the joke about someone called De'ath being in the funeral business. Everybody made the joke. I was showing him our gallery, and he was selecting the material he wanted in her coffin.

I said, "It's even more ironic that I paint still lifes. You know that it is a euphemism for death, of course. Life Is Still. And there are other kinds of death than the end of life. Those friends, forgotten as if they never existed. They say if you remember someone they will never truly die. A loved one's essence remains somewhere. Like secondhand clothing that never washes through. We want to be sure that person is gone, that we do nothing to anchor them here. So I paint their still life. To set them free. It's kind of like a memory of life. Rather than a memory of death."

In sunlight I could see tiny globules, like shiny tiny orbs of oil. They settled on surfaces. If I let my art sit for long enough, the globules will settle. This is why an item will feel sticky or slimy if it has sat still for a long time. The essences settling.

"Wow," this son said. "I didn't expect any of this. You're pretty amazing."

"I'm just making it up as I go along."

I'd convinced him. He came back with a box of belongings, things I suggested he bring. There were sandwiches in the kitchen of the funeral parlor, and other leftovers, but I went all out and bought sushi to share. I didn't want to turn him off. He didn't stay, though. He dropped the box and ran. I guess my family are used to the idea of eating in the vicinity of the dead. One thing about Gary; he never cared about that.

Still, I painted that mother a beautiful picture. He'd chosen a wooden spoon, a book of poetry, a bunch of lavender, and a pumpkin. Not for me to ask what any of it means. As I made the final touches, I felt that she was released. Dispersed. Just as every sip of water has a molecule from Julius Caesar or whatever that quote is, so does every breath you take contain the multitudes. A little bit of everyone who has ever lived.

If nothing else you'll be absorbed into the clothes on your back.

It's why I only wear new clothes.

While I painted, I fantasized that the son fell in love with me because of my art. Hidden depths, he'd say. Great movement of emotion that can't be seen on the surface. He did talk like that. He had a radio show, Sunday morning chat.

Once his mother was buried I never saw him again. I listened for a few weeks, until he said on his show, "Thanks to the De'aths, yes the De'aths, who are gentle and kind and showed my mother the deepest respect. You can even get a piece of amateur art done, if you ask."

Amateur!

And he used all I told him on his radio show, just using my thoughts and words, our generations of knowledge, even saying "not so much a memento mori but a memento vitae, if you will." Thief.

I was reading in the back garden a couple of days later, snoozing and reading, when I heard Johnno call my name.

"If you want me to go round and thump him, let me know," he said. "That radio arsehole. He shouldn't be making fun us like that. Your paintings are really good."

I was speechless. I'd never heard a kind word come out of this man's mouth. He'd brought beer with him and he offered me one.

He said, "I love your sister. I truly do. She's a good wife. But you remind me of my son's mother. My first love." I couldn't figure out what he was up to at first, but remembered overhearing my sister saying, "I've got him on a sex ban."

Seriously? That's what he wanted from me?

"She sickened and died." There was something about the way he said this, about his first love, his first wife. The way he rubbed his mouth, and I knew he'd done something to her. He leaned toward me and I pulled away. He gave me this grin, this "I can wait" look and left me alone.

It was later that afternoon when my phone rang: Mum.

"It's your sister. She's in hospital."

"What happened?"

"She fell down the stairs. Drunk." Even in Mum's voice I could tell she didn't believe that. My sister didn't drink. "Can you go by her house and get a few things for her?"

"Why can't Johnno?"

Pause. "He and the boy have gone fishing. It's been planned for weeks apparently. Just get her things, Sarah." Her voice cracked on that. We hung up.

My sister looked terrible. Her nose bandaged. Lacerations all over her face. Hand and wrist in a cast. She was in and out of sleep, drugged up. I packed the books, magazines, clothes, and snacks into the bedside drawers. "Was it Johnno?" I asked. She squeezed her eyes shut.

The thing is? Even if she left him, he'd move onto the next one and get stuck into her.

A nurse brought in a huge bunch of flowers from Johnno.

"He's a wonderful husband," my sister said, a whisper I could barely hear.

I had a still life to finish so I went back to the funeral parlor, thinking I could channel my distress about my sister into my work.

Dad sat in the garden in his full funeral director suit. The sun shone but it was like he was in shade, as if darkness covered him. He had a family photo album on his lap.

"Dad?"

"You can see when it changes," he said. "You see? When my father was alive, and then he was gone. And then Johnno joined the family." I could see it. From shadow to sunlight and back. From photos of people not looking at the camera, children crying, to raucous photos of everyone enjoying themselves, to our most recent group photo. I remembered that one; it was an exercise in torture.

"I hate him," I said.

I looked at photos of my grandfather sitting there in the middle of everyone. His wife, my grandmother, looking at him, not the camera. A large ornate walking stick resting on his knee. Rosewood. A lion's head handle. I'd never noticed this detail before. But I'd painted that stick any number of times. It was Uncle Hermit's stick, from the hermitage.

"Why did Grandfather have Uncle Hermit's stick?" I asked.

"It's his own stick. Not Uncle Hermit's." He hadn't realized what this meant. What this told me.

I put my finger on the photo. "That's the walking stick in the hermitage. Is the skeleton my grandfather?"

Dad looked at me. "Smartest of them all," he said.

He told me then. Halfway through I got my sketchpad and pencils, because it was hard to hear and sketching gave me an easier focus.

Dad told it with his eyes shut, his head turned away. It *was* my grandfather in the hermitage. It was an accident, at first. Dad hitting him with a fry pan to stop him beating up Grandma. And deciding to lock him in the hermitage to teach him a lesson. They had help but Dad didn't say who.

"We tied him to Uncle Hermit's chair."

"So Uncle Hermit's skeleton never actually sat there?"

"No. He had a good Christian burial a long time ago. We did it ourselves, you can't say we don't know how to do that. He's behind the hermitage where he would have wanted to be. We planned to leave my father overnight and then see if he was sorry, but when we got back he was done."

Dad mimicked throat cutting. "Your grandma said it was Uncle Hermit, back from the dead to look after her, to say thank you for not forgetting him. He came out of the walls to do the job. She takes those plates of food for both of them. The day she confuses the two is the day I start to worry about her."

I worked on my sketch. My sister sent me a text asking me to bring more underwear. "I'm bleeding like a motherfucker," she said, and I laughed out loud. This was my real sister, my pre-Johnno sister, full of verve and pep. Even having him at a distance helped.

I flicked through the photo album. I could see it so clearly, like Dad did, the influence these men had over the whole family.

In perfect timing, Johnno sent me a photo of himself, shirtless, on the end of a pier, holding his fishing pole. His son must have taken the photo and I hated the two of them, there with my sister in hospital.

I hated the way my heart flipped a bit.

I hated that Johnno had picked me out as if he knew I was weak enough for him.

I showed Dad the photo. He leaped to his feet, his chair falling backward to the ground with a soft thud.

"I hate that kid as much as I hate Johnno," I said.

Dad said, "It's never too late. Get rid of the bad influence and the kid still has a chance. Look at me. Imagine who I'd be if we hadn't."

He paused. They say your life passes before your eyes when you die and this felt like the same thing; his other life, his possible life, flickering in a flash. "Would Johnno come to the hermitage if you asked him? He likes you," Dad said.

I hated how much I liked hearing that. Hated myself for understanding what he was suggesting.

We had to bury my grandfather first. My dad did that; he said I didn't need to be there. I wanted to, though. To see those bones bundled into a pile and lose any sense of "who."

I left Dad managing that and went to the pub, where I'd asked Johnno to meet me. He had a drink waiting for me, and he had a good shirt on, a date shirt.

"I've always liked you," he said. "In a different world, things would be different."

I despised him. But he smelled good and I was tempted. Seriously tempted. He was so big.

"You must miss her," I said. I didn't mention his wife was in hospital because of him. "Although . . ."

He stopped eating and looked at me.

"Although she can be such a bitch. To be honest."

"Good to be honest," he said.

I took a big swallow of whiskey. My hair looked good, clean, straight, smooth. I wore a singlet top that defined my shoulders. Adorable splashes of paint on my arms. Perfume musky.

"You must be lonely," I said. "I told you Gary and I are taking a break. I don't miss him much. He's good with his hands but not that good, if you know what I mean," and I'm tossing my head back, showing my throat.

We'd ordered chips and spring rolls and chicken wings, none of which we'd eaten.

"Let's take a plate to Uncle Hermit," I said.

This confused him.

"Believe it or not, it's a cover. We've used it forever." I licked my lips. "This is going to sound weird, but I'd love to paint you naked." His vanity and his libido, and his joy in cruelty to his wife, his thought he can use it against all of them, made him say yes.

It doesn't take much for a man like him. He easily believes every woman wants him.

I had a basket in the car. A thermos of Irish coffee, drugged. Condoms hidden/not hidden under a cloth to distract him. Paintbrushes and paints. "Hold on to the basket," I said. "Have some coffee."

"You hold it," he said. He took my keys. This was not a man who let others drive.

I directed him to the hermitage. He talked the whole way, telling me stories, big-noting himself. As if he was trying to seal the deal.

He parked the car. "What is this place?"

"I've never brought anyone here before. I'm nervous."

I took a fake sip of the Irish Coffee, handed the thermos to him. "Come on," I said. "Make me feel better."

I led him to the hermitage, both of us stumbling and laughing in the moonlight.

There was a glow inside.

"This is pretty sweet," Johnno said. *Thish,* he said, and *shweet,* his voice slurred.

I pushed open the door. "You sit," I said. I put my basket on the table, took out my paintbrush. I undid the top button of his shirt. "When I said, paint you," I dusted my paintbrush along his cheekbone, along his collar bone, "I meant paint you. You need to strip off."

Everything in there was grimy to the touch.

He laughed. "Ya coulda just asked." He drank the last of the Irish coffee and fumbled his clothes off. The walls pulsated around us. He nodded his head to his chest.

I texted Dad. We hadn't decided yet what to do. An overnight scare? Or more? I tied Johnno to the chair with some rope we'd brought with us, Dad watching from the doorway. Johnno awake enough to go "Whaat?"

"You haven't mentioned your wife," I said, and you could see him come back to reality with a thump, some kind of realization hitting him. He shivered; it was cold. The walls breathed and I could smell dry grass, fresh-cut grass, something odd.

The walls seemed to close in on me and I stepped back, outside, and the door creaked closed as if in a gentle gust of wind. As it closed I saw Johnno's head tilt back as if pulled, and as we walked away I heard a gurgling.

I went back to the hermitage and painted his still life in secret. No one else needs to see it. I have it in my bedroom cupboard, face to the wall. Only I know it's there. I won't be going back to the hermitage for a while. I feel a sick comfort, knowing he'll be there forever, in the walls. A bottle of beer. A steak I took in and out of the fridge because, much as I loved how things changed, I didn't want the smell of rotting meat in my place. A red rose. And a well-thumbed porn magazine.

"Here's a toast," my dad said. He was tipping over drunk and we all laughed. My grandmother chuckled as she made up the Uncle Hermit plate, adding a bottle of hot sauce. She'd worked out what had happened, for sure. My sister was tired, looking after the kids on her own and working a full-time job. But she was smiling for the first time in years. She wasn't grinding her teeth, clenching her fists. Gary went around filling the glasses, making sure everyone had what they needed. I didn't regret taking him back. He was still our carpenter, and he was different with Johnno gone. A good, kind man doing his best.

And if he ever changed for the worse, there was the hermitage, and Uncle Hermit, and I'd paint a still life for Gary that would break my heart but be utterly beautiful.

ABOUT THE AUTHORS

Paolo Bacigalupi (www.windupstories.com) is an internationally bestselling author of speculative fiction whose debut novel, *The Windup Girl*, appeared in 2009 and was followed by the Shipbreaker trilogy, *Zombie Baseball Beatdown*, *The Doubt Factory*, and *The Water Knife*. He has won the Hugo, Nebula, World Fantasy, and Michael L. Printz awards and was a National Book Award finalist. His latest book is *Navola*, which shares a world with this short story.

Elizabeth Bear (www.elizabethbear.com) was born on the same day as Frodo and Bilbo Baggins, but in a different year. She is the Hugo, Sturgeon, Locus, and Astounding Award–winning author of dozens of novels; over a hundred short stories; and a number of essays, nonfiction, and opinion pieces for markets as diverse as *Popular Mechanics* and *The Washington Post*. Her most recent novels are space opera *The Folded Sky* and fantasy *Angel Maker*. She lives in the Happy Valley of Massachusetts with her spouse, writer Scott Lynch.

Vajra Chandrasekera (vajra.me) is from Colombo, Sri Lanka. His novels *The Saint of Bright Doors* and *Rakesfall* have between them won Nebula, Ignyte, Locus, Crawford, and Otherwise awards, been selected as *New York Times* Notable Books of 2023 and 2024, and been nominated for the Le Guin Prize for Fiction and the Hugo, among others. He is one of the 2025–2026 Fellows of the Dorothy and Lewis B. Cullman Center for Scholars and Writers at the New York Public Library.

Indrapramit Das (www.indradras.com) is a writer and editor from Kolkata, India. He is a Lambda Literary Award winner for his debut novel *The*

Devourers, a Shirley Jackson Award winner for his short fiction, which has appeared in a variety of anthologies and publications, including Tor.com, *Slate Magazine*, *Clarkesworld*, and *Strange Horizons*. He has also won a British Fantasy Award for novella *The Last Dragoners of Bowbazar* and his anthology *Deep Dream: Science Fiction Exploring the Future of Art* was short-listed for the Ignyte and Locus awards. Das is an Octavia E. Butler Scholar and a grateful member of the Clarion West class of 2012. He has lived in India, the United States, and Canada, where he received his MFA from the University of British Columbia.

Writing honors for **Andy Duncan** (https://linktr.ee/andy_duncan) include three World Fantasy Awards, a Nebula Award, a Theodore Sturgeon Memorial Award, and a Mary Kay Bray Award for criticism from the Science Fiction Research Association. Recent fiction includes "Criswell Predicts" in *Storyteller: A Tanith Lee Tribute Anthology*. Recent essays are in *Journal of the Fantastic in the Arts 35.1* and *More Than Love: The Enduring Fascination with Edgar Allan Poe*. He reads nine of twelve stories on the audiobook of his most recent collection, *An Agent of Utopia*. A tenured writing professor at Frostburg State University, he explores his backyard in Weird Western Maryland (www.frostburg.edu/personal-arduncan).

Jeffrey Ford (www.well-builtcity.com) is the author of the novels *The Physiognomy*, *Memoranda*, *The Beyond*, *The Portrait of Mrs. Charbuque*, *The Girl in the Glass*, *The Cosmology of the Wider World*, *The Shadow Year*, *The Twilight Pariah*, *Ahab's Return*, and *Out of Body*. His short story collections are *The Fantasy Writer's Assistant*, *The Empire of Ice Cream*, *The Drowned Life*, *Crackpot Palace*, *A Natural History of Hell*, *The Best of Jeffrey Ford*, *Big Dark Hole*, and *Pandemonium Waltz*. Ford's fiction has appeared in numerous magazines and anthologies from Tor.com to the *Magazine of Fantasy & Science Fiction* to *The Oxford Book of American Short Stories* and has been widely translated. It has garnered World Fantasy, Edgar Allan Poe, Shirley Jackson, and Nebula awards and a *New York Times* Notable Book of the Year.

Daryl Gregory (www.darylgregory.com) is a Seattle writer whose novels and short stories have been translated into a dozen languages and have won multiple awards, including the World Fantasy, Shirley Jackson, and Crawford awards, and have been short-listed for the Hugo, Nebula, Edgar, Dragon, Locus, Lambda, and other awards. His latest novel is *When We Were Real.* His seven other novels include *Revelator* (a *Washington Post* book of the year), *Spoonbenders* (an IndieNext pick), and *Pandemonium.* Other books include the novellas *The Album of Dr. Moreau* and *We Are All Completely Fine*, and the collection *Unpossible and Other Stories*, a *Publishers Weekly* best book of the year. He has also written for comics, video games, and television, and frequently teaches creative writing.

Stephen Graham Jones (www.stephengrahamjones.com) is the *New York Times* bestselling author of thirty-five or so novels and collections, and there's some novellas and comic books in there as well. Most recent are *The Buffalo Hunter Hunter* and *Killer on the Road.* Up soon is *Off the Reservation.* Stephen lives and teaches in Boulder, Colorado.

Cassandra Khaw (cassandrakhaw.substack.com) is an award-winning game writer and former scriptwriter at Ubisoft Montreal. Khaw's work can be found in places like the *Magazine of Fantasy & Science Fiction*, *Lightspeed*, and Tor .com. Khaw is the author of five novels: *The Last Supper Before Ragnarok*, *The All-Consuming World*, *The Dead Take the A Train* (with Richard Kadrey), *Bells Hells: What Doesn't Break*, and most recently *The Library at Hellebore.* Khaw's first novella, *Hammers on Bone*, was a British Fantasy Award and Locus Award finalist, and their latest novella, *Nothing but Blackened Teeth*, was a *USA Today* bestseller, Bram Stoker Award nominee, and World Fantasy Award nominee, and their short fiction has been collected in *Food of the Gods* and Bram Stoker Award winner *Breakable Things.*

Isabel J. Kim (www.isabel.kim) is a Korean American speculative fiction writer based in New York City. Her debut novel, *Sublimation*, was published in 2026. She is a recipient of a Nebula Award, Shirley Jackson Award, and a BSFA Award and has been a Hugo, Locus, Sturgeon, and Astounding Award finalist. Her short fiction has been published in *Clarkesworld*, *Lightspeed*, and *Strange Horizons*, among other venues. Her work has been reprinted in the *Best American Science Fiction and Fantasy 2023* and *2024* and elsewhere. When she's not writing, she's cohosting *Wow If True*, a podcast about internet culture.

Darcie Little Badger (www.darcielittlebadger.com) is a Lipan Apache writer with a PhD in oceanography. Her critically acclaimed debut novel, *Elatsoe,* was featured in *Time* magazine as one of the Top 100 Fantasy Novels of All Time. *Elatsoe* also won the Locus award for Best First Novel and was a Nebula, Ignyte, and Lodestar finalist. Her second fantasy novel, *A Snake Falls to Earth,* received a Nebula Award, an Ignyte Award, and a Newbery Honor and was on the National Book Awards longlist. Her third book, *Sheine Lende,* is the prequel to *Elatsoe* and was a *USA Today* bestseller. Darcie is married to a veterinarian named Taran.

Samantha Mills (www.samtasticbooks.com) is a multiple award–winning SFF author living in Southern California. You can find her short fiction in *Uncanny Magazine, Beneath Ceaseless Skies, Strange Horizons,* and others, as well as in the best-of anthologies *The New Voices of Science Fiction* and *The Year's Best Science Fiction and Fantasy 2023.* Her short story "Rabbit Test" won the Nebula, Locus, and Theodore Sturgeon Memorial awards. Her science fantasy novel, *The Wings Upon Her Back,* won the Compton Crook Award for best SFFH debut and was a finalist for the World Fantasy Award for Best Novel.

Premee Mohamed (premeemohamed.com) is an Indo-Caribbean scientist and speculative fiction author based in Edmonton, Alberta. She has been a finalist for a number of awards, including the Crawford, British Fantasy, Locus, Aurora, British Science Fiction, Hugo, Ursula K. Le Guin, Georges Bugnet Award for Fiction, and Robert Kroetsch City of Edmonton Book Prize. To date she has won the Nebula Award and World Fantasy Award for her novella *And What Can We Offer You Tonight* and the Aurora Award for her novella *The Annual Migration of Clouds.* In 2024 she won an Alberta Literary Award, World Fantasy Award, and Ignyte Award for her collection *No One Will Come Back For Us.* Her short fiction has appeared in many print and audio venues. In 2017 she was nominated for the Pushcart Prize for her story "Willing" (Third Flatiron Press). In 2024, Premee was the writer-in-residence at the Edmonton Public Library. She was also an assistant editor for the short audio science fiction venue *Escape Pod* from 2020–2024. Previously she was a Capital City Press featured writer for 2019–2020 with the Edmonton Public Library. Her guest editing positions include *Small Wonders* magazine, Interstellar Flight Press, and *Apparition Lit*. She has judged short fiction competitions with CBC, Dream Foundry, *Alberta Views* magazine, and others. Her latest book is the novel *Wickhills*.

Tamsyn Muir (www.tamsynmuir.com) is a horror, fantasy, and science fiction writer. She is the author of the *New York Times* bestselling Locked Tomb series, which begins with *Gideon the Ninth*, continues with *Harrow the Ninth* and *Nona the Ninth*, and concludes with *Alecto the Ninth* (forthcoming), and the novella *Princess Floralinda and the Forty-Flight Tower*. Her short fiction has appeared in *Nightmare Magazine*, *Magazine of Fantasy & Science Fiction*, *Fantasy Magazine*, *Weird Tales*, and *Clarkesworld*. She has won the Locus and Crawford awards, and been nominated for the Hugo Award, the Nebula Award, the Shirley Jackson Award, the World Fantasy Award, the Dragon Award, and the Eugie Foster Memorial Award. A Kiwi, she has spent most of her life in Howick, New Zealand, with time living in Waiuku and central Wellington. She currently lives and works in Oxford, in the United Kingdom.

New York Times bestselling novelist **Garth Nix** (www.garthnix.com) has been a full-time writer since 2001 but has also worked as a literary agent, marketing consultant, book editor, book publicist, book sales representative, bookseller, and as a part-time soldier in the Australian Army Reserve. He has written numerous books, including the Old Kingdom series beginning with *Sabriel*; the Keys to the Kingdom series; *Frogkisser!*; and many others. His most recent novels are *Massif*, *The Sinister Booksellers of Bath*, and *We Do Not Welcome Our Ten-Year-Old Overlord*. He also writes short fiction, with over sixty stories published in anthologies and magazines. More than seven million copies of his books have been sold around the world and his work has been translated into forty-two languages.

Tobi Ogundiran (www.tobiogundiran.com) is the award-winning author of the Guardian of the Gods duology (*In the Shadow of the Fall*, *At the Fount of Creation*) and the critically acclaimed short fiction collection, *Jackal, Jackal*, which was a *Publishers Weekly* Top Ten Summer Read. He is the recipient of the Ignyte and British Fantasy awards. He has also written for the *Overwatch* and *Magic: The Gathering* universes. Ogundiran has been a finalist for the

Locus, World Fantasy, British Science Fiction Association, Shirley Jackson, and Nommo awards. His short fiction has been featured in original anthologies such as *Africa Risen* and *The Book of Witches*; in several educational and Year's Best anthologies; and twice on the hit podcast *LeVar Burton Reads*. Born and raised in Nigeria, he now lives and works in the United States.

Silvia Park (www.silviapark.com) is the author of *Luminous*, which is a finalist for the Los Angeles Times Book Prize, and has been longlisted for the Dublin Literary Award, Waterstone Debut Fiction Prize, and British Science Fiction Association Awards. She splits herself between Seoul and Lawrence where she teaches fiction at the University of Kansas.

K. J. Parker (aka Tom Holt) (www.tomholt.com) was born in London in 1961 and has been, at various times, not very good at coin dealing, lawyering, farm laboring, lumberjackery, and auction house portering. He is an indifferent metalworker, inept carpenter, two-left-footed fencer, timid horse-rider, lackluster archer, so-so armorer and swordsmith, barely adequate stockman and forester, run-of-the-mill mid-list novelist, skilled textile worker and crack shot who won the World Fantasy Award for novellas two years running some years ago and has since produced relatively little of note.

Kelly Robson (www.kellyrobson.com) is a Canadian writer of science fiction, fantasy, and horror. She is the author of the short fiction collection *Alias Space and Other Stories*, the time travel adventure *Gods, Monsters and the Lucky Peach*, and the fantasy stoner comedy *High Times in the Low Parliament*. She's been a finalist for many major awards, and won the Nebula Award in 2018 for her novelette *A Human Stain*. Kelly grew up in the foothills of the Canadian Rockies, and as a teenager was crowned princess of the Hinton Big Horn Rodeo. Kelly consults as a creative futurist for national and international organizations. She and her wife, writer A. M. Dellamonica, live in downtown Toronto.

Priya Sharma (priyasharmafiction.wordpress.com) writes short stories and novellas. She is the recipient of several British Fantasy Awards and Shirley Jackson Awards, and a World Fantasy Award. She is a Locus Award and a

Grand Prix de l'Imaginaire finalist. Her work has appeared in venues such as Tor.com, *Interzone*, *Black Static*, and *Weird Tales*. She lives in the UK, where she works as a medical doctor.

Angela Slatter (www.angelaslatter.com) is the author of the gothic fantasies *All the Murmuring Bones*, *The Path of Thorns*, *The Briar Book of the Dead*, *The Crimson Road*, and *A Forest, Darkly*. Slatter is also the author of the Verity Fassbinder supernatural crime/urban fantasy series, as well as twelve short story collections, four novellas, two books about writing, and a Hellboy Universe collaboration with Mike Mignola, *Castle Full of Blackbirds*. She has won a World Fantasy Award, a British Fantasy Award, a Shirley Jackson Award, a Ditmar, three Australian Shadows Awards, eight Aurealis Awards, and a Premier Ignotas Award. She's been a judge for the World Fantasy and the Aurealis Awards. Her work has been translated into Bulgarian, Chinese, Russian, Italian, Spanish, Dutch, Japanese, Polish, French, Turkish, Hungarian, Czechoslovakian, and Romanian.

Wole Talabi (wtalabi.com) is an engineer, writer, and editor from Nigeria. He is the author of the speculative thriller *The Fist Of Memory* and the critically acclaimed *Shigidi and the Brass Head of Obalufon*, which was one of the *Washington Post*'s ten best science and fantasy novels of 2023, nominated for the Nebula, World Fantasy, Locus, and other major awards. His short fiction has appeared in *Asimov's*, *Clarkesworld*, and *Africa Risen*, and is collected in *Convergence Problems* and *Incomplete Solutions*. He has also been a finalist for the Hugo, Nommo, BSFA, Sidewise, Ignyte and Crawford awards, as well as the Caine Prize for African Writing. He has edited five anthologies, including *Africanfuturism: An Anthology* and *Mothersound: The Saúútiverse Anthology*. He likes scuba diving, elegant equations, and oddly shaped things. He currently lives and works in Perth, Australia.

Paul Tremblay (www.paultremblay.net) has won the Bram Stoker, British Fantasy, Sheridan Le Fanu, and Massachusetts Book awards and is the *New York Times* bestselling author of *Horror Movie: A Novel*, *Another*, *The Beast You Are*, *The Pallbearers Club*, *Survivor Song*, *Growing Things and Other Stories*, *Disappearance at Devil's Rock*, *A Head Full of Ghosts*, and the crime novels *The*

Little Sleep and *No Sleep Till Wonderland*. His novel *The Cabin at the End of the World* was adapted into the Universal Pictures film *Knock at the Cabin*. His essays and short fiction have appeared in the *New York Times*, *Boston Globe*, *Los Angeles Times*, and numerous "year's best" anthologies. He lives outside of Boston, Massachusetts, and has a master's degree in mathematics.

Cadwell Turnbull (www.cadwellturnbull.com) is the award-winning author of *The Lesson* and the *Convergence Saga*. His short fiction has appeared in *The Verge*, *Lightspeed*, *Nightmare*, *Asimov's Science Fiction*, and several anthologies. His novel *The Lesson* was the winner of the 2020 Neukom Institute Literary Award in the debut category. *No Gods, No Monsters* was the winner of a Lambda, a finalist for the Shirley Jackson Award and the Manly Wade Wellman Award, and longlisted for the PEN Open Award. *We Are the Crisis* was a finalist for the Manly Wade Wellman Award and an Ignyte Award. Turnbull grew up on St. Thomas, US Virgin Islands.

Catherynne M. Valente (www.catherynnemvalente.com) is the *New York Times* bestselling author of forty works of speculative fiction and poetry, including *Space Opera*, *The Refrigerator Monologues*, *Palimpsest*, the Orphan's Tales series, *Deathless*, *Radiance*, and the crowdfunded phenomenon *The Girl Who Circumnavigated Fairyland in a Ship of Own Making* (and the four books that followed it). She is the winner of the Andre Norton, Tiptree, Sturgeon, Prix Imaginales, Eugie Foster Memorial, Mythopoeic, Rhysling, Lambda, Locus, Romantic Times' Critics Choice, and Hugo awards. She has been a finalist for the Nebula and World Fantasy awards. She lives on an island off the coast of Maine with a small but growing menagerie of beasts, some of which are human.

Nghi Vo (www.nghivo.com) is the bestselling author of the novels *Siren Queen*, *The Chosen and the Beautiful*, and *The City in Glass*, as well as the acclaimed novellas of the Singing Hills Cycle, which began with *The Empress of Salt and Fortune*. Her work has been nominated for the Nebula, Locus, and Lambda Literary awards and the Los Angeles Times and Ursula K. Le Guin prizes, and she has won the Crawford, Ignyte, and Hugo awards. Born in Illinois, Vo now lives on the shores of Lake Michigan. She believes in the ritual of lipstick, the power of stories, and the right to change your mind.

Kaaron Warren (www.kaaronwarren.wordpress.com) is the author of the novels *Slights*, *Walking the Tree*, *Mistification*, *The Grief Hole*, *Tide of Stone*, and *The Underhistory* and the short story collections *Through Splintered Walls*, *The Grinding House*, *Dead Sea Fruit*, and *Primer to Kaaron Warren*. Her fiction has won Shirley Jackson, Australian Shadows, Ditmar, and Aurealis awards. She lives in Canberra, Australia.

E. Lily Yu (elilyyu.com) is the author of *On Fragile Waves*, which won the Washington State Book Award for Fiction; *Jewel Box*, a finalist for the Los Angeles Times Book Prize, the World Fantasy Award, and the Washington State Book Award; and *Break, Blow, Burn, & Make*. More than forty of her stories have appeared in venues from *McSweeney's* to *Boston Review*, as well as fourteen best-of-the-year anthologies.

ABOUT JONATHAN STRAHAN

Jonathan Strahan is a World Fantasy Award–winning editor and anthologist and Hugo Award–winning podcaster who has edited more than one hundred books. He is a reviews editor for *Locus*; a consulting editor for *Reactor*, Tordotcom Publishing, and Subterranean Press; and a cohost and producer of the Hugo Award–nominated *Coode Street Podcast*. Find him online at jonathanstrahan.com.au.